DESTINY'S GAME "LOVE OR HONOUR" BOOK 2

Destiny's Game
"Love or Honour"
Book 2

Marcus Dizon

Contents

This is a tribute to my grandmother, Salvacion Pancho, and my grandfather, Leonardo Pancho, who raised me and shared their wisdom. My grandfather was a strict disciplinarian, yet he also had the ability to infuse humuor into moments when it was necessary. I am profoundly grateful to them for being a source of inspiration as I complete this sequel, and I missed you so much my dear grandfather. To the rest of my family, thank you even when there were times of uncertainties but understanding stood the toughest test of time. And last but not the least, the universe is always full of patriotism and heroism.

Disclaimer

One

The Backup Bodyguard

As he lay in bed, brimming with excitement at the thought of how far he had come, he reflected on how much it had once meant to him; before this whimsical and yet strange conflict began. He could still clearly remember each detail from the day of the incident, the moment when the near collision almost compelled him to rush forward and rescue Osmond. But it turned out to be a false alarm, nothing more than a typical mishap while parking a vehicle. Yet, what seemed ordinary at first quickly transformed into an extraordinary, almost surreal moment. It all began when he noticed the woman in the purple turban and sunglasses, her presence revealed slowly as the tinted car window rolled down. He had frozen in place, choosing to wait and watch, his curiosity was getting deeper as Osmond stepped out of the car to inspect for any damage. The details of their conversation eluded him; he couldn't decipher much. However, the woman's demeanour caught his attention. She was making a determined effort to remain anonymous, a fact he couldn't ignore. Then Cedrick closed his eyes after he took a deep breath and dismissing the possibility of thought in his mind about Ms. Alex's reaction tomorrow morning.

In the other room, Osmond was reflecting on a certain event from his past. He had no idea why these memories suddenly resurfaced, but he had just realised it must have happened for a reason.

As someone watching grabbing every piece of clothing from the drying rack near the wooden kitchen countertop table and gave no response, it was autumn season, and a light breeze stirred the two lemon trees in the backyard. The soft patter of raindrops on the windowpane stood as the only silent witness to the tension between them. She let out hot water from the kettle and closed her eyes for a brief moment before speaking again.

"Look, it's pointless to keep doing that just to make so ad also witnessed an ill-fated event that ultimately changed his life. Yet, she felt compelled to keep reminding him of the consequences, where this path might lead and how it might all end.

"You are still young and may not fully understand everything right now, so we can't predict or say what truly belongs to you at this point," she said. "You should enjoy being a teenager and make friends," she added. The boy, however, simply stared at her before turning his gaze back to the object she had noticed earlier when she had walked into the kitchen after her late afternoon nap. Then she heard his response.

"Your suggestions aren't helpful because I already have a way, and that's the scholarship program I found inside of my backpack when I was rescued before. Sorry, but I'm going to my room." He grabbed the pile of carefully folded clothes and suddenly realised how stifling the situation had become for both of them. Just as he was about to leave, he hesitated, looked back at her, and said, "I made pasta for dinner and already ate." Without waiting for a reply, he turned and walked to his room.

The woman let out a sigh while her eyes fell on the washed plate and a few utensils resting on the stainless-steel drying rack. She felt certain of two things: a deep pity for the boy, struggling to cope with their current reality, and a gnawing fear of what the future might hold. She worried his longing for something beyond their reach could lead to dire consequences, perhaps even putting his life in jeopardy.

Meanwhile, when the teenage boy entered the room, he carefully placed the pile of his clothes on the bed and closed his eyes. It had been almost eight months since he left his parents after Isabelle was abducted. He had ended up at his nana's place because his mother and father didn't really like the idea of him becoming a secret agent one day, just to find his childhood best friend, Isabelle. Now that he had the means to become one, he was determined to follow his desire, no matter what it cost, when the day came. Then another final event shifted to his mind after recalling from his teenage days, the final candidates were all in the Headquarters of Australian Secret Intelligence Service they were in unspecified room and each of them before they went inside there was an officer standing in front of single white door with the golden doorknob then on the table there was a pile of silky white bandana, he grabbed one to blindfolded them, when Osmond got inside, he remembered the time interval was every less than five minutes and he was second to the last when someone started to speak.

"I am not surprised how all of you men made this far from the very beginning of immersion and to that, the only reason why all of you are blindfolded is to put everyone to the test; shall I say, the battle of the fittest for this batch," the authoritative voice was familiar to everyone while nodding, it was the Director-General.

Osmond's mind was perplexed if what was waiting for them after the announcement from their superior and for sure all of them was deserving at this point, and everyone will do the finest of their skills just to win the last challenge. And he must trust himself more at this time to fulfil his mission.

"Any question?" The Director-General asked then no one answered when few seconds has passed, "it seems all of you is ready and I am glad to know it. And keep in mind this is the final test. I'll see you all once it is done and there is no specific count of days for this, but it is totally depending to each one of you. Whoever could make it, then it is officially done and clearly, that candidate is the winner." Then he automatically took the phone on his desk, "it is about time."

Then everyone heard the door opened followed by gentle multiple footsteps inside.

"Everyone will take to the military airport, and I assigned someone to give an instruction. Any question?"

"No sir!" Everyone responded.

"Good, and good luck gentlemen."

It was nearly midday when the two Australian Bushmasters arrived beside the C-17A Globemaster III at the designated location. The officer was already there, standing next to the military jeep. Excitement filled him as he looked forward to the beginning of the journey. He was rooting for three to five of the ten final candidates after the other five had been eliminated. Having witnessed their potential during training at Thames House in London, he knew it was all about their personnel skills in security, intelligence collection, and investigation to prepare them for their designated roles. Slowly, he scanned them one by one, observing their heights and body structures, then what made them who they were—until he began to speak. He worked for the CIA, as his American English accent was evident. Only the Director-General and he truly knew about the final candidates' training. Then he started to speak.

"Men, before we proceed and before taking off the blindfolds, congratulations to all of you. I have no doubt about each of you, as the Director-General said after the final selection: you all deserve to be here. However, let me remind you that after a cycle of rigorous training, this final stage is the ultimate test. Only the finest will succeed, as the failure rate is high. So, are you all ready?"

"Yes, sir!" They responded firmly, clearly prepared for what lay ahead.

"Good! Now, everyone may remove your blindfolds." The officer said, pacing back and forth with his hands clasped behind his back. When the officer's eyes fell on Osmond, he smiled briefly before his gaze landed on the man with the potential to win. However, Osmond's different traits made the officer doubt his chances of victory. The officer then turned his attention to the rest of the group. Meanwhile, the man with the potential to win concluded a plan in his mind.

He had already discussed his final move with his two trusted allies, and both felt the same way about Osmond. They had no idea about the total number of people who passed the training in London during that event, as they were all in separate areas, and one thing was for sure to them: always expect Osmond to be in the final stage of their training.

"Osmond, you can do it," Osmond said to himself. "Just do the right thing to win this final stage. If you fail, no regrets. As long as you did your best and always remember failure will never stop you from finding Isabelle." Osmond said to himself while the man in front of them pressed the button of his earpiece.

"Bring the bottles of water and helmets for them. They are about to leave soon," the man requested in a commanding voice.

Osmond remembered Cedrick McKain, who had been friendly to everyone. He found himself rooting for Cedrick to win, rather than the man who, from the very first day of training, had shown a deep dislike for him. Osmond didn't let that bother him either—until they saw a man in uniform carrying a bag with their drinks. The man gave a salute to the officer, then opened the bag in front of them.

"From the left, in order. You may start taking your water now and then proceed inside the plane," the officer commanded.

"Yes, sir!" They responded. Osmond watched as each person lined up perfectly while grabbing their drinks. When it was his turn, he took the two items and proceeded to the plane's ramp, the aircraft hummed loudly in the area, the sound helped him feel more optimistic at the moment they arrived as it was diverting his worries. When he got inside, he situated next to Cedrick then glance to the specific part of aircraft, seeing the folding toe plates as they about to take off after the pilot announcement.

"I am not surprised you made it this far, mate," the man said, staring at Osmond before scoffing.

"Mate, as the Director-General said, we all deserved to be here." Osmond calmly replied.

"Alright, as you've said. But let me remind you that I will do my best just to win." The man replied firmly to Osmond and shifted his gaze to his trusted allies, and they exchanged fist bump followed by silence between the men. Until the pilot announced that they were about to descend the altitude and told them to be ready once the ramp started to open slowly. And everyone nodded in agreement as they looked at each other, then until they heard the pilot started to announce that they were now at less than 5,000 feet, and they stood up confidently until Osmond saw the three quickly jump off the plane, then one by one followed them, and Cedrick tapped his shoulder and nodded at him before jumping off. Then he took a deep breath before he followed Cedrick and deployed the parachute, and Osmond remembered something while seeing that they were all doing the same: the free fall style so that they were close to the designated point.

Then he remembered the most crucial part of that day, even he was able to dodge all the traps and after those incidents, he was wounded and did his best to keep moving. As he knew, none of his batch mates had been in the area after he scanned the surroundings carefully. From the wild grasses, vines, and trees, everything seemed untouched by any human. Then he smiled, despite the extreme feeling of pain in his legs and arms whenever there was any incoming sharp object towards him, he paid no mind to whether his body would end up in anything in the area as long as he could avoid getting hit. From the large roots to the rock, he endured the pain as much as he could. Every drop of rain with the chilling wind was rough for Osmond while he was taking a rest under the big tree, as he gazed towards the part of the east; a certain part of that direction gave him a reason to smile with tears, as he already knew what's next. And the sudden thought came to his mind, gasping his breath, that he needed to proceed as soon as he could, though his body was shaking heavily. Then, Osmond's mind drifted back to the present as he started to feel sleepy and smiled while seeing Alex's face in his mind.

The next morning, after Alex had finished her morning rituals, she was completely surprised by what she saw. Osmond was in the lounge area with someone who looked familiar as she made her way to the kitchen for breakfast. Then she noticed the man stand up from the couch and smile at her.

"Hi, good morning!"

"Morning," she replied casually. "Sorry, what's your name again? You look familiar." The man glanced at Osmond and simply nodded in response before speaking while looking at her.

"Alright, let me introduce myself again, Ms. Margarette Alexandria. I am Cedrick McKain, your second bodyguard."

Alex merely nodded and shifted her gaze to Osmond. The way she looked at him seemed to say, "What the hell is this?" Osmond, however, ignored her reaction, though he couldn't deny feeling unsettled by how Cedrick had introduced himself to his client. A moment later, Alex turned her attention back to Cedrick.

"How polite of you, Mr. McKain, though perhaps not at the most appropriate time. I'm just feeling rather disappointed today." With that, she turned and walked back toward the guest room, leaving the two men staring at each other—Cedrick filled with questions, while Osmond tried to mask his reaction behind furrowed brows.

"Anyway, when are they coming back?" Cedrick asked, referring to his parents.

"In two days," Osmond replied.

"Alright. You mentioned before that your mother is a great cook, but I can manage that," Cedrick responded, while Osmond nodded before answering.

"That's good, since I want to be extra careful about guarding her."

"Yeah, as the finest agent. And her dad is likely expecting a lot from you in that role," Cedrick said. Osmond grabbed his coffee from the table and felt that same uneasy feeling again after Cedrick's introduction to Alex. He quickly dismissed the thought, knowing it made no sense to dwell on it. He took a gentle sip from his cup.

"So, are you preparing breakfast soon?"

"Well, I can if you want me to," Cedrick answered after finishing his coffee.

"Alright, I'll let her know," Osmond said, starting to walk toward the room after finishing his drink. Standing in front of the door, he recalled why Cedrick had become her second bodyguard. Now, he hesitated to knock, already sensing he would hear her harsh words—though only Alex ever made him feel this kind of fear, as she truly meant a lot to him.

She stood by the window as the cool breeze rustled the plants and their flowers, helping to ease her frustration with the two men. Osmond's behaviour had irritated her, tempting her to reprimand him, but she opted for silence. She was aware that the extra guard's presence was meant to stop her from fleeing once more until she heard the soft knock, walked towards the door as she knew it was Osmond behind that door and was glad that she could finally confront him about having Cedrick as the second bodyguard.

"Yes?"

"Cedrick is preparing breakfast now. I'll let you know as soon as it's ready."

"Alright, but Osmond, I'm not happy with what you did. You made a decision without consulting me—how could you?" Alex said firmly.

"Ms. Alex, please try to see things from my perspective. I'm aware of what you did last time," Osmond responded.

"You have no idea how that feels, Osmond," Alex shot back, rolling her eyes. "By the way, how long is he going to stay?"

"That's precisely the part I can't tell you," Osmond said seriously, locking eyes with her, "especially, after what I witnessed last time in my room, Ms. Alex. Why did you do that?" His words seemed to pierce straight to her soul. She smiled bitterly and shook her head.

"Osmond, you have no idea where I'm coming from. It was a difficult choice for me as well."

"Okay then. So, liberty without security, or security without liberty?" Osmond asked while maintaining himself not to disrespect the heiress of Mr. Enrique.

Then Alex was in silence after she heard those words from Osmond, until she realised, she was hugging the man with tears.

"It's okay, but I am sorry as well. I just had to give you a harsh option so I could totally secure your safety, even if it was painful for me," Osmond said while he now also hugged Alex. He held her hand and they kissed for the second time.

"I apologise if I had to give you a harsh choice to ensure your safety, even though it was painful for me," Osmond said as he hugged Alex. He held her hand, and they kissed for the second time.

Cedrick was on his way to the lounge room to inform them that their food was ready. When he saw Osmond sitting on the couch with the television on, Osmond felt relieved that Cedrick hadn't witnessed the intimate moment between him and Alex. Otherwise, it could have caused serious trouble or controversy—especially since no one could predict Cedrick's reaction if he had caught them kissing.

Osmond saw Cedrick heading to the toilet and seized the opportunity to inspect the food. He wanted to ensure it was safe for them to eat, knowing that any alibi Cedrick might offer meant they needed to eat first. Taking a deep breath to focus, Osmond carefully smelled the food on the table. As Alex's main guard, he couldn't risk anything harmful happening. Satisfied that the food was safe, he felt relief and returned to the lounge room to continue watching what he had been watching.

Two

The Past

Osmond had just finished his shower and was aware that Alex was in her room, while Cedrick was in the kitchen preparing their lunch for the day. As he picked up his white shirt from the bed, his cellphone rang, displaying his sister Cathy's name on the screen. He was taken aback by the unexpected call. Rather than putting on his shirt, he opted to answer, thinking it might be significant.

"Yes, Cathy?"

"Hey you won't believe what I saw last night," his sister started, her voice brimming with excitement from the other line.   "What is it?" He asked casually.

"I'm not entirely sure if I saw the right person, but there was someone who looked just like your childhood best friend, Isabelle."

"Are you sure? Did you try to approach her? It could be her. " And now his heart racing as he felt its rapid beat.

"Unfortunately, I didn't because we were crossing the road at that moment, and when I looked back at the group of teenagers, she had vanished. But I'm quite sure that even though the last time I saw her was fourteen years ago, her appearance is etched in my memory," his sister replied confidently about what she had witnessed.

"Which street and what time?"

"I can't recall the exact time, but it was right next to my workplace, Rankin Street." At that moment, Osmond felt a chill run down his spine upon hearing the location.

"Why didn't you call me last night? I could have gone to check that place to find her," he said, frustration evident in his voice.

"Remember, Osmond, you need to look after Ms. Alex, and I'm sure you would hesitate to leave," his sister replied seriously.

"Alright, that's fine. Thanks for informing me," Osmond said, gazing out the window as he contemplated his next steps after receiving the news from his sister.

Meanwhile, after Alex entered the room, she made a decision from now on that she needed to forbid her feelings for Osmond. There was no such reason to look forward to after she heard everything when she was about to knock on the door. Until a scenario came to her mind: one day there will be a possibility of Isabelle's presence in his life. And she closed her eyes after that. Then she remembered Cedrick, again as what she had thought before when she saw him the first time. Even though he was possessing a different kind of demeanour, she never felt any similar feelings to those she felt toward Osmond. She closed her eyes and kept trying to think about any backup plan on how she could manage to go back to Melbourne. Then she shook her head. There was no way for her to do that; instead, she must accept the reality of Cedrick as her second bodyguard.

During their lunch time, Cedrick seized the moment to capture Alex's attention while he noticed Osmond lost in thought. An hour earlier, he had decided to serve pasta on Alex's plate and refill her water glass. When Alex glanced at him, she smiled and simply said, "thanks."

"What kind of snack would you like later, Ms. Alex?" Cedrick inquired.

"Anything is fine since Osmond told me you're responsible for preparing meals," she responded after sipping her water and wiping her lips by napkin. She tried several attempts to make eye contact with Osmond were in a deep thought, as he remained preoccupied.

"I believe I can prepare a chocolate pizza later," Cedrick cheerfully responded, followed by an overwhelming sensation as he had to admit to himself that day that the lady had stirred feelings within him, an irresistible urge that he couldn't dismiss. So, when Osmond called him for assistance as a backup bodyguard, it turned into an unforgettable night for him. He even reread the relevant details about her provided by the Director-General to convince himself that it was truly happening, that he would see her again. Even though she was not an ordinary woman, or rather, an heiress, those details never caused him any hesitation. He found it delightful how he managed to get to know her, and now it was unfolding, and he eagerly anticipated the outcome. He felt a strong sense of optimism, believing that if he continued to do what was right, a positive result would follow.   "Hey mate, I'll whip up a chocolate pizza later. Do you want anything else? Ms. Alex didn't mention anything extra," Cedrick inquired of Osmond, seizing the opportunity after noticing the sudden shift in Osmond's demeanour as he continued eating.   "Sorry, mate, I can't think of anything, but it's entirely your call. Just check the pantry. If I come up with something while you're making the chocolate pizza, I'll let you know," Osmond replied. He realised he was lost in thoughts about Isabelle after his sister's call. Damn. But he felt no shame in that, and he had no regrets. Despite the unexpected news and the chance of reuniting with her, he was determined to stay true to his responsibilities, even if it meant a conflict with Alex. Then he noticed a different expression on Cedrick's face, which made him wonder what it was, but he gradually dismissed it as he was consumed with thoughts of how he might find Isabelle. Alex was certain of Osmond's thoughts—it was undoubtedly Isabelle.

They were just had their meeting and Enrique was standing in front of the bar area and recalled a particular incident from over twenty years ago. He inhaled deeply as memories flooded back, still lingering in his mind while he sipped his vodka. The recollections were vivid, especially the afternoon he spent in the parking lot, contemplating recent happenings in the dining area before heading to the office. His father, Alfredo, continued to show disappointment despite

Enrique's diligent efforts for their business. This was not merely a typical business transaction; it represented a groundbreaking opportunity for a substantial partnership, yet his father opted to highlight the ideas of his younger brother, Emilio. His thoughts were suddenly disrupted when he sensed someone approaching and recognised it was his wife, Evangeline.

"It seems like you're lost in thought," she said while placing her hand on his shoulder, prompting him to take another deep breath before responding.

"I was just reflecting on our business and particularly on our daughter," Enrique replied, smiling at his wife.

"Oh, I felt the same earlier. But remember what you said, Alex is safe with Agent Gomez," Evangeline reassured him.

"Yes, I understand that. Regardless, we need to get ready soon for the event we must attend. A charity event, and Mr. Lucas Emsworth will be present."

"Really? I thought he wouldn't be able to make it tonight?"

"Since Mr. Amadeus is unavailable, Lucas will represent him due to some issues," Enrique explained.

"Oh, I see. I hadn't considered that. I really admire Mr. Amadeus, but I have nothing against Mr. Lucas. However, I do prefer his grandfather more."

"Well, let's set that aside; what truly matters is our attendance as major sponsors, and we should prepare quickly since I need to meet someone important before we head to the event," Enrique stated, kissing his wife gently before departing, leaving Evangeline shaking her head with a smile at her husband's response.

It was late afternoon when Alex was in the shower, and Osmond could no longer hold back. He rose from the couch and seized the opportunity to satisfy his curiosity.

"Is everything alright, mate?" Cedrick inquired, while curiosity was in his eyes, "you seem troubled today."

"Well, sort of mate and I need to find out something. Could you do me a favour? I'll be quick. Can you keep an eye on her? I'll be back in less than half an hour," Osmond asked. Certainly, anyone would find it unfair to agree to such a favour during their duties, but for Cedrick, it was an appealing opportunity; even if Osmond was gone for the rest of the day, he felt confident he could protect Alex at all times.

"Alright, mate. Take your time," Cedrick said, patting his shoulder in agreement.

"Thanks, I'll head out now and won't knock on the door since I have a key," he replied as he began to leave. Once outside, he surveyed the area to ensure everything was safe, and after confirming there was nothing suspicious, he casually walked to the open garage. He glanced at his father's motorbike, retrieved the key from his pocket—dressed in a grey tracksuit and black sneakers that day—grabbed a black leather jacket from the corner to cover his black long sleeve shirt and put on his helmet. As he drove, several people waved at him, and he waved back, maintaining the required speed. He recalled the man who would assist him in uncovering the mystery of the figure his sister had seen the previous day. They were familiar with each other, as the man had lived in that town for over a decade, which had a population of less than a hundred at that time. Upon arriving at his destination in under ten minutes, a few more people recognised him.

After parking his motorbike in the car park and placing his helmet inside the top box, he was greeted by several individuals carrying shopping bags towards their car, while others leisurely walked along the nearby footpath. Following their exchange of greetings, he casually made his way to the building he intended to investigate. As he approached the building, he felt fortunate to spot the man finishing his cigarette in the left corner of the premises, recognising him despite the visor he was wearing.

"Hey Osmond, how are you?" Lester asked as he disposed of his cigarette in a nearby bin.

"I'm doing well, thank you. So, how has your day been?"

"It's been alright, but a bit dull today compared to yesterday. However, now that you're here, it's definitely better! Haha!" The man embraced him, and he patted his back, mirroring the same gesture.

"What brings you here?" The man began.

"The reason I'm here is that I can only reveal the truth with your assistance," Osmond responded after their friendly greetings.

"Oh, that? Haha! No worries, mate! If I can assist, I'm all in!" The man replied.

"Thanks, mate!" After that, he surveyed the surroundings before turning back to him.

"It's about Isabelle, mate," he said, his tone shifting noticeably. The man was aware of the entire situation regarding Isabelle, as they had previously discussed it when they reconnected after his graduation to become an Agent. The man smiled and nodded, giving him a gentle tap on the shoulder.

"So, what's the sudden concern about her?"

"My sister saw someone who looks a lot like her on this street the other night, mate," he explained, glancing around the area again, hoping to catch a glimpse of her. He wished for fate to give him a chance to see anyone who could provide a clue that it was her. Even though many years had passed since he last saw her, he would never forget the face of his childhood best friend.

"Are you implying that you want to review the CCTV footage?"

"Absolutely, since you're in charge of that department, I believe it would be a great help in determining our next steps once I have more details."

"Okay, I can set that up, but we have to do it quickly because we could get into trouble if my boss finds out. Still, since we're friends, I'm more than willing to help you out."

"Thanks a lot, buddy!" He said, giving him a hug to show his appreciation, and then they started walking inside, taking a right at the end of the corridor before entering the room. As Lester began searching for the previous records, Osmond sat beside him, and they both started looking at the screens from CAM 1 to CAM 5. Eventually, they saw a group of teenagers on CAM 4, but the light was too dim to clearly see the face of the unknown person with them. After a few seconds, the woman turned left, indicating she wasn't part of their group, and he asked to zoom in to see if it was Isabelle. Unfortunately, the image became pixelated. He let out a deep sigh while Lester shaking his head.

"I'm sorry, mate," Lester said, then he suggested checking more footage, and Osmond agreed, but after some searching, they found nothing except for the woman on CAM 4, who was wearing a black snapback, white long sleeve shirt, a straight-cut jeans, and sneakers.

"It's all good, mate, no worries. I believe there will be another chance for either of us to spot that mysterious person again since we all know exactly what she looks like, and I'm sure we'll be notified."

"Yes, I still remember her from the time you showed me her picture. So, I can definitely say if I see someone who resembles her."

Then he realised it would ultimately be very painful for him if his sister confirmed that it was indeed her, and he verified for himself that day that if it was his best friend. But for the moment, he would no longer be troubled as he had seen the result. He finally made the decision to leave the room, allowing Lester to resume his duties after he said goodbye. He was just about to press the button on the motorbike when he felt something; his instincts kicked in quickly, and with reflexes, he took a step forward to retrieve whatever it was to show the attacker that it was not the appropriate time for such actions. Upon checking the item, it turned out to be just a piece of marble. He then scanned the area and no one was around, except for a busy woman pushing a pram towards her car. Shifting his gaze to the other side, he saw nothing but a lush arrangement of ornamental plants in a flowerpot beneath the trees.

He then remembered Cedrick's last encounter with the unknown assailant, and a wave of fear washed over him. Instinctively, he hopped on his bike, determined to return to their home as quickly as possible. As he rode, a whirlwind of emotions flooded his mind: could this be linked to the mysterious threat against Alex, perhaps a potential enemy of her father? Or maybe a band of mercenaries had invaded their home, leaving Cedrick struggling to protect Alex? His grip on the handlebars tightened, and when he glanced at the speedometer, he realised he was traveling at over eighty kilometres per hour

When he got home, he felt a wave of relief seeing how peaceful it looked from the outside. But once he stepped inside, the scene was totally different. Cedrick and Alex were busy in the kitchen, and he caught a glimpse of his hand as he cheerfully guided Alex, who was listening intently and nodding along. He shook his head, thankful they hadn't noticed he was back, so he didn't want to interrupt them. He stepped outside to calm down after rushing to get there, but then he saw that annoying view. So, he decided to hop back on his motorbike and take some time for himself. He rode more than a kilometre away from their house when he noticed someone waving at him. He slowly pulled the handle to reduce his speed until he finally came to a stop in front of the gate.

"I knew it was you, Osmond! It's wonderful to see you again after six months!" The man exclaimed after switching off the mower he was operating.

"Yes, I'm really glad to be back, Eddie!" Osmond responded with a smile.

"How are they? Martin and Celine?"

"They're doing well, and they might return tomorrow since they went camping." Osmond said as he dismounted from his motorbike.

"That's fantastic news, especially since they were busy with the farm. So, how are your brother and sister?"

"They're good, enjoying their families."

"That's great to hear! How's work treating you?"

"Not too bad; I'm here to relax and unwind."

"Good for you, man! I'm really happy to see you here again," the man replied, wiping the sweat from his brow as the temperature felt like it was over twenty-five degrees. Just then, the main door opened, revealing a woman in her late forties who called for her husband to come inside, needing assistance with something. She waved at him with a smile, and he nodded in return.

"Alright, Osmond, my wife needs help inside, so I'll go for now. See you next time, and please send my regards to your parents." He extended his hand for a handshake, which Osmond gladly accepted. He then decided to leave the area, planning to visit a place to spend some time. He left his phone behind so Cedrick wouldn't be able to reach him, as it had been nearly half an hour since he departed. He was now heading to the nearest stream, and after less than five minutes, he arrived at his destination. He parked the motorbike by the roadside, took a deep breath to calm his emotions, and removed his helmet and leather jacket. As he listened to the sound of the bubbling stream, he smiled, recalling the last time he was there with Alex and his nephew. However, circumstances changed when Alex attempted to flee from him, leaving him with no option but to request assistance. He shook his head and took a few steps closer to the water, picking up some pebbles which he casually tossed into the centre of the river. Once he ran out of pebbles, he gathered more and repeated the action, listening to the sound of the water as it hit the surface before finally disappearing beneath it.

Meanwhile, at the Gomez household, Alex and Cedrick were nearly finished with their baking. She observed the table, noting how they had arranged the food alongside slices of assorted fruit. The drinks selection and vanilla ice cream were their top choices, complemented by chocolate syrup.

"Are you certain he mentioned he would return in less than half an hour?"

"Yes, Ms. Alex, but perhaps something unexpected occurred, which is why he is still not here."

"That may be true, but he should have asked for my permission before leaving. This is simply unbelievable, Cedrick."

"But I am here, right?" Cedrick replied, realising too late that he had spoken out of turn to Alex.

"Excuse me?" Alex responded, her expression one of confusion as she looked at him with a questioning gaze. Meanwhile, Cedrick was scrambling to justify his earlier words.

"What I meant was, I am here as your backup bodyguard," Cedrick quickly clarified, relieved to have rectified his statement, as he did not want her to think he was trying to take advantage of the situation.

"Yeah, I know that, but still, he must let me know. But anyway, shall we eat soon, or we still must wait for him? Oh, I remember someone, and how I wish, Andrew is here for sure he would love this food!" Alex exclaimed.

"Who's Andrew?" Cedrick asked while he took the phone from the pocket of his short and he was now taking a picture of food from the table. This would be a memorable for him, as they bonded well today.

"Osmond's nephew. His sister's son, and he loves sweets!"

"Alright, it is okay, but we can make another this kind of snack when he visits us here."

Then Osmond arrived and noticed they were about to begin eating the snacks. He made loud footsteps to alert the two that someone was nearby. He felt completely fine now and recognised that he had been overthinking Cedrick's playful antics, which affected his perspective. If Alex were to inquire about his whereabouts, he certainly would not say that he had investigated based on what he heard from his sister, since it would ignite her frustration once she knew about Isabelle, and he conducted an investigation on that day, the reason why he had gone for almost an hour.

Three

The Unseen Threat

Enrique remembered a certain event from more than two decades ago. He took a deep breath while recalling the past, which still haunts him in some way while drinking his vodka. It was still clear in his mind how he recalled the past. It was in the middle of the afternoon when Enrique gathered his thoughts in the parking lot, reflecting on recent events in the dining area before heading to the office. His father, Alfredo, still expressed disappointment despite Enrique's best efforts for their business. This was not just an ordinary business deal; it was a record-breaking opportunity with the potential for a significant partnership, and his dad had chosen to present his younger brother Emilio's ideas. His reminiscing was abruptly interrupted when he sensed someone approaching and saw it was his wife, Evangeline.

"It seems like you're recalling something," then he felt her hand on his shoulder, and he took a deep breath before he replied.

"Well, I was just thinking about our business and especially our daughter," Enrique said and smiled at his wife.

"Oh, I just felt the same way earlier. But remember what you've said, Alex is fine and safe with Agent Gomez," Evangeline said.

"Yes, I know that. Anyway, we have to prepare soon since we have an event that we need to attend to. A charity event, and Mr. Lucas Emsworth will be there."

"Oh, Mr. Emsworth! I thought he couldn't attend tonight?"

"Since Mr. Amadeus can't attend. So, Lucas will be his representative due to some matters," Enrique replied.

"Alright, I never thought about that. Since I am very fond of Mr. Amadeus, but I have nothing against Mr. Lucas though. But I like his grandfather more."

"Well, forget about that, what really matters is our presence as major sponsors and we better prepare soon since before we go to the event, I need to see someone and it's important," Enrique said while kissing his wife on the lips and he left while Evangeline shaking her head and simply smiled how her husband responded about what she said between Lucas and Amadeus.

He simply nodded as the security personnel opened the main entrance of the medium-sized suite for the evening. With only a select few invited to this special charity event, he was in a rush after exiting the vehicle, having finally found a parking spot. In his haste, he even neglected to thank his driver. However, he felt a sense of relief upon noticing that the speaker was about to begin. He was confident he had arrived on time, as some attendees were just taking their seats. Among them, he spotted Enrique with his wife, Evangeline. Fortunately, his assigned seat was positioned behind the couple, allowing him to indulge in watching the man he despised the most.

"Enrique, you may relish the upcoming days, as I understand your feelings about bringing your beloved daughter to Queensland. But rest assured, I will ensure that everything unfolds according to my plan. And, of course, I am not entirely malevolent; there are plenty of days and time to enjoy and appreciate my preparations." Lucas smiled as he wrapped up the most mischievous scheme he had ever devised. Even his most trusted associate was unaware of the main event; their only task was to follow his directives.

When the program concludes, everyone was engaged in socialising while enjoying their drinks, once again, Enrique attempted to persuade him for a second time regarding his grandfather's construction company being involved in one of his future business sites.

After they clinked their glasses of wine, he replied, "it is an honour to hear that once more from the wealthiest man in this country. However, there are matters I must discuss regarding my grandfather's approval. Since I began my involvement in his world, I have never found any record of our company having partnered with you when I reviewed our historical files."

"Oh, come on Lucas, please don't do this again. I assure you, once we embark on our business venture, you and I will become one of the most powerful business alliances in the Asia-Pacific region," Enrique remarked, his tone indicating that they would indeed be an unstoppable force once the deal was initiated.

"I appreciate your words, and they remind me of my grandfather, whom I represent tonight. To summarise, he previously declined your offer for a partnership. However, perhaps in the future, he might reconsider. Although I currently oversee our business, I still seek his approval, and I hope you can understand my position."

He then took a sip of his drink, glancing at Evangeline as she engaged in conversation with a group of socialites by the nearby window. Deep down, he sensed that Enrique's wife harboured some disdain for him, but he chose to let it be. He had never shown any overt signs that could be interpreted as malicious towards the couple. He casually turned his attention back to the man in front of him and gave his right shoulder a light tap.

"Anyway, I must be on my way soon, Enrique, as I have an early commitment tomorrow. Once again, I am pleased that we could reconnect for this significant event that holds a special place in our hearts."

Every time he remembers the horrific accident of his brother, he can't bare the amount of regret he feels, plus he never had the chance to confess his ill feelings towards his brother and the fact that their parents were always giving him credit and the attention. Until the day came, that he acquired the vast wealth of their family, but still the past haunting him in so many ways. If his brother never died, he would never get this kind of status; so, when his daughter got a mysterious threat, he did the best possible way to keep her safe as he can never endure the same experience from the past. Then he recalled the last update from the Director-General as they slowly getting the mystery of the puzzle, he sighed as he missed his daughter so much. But then, all awhile he was still in confusion why Lucas and his grandfather Amadeus still never accept his proposal.

It was almost midnight, and Alex couldn't sleep. She sat in the chair, staring at the silence of the dark front yard while the calm wind bracing her. She made sure the two men in their respective rooms were asleep and then walked towards the veranda. She wanted to spend minutes assessing things, taking the chance to get out of the guest room. It bothered her about hearing the conversation between Osmond and his sister Cathy earlier, which had given her a reason to disregard the mutual understanding she had with Osmond. But now, with Cedrick serving as a backup bodyguard, her plan to return to Melbourne was finally compromised.

She let out a deep breath. "This can't be happening," she thought. "It's so frustrating." She had to do something. Just as she was about to conclude her next thought, the lights from the lounge room quickly flickered on, revealing where she was.

"Sorry for disturbing you," Osmond said, standing there. "I've been standing here while watching you. Is everything alright?"

Alex was in disbelief that she had never felt any presence or noise. She quickly managed to respond.

"Yes, I just couldn't sleep and realised I needed to spend some minutes here. It might help me fall asleep when I go back to my room," she replied.

"Okay, but please, Ms. Alex, next time, just a soft knock on the door then call my name to let me know whenever you want to leave your room during this kind of hour. I must ensure that I can always keep an eye on your safety. Please, don't do this again," Osmond said, his voice casual yet firm. Behind his firm words, he tried to keep his emotions in check, not wanting her to repeat the same thing a couple of days ago.

"My apologies," she replied, realising that Osmond was fully aware of what she had tried to do. It was evident in the way he had uttered his words, she knew there was no way to disagree. It was part of his responsibility, and she attempted to compose herself as she walked back toward the room. When she was just a few steps away from him, she gently nodded and wished him good night, to which he responded.

"Good night as well, Ms. Alex. By saying this, I hope you fully understand where I am coming from with those words."

Their eyes met, and she searched within herself for a way to articulate her response, ultimately deciding to keep it casual.

"It's alright, and there's no need for an explanation; I completely understand you," she said, smiling at him before continuing her walk. At this point, she found herself feeling quite confused.

Once she entered her room, another thought crossed her mind: if she were not a client, would Osmond still show her the same level of care and attention that he gives to Isabelle? She sighed, troubled by this realisation. Additionally, she felt irritated by the presence of another person acting as a guard without her consent. Yet, deep down, she recognised it was her own fault, as Osmond was aware of her intentions from a few days' prior.

Upon waking up at that morning and glanced at the clock, Osmond saw it was only five thirty. Peering out the window from his bed, he saw that it was still dark. He shifted onto his side, clasping his hands on the pillow after closing his eyes once more, thinking of Isabelle. If only he had no responsibilities, he would spend a great deal of time searching for her. The fact that his sister had spotted someone who looked remarkably like her was a sign that she was still alive! However, despite his efforts yesterday to confirm that it was really her, he had been still unsuccessful. Then a thought occurred to him; he realised he had another opportunity to uncover the truth behind the sudden appearance of someone resembling Isabelle. After nearly an hour, Osmond decided to head to the bathroom, as nature called. Upon opening the door, he encountered Alex, who had just exited.

"Hi, good morning, Alex." He asked while trying to fix his white shirt to cover his boxer shorts as he looked at her.

"Morning, Osmond," Alex replied, then recalled something she hadn't had the chance to ask since Cedrick was with them when he arrived yesterday.

"Anyway, Osmond, since I have the right to ask you this, where were you yesterday?"

"I just checked something."

"Really, about what? Osmond, this is the first time you've done this, which is quite strange. But anyway, I hope it won't happen again."

Osmond furrowed his brow while looking at her, then nodded instead to avoid any further questions.

"I'm sorry about that, Alex; it won't happen again." After hearing Osmond's response, she remained silent, gazing at him without any hint of doubt. One thing was clear: Osmond was concealing something from her, and she chose to wait before responding.

"Okay, I'll head back to my room since it's still early. See you later."

"Alright, see you." Alex then turned to leave the front of the bathroom door and made her way to her bedroom without glancing back at him.

After using the restroom, Osmond glanced at himself in the mirror after washing his hands and noticed that he hadn't gotten enough sleep. He couldn't rest the previous night, preoccupied with thoughts about the results from yesterday. He pondered why, of all places and people in the world, he was suddenly entangled in a series of strange and perplexing events involving Mr. Enrique's heiress. The threat to Alex, marked by a cryptic email and an unusual riddle, and Cedrick had a strange encounter from a skilled attacker, while to him was a warning or message had been directed at him yesterday, leaving no clues behind. One thing was certain; the person who threw that marble at him was exceptionally skilled, as the precision was clear and well-practiced. He washed his face again to calm his racing thoughts, then looked back in the mirror at the water dripping from his face. With a sigh, he reached for the face towel in the drawer and gently dried his face before exiting the bathroom.

The morning went normal for them as Cedrick prepared the breakfast while Osmond checked the CCTV footage and he was glad that nothing was peculiar, but the sudden scenario appears in his mind between Alex and Cedrick yesterday, he tried his best to bear what he had witnessed between them. Until a question came to his mind; during the first day and second, they met, Alex was totally different compared how she treated him, while Cedrick on his first day afternoon they got along well.

During lunchtime, Cedrick remembered something and mentioned it to Osmond just as he was about to refill his bowl with soup.

"Mate, there's been ongoing news circulating globally about the assassination of several high-ranking officials during their secret meetings."

Osmond felt uneasy about the news he was already aware of, not wanting Alex to experience any additional fear, as the threat to her was already alarming enough for the de Ayala family. However, he composed himself to respond after taking a sip of water from his glass.

"Of course, mate, since it has been a significant international issue, even now, as authorities have uncovered that these officials were plotting to instigate a war for political gain. That incident happened a week before I became her bodyguard," he said, glancing at Alex while she wiped her mouth with a white napkin.

"It's a good thing my father isn't involved with any political party; otherwise, I can't imagine what my life would be like," she replied, noticing the two men nodding at her before they resumed their meals.

Osmond then attempted to analyse the important news from earlier and casually dismissed it, convinced it had no relevance to the cryptic email and riddle, as it was a political dispute among government officials, while Ms. Alex's situation was clearly tied to a conflict among corporate individuals. He recalled what he had encountered the previous day, but it wasn't the right moment to bring it up that time.

"Excuse me, I'll return shortly."

As Alex walked towards the bathroom, Osmond realised he needed to confess something that had been on his mind since yesterday.

"Mate, while I was about to come back here from the parking lot, someone threw a marble at me. I tried to find out who it was, but I couldn't see anyone who matched my instincts about a potential attacker.

This led Cedrick to ponder another question. Could this be linked to his previous encounter before arriving in Queensland? Or was someone monitoring them and testing their ability to protect Alex? Knowing the General-Director, he always had plenty of surprises in store since the beginning of their training.

Four

World's Top Assassins

The officials were curious about the noise coming from the ceiling while exchanging glances until one of them turned to the staff member in military attire and asked for maintenance to investigate, just as the main course was about to begin. Then was no more reason to stay, as the next moment will slowly unfolded anytime soon. As the door to the exit swung open, someone was lurking behind, and that individual sensed the metallic sound. A swift movement to alert the assailant that it was finished, by shaking the head wearing a military cap then another attack came from a different direction, but it was futile; until the remaining one finally saw single kick from the intruder; By forwarding with the rear leg, then raising the opposite leg and swinging it in a crescent shape and the motion resembles of an axe kick. The executor saw how it landed on the target's neck.

"Don't tell me that I didn't warn you," Hooded Pitohui said to the last man standing who attempted to stop from leaving the area.

"Replaced them, with this. And I'll let you live." As Hooded Pitohui clearly instructed the chef after eliminating the guards from inside and outside of the kitchen area, that was the scene before the main objective concluded.

It was almost past eleven in the evening and there was a normal establishment, a wide two-story building. Someone was in the isolated car park, separate from the main parking lot, silently watching the final moments of the event on the screen inside a black sedan, they were immobilised in their seats before they died from consuming their food laced with liquid Sarin. And a few of them wanted to start a political conflict that should never be happen. Then, that person took the phone from pocket to make a call after sending the video footage to the respective superior via laptop.

"Two hundred individuals have been eliminated, among them several high-ranking officials. With the final mission already completed, there's no need for me to head to HQ."

"Impressive, very impressive, Freya. There's no doubt why I chose you to carry out this most dangerous and difficult mission prior to your resignation. Anyway, good luck to you. I've already sent the payment to your account. Goodbye."

When the conversation ended, the unknown figure sat in silence, taking a deep breath, followed by tears. Tears of happiness, accompanied by a flood of unspoken words that needed to be shared with someone but there was nobody, except the existence of the unknown figure. Then until a realisation came to mind, the past and the future. Even everything was already carried out by plan, there was an enormous amount of courage to take for that decision. Then the engine started. Within a few seconds, the car began to fade into that area, and the dark empty parking lot stood and the surrounding area as the silent witnesses to the event that ended the lives of a couple hundred people and the unbearable feelings of the executor.

On the other side of the location, in a dimly lit lounge room, a man wearing a white robe stood deep in thought after the conversation, until a certain event from the past came to mind how it had all begun with one particular person. That day, he had been both a visitor and an instructor, keenly observing the students inside the dojo. They all had potential, but one stood out to him. The young student possessed a unique aura; their movements were swift and precise. Then he carried out calculate plan, and it was accomplished effortlessly. And now, the codename Hooded Pitohui was hailed on the other side of the world as one of the most lethal assassins on the planet. Even though there was no contract, the executor provided an exceptional amount of skill, which led him not to reject the resignation before executing the final mission. Then someone came to the living area as he put his phone inside of pocket of his robe.

"Father, I am sorry, but I can't help thinking about this. Even though I know you already discussed it with Freya, the Hooded Pito-hui, what if there is an event of double-crossing us? Like revealing our identity and the secret of this underground organisation?" The Expert's codename asked.

"Don't worry too much about it. We discussed the whole thing before I accepted the resignation, and I will not hesitate to make my next move if it happens." He replied to his son, while looking at him. "Anyway, are you done examining your next task?"

"Yes, father. And tomorrow I'll do my surveillance so I can accomplish the mission by nightfall," he replied to his father.

"Great to hear, I'll go ahead now to sleep. As I have also plan to do for the entire day. Good luck to your next mission, good night The Expert."

"Good night too, Dad," he said while looking intently at his father as he left the lounge area. He gathered his phone from his pocket and unlocked it, swiping through the contact list until he finally found what he was looking for. The abbreviated codename "H.P." belonged to someone who had recently quit the organisation. He was about to press the call button but hesitated, realising it was pointless to contact the former member. He then recalled their last mission; a back-to-back operation, but there was a main fact about his colleague; he had never seen the face behind that metallic mask wearing a hooded black jacket. The usual trademark of killing multiple people at once was truly striking, a feat only achievable by the sole member of the organisation capable of executing such a meticulous process to hit numerous targets. Meanwhile, he had eliminated the rest from the outside of the building in broad daylight, serving as a sniper to take out the watcher, their targets, and their bodyguards. After recalling the event, he quickly pressed the delete button, locked the screen, and walked toward the switch of the dimly lit room to turn it off, as he also needed to sleep. He left the living room so he could start his mission early the next morning.

As he entered the rented car under a different identity two days ago, wearing reading glasses and a nerdy styled long black wig, The Expert was completely satisfied with his look. All he needed to do was pretend to be a normal individual at the hotel when he checked in, and the rest would follow as he performed his task. He had made sure the night before that everything he needed was already organised in the trunk. Then, he started the engine. While driving, he realised that sometimes his father's organisation wasn't entirely evil. They had killed and would continue to kill lawless people. That was the mission: to eradicate them. He took four hours of driving before he arrived at his destination. As usual, checking in was effortless for him. He strolled casually toward the elevator, stepped inside, and pressed the desired floor number, standing silently as he faced the double doors until they closed gently. By after twelve in the afternoon, he would begin observing the next two blocks, focusing on the hotel where his target was expected to spend the night. After settling into his suite, he grabbed a drink from the minibar and sank onto the couch. Picking up the remote from the coffee table, he turned on the television, then he changed the channel until he saw the news was covering the controversy involving Mr. Enrique's only daughter, Ms. Alex, and her best friend Elissandra, the international model, in Madrid, Spain. It was already headline in the news last week then even up to now, and this morning too when he was browsing his phone, then he saw it again. Then he smiled as the media maybe wanted to know more about the controversy between the three ladies who had involved; uninterested in the story unless it had business relevance, he switched to another channel for the second time. Finally, he landed on a music program, choosing to watch a classic music show. He adjusted the volume to ensure it wouldn't disturb the neighbouring room. A sudden realisation struck him again, the shocking fact that someone had left the organisation. He had never seen the co-dename Hooded Pitohui engage in hand-to-hand combat during their missions, as always assigned to a very specific task. Then there was another incident, that they both captured the main key to find the head of the criminal group and brought him to the safe hideout whenever an interrogation is required. Then the man tried to escape by demonstrating his martial arts skills, even though both of his hands were tied tightly. He used his right elbow to deliver a brutal blow to HP's stomach. Immediately afterward, the man attacked again, striking him with a surprising roundhouse kick to the jaw. The blow was deadly, as his surroundings began to blur. He barely noticed his companion quickly grabbing a machete from a nearby stainless-steel table and pointing the weapon at the man's neck as a warning.

"How would you prefer to die? Painfully or painlessly? You can share your answer now or later. Although it is not my trademark, I will not hesitate to decapitate you if you dare to do that again," the Hooded Pitohui warned the man.

He then quickly expressed his thoughts, touching the base of the long machete as if trying to convince his companion.

"Hey, don't scare him. We still need to extract some information about this mission," he said to his partner. Then Hooded Pitohui looked at him, then nodded and shifted its gaze to the captured man and started to speak.

"My companion was right. You are lucky," said by Hooded Pitohui to the man then looked at him again, "I'll leave it all to you since I need to update the superior." With that, the woman walked towards the private room.

When his companion finally entered the room, he turned his attention back to the man, noting the overwhelming anxiety on his face. It was a fear that could only be seen in someone who had come dangerously close to a near-death experience.

"My colleague was serious. If I were you, I'd say what needs to be said. Maybe then we can still negotiate," he told the man firmly.

In the end, the operation turned out well. They retrieved what they needed, and as for the man? They let him go once the mission was complete. After all, he was not the main target. They always stuck to the plan, no matter what.

His thoughts drifted back to the present, a faint pang of regret flickering within him. He wished he had witnessed one of Hooded Pitohui's legendary combos—something deadly and awe-inspiring. With a sigh, he pushed the thought away, focusing instead on the TV. Taking a sip of his soda, he considered ordering room service for lunch. Visiting an establishment outside his room didn't appeal to him today. Having scouted the area two days ago, he does not need to put much thought into his first move this afternoon to carry out his latest mission. He smiled, since there will be no other involved according to the report, so it will be an easy for him to eliminate the target.

The early evening was lively with pedestrians filling the street, while numerous cars were stopped at a red light, patiently waiting for their turn. On the other side, every driver was benefiting from a green light, enabling their travels to proceed toward their destinations. A particular car parked on the right side was hosting an important event for someone. Inside the vehicle, the sky was beginning to fill with early stars as the silhouette looked straight ahead from the driver's seat. After watching a news segment about the assassination of a notorious criminal leader, the individual was already aware of who was responsible. After locking the screen of mobile device, a vision of something significant and a new beginning appeared, followed by a nostalgic moment that brought a slight smile. Looking at a small bag, it was now time to chase something important as per the plan. The person stepped out of the vehicle and moved to the boot to open it. While examining its contents, a simple nod after checking inside, grabbed the bottle next to it, opened the bag, and poured the liquid inside. Smoke started to rise into the air, and after a few moments of satisfaction, the individual made a way to the nearest rubbish bin to dispose of the bag and its contents.

On the opposite side of the Australian continent, after an hour had passed, a figure donned a mask, this time in a striking gold hue. The laws of motion had become critical for this individual, as it marked her third attempt to complete the mission. The location was unsuitable at that moment, with environmental noises disrupting her concentration. Suddenly, a specific idea sparked as she oriented herself towards the target, traveling at approximately sixty miles per hour, requiring her to act within five seconds. Taking a deep breath, her gaze finally fixed on the two, then when a loud scream and chaos erupted from the crowd and the seagull changed its course upon noticing the approaching object. Meanwhile, security personnel scrambled to identify the culprit, some attempting to communicate through their earpieces, while one person casually departed, having no reason to linger regardless of the outcome. The weapon was lethal enough, even if it failed to strike the vulnerable point.

"Oh you guys, still want to play?" Someone asked as she was wearing a leather coat with belt that paired with below the knee black boots, while the blonde hair was set in a bun while gazing at the men taunted from the floor, where most of their joints were dislocated, the gun spinning on her index finger to demonstrate its futility once the advantage shifted in her favour. The earpiece beeped, but she remained silent, as the sounds of their agony over the line sufficed to confirm her success. The call ended, but if the Superior reconsidered to proceed about the next decision, she would take pleasure in eliminating them all. However, that was not her intent; it served as a warning from the one who had commissioned this task.

Meanwhile, on another part of Australia, Addison was utterly baffled by the sudden cancellation of the mission from the previous day, especially since it had been the perfect opportunity for him to execute the task, which he had instead assigned to someone who had just completed it half an hour earlier. He was satisfied of the outcome tonight; they were the best! But the word opposite came in his mind when he got a call from someone earlier; a certain member who has a significant value to the organisation; this is the first time to turn down a very simple task to his member.

Upon his arrival, an envelope was presented to him, and after he nodded in understanding, he grasped the contents within.

"So, this is the reason?" He asked, then seeing him in a casual nod.

"Actually, this is not acceptable as someone who recently had done this but since it would entirely affect your every mission, then there is no way for me to refuse."

"Thank you Superior."

"But once you crossed the line of this organisation, you must remember this; any one of your colleagues can find you and to execute the next step."

"I truly I understand that, but nonetheless I always value about my loyalty to the group as it holds a remarkable experience to me."

"Great to hear, and I will count on that "Umbra," and I am wishing you all the best."

Five

Ezekiel and Esmeralda

At six thirty in the morning, a twenty-five-year-old Ezekiel knocked on the double doors of the library and entered wearing a powder blue polo shirt and black slacks, which were slightly dirtied. His primary intention was to politely decline the favour regarding the event scheduled for the following week, as he already had other commitments. Inside, he saw his father, Amadeus, smiling warmly at him then folded the newspaper, placed it on the antique table, and took a sip of his brewed coffee, its strong aroma filling the room as Ezekiel settled into the chair.

"Thanks for coming, even though I know you're tired from your latest project," Amadeus began. "I am sure your mother gave you a heads-up about what this is all about," he added with a smile, clasping his hands on the table.

"Dad, can you please send someone else to that event instead of me? I'm busy that day," he asked his father, looking at him intently and hoping for his consideration until he noticed his dad sigh heavily.

"I wish I could, but I can't attend either as your mother and I would've an important task that night. Remember, we're both guests at this event, since we've been supporting the group for quite a few years. I don't want to tarnish our reputation by not attending," his father replied in a serious tone.

"Oh god, I thought it wasn't them that we both actively supporting," he said, biting his lower lip as he tried to figure out how to manage his schedule. "Alright, Dad, I'll attend the event, but can I leave once my part is over? I don't want to miss my other commitment entirely. I'll ask my personal assistant to speak on my behalf while I'm not there," he concluded.

"Well, it's up to you. What matters to me is that either you or I am would be there since I've already mentioned this to the team."

"Alright, Dad. I'll be there, but I need to sleep now. Can I go?"

"Sure, rest well, and thank you." Amadeus said as he watched his son stand up, walk to the door, and look back.

"I'll see you around, Dad," Ezekiel said before the door finally closed.

"Poor Ezekiel. Still, I'm hopeful that your sister will eventually show an interest in the business, so I'll have two people to work with. For now, though, I'm relying entirely on you as my most trusted ally, next to your mother."

After a quick shower, he dried his deep black hair. As Ezekiel lay in bed wearing a white shirt and blue boxer shorts, he pondered the event that was a week away. He exhaled deeply, closed his eyes, and tried to shake off the anticipation, reminding himself of the countless gatherings he had attended before. Yet, something inside him felt a compelling pull to look forward to it.

"What could it be?" He wondered to himself, but surely it was just another formal occasion, much like those he had grown accustomed to. Several minutes passed, until Ezekiel fell asleep from exhaustion due to his overnight work at the family business.

It was a demanding week for father and son as they handling the primary responsibilities of their business. Owning the largest construction company in the country, Amadeus remained actively involved in overseeing every major project, while his son, Ezekiel, managed the smaller ones. This approach served as a valuable stepping stone for Ezekiel, preparing him for his future role as CEO. By seven in the evening, the lights were off in the two-story building, except in one particular room where Ezekiel was surrounded by a towering stack of folders in his office. He diligently reviewed the paperwork on his desk, which included comprehensive reports on his latest project. These reports encompassed financial summaries and monitoring systems designed to ensure precise control mechanisms were in place in every department. He was grateful to his secretary, who had helped him that day. Now, with only a few folders left to scrutinise, he felt close to completing his work. Suddenly, a strange feeling swept over him, and his eyes were unable to divert their gaze from the piece of paper he was holding. He sighed deeply, trying to control the unwelcome sensations so he could finish his remaining tasks for the night. He needed a full day of rest tomorrow to prepare for the evening event organised by a group that helps underprivileged individuals for their educational finances. Before going home, Ezekiel decided to have dinner at the famous fast-food restaurant, and he quickly consumed the meal as he wanted to sleep once he arrived their home after a quick shower. By the next morning, all Ezekiel did was spend the entire day in his room, taking a satisfying rest after organising his attire for the event.

It was already past six in the evening and Ezekiel stepped out of his black Jaguar 420G in the reserved parking area about a hundred metres from the main carpark, dressed in a black three-piece suit and black leather shoes. His hair was neatly styled with pomade while his companion, Arthur, who attired in a grey suit, joined him and agreed to his suggestion of avoiding attention at the main entrance by walking directly from where they had alighted. When they finally arrived at the main entrance, they saw a group of people and Arthur whispered to him.

"One of them is an old friend, will join them for a while."

"Sure, take your time. I'll go inside and see you around," he replied, tapping his companion's shoulder before continuing toward the opened huge double doors of the hall. As he entered, he heard a melodious sound coming from the left corner of the hall, just a few steps away, attended by two men from the sound and audiovisual team. The captivating aroma heightened his senses and rejuvenated him until someone caught his eye on the right side of the room, similar to the golden ambient lights from the ceiling created a serene atmosphere. Slowly, he walked toward that spot after grabbing a glass of wine from the satellite bar attended by waitress. The woman he had noticed was holding a pile of pamphlets, engaged in several conversations with a few people dressed in the same white, collared clothing. Exhaling gently, he decided he would find the right opportunity to get to know who the woman was. Then he suddenly realised, the particular but not clear from the previous week.

"Maybe it was a sign and would finally prove me right later about this feeling," he calmly said to himself as he tried to get a closer look at her. Taking his time, he walked slowly toward the group. As he walked past them and saw her smile, an instantaneous sense of tranquillity washed over him. The moment felt magical, causing him to quickly divert his gaze to the nearby round tables to avoid being caught staring and saw how the tables were elegantly prepared with a silk white cloth and a set of fresh assorted flowers in the middle.

"What should I do to get to know her name?" Ezekiel asked himself, while watching several staff tidying up the tables and one of them smiled at him so he smiled back. Then, he took another sip of his drink until he saw the woman was now heading towards where he was after she spoke with her companions and Ezekiel was able to think quickly how he would get the attention of the woman after he put the glass of wine on the table until his expectation happened and their bodies collided.

Then the woman started to look at him for a few moments before she speak.

"Whoever you are, could you please be mindful of yourself as a human?" Behind of her words, there was a certain thought in her mind while they were exchanging glances. The trace of confusion in his eyes while hers was exuding of confidence.

"Oh, please, don't think that way and sorry for how I approached you. I never intended to be rude. Please, don't walk away," Ezekiel apologetically said, and she simply smiled at him before she replied.

"Apology accepted, excuse me," and then watched as the woman walked away without a backward glance. He shook his head and smiled, his right hand resting on his hip while he scratched his head with his left. The woman was quite charming yet difficult to get to know. Suddenly, an idea struck him as he saw his companion, but his intention never happened as he spotted his mother, Sylvia Emsworth, with her most trusted associate Lucy as they were both drinking a glass of champagne. "*What are they doing here?*" He asked himself and as far as he knew, they were with his father at an important event right now. To satisfy his curiosity, he decided to approach his mom.

"Mom, why are you here?" He asked, as his eyes scanning the room for someone before landing his gaze on her.

"I'm here because your father and I had a bit of a disagreement," his mother answered serenely. "But there's no need to worry, it was just a minor issue. I thought coming here would help lighten the mood. Plus, I wanted to give the speech on stage later because I was really impressed with what I witnessed earlier."

Ezekiel knitted his brows as he looked at his mother before speaking.

"What do you mean, mom?" He inquired, picking up a glass of wine from a passing waiter's tray. He swirled the glass to his satisfaction, took a slow sip, and watched as his mother, who just gave him a single smile as she gently placed her two fingers on the peak lapel of his suit to fix the vintage Tiffany mid-century rose pin brooch piquing his curiosity even more.

"Must I truly reveal what it was all about?" She looked at his eyes before she continued, "trust your feelings Ezekiel, and I'll see you around by chance."

His mother departed with a pleasant smile while her words of encouragement lingering in the air, he felt a surge of determination. Her simple advice to trust himself resonated deeply, serving as a catalyst for introspection and newfound resolve. He understood that he didn't need to reveal every intricate detail of his intentions; instead, his actions would speak itself. With the right courage and mindset on proving his true character, Ezekiel prepared himself and would look for the woman who had previously misjudged him. He slowly nodded, his mind a whirlwind of thoughts, as he watched his mother socialising among a circle of guests. That night, his main purpose shifted unexpectedly, presenting an opportunity he couldn't afford to miss. Most of the attendees were unaware of his identity, as he preferred to maintain a low profile. He took another sip of wine and began searching for the woman, since the group was no longer where he had seen them earlier. He remembered his commitment, then scanned the area to find the head of the organiser so he could ask about where he could use a telephone. He needed to notify his assistant that he couldn't make it and assigning him as a representative for the occasion. After few moments, Ezekiel spotted one of the event organisers and approached him to ask for the telephone. The man who's almost same age as him responded politely and raised his right hand to get the attention of a waitress, and he clearly instructed her to escort Ezekiel to the organiser's room to use the telephone and he found out that it was just next to the cloak room when they were exited the main entrance.

"Thank you for bringing me here," Ezekiel mentioned to the waitress.

"You're welcome, sir," she replied to him with a smile before she left and closed the door.

As he approached the Oakwood table, Ezekiel took a small notebook from his suit pocket to locate the phone number of the place where his assistant was. After dialling the number, he waited barely ten seconds before someone picked up.

"Hi this is Ezekiel Emsworth, I would like to speak with my assistant please."

"Alright sir, hold on," the lady replied from the other line.

And as expected, Ezekiel never waited for long as he heard the familiar voice from the other line.

"Yes, Sir Ezekiel?"

"I can't make it there tonight. So, I'm wholeheartedly trusting you to do my thing. And also, I am expecting you to make a valid reason for them."

"Alright sir, you can count on me with that and good luck to the event where you at now."

"Sure, thank you," then Ezekiel hanged up the call while the smile escaping from his lips until he heard the door opened and was totally surprised who behind that door when he looked at it.

"How does it feel?"

"What do you mean?" Ezekiel asked. He noticed the woman roll her eyes before she replied to him.

"I know you were looking for me before you came here."

Ezekiel smiled while shaking his head, observing her in silence as she approached him, he finally understood what she was implying and extended his right hand in introduction.

"I'm Ezekiel, and you are?"

"Nice to meet you, Ezekiel. I am Esmeralda," she said with a smile. Hearing his name intrigued her even more. However, when she attempted to kiss him, Ezekiel was taken aback.

"That's so fast," Ezekiel said, shaking his head.

"I wasn't expecting that from you," Esmeralda replied, smiling and shaking her head as well.

"I thought you were-"

But Ezekiel never had a chance to finish his words. The woman in front of him kissed him gently on the lips, leaving him in shock until he eventually found himself responding to her kiss. That moment lingered for nearly a minute.

"This is the right place for us," Esmeralda said after they kissed, seeing him smiling while nodding.

"Uh, yes. That's right," Ezekiel agreed, still smiling at her.

"I guess, we are on the same page?" Esmeralda asked him.

"There's no doubt about that," he replied.

"I'll go back now to the main hall," Esmeralda said as she grabbed some pamphlets from the table next to them.

"Hold on," said by Ezekiel as he held her hand while looking in her eyes then the woman looked how he was holding her hand and their gaze locked at each other.

"Can we meet later like within half an hour?" He asked since the speech would be after thirty minutes, "I mean not here, do you know where the other car park is? Not the main one."

"Yes, of course. And sure, see you around," she answered to him.

When Esmeralda finally left the room, Ezekiel smiled and shook his head, still unable to believe what had just happened. Nevertheless, he felt no regret about any of it. After waiting a few moments, he returned to the main function room and spotted Arthur, who was now alone, sipping a glass of wine at the satellite bar. Then he saw his companion begin walking toward their designated table, and he casually approached the table as well.

"Where did you go?" Arthur asked.

"I just went to the organiser's room to use the telephone to make call since I can no longer attend the next event," Ezekiel answered promptly to his most trusted companion.

"Alright, whatever the reason was, I am happy for that. Since it would be totally tiring for you to attend the next one since tomorrow is Monday and I'm happy that both of our moms are here," he replied. "So later, I'll go with her once this event is over."

"Yes, sure. And if, by chance, you can't find me later, it's probably because I'm caught up with something. Don't worry about it, just enjoy yourself tonight." Ezekiel said, tapping his companion's shoulder. He glanced at the group of people and saw his mother and Lucy still engaged in conversation. Then his eyes landed on Esmeralda, who was also busy socialising with another group.

The soothing melodies of background music captivated every guest in the room, complemented by the dimmed lights from the ceiling that harmonized with the jazz. Ezekiel was relishing the moment as he observed Esmeralda enjoying her time with her colleagues. He then glanced at his watch, smiling as he realised that in less than thirty minutes, he would head to the location they had agreed upon for their meeting. Just then, he spotted Arthur, who was conversing with a group of people. Earlier, when Arthur had left their table, he had simply mentioned he was going to the restroom. Upon returning to their designated spot, Arthur patted Ezekiel on the back and whispered,

"Ezekiel, I see another group I know. I think I'll join them since it's been a while. Is that okay?"

"Absolutely, as I mentioned before, enjoy yourself. Don't worry about me; I have something to take care of shortly," Ezekiel replied. Arthur then made his way to the nearby table, waving at them until Ezekiel noticed a familiar group closer to the stage. To his surprise, he saw his mother and Lucy joining Esmeralda's group. Then, something unexpected happened: the woman who had caught his eye that evening glanced at him for a brief moment, and time seemed to slow down. He recalled his mother's reaction as they exchanged glances; she clearly delighted in the chemistry they shared. He smiled and took a sip of wine, and for the remainder of his wait, all he could think about was how much his mother and Esmeralda enjoyed each other's company, as their conversation flowed effortlessly. Then he witnessed the next scene: his mother gently tucked a strand of hair behind Esmeralda's ear. He knew his mother well; if she truly liked someone, she would certainly express it. His heart raced; if Esmeralda accepted his proposal the following day, then the wedding will take place as soon as possible, as he cannot imagine being single for the next few months. He was aware of this and felt confident about her. They were destined to be together, and this occasion was a sign for them, prompting him to smile. As he awaited the moment he had been looking forward to, he casually rose from his chair while a woman ascended the steps of the stage to announce the next segment of the event.

"Sylvia, I thought Ezekiel would be giving the speech?" Lucy inquired after seeing her friend's son exiting the function hall.

"It's alright, Lucy," Sylvia replied with a smile, having already informed the organiser that she would be delivering the speech instead of her son. She then turned her attention to the stage as the speaker began reading some important honourable mentions for the evening.

Meanwhile, Ezekiel was thrilled as he arrived at the designated parking area. He looked up at the sky, which presented a magnificent view that night. The cluster of stars was breathtaking, and the moon shone brightly, even in its waxing quarter phase. He checked the key in his slacks pocket to ensure it was there, nodding in satisfaction as he felt the metal pieces of the key chain. He glanced towards the reserved parking area, hoping to see someone approaching, but there was no sign of anyone. After checking his watch, he decided to take a stroll while he waited. He took a deep breath when he heard footsteps approaching, and when he turned around, he smiled upon seeing her. It was Esmeralda walking towards him, and he instinctively moved to meet her. Time seemed to slow down as he embraced her and kissed her for the second time, which she happily reciprocated while they held each other close. After a few moments, they released each other from the hug.

"I apologise if you had to wait for me here for a bit," Esmeralda said, holding both of his hands.

"Esmeralda, it's perfectly fine with me. Now that you're here, it doesn't concern me." He responded, kissing her hands.

"Ezekiel, this feels incredibly surreal for me. I've never experienced this before, and I can't quite grasp why I struggle to envision myself in a relationship. However, everything changed when we met tonight, in a way that I can't explain." After expressing her thoughts to Ezekiel, she noticed him gazing at her intently, and then he smiled while gently stroking her right cheek.

"Believe it or not, we share the same feelings, Esmeralda," he said, continuing to tenderly caress her face. As Ezekiel noticed her nodding while still clasping her hand, he began to stroll forward, never releasing his grip. The joy radiating from her expression was unmistakable, as she bit her lower lip and gazed around them.

"What a magnificent night, wouldn't you agree?" Ezekiel's voice broke the silence.

"Indeed, it is. And I adore it," she replied.

Then, they both explored their surroundings, still clasping hands, and any observer of that moment would undoubtedly describe them as high school teenagers. However, no one was present to witness how they relished and savoured every fleeting second of their experience. Eventually, they began walking back to where his car was parked. At that moment, Ezekiel turned to her, and this time, the intensity of his gaze was profound, akin to a fire; each breath he took while looking into her eyes seemed to transport them both on a journey of eternal bliss. Finally, he reached for his keys in his pocket and glanced at her, while Esmeralda's eyes also began to reflect a passionate longing, revealing a deep desire for the man standing before her.

She continues to experience discomfort in a specific area of her body; the man was nearly inside her. She ran her hands along his back, gently exploring the medium muscular physique of Ezekiel, until she heard him begin to moan uncontrollably, and she too realised she was on the verge of screaming. Then Ezekiel tenderly kissed her lips, silencing her from making any sound in their current position until she reciprocated his kiss, leading to an increasingly intense and adventurous form of lovemaking they engaged in. The drops of his sweat on her and her sweat on the leather seats of the car were both passionate; until they both reached the glory of their earnest attraction from the moment their eyes met. A solemn of silence envelope inside of the car, while their breath was gasping with joy until Ezekiel broke the stillness as the radiance of the moon was now starting to cover by a thin cloud above of the peaceful night.

"Did you know that a week before attending this event, I felt an emotion I couldn't fully comprehend? It was the first time I had such a feeling. Everything shifted when I saw you. I recall telling God that I would place my trust in Him, regardless of the circumstances. I must admit, God truly understood what was best for me, and that was the moment I first saw you," he spoke softly to the woman as she rested her head on his chest. He found himself entertained as he played with her long, glossy brown hair with his fingers, then he gently kissed her forehead.

A few moments later, Esmeralda mentioned something about him that he wished she had never said.

"Ezekiel, I realise this might seem quite ordinary, but since we are here, I feel compelled to share it now." She gazed at him while her left hand softly played with his chest.

"Of course, what is it?" He replied, his hand still tenderly playing her hair.

"I don't belong to any group associated with your background, and I'm sharing this so you can understand who I truly am. I'm just a simple woman who works whenever there's a job opportunity available to me." She recognised that Ezekiel, from his demeanor and body language, came from a wealthy family.

"That's not a problem, Esmeralda. From the moment I laid eyes on you, I understood what kind of woman you are, which is why I was drawn to you, especially when your candid words struck me directly." Then he heard a soft laugh escape her alluring lips, a gesture so infectious that he found himself laughing too, and they began to kiss. Before they returned to the event room, Ezekiel agreed to her suggestion that he should leave first, just as they had done about half an hour earlier, to avoid raising any suspicions or gossip from anyone who might see them return together. She understood how this world operated, so she preferred to keep it a secret for the time being, knowing that everything would unfold when the moment was right for both of them. Upon reaching the hall, the lights remained dim, prompting

Esmeralda to quickly jot down an address on a piece of paper from the nearby satellite bar, indicating where they could meet the following day. Glancing inside, she noticed people beginning to leave, seizing the opportunity to take several copies, discreetly placing the paper beneath the specified one before casually approaching the group of people who had requested copies when she arrived, and then making her way to the table where Ezekiel was seated.

Then he found himself puzzled by the pamphlet until he flipped through two pages. Upon noticing a message inscribed on a piece of paper, he suddenly remembered where it was located, and they had plans to meet the next day around three in the afternoon. This timing was ideal since he had already accomplished several important tasks the day before, enabling him to leave his office before one o'clock. He cast a glance at Arthur, who was still mingling with a group of people. If the chance presented itself, he would let him know that he had finally discovered the right woman he intended to marry. Before leaving the event, they exchanged knowing looks and shared smiles while he watched her busily packing their things with her colleagues in the corner of the room. The peacefulness of the night was interrupted by the sounds and lights of a vehicle making its way home. The area around them had an unsettling vibe, with tall native trees flanking both sides of the road, yet inside the car, a lively conversation flowed between mother and son.

"Ezekiel, if she's truly the one for you, then go for it. I genuinely admire her character; she is very accommodating when she feels comfortable, and I don't think she's the kind of woman who would exploit a man from a wealthy family."

"Actually, mom, we're meeting tomorrow at three in the afternoon, so I was lucky that I managed to finish some significant tasks last week in preparation for the days ahead." He then remembered the piece of paper she had given him before they left and wanted to show it to his mother, as she had a passion for calligraphy. However, he quickly realised that the paper was no longer in his slacks. As he adjusted his left hand on the steering wheel, he used his right hand to check the right pocket of his slacks, only to be taken aback that it wasn't there. Just then, his mother began to scream, pointing at the windshield of the car.

Six

Amadeus Emsworth

The corporate lunch meeting unfolded in an executive suite; a space designed to exude exclusivity. Floor-to-ceiling windows bathed the room in natural light, offering breathtaking views of the city skyline. The contemporary decor featured sleek furnishings in neutral tones, accented by polished chrome details and tasteful artwork, creating an atmosphere of understated elegance. A long conference table served as the centrepiece, adorned with fresh floral arrangements and pristine white linens. Selected guests, were carefully chosen for their ability and influence, engaged in lively discussions over a gourmet spread of artfully plated dishes prepared by a private chef. The soft hum of conversation was complemented by the faint strains of ambient music, ensuring a relaxed yet professional ambiance, Mr. Amadeus entered the suite after stepping out, accompanied by the host's announcement.

"Oh, there he is! Before we conclude this event, I have an announcement. I have decided to renew the contract with AE company to construct several of my future projects, as I see no reason to change builders. Thank you all for coming," the entrepreneur said, followed by a round of applause filling the opulent room while he was intently looking at Mr. Amadeus Emsworth.

"Thank you so much, Mr. Saunders!"Amadeus exclaimed, his voice brimming with genuine gratitude as the two men clasped hands in a firm handshake. The exchange was brief yet meaningful, a silent acknowledgment of mutual respect and understanding. As the moment lingered, Amadeus could not help but feel a surge of appreciation for the man standing before him, someone who had undoubtedly played a pivotal role in the opportunity that now lay ahead. With a grateful nod, he turned and approached his seat, carrying with him the weight of optimism and a renewed sense of purpose.

"Mr. Amadeus, congratulations!" Lucy exclaimed warmly as he settled into his chair.

"Thank you! But how I wish my wife and Ezekiel were still alive, as I am unsure if my daughter is interested in assuming the position once I decide to resign. I would prefer my successor to be from the Emsworth family bloodline. However, my grandson is still young at just fourteen," Amadeus said, referring to his daughter's son. "Ezekiel was a workaholic and never had the chance to become a father, nor did I have the chance to be a grandfather to his child. Sometimes I cannot help but blame myself after all these years," then he looked at her and deeply sighed with sadness in his eyes.

"Well, I must admit that I initially thought your late son was quite the workaholic, Mr. Amadeus. However, my perspective changed the last time I saw him with that lovely lady at the event," the woman replied seriously.

"What do you mean?" Amadeus asked.

"That night, during the event, your son and the lady both disappeared while Sylvia was giving her speech on stage."

"Why have you never told me this before?" Amadeus exclaimed in disbelief.

"I only remembered what I saw when you spoke about the past, but at the time, I chose to ignore it," the woman replied after taking a bite of her dessert.

"I owe you so much Lucy!" He said, after taking a moment to gather his thoughts about the big plan forming in his mind. The next morning after arranging a task with a certain man the night before via phone call, Amadeus waited calmly in his office then several minutes passed before a soft knock came at the door.

"Come in," he said casually, while examining the piece of paper then the door creaked open, and Amadeus finally lifted his gaze, meeting the familiar face of the man he had been expecting. Behind him, a staff member entered with silent efficiency, balancing a silver tray laden with a steaming coffee pot, two pristine white cups resting on delicate saucers, and matching containers of milk and sugar, then a few pieces of chocolate croissant in a bread basket. The faint clink of porcelain accompanied the tray being placed on the side table, filling the room with the comforting aroma of fresh coffee.

"Thank you for coming, Detective Gregory," Amadeus said, after he glance at the big antique shelf with analog clock that stood on the right side of the room. With a gesture, he invited Mr. Gregory to take the seat across from the intricately crafted table while his expression was already composed but his mind already racing ahead, anticipating the conversation that would follow after their cups of coffee were carefully placed on the table by the staff.

"The pleasure is mine, Mr. Amadeus," the man replied as he settled into the chair.

Amadeus, exuding a sense of urgency, entrusted the man in the black suit with a task that clearly weighed heavily on his mind.

"I trust you to complete this task as soon as possible," Amadeus said, handing the dirty white envelope to the man in the black suit. "Also, please provide me with daily updates; this is really important to me," he concluded.

"No problem, sir. I'll keep you posted," the man said, quickly scanning the papers from the envelope. The detective took a sip of coffee.

"Thank you," Amadeus replied, lifting his cup to take a sip as well.

"I'll head out now, sir. Since it's urgent, so my partner and I will begin the first step of this assignment today," said the man, who appeared to be in his mid-forties, as he stood up and offered a handshake.

"Great! I look forward to receiving the latest report tomorrow before evening," Amadeus said joyfully, accepting the handshake as he stood. "I will do whatever it takes to explore the possibility of my theory," he said to himself while taking a deep breath as he watched the man leave the room, then steadied himself to tackle the rest of the tasks he needed to complete that day.

It was just past noon two days after when Amadeus was discussing his itinerary for the next four days with his assistant. As they walked through the lobby of the main building, heading to visit the current project, his secretary's voice cut through the air as she approached them.

"Sir, someone is on the phone, and it is urgent," the woman said.

"Who's the caller?"

"Sir, it is Mr. Gregory."

Amadeus felt a sudden mix of feelings. He glanced at his assistant before he spoke.

"We will not be able to visit the site now. Please cancel the rest of the appointments for today," he politely requested.

"Alright sir," the man replied.

"Let's go," Amadeus said to his secretary, in less than five minutes they finally arrived at the designated floor.

"Anna, please transfer the call to my office now," Amadeus said, as he stepped out of the elevator and hurried toward his office, he heard his secretary respond, "yes, sir."

Amadeus took a deep breath, inhaling and exhaling before lifting the device to answer the call.

"Yes, Detective Gregory?" He began.

"Sir Amadeus, I apologise for yesterday if the key element of the report was missing. However, we now have all the details," the man responded, "and we are now heading there from Queensland, and I will discuss every detail when we meet tonight at your residence."

"Great! Thanks! And I can't wait to know everything about the entire investigation," Amadeus exclaimed.

"Alright sir, I'll see you later."

"Yes and thank you."

That evening after dinner with his assistant, Amadeus was waiting inside of his office. He felt a sense of relief knowing that his daughter, Audrey, was on vacation in Europe with her family and would return in two weeks. Taking a moment to himself, he sipped from a glass of Lark Legacy Cask 1 Single Malt whisky, until he heard the sound of the incoming vehicle from the outside. He already instructed his butler for a few protocols for that night, no calls and visitors at all costs except for Mr. Gregory. He stood from his chair and walked towards the large family portrait, the faces within the frame radiated joy and togetherness, yet his eyes instinctively sought one in particular.

"I am hoping for the best, my son. And wishing that whatever Lucy saw it has a result for the positivity of my conclusion," Amadeus softly whispered to himself while looking at the photograph until he heard a soft knock on the door and quickly approached to open it.

"Good evening, sir," the man greeted him with a smile while shaking his hand. Behind the detective stood another man in a black suit, who was familiar to him, his partner Maverick, for the investigation. The partner also offered him a handshake before he proceeded to his table.

"I never thought it would be quicker than I expected for you and your partner to find the answers," Amadeus started as he sat on the black vintage swivel chair.

"Actually sir, they were totally fine, but everything became complicated until Mr. Enrique de Ayala's desire happened," the detective answered. Amadeus furrowed his brow as he listened, his expression tightening until the detective handed him an envelope. He swiftly scanned the report inside, piecing everything together as he finished reading. Then he came to the last item, a photograph that left him completely shocked by how everything had unfolded.

"Detective, I need your help. I want to leave for Melbourne tonight."

"Sure, Mr. Amadeus. As I had already predicted this plan, I informed my team accordingly."

"Great! I'll be back, gentlemen. I need to sort some things out," Amadeus said as he began to leave the room.

After an hour and half journey aboard the private jet, they touched down in Melbourne and the hum of aircraft fading into the stillness of the airport. As the jet's steps unfolded and the trio began their descent, Amadeus, with his usual air of authority, turned to the detective and his partner.

"This search must remain discreet," he clearly instructed, his sharp gaze cutting through the cool night air. The weight of his words was unmistakable; finding Lucas was paramount, but it had to be done without drawing unnecessary attention. The detective nodded silently, understanding the gravity of the situation, while his partner adjusted his jacket against the breeze, ready to act; They finally got into the SUV and began leaving the airport, heading toward the city of Melbourne with its secrets waiting to be uncovered. The hunt for Lucas was about to begin. It was already past one in the morning, and the current temperature was minus two degrees celsius and Amadeus lay restless, unable to succumb to sleep as the weight of anticipation consumed him. The result of the search lingered in his mind, a silent spectre that refused to let him find peace. Before arriving in the state of Victoria, he had meticulously reached out to his trusted confidants, ensuring every detail from accommodation to his immediate needs was flawlessly organised. Yet, even their reliability could not quiet the storm within him. The room was still, save for the soft crackle of the wind against the windowpane. He stood by the frosted glass, gazing into the darkness, letting the biting chill of the night seep through to dull his mounting anxiety. With a deep, deliberate breath, he brought the steaming cup of tea to his lips, it's warmth a fleeting comfort as he braced himself for what awaited. He almost fell asleep when he heard the incoming footsteps towards the door and Amadeus quickly got up from his bed to open the door since he already knew who they were as he already secure the safety of the premises.

"Mr. Amadeus I am glad that you are still awake," detective Gregory started as they walked towards inside of the room while Amadeus closing the door behind them.

"Just as I was about to fall asleep, I heard footsteps," he replied.

"We already know the name of the group, but sadly, the leader of this underground criminal network is cunning. His real identity remains unknown, and, for now, he's outside the country. However, I've managed to discover the name of the individual who with Lucas," the detective said as they sat down. Amadeus settled into a single armchair, while the other two took seats on a larger couch.

"Detective, can your team track down the whereabouts of the person Lucas was with?" Amadeus requested as he stood, he opened his attaché case from the nearby kitchen table, grabbed the envelope from inside, and walked back toward the two men.

"This will be more useful for them to find what we are really looking for," Amadeus said as he handed the envelope to the man in front of him.

"Absolutely, Mr. Amadeus," the detective replied when he saw a thick pile of hundred-dollar bills inside the envelope.

"I have a strong feeling we need to find Lucas as quickly as possible, given everything we've uncovered so far," the detective assured him.

"Yes, please," Amadeus responded, his gaze conveying the urgency of the matter. The man placed a reassuring hand on his shoulder before replying.

"Don't worry, we will. This time, I'll do everything I can to ensure my team finds the man. He's the final piece of the puzzle."

"Thank you, Mr. Gregory. For now, we both need to rest and allow your team to continue the search. Tomorrow, we'll need our energy for the next phase. You can now head back to your room," Amadeus said, glancing at the sleek stainless-steel wristwatch on his arm.

"Got it, thanks," the man responded. Turning to his companion, he said, "I'll head back to my room now and gather the rest of the team there so I can lay out clear instructions for the night ahead." Both men stood, exchanging a firm handshake with the head of the Emsworth family before making their way toward the exit.

The following day dragged on endlessly for Amadeus, each ticking hour stretching his patience to its brink as he anxiously awaited the final verdict. His nerves frayed, his body coiled with tension, he wrestled with a restless mind after enduring a relentless stream of follow-up calls from Maverick, he suddenly noticed the detective, who had offered to find in some places. As the clock inched past four, a new wave of concern arose; the detective still hadn't returned. Anxiety began to settle in as the faint hues of twilight signalled the approach of evening. Standing alone on the hotel balcony, the cool breeze grazing his face, Amadeus exhaled a deep, weary sigh, his thoughts tethered to a single hope: that clarity and resolution would arrive before another day shrouded in uncertainty. Then, he heard a knock at the door. He was certain it was the detective, as he had clearly instructed his driver that he did not want any disturbances except from Mr. Gregory or his search team. When he opened the door, it was him shaking his head, signalling that he had failed in that moment.

Amadeus gazed at the detective for a moment, then gave a slight nod before speaking.

"Let's wait for Maverick and his team. I haven't lost hope. Thank you for the update." With that, he quietly closed the door.

Several lights from the vehicles on the road pierced through the large windows of the hotel's restaurant, casting different glows over the neatly arranged tables and the soft hum of conversation. Mr. Amadeus, seated at a corner table, was carefully slicing a piece of porterhouse steak while his driver chewed his food beside him, their quiet exchange punctuated by the occasional clink of silverware. Detective Gregory leaned back in his chair, his sharp eyes scanning the area even as he stirred his Asian noodles. The tension in the air lightened abruptly when the leader of the investigative team strode in, a confident smile on Maverick's face and an unmistakable glimmer of success in his eyes. As he approached the group, his words cut through the hum of the restaurant with clarity.

"Sir Amadeus and Detective Gregory, we found the key," he said carefully as he took a seat next to the detective.

"I was waiting for such big news, and finally, we have him!" Amadeus exclaimed after finishing his red wine. A wave of relief and anticipation swept over the table, the weight of uncertainty lifting as the pieces of their puzzle finally began to fall into place.

"Excellent!" The detective replied, taking a sip of his drink. "So, did you take him to the place?" He set his glass on the table, glanced at his partner, and saw him nod. Turning his attention to Mr. Amadeus, he nodded again.

"Great work, Maverick. Your efficiency is much appreciated," Amadeus said after exchanging glances with the detective. Shifting his gaze to Maverick, then he continued, "you and your team can take a break for now, Gregory and I will handle that man." Amadeus spoke with finality, then took another sip of his wine before standing up from his chair. "Men let's go. We need to finish our objective here in Melbourne as much as possible," he was followed by the driver and Detective Gregory as they made their way toward the hotel's car park.

Seven

The Rescue Mission

They had finally found the man they'd been seeking, seated in a battered chair, his arms tightly bound, and his eyes hidden by blindfold. The air was heavy with tension as Amadeus exchanged a brief glance with the detective, a silent understanding passing between them. With a slow, deliberate nod, Amadeus stepped forward, his sharp gaze fixed on the figure before him. He exhaled deeply, his calculating mind assessing the man's age to be somewhere in his late twenties or early thirties. After a moment of silence, Amadeus spoke, his voice calm yet laced with authority.

"You're not innocent, so there's a reason you're here. I expect your cooperation and honesty, what's your name?"

The man flinched at the sound, his bound body shifting nervously.

"Who are you?" He stammered, panic edging his voice.

"Please, I have nothing worth kidnapping. There's no reason for this-"

Amadeus cut him off sharply, his tone cold and unwavering.

"Do not test my patience. What's your name?"

The man hesitated, trembling as his words stumbled out.

"I-I am Sean."

Amadeus's eyes narrowed. "Sean," he repeated, his voice heavy with intent, "where is Lucas?"

"Who- who's Lucas?"

Amadeus couldn't contain himself and delivered a heavy punch to the man's stomach. He watched and listened intently as the man reacted to the blow.

"Please! Stop! I don't know who Lucas is!" The man cried out in pain.

"I'll stop when I hear the truth!" Amadeus shouted back. "Where is he?!"

"I really don't know! Please, let me go!" The man pleaded, his voice trembling with fear and agony. Amadeus inhaled deeply, exhaled slowly, and ran a hand through his hair in frustration.

"I'm running out of time," he said in a low, tense voice, shaking his head as he looked down at the man.

Meanwhile, the detective watched silently, fully aware that Mr. Amadeus understood the consequences of his actions that night and feeling no inclination to place blame on the entrepreneur. Hoping that everything will turn out well for good.

"I'm not a killer," Amadeus said coldly, "but if killing you would ease my disappointment, I wouldn't regret it for a second." He turned to Detective Gregory, who gave a silent nod and stepped forward with the .45 caliber gun in hand. The dimly lit room crackled with tension as Amadeus's voice cut through the suffocating silence, his words laced with a chilling finality.

"Now, what are your last words?" He asked, his tone steady, almost dispassionate, as the cold steel of the gun rested against the man's forehead. Amadeus's piercing gaze bore into him, unyielding and void of mercy, as if daring him to utter something profound, defiant, or even pleading. In that moment, the room held its breath, the air thick with the unspoken—the fragile dance between life and death hanging precariously in the balance.

"I-I left Lucas along Summit Road on Mount Buller! Since I needed to retrieve something from him. Please, sir, may I go now? I have a family!" The man pleaded; his eyes filled with tears under of blindfold with fear.

"Where in Summit Road?!" Amadeus asked as he needed the exact detail to be easier for them to find Lucas.

"In the Village Toboggan Park!" The man replied.

"Are you telling me the right information?" Then Amadeus saw the man nodded at him more deeply at that moment then shifted his gaze to Detective Gregory. He quickly evaluated the plan for the night, seeking a definitive answer to his theory, for sure Lucas is not totally safe in that place especially in this season and it was more than three hours' drive from the city of Melbourne.

"Detective, I need you and some of your men to search for Lucas. One should stay here to keep an eye on him," he said, pointing to the man who was now beginning to sob. "Since I'm not finished with this one yet," with that, Amadeus turned and exited the room.

The detective silently nodded to two of his men before turning to the last one.

"Conrad, he's still dangerous. Keep a close watch on him at all costs—we need to see this case through to the end."

"No problem, sir, you can count on me," the man replied as he watched them walking towards the exit. And he started to inspect the whole area to secure every corner just in case he tried to escape, once he was done, he went to the nearest table and consume the rest of the night while waiting for his team. The darkened city streets blurred into streaks of light as Amadeus sat in the passenger seat, his gaze fixed on the horizon with a grim determination. The detective's car and his team trailed closely behind, their headlights slicing through the night like beacons of urgency. Amadeus's jaw tightened as the driver voiced his concern, suggesting enlisting additional help from the authorities.

"That's an option but not appropriate," Amadeus said firmly, his voice low but resolute, "we don't have time for bureaucracy. This mission is personal, and I intend to keep it that way." The driver nodded in understanding, his hands gripping the wheel as he pushed the SUV to the road speed limit, the engine humming with strain. The air between them was heavy with unspoken tension, a shared understanding that every second counted. Then until finally they reached the destination, after parking the car at the Toboggan Park parking lot, Amadeus reached into the backseat, pulled out the appropriate footwear for the terrain, along with flashlights, and radiotelephone handed them to his team.

"Alright, men, let's approach this the best way we can. We need to find Lucas. Let's split up—one group heads east, the other west—and we'll regroup at the far end of the park," he instructed, trying to keep his emotions in check. As he scanned the area, shaking his head slightly, the detective replied.

"He's right. This place isn't safe. It's been four hours since that bastard left Lucas here, and we have no idea what might've happened since or what condition Lucas is in after the encounter." With that, they turned on their flashlights and began walking in their separate directions. "My son Ezekiel, I'll do everything just to get what really matters. And that is Lucas," Amadeus said to himself.

"Lucas!" Amadeus shouted, his voice echoing through the night as he and his driver repeatedly called out the name. Nearly twenty minutes had passed since they began searching for him. They scoured every shadowy corner and patch of wild, tangled grass, their flashlights cutting through the darkness in the hope of finding him. But there was no sign of anyone, and the biting wind of the chilly night grew stronger. Meanwhile, detective Gregory saw almost lifeless figure sprawled on the dark the icy terrain, while approaching and the flashlight he's holding was focusing on to someone's face.

"Oh god, Lucas!" It was him, and not moving while his fragile body teetering on the edge of mortality, his breath shallow and fleeting under the relentless grip of the cold. The team's determination had unearthed the truth, but at a grave cost, leaving Gregory with the weight of not only capturing the culprit but also confronting the grim reality of Lucas's condition. The frigid air carried an unspoken urgency, as they knew every second counted in the fight to save him from the clutches of death. Suddenly, Amadeus heard a voice crackle through the radiotelephone. It was Detective Gregory.

"Mr. Amadeus, do you copy?" The voice from the other line emerged.

"Yes, Detective?" Amadeus replied, after pressing the button to respond when he pulled the device from his pocket.

"We found him! We're close to the end. Do you copy?"

"R-Roger that! We are on our way!" He answered, his heart pounding wildly. He turned to look at the driver.

"Let's go," they said, then walked hurriedly to their destination. When they arrived at the location, Amadeus saw Detective Gregory carrying Lucas, and as he approached them, it was evident that his grandson was on the verge of death.

"We need to hurry!" Gregory shouted. "His vital signs are fading!"

Amadeus nodded, struggling to control his emotions at what he had just heard and seen. As they walked back to the car park, they knew they needed to act as quickly as possible to save Lucas.

"I have a close friend who lives near this area. He's a doctor since I don't want to take my grandson to the hospital to avoid any unwanted conflict with the gang, just in case." Amadeus said after they had settled Lucas in the backseat of the SUV. His gaze then turned to the driver, and he nodded, signalling that the driver understood what he meant while seating next to his grandson and he held his hand as he totally knew behind of his condition Lucas can still hear and feel him.

"I'm with you Lucas, just hold on, okay? We are on our way to the place that can totally save you," Amadeus thought at the back of his mind while looking at his grandson.

"Got it, Mr. Amadeus," the driver replied. He went to the driver's seat, closed the door, and started the engine.

"All right, Mr. Amadeus, we'll be right behind you," the detective said. He turned and walked toward his car. The two automobiles started to leave the dark place; the weight of the night hung heavy as the cars disappeared into the distance, leaving behind the echoes of a place that would not soon be forgotten. The following day, Amadeus finally resolved the conflict with Sean after Lucas was rescued and treated by the doctor. Acknowledging the danger surrounding their circumstances, Amadeus confronted Sean, insisting that he must leave the gang to ensure Lucas's safety. Though it was a difficult decision, Amadeus released Sean, still blindfolded as a precaution, and urged him to start a new life. Despite Sean's past actions, Amadeus remained grateful for his role in saving Lucas. The doctor revealed that Lucas had been injected with general anaesthesia but was fortunate to survive, and, as a parting gesture, Amadeus provided Sean with enough money to begin a new life. With matters settled, Amadeus returned to the private residence of his trusted friend, burdened yet hopeful about the path ahead.

As the door creaked open, Amadeus saw the private nurse carrying a tray laden with empty plates, bowls, and a drained glass of water. A relieved smile crossed his face as he gave a cursory glance at the remnants of the meal.

"I'm glad he ate everything," he said, his tone warm with gratitude. "How's he doing?" The nurse returned his smile, though hers carried a soft, reassuring confidence.

"Mr. Amadeus, he's on the path to recovery. The trauma still lingers, but I can see his resilience. He's giving his all to regain his strength, especially after taking his medication." Amadeus nodded appreciatively, the weight on his shoulders easing slightly.

"Thank you so much," he replied simply, his gratitude evident in his voice.

"You're welcome Mr. Amadeus. I'll go ahead now to give an update to your friend," the nurse replied.

"Alright, sure," said Amadeus. When he opened the door, he saw his grandson staring out the window wearing an all-over white colour lab gown then he felt the immeasurable sadness and pain that undeniably evident in him. Amadeus quickly composed himself, thinking of how to ease his grandson's feelings. Lucas turned to look at him, offering a faint smile, before shifting his gaze back to the window. A thought came to Amadeus's mind, how to alleviate the weight of the horrendous event his grandson had been enduring since the ill-fated incident. Until he finally heard his voice when Lucas glance at him again.

"Whoever you are, thanks for saving me," said by Lucas.

Amadeus didn't answer, he simply smiled while approaching his grandson.

"I am well aware of the entire story, and the resemblance is so uncanny," Amadeus said as he sat down, still looking at him. Then he took out his wallet, grabbed a photo, and handed it to Lucas, who silently accepted it.

"His name is Ezekiel Emsworth, the eldest of my two children. He's your father, and he died in a car accident with Sylvia, your grandmother. Lucas, from this time forward, your life will be different, and I am glad that we've made it." Amadeus then stood from his chair and approached the patient to hug him.

Meanwhile, Lucas was speechless. He carefully examined the photo of the two men. The man hugging him; his grandfather and the other one in the picture looked exactly like him, Ezekiel.

"He is your father, and I know that your mother is Esmeralda Courteney," Amadeus continued, "I was so fortunate and thankful to God that Lucy was the key for me to start this mission, and that mission was to find you." When he looked at his grandson, the expression was a swirl of emotions that words could never capture a blend of sorrow, weariness, and a fragile hope buried beneath the shadows of his trauma. The older man sighed, his heart heavy yet tender, and offered a gentle smile as he tried to process the depth of what he saw in those young, tired eyes. He placed a reassuring hand on his grandson's shoulder and spoke softly, his voice carrying both comfort and promise.

"Rest well, Lucas. Take all the time you need to heal. And when you're ready, we'll set off for Sydney. It'll be a fresh start, your new home. You'll meet your Aunt Audrey and your cousin once they're back from their holiday," his words lingered in the air, a quiet assurance of better days ahead, even as the weight of the past loomed in the silence between them then he saw him gently nodded at him and simply smiled.

It has been two days since Lucas was rescued, and since last night, he has been able to take a bath. He still remembers the sizes of clothing for his late son, Ezekiel, making it easy for him to select the outfits he purchased yesterday. Amadeus felt completely satisfied throughout the day after his conversation with his daughter, choosing not to mention Lucas, as he wanted it to be a surprise for them. As he walked into the room after chatting with the doctor outside while enjoying a coffee, he noticed Lucas still asleep. He took a seat in the chair, watching him. At that moment, he wished for nothing more than to see his grandson in such peaceful slumber. He adjusted the Vulcan Quasar heater and the white blanket covering Lucas. Then, he recalled Mr. Enrique and pondered why his grandson had fallen victim to such circumstances, despite the many people in the country. Perhaps there was a reason behind it that only fate could truly comprehend. Therefore, he needed to keep the file secure, ensuring that no one could access its contents, revealing nothing to anyone except those he worked with during their mission. The potential for war loomed, and Mr. Enrique was just as powerful and influential as he was; he had also briefed others about the incident. Amadeus wanted to avoid any conflict, as it was purely an accident that no one had planned. Lucas and his family were victims of a cruel twist of fate. Suddenly, he felt movement in the bed and saw Lucas slowly opening his eyes and glancing at him.

"Finally, you are awake, Lucas. How do you feel now?"

"I feel better now, grandfather," Lucas replied, scratching his eyes.

"That's wonderful to hear. I just spoke with your aunt a little while ago, and I didn't mention to her that I am here in Melbourne and had a whirlwind experience, but of course, it turned out to be quite fascinating because you are the reason for it." He then slowly stood up, pulled the chair closer to the bed, and began to caress his grandson.

"Although your father and grandmother are no longer with us, and of course the family that you grew up with, but you given me a reason to find happiness every day. The day they both left, my life felt cursed; I questioned what I had done to deserve such pain, especially since Sylvia and I had only had a minor disagreement that night, which spiralled into a nightmare. In that moment, I realised that within every suffering lies a glimmer of hope, and that hope is you, Lucas; I wish for you to feel the same way." He then kissed his grandson on the forehead.

"Thank you, grandfather. I promise that from this day forward, we will always find happiness together," Lucas replied, beaming with a radiant smile as he looked at him.

"Ah, that's my grandson! Haha!" He chuckled, giving Lucas a gentle shake of the shoulder to emphasise that this moment was special for him. The following morning, Lucas awoke to find two unfamiliar men in the room. He glanced at his grandfather, confusion evident on his face as he wondered who they were. After receiving a reassuring nod from his grandfather, who smiled joyfully while approaching him, he sat up in bed and tousled Lucas's hair.

"Before we head to Sydney, I want to introduce you to them; without their help, we would never have met. Today, we are saying our farewell to them. The man sitting next to you is Detective Gregory, and beside him is Conrad. And of course, you already know Doctor Bronte, who has been taking care of you," Amadeus concluded, standing up to offer handshakes as the men moved closer.

"I am very pleased to see that you are finally well, Lucas. I wish you all the best as you embark on this new chapter of your life with your grandfather, and of course, with your aunt Audrey and her family. I've met them a few times, and I'm sure you will enjoy their company," Detective Gregory said warmly. Amadeus couldn't help but admire the way Detective Gregory expressed his words for Lucas, and he couldn't blame him, as they had known each other for quite some time. So, it was indeed that he cares for him like his son.

"Thanks for helping my grandfather to find me. I owe my second chance of life from you," and he looked towards to the other man and to his grandfather, "and thanks to you too but also I will do my best to live a good life after finding out that I still have a family." He calmly said and smiled at his grandfather. "Thanks for helping my grandfather to find me. I owe my second chance of life from you," and he looked towards to the other man standing next to his grandfather, "and thanks to you too but also I will do my best to live a good life after finding out that I still have a family." He calmly said and smiled at his grandfather, they stayed for almost an hour in his room and spent the moment with laughters until they dropped them off to the airport and by concealing their identity; Amadeus and Lucas both wearing a visor and a cap that paired with their black jackets before they alighted from the SUV. At first, Lucas was hesitant to wear the sunglasses but his grandfather insisted just to remained unknown both of them from public eye. And while the driver getting their things from the boot, his grandfather gently tapped the shoulder of Doctor Bronte after of their manly hugged, followed by Detective Gregory and his assistant Conrad, while the airport staff were doing the final inspection to the aircraft while the hum of its turbine was causing a strange feeling to Lucas, until their gazes met, his grandfather.

"Grandfather, I never thought that we would go to Sydney by plane," he said after his confusion.

"Sorry, I forgot to mention this to you. As an Emsworth, this is our usual way of travelling by air," then he rumple his hair and both of them were now looking at the jet.

"Alright," Lucas casually responded and was about to help the staff for their two carry bags but his grandfather held his hand.

"It's okay Lucas, let him handle those carry bags."

"Sir Amadeus the inspection is finally all clear." The detective said, then they were now proceeding to the jet steps after they waved their goodbyes to Doctor Bronte and his driver.

Eight

New World

As Lucas looking outside of the window after the jet's take off, while his grandfather reading a newspaper, he closed his eyes for about a minute and when he opened them, everything from the ground was slowly fading to his sight and had hoped that his dark memories will be the same as what he last had seen before the window's pane of the plane was now covering of white clouds while he heard the detective and his partner was discussing about their job for the next day as they were both sitting opposite of their seats. After ninety minutes of flight, the jet finally landed in Sydney at Bankstown airport, about twenty-six kilometres away from the city.

Before they entered to the vehicle, Lucas was in awe after seeing the colour black Jaguar XJ Series III as his grandfather mentioned it to him while the driver waved while waiting for them at the tarmac, then the detective and Conrad had made their way to the carpark outside after the formality of farewells between them since they have to work on things for that day. After more than half an hour of travel from the airport, he was now glancing at the stately home; the lawn was vast that adorned with Sir Grange Zoysia which he quickly assessed its kind of grass, then the assortment of flowers was overwhelming since it was like a botanical garden as he smelled their scents while they were standing along the driveway.

"I don't know that my father came from this kind of life," Lucas said as he can't believe as his eyes saw and felt the ostentatious experience on that day. "All I knew that he belongs to a very decent family, as my mother mentioned to me before."

"Oh, since they had never discussed any further things after they made you! Haha!" The old man laughs after ruffling his hair. "Can you see those trees?"

Then he followed his grandfather's finger where he was pointing, by his index finger. He saw the well aligned Bottlebrush from left to right of the garden while in the center was around five bar in length of steel electronic gate, then he nodded and looked at him.

"That was the favourite spot of my children during our weekend picnic after we moved here from the ancestral house." Amadeus said gently while gazing to it.

Lucas saw how his grandfather shifted his facial expression about mentioning the memories from the past, then he put his arms toward his shoulder to console him.

"Do not worry my grandfather, I am finally here! As you said before I am very much look like my father, right?" He asked gleefully.

"Sorry, my grandson. I just missed your father so dearly. But we will recall some of our finest moments once I show to you the collection of our photos." Then he signalled the butler and one of the staff to take care of their belongings. Before they arrived he already informed the whole staff about Lucas, and were all surprised about the existence of unknown child of his late son, but then all were so glad that there will be another Ezekiel from that day, as they misses him so much.

As they entered the spacious living area followed by the staff, Lucas was amazed of what he saw. From left and right, there was a two huge Palladian windows in the middle of two arc top style and the four corners has a giant bird of paradise kind of indoor plant in a huge white circular flower pot. Then a three seater large leather couch in a beige colour facing the main door, a coffee table with a stack of magazine, while the rest of the two single leather couch was facing against each other, and then they greeted by Discovery Manor Grand Staircase with a maroon carpet facing the large couch and two chandeliers traditional style in a chrome colour; one at the centre of the staircase, and the other was in the middle of living area. Then at the right side corner when he glanced at it, there was a three level of bookshelf and the type of wood was an American Oak then Lucas quickly ran into it due to his excitement, while Amadeus was smiling looking at him, until he saw him shifted his gaze towards him still smiling.

"You will enjoy more once you see the main library at the second floor." Then he looked at the staff behind him and nodded to them, which was his usual signal for whatever task they have in hand.

"Wow! This is so amazing to know and feel that we have this here and also the big library upstairs!" He said jovially and now his eyes were examining them, touching every spine of books that he see and almost of them were in hard cover; the top was general-fiction, second was politics and history while the last was encyclopaedia and dictionaries.

"Well, actually that bookshelf was organised by one of the staff as I asked before we came here because I know that you are fond of them." Amadeus said while approaching his grandson.

"Thanks for that! And now, I already have two favourite spots!"

"Well, there is another one that you have to see. Since, I know from the next day after we rescued you, it also came to my mind. So, shall we proceed upstairs?" His grandfather asked while his hand gestured towards the stair.

"Sure! And I can't wait to see that!" Lucas replied after he put back the book on shelf after inspecting the front and back cover.

Amadeus gently wrapped his arm to his shoulder while they were now ascending through the steps of staircase and he looked around from the ground to the ceiling while the lights were on. It was his first time to see such a magnificent abode. The intricate details of the huge painting matching the wallpaper on the wall was also striking when they reached the second level. Then several antique art pieces were also located facing the stair, the huge vases that come in a variety of colours and shapes and the medieval armour of a cavalry with shield and sword in a silver colour is also notable.

"Wow, the craftsmanship of that painting speaks for itself!" He said then quickly approached it to touch the piece of work by his right hand.

"Haha! You remind me of your grandmother, she won that piece during the auction when your father was only a teenager, the name of that painting is *"The Parisian Life"* painted by a famous Filipino painter, he's name is Juan Luna." Then he saw his grandson nodding while still examining the painting.

"Next time, I will check the rest of them! Do we have more paintings?" He asked while looking to the rest of paintings along the wide hallway as they walked to the right side of the corridor.

"Yes, inside of the library." Amadeus replied.

"Then I also forgot to inspect some of them downstairs when I saw the bookshelf."

"Do not worry, as I am also fond of paintings I am planning to collect more." Amadeus replied while they were now heading to the specific room and they turned left when they reached the end of the hall. Then, he opened the door and Lucas was amazed when he saw the entirety of the room.

"This was your dad's bedroom. And from now on this is yours now. His clothes are still here inside of the cabinet, if you want to use them it's up to you,"

"I never knew that you will take me here! And that would be a great idea, since wearing them is like, I already have my father in my life without his presence."

"So, keeping them here is very reasonable then." Amadeus replied.

"Thanks for it grandfather."

"You're welcome. Anyways, I'll let you to sort out your things for now. And let's meet later downstairs once you are done here. And I need to discuss some matters to the security and to the rest of the staff.

"Sure, and see you later grandfather." Lucas said, then before the old man left, he gently tapped his shoulder and smiled. Then to show his appreciation, he hugged him with tenderness before he finally walked toward the door, then waved at him and he wave back then saw how he gently close the door of the room then after hearing the sound of locked, he gazed at the entirety of the place where his father used to sleep every night. He smiled even he felt a pinch of pain in him, he lost his biological father without seeing him personally. Then at the day of his graduation, an ineffable series of events in life happened. He closed his eyes, then he opened it again in a matter of seconds to keep himself from any surge of sadness from that time.

It has been a few days when Lucas personally groomed by someone that his grandfather really knew, then Amadeus started to teach Lucas about things that he needs to learn, from proper wearing different clothes on every occasion, then the table etiquettes from three to five course meal. One night, while the grandfather and grandson having their moment in the living area after dinner and to the other area of ground floor which was the main kitchen, all staff was smiling while conversing in a minimal tone of voice about their thought from several days that they witnessed how things changed inside of the mansion.

"I can't still move on whenever I see him, my thought in my mind is seeing the late sir Ezekiel, since the day he arrived with sir Amadeus. They are so identical." The butler said while standing in front of the two staff and watching as they polishing the silverware.

"Sir Amadeus was a hundred percent correct when he informed you about him. And the way he walk and talks, it was almost the same of his father!" The lady in her early fourties' replied, then she ended her thought and made her two colleague smiled. "That's why sir Ezekiel was my first ever crush!" Then she giggled like a high school student while gently placing the forks and spoons on the tray. "Oh, I remember the time he asked me to join him in a late afternoon snack! How I wish it was an endless tale of dream!" Then the woman can't stifle her laughter as she was now covering her mouth by napkin. Then the butler just shook his head while slowly laughing and took an extra napkin from the nearby table and gave to her to use as replacement from the napkin that she used to cover her mouth.

The butler still smiling as he saw the two was still having a conversation, since the woman were continuing to recall the rest of other moments she had and having a huge crush to the late son of the patriarch, he even remembered the three of them were started to work to the family of Emsworth more than twenty years. Until the other member of the family, Mrs. Audrey Windsor entered to his mind, as for sure she will have the same thought that her brother is alive when she arrive next week with her family, then he check the time on his watch, it was half past eight and gently nodded and looked to the two women.

"Alright, tonight I tolerate this kind of silliness as an extension to celebrate about welcoming the son of late sir Ezekiel, but tomorrow good luck ladies and good night." The butler said before he waved his hand to the two as he needed to tend some duties outside of the estate before he finally takes his good sleep later that night.

It was now another week and also a new look of Lucas after they have done the steps for him. He looks presentable now; while Amadeus and the rest of staff were clapping when they saw him in a colour black of three piece suit. Then everyone proceeded to the ground floor and they went outside to have their lunch together facing the garden as his grandfather announced last night that everyone must join to gather as a celebration, and also for helping him to make him smile genuinely after the passing of his wife and son. After their lunch, he and his grandfather were waiting at the living area for the whole family to arrive as they spoke to the butler via phone when the patriarch of the clan was busy in his office the other day.

He saw his aunt wearing an all black trench coat, while the man next to her was wearing a black jacket paired with navy blue jeans and high cut boots, while his cousin Lawrence wearing a black jumper and a khaki pants and a sneaker.

"Oh my! Dad, what is going on? Am I dreaming?" Audrey gasped as she spotted the figure behind her father after dropping her handbag in disbelief, while her two hands brought to her mouth in shocked then shifted her gaze to her dad, confusion clear on her face as she saw him laughing while her husband and son were also joining him to laugh until her father slowly stopping himself from laughing before he speaks.

"Audrey, please take a deep breath, okay? I know how you feel because I went through the same thing," he answered, feeling a mix of emotions as he watched Lawrence and Lucas greet each other with smiles and waves.

"Alright, this is Lucas. He is your brother's son."

Amadeus still couldn't completely suppress his laughter as he noticed another expression when her eyes grow wide while she staring at him, then she rushed over to Lucas and wrapped her arms around him that filled of warmness while smiling.

"I had no clue I had a cousin before, until grandpa mentioned it to us last time when dad and I spoke to him by phone call while we were in Europe." Lawrence exclaimed as he walked up to Lucas for a handshake after his mother embraced him.

"Great to meet you, Lucas. I'm Lawrence, your one and only cousin." Then Lawrence saw his mother was now looking at him after she looked at his dad, and her eyebrows were now raising while tapping her right cheek by her index finger, indication that she was not dreaming.

"It's wonderful to meet you, Lawrence. Actually, our grandfather talked about you a lot, as well as Aunt Audrey. It's fantastic that we finally got to meet," Lucas replied, and he was completely captivated by his cousin's manners at such a tender age; just fourteen years old, yet his etiquette resembled that of a fully mature adult.

"So, when you two talked to dad last time while I gave the phone to you," now her finger was pointing and at the same time looking at her husband, Clarence. "Anyway, I don't mind at all. Lucas, meet my husband Clarence Windsor." She was now smiling again then her husband approached Lucas for a handshake. Then she looked at her father.

"Dad, you really need to clarify this! I deserve a thorough explanation! How can it be that Ezekiel has a son, and just look at him now! He's already all grown up! Haha! Oh my goodness! But welcome to the Emsworth family, Lucas!" She embraced him once more, while Lucas fought to keep his emotions in check. The warmth of the family he had lost wrapped around him, yet he managed to maintain his composure.

"Well, it's quite a tale, but I promise to share it with you next time."

"Okay, so Dad, we absolutely need to celebrate this! I mean, a grand celebration, right?"

"Absolutely!" Amadeus responded to his daughter, giving a thumbs up in agreement.

However, Lucas felt uneasy about the idea, so he proposed an alternative.

"Do we really need to do that? I don't think I'm ready for it."

"Why not, Lucas?" Amadeus inquired.

"Because I'm not prepared yet; I'm not accustomed to such things, like a grand celebration. A simple gathering would be perfectly fine." Then he noticed his grandfather and aunt exchanging glances, and Amadeus nodded.

"Alright, if that's your preference. But one day, you will have to embrace your new life. I believe a special dinner tonight would be just right, and remember, Lucas, you are an Emsworth; soon enough, you will take on the family business and everything that comes with it."

"You're absolutely correct dad! So Lucas, be prepared at any moment! Haha!" Audrey exclaimed, glancing at her husband, who was quietly observing them, and smiled back at her.

Then after several days, his auntie and her husband gladly helping the Patriarch of the clan to refine everything that he needs so he will be able to handle his obligation as an Emsworth.

Nine

New World Part Two

After a half day of training, it was a bright and cool Monday, creating a similar ambient vibe between grandfather and grandson as they enjoyed their leisure time in the living room. Suddenly, they spotted someone on TV that Amadeus hoped never to see with Lucas, and a gradual shift in his mood occurred, unnoticed by Lucas. It was Enrique appearing on the screen, while Amadeus struggled to maintain his composure sitting beside his grandson. Meanwhile, Lucas was enthralled by the image of a man in a black suit displayed in the top left corner of the screen, as the introduction of the media personality named Enrique seemed quite appropriate.

"Now, this year he is another additional to one of the most important pillars of the country's business industry, and as the sole heir to their business empire, the burden of responsibility on his shoulders is tremendous," the reporter stated while observing the crowd of people leaving the main entrance of the building.

"Grandfather, he seems like such a kind and intriguing figure in the business world," Lucas exclaimed as they both sat on the large couch, his eyes glued to the screen. He caught a glimpse of his grand-dad casually nodding in response, though he didn't reply to his comment.

"And we're about the same age!" He continued, "it feels like I could learn so much from him! Just think about it, he's the one making all those corporate decisions? Wow! What a responsible and admirable trait, don't you think, grandfather?" He asked, his admiration for the man in the striking charcoal suit was unmistakable. He took a sip of his Mixed Berry Smoothie, while in front of them was an Italian Grazing Board with Roasted Tomatoes, and his grandfather slowly took sip of his orange juice in a highball glass. Then, the moment finally arrived when the TV reporter turned to the young businessman, who was eagerly awaited as security tightened around the area.

"So, Mr. Enrique, as the successor to your parents, how does it feel after finishing the first day as CEO?" The first question from media personality , holding the microphone towards him and everyone could see the striking and confident demeanor of the young heir as he smiled and engaged with the media crowd before he began to respond.

"Well, it has certainly been challenging, but also incredibly rewarding. I must acknowledge my father, or rather our parents and give credit to my late brother Emilio, as we both entered the business world at such a young age. I truly wish he were still here so we could support each other in contributing to the economic growth of our country," the young man said warmly and his gaze shifting between the media crowd then to the cameraman. The sunlight glinted off his dark brown hair, making it even more noticeable before he continued.

"In the end, my other goal is to emulate my parents by committing myself to charitable endeavors for those who are less fortunate, as this world truly lacks meaning without acts of kindness, wouldn't you agree? To summarise, my fiancée shares this same passion, which fills me with immense gratitude for the insights I have gained about them." He concluded then chose not to respond to any further inquiries from the media after a particular person standing to his right whispered to him.

"I apologise, but I must attend to an urgent matter. So, please forgive me." He and his personal assistant swiftly proceeded to the black Mercedes Benz sedan that had just arrived in front of them. The cameraman recorded the scene as the car slowly faded from sight, making a right turn when the red light turned green.

Concurrently, Lucas was trying to form a plan to his mind how he would meet the man that he recently saw on the screen of television when the right moment finally came, then he continued drinking his smoothie while his grandfather was in silence after switching the channel which he casually thought that he was thinking for the next paper works that he mentioned earlier.

After having his breakfast, then he went outside for a smoke while holding the cup of his coffee then he realised to take his time as he opted to wake up that early to prepare everything and to double check his notes. As the sunlight starting to envelope the surrounding, he opted to sit in outdoor garden bench wooden wagon chair and took his breath while gazing to surrounding, the memories from the past made him realised that if only they were still with him, his life wouldn't be incomplete, it was comparable to the early cold morning that embracing his whole being; but he managed to remained calm to handle his task later on. His internship was finished after six months, and also he worked at the small office as an assistant after that as part of his immersion. It was a tough during that period for him but nevertheless he enjoyed the most vital part, since it was a prerequisite to be part of his grandfather's world.

When he finished wearing the corporate attire, he was glancing himself in the front of mirror, he smiled when he saw his reflection, a dark blue two piece suit, and a white long sleeve underneath, then a dark brown leather shoes. He was now finally calm at that time and before he slept last night, he made sure that he reviewed a few times after taking a shower the most important part of his presentation for that day. Today would be his first time to discuss about his perspective for corporate meetings, and there was no way to turn his back on that kind of obligation, then he sighed and switch off the light of his bathroom.

He composed himself after finding out that the car was already in the basement of the building, but then before they entered there, he glanced to the entirety of it, a four level of edifice, and the meeting conference room was located at the second floor, his grandfather mentioned about the details per floor before and the day after they went there so he can personally see how it looks like and also he already introduced him to his business associates and to the staff. Majority of them were amused when they saw him, while the usual word of reaction from his family were just the same after they expressed about the similarity between him and his father, Ezekiel Emsworth.

"Amadeus, I am glad that one day this young man will be here for everyday, as I missed so much your late son, Ezekiel. I remember when we were working together then I never thought that he will be so secretive that night during the event! Then the last time I visited to the mausoleum of your family, I asked him where did you go when I was looking for you? Since the last time I saw him when I left from our table. Then the answer is here, in front of us! Such a silly man, haha!"

"Arthur, thanks for mentioning it and now there is more reason for me to be still grateful after my wife and son passed away. Both of them gave me a precious one." Then Amadeus tapped the shoulder of his grandson while laughing with Arthur.

Meanwhile, all of his doubts and worries had fade when he saw the ambiance inside of the office, while they have still less than half an hour to go before the conference will start as Lucas gazed to his watch.

"Oh, it is such a big compliment on my part sir Arthur, and I hope I can do the same thing as what he does before, since as an Emsworth, there is an enormous challenging responsibility lies on my shoulder."

"See that, Arthur? Even his presentation is not about to start but look, he came prepared! Haha!" Amadeus said while looking at the man named Arthur, then looked at him while still laughing and caressed his head as he was sitting next to him.

"Thanks grandfather." And he was about to say more but then their attention shifted to the specific part of the room, then until they saw behind that door. It was his Aunt Audrey, wearing a black and white corporate attire while her feminine perfume was starting to fill the room.

"Good morning everyone!" She greeted them gleefully.

"Good morning too Audrey! Thanks for coming today even though last Saturday you mentioned during our dinner that you are not quite sure if you can come, but here you are to show your support to your brother's son."

"Haha! Oh, don't say that dad! As you know me, sometimes I am so unpredictable, and nevertheless I am committed to show the best way I can!" Then she gave him a peck on his cheek then she looked at her nephew.

"Oh, you look great in that suit Lucas, makes you even more handsome! Same as my late brother." Then another gesture she gave to her nephew and saw Arthur was looking at them, which she casually offered him a handshake. It was known to her father and Ezekiel that this Arthur once confessed his feelings towards her, but that time she already found what's for her, and that was the father of her son Lawrence. She did the best way to greet him, since even up to now; the man in front of her was still single.

"Hi Audrey, it is nice to see you here today."

"Thanks Arthur, and I hope your weekend was great!"

"Yeah, it was! And I can't wait to see your nephew's presentation for today."

"Same here, but for sure Lucas will do well today as he is an Emsworth, right dad?"

"I shall no doubt about that, as I reviewed all of his performances and I was impressed!" Amadeus replied to his daughter while smiling to them.

"Yes, I agree that's why I came here since the last time I asked dad about the updates but he kept refusing to divulge." Then she smiled.

"Haha! Well, look you are here! So, my approach to my plan really works!" Amadeus replied while expressing his amusement to his daughter.

Lucas was even more inspired after seeing the banter between his grandfather and aunt, then he was now looking forward for his presentation later since he prepared himself last night. He was silently observing his grandfather while speaking to the front, then he was also taking notes so he can review them for the next time while the duration of the presentation was almost less than twenty minutes until it was his turn as his grandfather looked at him.

"Now it's your turn Lucas," as Amadeus gazed to his grandson, and smiling at him then saw Audrey was looking at her nephew as well and being proud of Lucas was evident on her face. Then Lucas was now taking his steps toward the front of the room.

"Good day everyone, thanks to my grandfather who gave me this kind of opportunity to present my idea and also perspective about this big responsibility which I really focused on the cost-benefit analysis," Lucas began, his gaze sweeping around the large rectangle table where the major shareholders were seated. He paused briefly as his eyes met the woman from the finance department—she had gathered the key data he requested. "It was also a learning opportunity for me, and I'm sincerely grateful to the finance team for their efforts. The findings suggest that this analysis will benefit everyone involved with the company."

At his signal, his secretary stepped forward and began distributing printed copies to each person around the table.

"As you'll see," Lucas continued as the slideshow flickered to life on the large screen behind him, "I've also included a section on Business Ethics. While we often label actions as 'good' or 'bad,' it's important to recognise that not everything is so easily categorised—or prioritised." He paused, scanning the room before adding, "that said, if any department head fails to uphold these ethical standards, we'll move the discussion to Corporate Governance. Accountability is key."

An energetic smile appeared on Lucas's face as he glanced at his grandfather at the centre of the conference table.

"My grandfather used to talk about something he called a 'retro-spectroscope'—a way of looking back with clarity. There's no doubt this company grew into the largest construction firm under his leadership. His vision and integrity were always be a remarkable influence to all of us." As he finished speaking, a respectful silence filled the room until a voice broke through.

"And I have a feeling you'll carry on in the same way, Lucas," Amadeus said, his voice warm and certain. Applause followed, echoing through the boardroom. Some stood to shake hands with both Lucas and Amadeus, a show of support and approval.

"This meeting is adjourned," Amadeus declared, and the room gradually emptied with quiet conversation and nods of satisfaction, then Lucas and his auntie Audrey exchanged of handshake then his grandfather asked his aunt about the reservation that she made yesterday, then they proceeded towards the main door to celebrate that he finally made the presentation went well that day and after their lunch his grandfather and aunt were had to catch up with her husband as they have another appointment while their driver took him to their residence. Inside of his room, as he gazed to the window something occurred in his mind and smiled.

Ten

Lucas Emsworth and Vivienne Romano

His grandfather was on his holiday for the entire week and informed him two weeks in advance. He felt happy for his grandfather, knowing he could finally take a break, especially since he had seen him tirelessly working as the founder of the AE company, even from home. There was a moment when he asked for a hug after preparing a snack and personally delivering the food to his office. Before knocking on the door, he made a promise to himself to do his utmost to help manage the family business.

"You know, if your father and grandmother were here, I truly believe they would be proud of you, just as I am," his grandfather said after placing the tray on the table. He noticed the familiar sight of stacks of folders, papers, and pens as he looked at him.

"Thank you, grandfather. And please take a moment to eat," he requested, taking a bite of the sandwich from the plate and smiling at him while sitting in front of his desk.

"Alright, I appreciate you bringing this food. It's quite timely, as I was just about to ask one of our staff to prepare something for me," he replied. The room was filled with cheerful conversation between them until a realisation brought him back to the present.

The ambient light was dimming the room, creating a darker atmosphere, while the candlelight on each high table emitted a fragrant floral aroma. The number of guests that evening was fewer than a hundred wearing a cocktail dress while men were in their suits and ties. Lucas was casually mingling after the conference and had even told his driver earlier that he could explore the city before heading upstairs, as the meeting would wrap up in nearly two hours. He noticed some women attempting to flirt with him, but he politely signaled that he was not interested in dating or any romantic involvement. This had been his mindset ever since he entered the world of affluence and it started four years ago.

Just as he was about to enjoy a sip of his wine, he noticed the group of men to his right turning their heads as the two doors swung open. And there she was, a stunning lady clad in a golden cocktail dress, her lustrous brunette hair elegantly styled in a classic chignon. The pearl drop earrings, embellished with tiny diamonds, sparkled brilliantly, enhancing her beauty. His gaze was irresistibly drawn to this remarkable woman, the most beautiful he had ever encountered.

"Damn," he muttered to himself, "I thought you were steering clear of women, yet here you are, captivated by her." He slowly shook his head, attempting to divert his attention elsewhere in the room, but his eyes were once again drawn to her, now engaged in conversation with a group of ladies. Until one of them noticed his gaze and waved, prompting him to return the gesture with a smile. That was Sarah Whitfield, a member of the association that organised the event, someone he had known for quite a while.

"Lucas, come and join us so I can introduce you to someone," she called out, gesturing for him to come over. He simply nodded after taking a sip of his drink and made his way toward her group. Their eyes locked, and the newcomer smiled at him, a smile he happily returned. Then until he saw Sarah whispered to their other two companions and separated themselves from them after nodding at her, until he finally got close to them.

"Vivienne, I would like to introduce you to Mr. Lucas Emsworth, the grandson of the chairman of the AE company. And Lucas, this is Ms. Vivienne Romano, a television personality."

"Oh, hi there, Lucas! It's a pleasure to meet you!" The lady exclaimed with enthusiasm, and they both instinctively greeted each other with a kiss on the cheek. Lucas found himself momentarily at a loss for words as he took a closer look at her, he was convinced that even without makeup, she would still be stunning. It took him a few seconds to collect his thoughts.

"Similarly, Ms. Vivienne Romano. Honestly, this is my first encounter with a television personality," he stated sincerely, his eyes still locked on her, a smile gracing his face.

"What a flattering remark, Lucas! I assume you don't watch any TV shows before seven in the evening, do you?" She asked, picking up on his comment about meeting someone like her for the first time.

"Well, actually, no," he answered, shaking his head while smiling at her.

"That's so unfortunate, Lucas but why is that?" Vivienne inquired, taking a sip from her champagne glass.

"Due to my obligations. I have to be actively involved in my grandfather's business," he clarified, pausing as a thought occurred to him.

"But from now on, I will." One thing was clear given by chance; he would discreetly give his business card to Vivienne later, wanting to keep their exchange of contact information private from the others in the room.

"Lucas, you should definitely check out her segment sometime; I'm sure you'd appreciate her as a TV host," the woman who introduced Vivienne suggested kindly.

"Well, perhaps one of these days," he responded, then Sarah raised the glass of her champagne which he and Vivienne followed.

"Cheers!" The three of them said the word then Sarah started to speak after taking a bite that she took from the nearby table, a sweet potato cream, seaweed black caviar and walnuts.

"Actually, I was quite surprised she made it tonight. Just last week, she mentioned she wasn't sure if she would come."

"Well, stop saying that. Haha! I'm already here, even though I'll be leaving before an hour since I have to review my script for my next show and, of course, the rest of my tasks," Vivienne replied, allowing a small smile to escape her lips, which she also came to the table and pick a piece of roquefort cheese, cream cheese, smoked salmon, fresh lemon and dill.

"What segment do you do Vivienne?" Lucas asked, while the lady was chewing her food, then after she wipe her lips by napkin, while the small laugh came from her lips was still tingling in his mind. It was magical and creates a hypnotising kind of music to his ears.

"It is a kind of segment that tap into current trends, humour, or any relevant social issues can make an impact to the audience." Vivienne answered.

"Oh, so it is about a cultural relevance." Then Lucas noticed that smile, and he was momentarily frozen in place, still captivated by her beauty and intellect. Unbeknownst to him, Vivienne was fully aware of his reaction.

"Oh, excuse me, I just need to visit the restroom," Vivienne said politely, casually placing her drink on the nearby cocktail table. He and Sarah nodded in acknowledgment. Then Sarah was approached by another lady, and they engaged in a brief whispered conversation before Sarah returned to their spot, glancing at him with a playful smile.

"Hmm. that look?" Sarah mentioned while smiling at him, "this the first time that I have seen that kind of smile from you towards the woman."

"Oh, that? That was nothing. I am just really surprised that I would meet a well known TV personality tonight and nothing else." He simply answered and smiled at her.

"Alright, fair enough. Since I had this kind of thought that you guys would be totally a perfect match but unfortunately, I have never seen strange towards her. I knew her very well and the way she speaks to you was the same toward the other men."

He was about to response when they both saw that Vivienne was now heading towards them.

"Sarah, thanks a lot for inviting me here but I have to go soon in less than half an hour since I need to meet someone before I do my review. But also, it was a pleasure to meet you Mr. Lucas Emsworth."

"It is an honour to meet someone like you Ms. Vivienne Romano." Lucas was in disbelief after hearing that the woman will be leaving soon, even though he can manage to gather information about her but seeing her in person like this moment is such a privilege to him. The rest of their moment that time went smoothly still talking about interesting facts, until he decided to go to the bathroom then he was in a hurry to be back to their spot then seeing now Vivienne was on her way to the main door as she waved goodbye to her friends, then Lucas took the opportunity to put his calling card when he saw her clutch bag was opened.

"Bye Lucas! Again, I was glad to meet you here." Vivienne said after they exchanged a graceful handshake.

"Same here Vivienne and oh, your bag is open." He said casually, then the woman zipped the zipper of her evening bag without noticing the unfamiliar piece of thing inside then smiled at him.

"Thanks."

"You're welcome. And please take care."

Then before she sleep, she saw something inside then she was wondering how it ended there, though her calling card was a different colour; then she was surprised seeing his name on it when she took the card; but she knew from herself, she was happy that the man did it for her. As day goes by, the setup was catching up with each other, but Vivienne requested a discreet for the meantime as she doesn't want any attention from anyone who works for media and also to protect Lucas as not part of any form of entertainment or media personality. They will show their affections when the right time comes. Until Lucas, ended their usual setup due to a reason that he did not divulge to her.

Every drop of his tears was evident that someone was in pain, then until the punches on the wall was getting stronger as he recalled their memories. Then he paused for a moment, then shook his head slowly, and followed by a bittersweet smile. His life was a terrible nightmare, then, concurrently, he bit his lower lip as he remembered their first night, as the woman showed the same feeling towards him. They were in her room as she called to his office before they met, then when they got into the room hence, she was the one who initiated to take off his suit and, while they were kissing passionately, he just found himself that his hand was moving towards her legs, and he started to caress the smooth and every inch of it makes him more excited until he realised that it was too late to turn his back when he did something. He pulled out her underwear from her legs, then they both looked at it, a red panty! Then she giggled at him while looking and he was amused by the way she showed her silliness. Then they kissed again. Now it was fierier between them while the woman was now caressing his body too as he is hurriedly taking off his long white sleeve, then she unzipped the zipper of his slacks.

"Oh god! I want to spend the rest of my life with this irresistible woman," he said at the back of his mind, but he opted to be that way, since it's still too early to make any permanent relationship that would lead to a proposal. It was their first night. Then instantaneously, he carried her towards the bed and gently put her onto it then the moment of silence stuck within him while glancing to the alluring physique of woman that truly captivated his attention.

"I love you Vivienne," he whispered while caressing her face, while they were looking at each other.

"I love you too, Lucas," she replied, and then kissed him until they started to remove the garments left on their bodies. Then a stain of blood on the bedsheets was more than enough to convince him about the purity of her love towards him. Then the flashback in his mind brought him to reality. Then he vowed to himself that everything would be chaotic as hell, but there was more to it. Then he wiped his tears, to make a plan while starting to leave the dark room as he needed to sort things out aside from this personal wrath.

"Vivienne, believe it or not, I love you. But there is a circumstance that prevents me from being with you. For now, it may be confusing, but I must leave it that way. When the right time comes, you will understand just how much I love you. I have to sacrifice our relationship to give you the best life possible." Tears streamed down his face as he looked at her with deep emotion, he had been patiently waiting for the right moment to propose, having already purchased a ring for her.

"How could you do this to me Lucas?" Vivienne slapped him hard, twice.

Then all along, Lucas saw the raw emotion in her eyes; tears welled up as she shook her head and then stuck his muscular chest with her hands.

"I am sorry, forgive me but it may not today but hopefully one day."

"Then please, Lucas, whatever it may be, let me stand by your side through the ups and downs. Please, don't do this to me." Vivienne began to cry, slowly moving closer to embrace him. Lucas then hugged her tightly, showing how deeply he loved her and closed his eyes, and he can still see how deep her sadness that even dictionary can't totally define, but he stayed firm to end their relationship and avoided himself watching a television from the following day, and he thought to himself; *"love is the most painful emotion."*

But sometimes, it's a human nature that we can never deny when things can be so tempting, on that particular early evening after a week, Lucas switched on the television, he spotted Vivienne on the screen and his initial sadness transformed into joy as he saw her smiling on camera during her segment. He then pressed the remote control to adjust the volume after hearing her co-host mention an announcement coming up after the break, followed by a cut to a commercial. Since meeting Vivienne, it had become his late afternoon ritual to watch her, and it consistently brought a smile to his face. Just like he remembered, her face radiated brightness, a stark contrast to their last encounter, which left him feeling regretful about how they parted ways. The night was vibrant with the lively atmosphere of spring, just weeks before summer, yet their hearts were victims of circumstance. His attention returned to the screen as he noticed the television network's logo accompanied by its theme music, and he focused intently until a knock on the door interrupted him. He quickly turned to see who was there, finding a staff member carrying a tray of food he had asked earlier.

"Please, I want to be alone for now. And take that back to the kitchen," he requested, watching as the staff member nodded. "Also, let everyone else know I need privacy while I watch television, thanks." He casually turned off the light as he stood up from the couch, allowing the small lampshade beside him to cast a dim glow.

"So, we are back, everyone, and thank you for joining us tonight for this special episode that we are experiencing together. This night is particularly memorable for me since..." It was Vivienne, and confusion washed over his face as he watched her live, making eye contact with her co-host while smiling. Yet, behind that smile, it seemed like a different story was unfolding.

"Okay, okay, this is not what I expected; it looks like something significant is about to happen before the program concludes." The co-host replied.

"You know, we have been doing this segment for nearly five years, and then something came up that I need to address, even though it wasn't entirely part of my future plans..." Vivienne was on the verge of tears as she hugged the woman in front of her to hold back her emotions. After a moment, they finally separated, and Vivienne continued.

"To avoid prolonging any discomfort, I want to say that this is all about me since tonight is my last night on this program. But I assure you, I have no issues with the management, production crew, or the rest of the team at this network. However, there are things I need to focus on, and perhaps one day I can return as a host. So, this isn't a completely permanent goodbye." Vivienne concluded her statement with a smile.

Lucas quickly left the room to gather his team and put Enrique under surveillance to ensure he wasn't involved in the sudden decision he had just witnessed on the screen. He knew her very well; she loved her job too much to quit without a valid reason.

"I'm assigning each of you to keep an eye on all of his colleagues and anyone associated with him because I need to confirm that he has nothing to do with the recent news I just saw. I want a name with a clear answer if my suspicions are correct, and this must be done within twenty-four hours, understood?" He asked, looking at them with determination, his hands tucked into his pockets.

And when he finally finds out the result after ten hours, he was even more curious about the event; and its main reason, then he finally figures out that it was him when he decided to end their relationship. At that point, his anger and pain were even more getting tremendously horrifying as he finally concluded his first step.

The choice she made was appropriate after realising that the love they had came to a fruition; she was excited to inform him about this, yet the decision she saw him make was enough to satisfy her. Lucas intended to end their relationship for reasons that remained unclear, leading her to dry her tears with napkin while she packed her belongings and prepared to go to a place she believed would help her find what she was searching for: a way to move forward and forget the painful memories that could trap her in a whirlwind of emotions. Still, she sensed that they would cross paths again for a fated reason, which would be related to their future child.

Eleven

The Horrendous Day

The ambient light in the room now merged shades of gold and blue, beautifully capturing the moment as Felix eagerly observed his wife on stage. Behind her were the guitarist, the drummer, and the pianist to her right, all supporting her in the midst of a timeless love song. From the moment she started to hum before the intro, his eyes were locked on her while he remained seated at their assigned table, feeling fortunate to be at the front, a privilege granted by the son of the celebrant. He reflected on their first meeting and how they had raised Lucas together, who was graduating today with honours and surrounded by affection. They had been the cornerstone of his upbringing, teaching him compassion, fairness, and a profound respect for God. His reverie was broken when the music changed. He recognised the song, which required another voice to achieve the perfect harmony until the conclusion. He glanced at the celebrant, who caught his eye and smiled. Without a moment's hesitation, he approached her to express his desire.

"Madam, since this is a duet, may I join with my wife?"

"Certainly, why not? Go up on stage and sing with her," Sofia responded with a smile. Felix then turned to the man beside her, presumably her husband, who nodded in agreement and he began to clap, encouraging the other guests to join in when he glance at them.

Esmeralda beamed as she saw her husband finally on stage. She understood his intention to sing with her, a tradition they had shared several times before. The song they were about to perform was their wedding theme, and she felt joy at the thought of sharing it with the crowd, symbolising their love on this special occasion for the de Ayala couple. Felix gazed at her with deep passion, and after the introduction, she watched him begin to sing, unable to contain her happiness.

At that moment, Enrique was overwhelmed with emotion. The joy reflected in his parents' eyes was something he cherished deeply as he watched them enjoy the duet on stage. "Finally, I made them proud of me today," he thought to himself, glancing at the woman beside him. It was Evangeline Bennet, the woman he dreams of marrying one day, his girlfriend. He then signaled to the waiter, ordering his parents' favorite drinks, and naturally, he included drinks for his girlfriend as well.

"Oh my god, Carlos, I never expected this surprise," Sofia exclaimed, taking her husband's hand to express her gratitude. "This is the most unforgettable birthday I've ever had." Tears welled up in her eyes as she gazed at him.

"I'm so glad you love it. We usually celebrate in a simple way, but this time is special," Carlos replied, kissing her softly on the lips.

"That's why I never hesitated to say 'yes' when you proposed. I knew you would be a wonderful husband. And please, Carlos, try to ease up on our eldest son, Enrique. I understand you have high standards, but it's important to accept his flaws too," Sofia concluded, addressing Enrique.

"Yes, I understand, my dear. Today, he showed me that he can bring us joy, and I truly appreciate his efforts despite his shortcomings," Carlos said, gently stroking his wife's hands and looking into her eyes.

Esmeralda's intermission for the event was now finished, and Felix waved goodbye to the event floor manager after paying him more than he expected and as his wife and mother-in-law decided to leave the banquet hall after the performance together with Lucas's teacher.

"Sir, this is too much." He said after counting the money.

"Oh, it's okay. Since Mr. Carlos gave another extra for it, to extend his appreciation and to ask an apology since he can't leave the main room as he and his wife is still busy with the guests."

"It's totally fine, and I am thankful for this, please let him know." Then the manager of the event nodded at him and he was now joyfully walking to his wife Esmeralda waiting him in the lobby of the hotel, and today was the graduation of his stepson, Lucas. They could celebrate the special day at the restaurant as he didn't want his wife to make an effort preparing earlier today. He could also buy a gift for Lucas, even though he declined when he asked him a few days ago. Then, he checked the time on his watch. There was another hour left, and he could still buy the gift.

"Oh finally, you're here, as my mother was already bored after I performed," Esmeralda said when she stood up and looked at her mother.

"Never mind that, Felix," Claudelle said.

"Good thing, Lucas is not here; otherwise, another one will be complaining too, as this is the day of his graduation." The teacher said.

"Yeah; haha! And finally, I can buy the gift that he wants before we can go to the graduation ceremony." Felix added.

"Oh, really?" Esmeralda exclaimed. "Oh, you're making him happier today, honey, thanks for that," Esmeralda ended.

"Well, of course! As he is my son." Felix said, and there was no reason for him not to say such a thing, as he was not capable of having a biological son, as he was impotent. Before he and Esmeralda got married, he already confessed about his condition, and Esmeralda asked him back. Even he tried so many times to court her, until he heard a poetic reply from the woman who captured his attention when he visited a local pub after his work. Then one night he gave her a bouquet of red roses.

"I hope you will give me a chance to show how much I love you and I am sincere about it, and I promise you that I'll make you happy everyday."

Then the woman scoffed at him while raising her left eyebrow.

"Wow, the way you enunciate the chemical chain reaction from your cerebrum is like a sweet siren. But the thing is, I don't have the heart to love you." Then until one day, when the moment he heard the sweetest words, he ever heard happened.

"You know that I am a single mother, and Lucas is my son. Therefore, marrying me is you're literally accepting the responsibilities towards me."

"Well, I have no complaint about that." Felix gleefully replied. Then, the civil wedding ceremony held in their local area witnessing by their closest friends and loved ones, and they chose to live in a small town where Esmeralda grew up with her foster mother, Claudelle Vandervilt.

The event went very well as every guest saw the happiness from celebrant's eyes as well as her husband, and their son Enrique, then meanwhile Sofia asked her husband about Emilio, as the floor manager said, that he will comeback before he left the area and now the mother and son saw the disappointment on the expression of patriarch.

"That Emilio, was such a headache today. He even humiliated me in front of our business colleagues, and friends. As they were looking for him, and now the special day of his mother is entirely finished and yet, he never show himself! I am sorry, Sofia but your son is too much today. I will speak to him later as I know where he went."

The wrath of their father was enticing to Enrique's ear, now it was his turn; the new favourite son. Then he smiled, as he waved to the several guest who were exiting the function hall.

On that day of afternoon, the bustling street clearly demonstrated how vibrant the local town was, thanks to the support of its people. Inside the bookstore, they were about to move towards the counter when suddenly, a loud scream erupted from outside the premises. It was too late for them to escape as a large truck crashed into the store, causing a cacophony of screams that was unbearable, followed by the horrifying sight of blood splattered across the shattered glass window, obscuring the view of what remained inside.

Meanwhile, at another location, a group of men seized Lucas while he was waiting for Wesley outside their school. He was on the verge of screaming and resisting when the group's leader struck him on his face, knocking him unconscious. They swiftly placed him in their black car, and two of the men moved to the front and drove away, leaving Wesley bewildered and confused about Lucas's sudden disappearance when he finally got back after checking out one of their classmates who lived nearby. If only he can ask the silent witnessed in that place; so, he could find the answer to his question while gazing to the surrounding.

The leader felt let down upon discovering that his two men had mistakenly took the wrong student to their hideout after wandering back and forth. He slapped both of them while shaking his head.

"You two are idiots! Sure, they are nearly the same height, but their appearances are completely different! But come on! You really couldn't tell the difference between this guy and my brother!?" He slapped them again. His frustration grew as he realised, he couldn't be with his sibling after his uncle had prohibited him from contacting them due to the nature of his business operations.

Sofia took the chance to speak with her son, whilst her husband was in the shower. After changing her clothes she saw Enrique went inside of his room, then she needs to do something to avoid future conflict between father and son, she doesn't want to see them in this distasteful argument; as the event went very well. After taking a deep breath before knocking on the door, and several seconds after, Emilio did not open the door until she started to speak to let him know that his mother was behind the door.

She seized the opportunity to talk to her son while her husband was taking a shower. After changing her clothes, she noticed Enrique entering his room, prompting her to take action to prevent any future conflicts between father and son; she wanted to avoid any unpleasant argument, especially since the earlier event had gone so well. Taking a deep breath before knocking on the door, she waited several seconds, but Emilio did not respond until she began to speak, informing him that his mother was outside.

"Emilio, are you alright? Let's talk; I'm not angry with you. I completely understand, and it wasn't your fault. I just want to know if you're okay after your father scolded you today." She sighed deeply and knocked once more, but still, her son did not reply, and she heard no footsteps approaching. A sense of unease began to creep into her mind, leading her to rush to the master bedroom to retrieve the duplicate key. She hurried back to unlock the door, anxious to uncover what was happening inside. Upon entering the room, she found it tidy; a gentle breeze fluttered the white curtains at the window, and her eyes fell on the bookshelves to the right of the bed, where the books were neatly arranged. However, her attention was drawn to the hallway leading to the walk-in closet, at the end of which was a single door that led to the bathroom. Her smile gradually faded as she approached it, her heart pounding in a way she couldn't fully understand. When her hand finally reached the doorknob, she found it unlocked. Despite a voice in her head urging her not to open it, she made the decision to see what lay beyond. As she opened the second door, she was met with the horrifying sight of her son's lifeless body, submerged in the bathtub filled with water.

"No!! My son!!" After Sofia's loud shout, she rushed to the tub and lifted the pale body of her youngest son from the water, her tears overflowing as her shoulders shaking tremendously. The body of Emilio felt as cold as ice in her hands. On the ground floor, several staff members heard their employer's voice. After exchanging glances, they quickly ran to the second floor to see what was happening. When they reached the second lounge area, they found Carlos, who was only wearing a robe, his hair completely wet, running with Enrique towards an open room, where another scream while crying could be heard as they all entered.

"Emilio!! Why?!!!" Everyone was left in shock and silence until the patriarch shook his head, tears of regret streaming down his face, and began to punch the wall in frustration. Meanwhile, Enrique was confused about what to do at that moment, torn between approaching his mother, who was holding the lifeless body of his brother, and witnessing his father's bleeding knuckles as he continued to strike the wall. It was only when he touched the top of his head that he began to understand the full implications of the situation.

The following day marked the darkest point in his life as he discovered the death of his family in the newspaper. He witnessed a newly arrived group of men handing something to their leader and instructing him to clean up the mess from their table to floor. Initially, he hesitated to obey the leader, but a painful kick to his stomach forced him to comply, tears streaming down his face. In that moment, he wished he could ask any of them to end his life, a desire he felt deeply. However, from that day forward, he vowed to himself that once he finally saw his family's grave, he would end his life with his own hands.

Twelve

Osmond Versus Cedrick

The two men were having their conversation for about half an hour after they had lunch, and Alex went out from her room, ready to greet them. Upon seeing her, Cedrick greeted her with enthusiasm.

"Hi there! Can I ask a favour?" Alex started while adjusting her hair before placing her white headband on.

"Sure, what is it?" Osmond responded, turning his head upon hearing her question.

"I was wondering if we could visit the stream again, and also about the firearm. I'd like to try it again since you taught me last time," Alex suggested as she took a seat on the left side of the single couch.

"Wow, I didn't know that. Yes, of course!" Cedrick replied, his eyes began to reflect his excitement while seeing in his peripheral vision that Osmond was looking at him, sensing that his colleague had something to say, but for some reason, he couldn't quite grasp what was holding him back from expressing it. Then he heard Osmond's voice in response.

"I don't think that will be necessary," Osmond replied simply.

"And why not? It's still near here, right? And having Cedrick with us I think, it's clearly enough to say that no one can harm me, or us. Right?"

"I agree with you Ms. Alex, since the Director-General called our tandem as *The combat duo* we are both unbeatable when we are together, right mate?"

"Yeah, it is." Osmond responded and he adjusted the way he seated.

"Great! So, that's great to hear then." Alex warmly replied.

Osmond found himself at loss for words, remaining silent as he watched the two in front of him share their excitement through their conversation. He saw her glance in his direction, still smiling, before her gaze shifted back to Cedrick. It was a painful sensation, an intense feeling he had never experienced before.

Meanwhile, Cedrick began to realise that his treatment of the heiress was becoming increasingly apparent. However, true to his friendly nature, Osmond would never suspect that Ms. Alex held a special place in his heart.

"Alright, Ms. Alex, just wait here while I prepare my firearm and gather the items we need." Osmond finally said.

"Okay, I am going now as well to the other guest room to get mine." Mentioned by Cedrick after hearing Osmond while smiling due to his excitement.

Inside his room, Osmond finds himself neither in agreement nor content with the upcoming activity they will engage in once they arrive at the location, or rather, his training spot during vacation. He wishes for that place to remain special between him and Alex, but now with Cedrick joining them, it feels like a different kind of pain, especially after witnessing their closeness right before his eyes.

Meanwhile, Alex couldn't help but smile at his reaction. Now, she was ready to relish the moment since it was her turn, while gazing at the closed door room of her bodyguard, who had unexpectedly become a love interest during her stay at his home with his parents. A whirlwind of emotions washed over Osmond as he gathered his gear, including transparent eye protection and earmuffs. A smile crept onto his face as he remembered how he had held her wrists, the way her eyes had flickered towards him, and how his smile and care for her transformed the heiress's experience into something blissful. He took a deep breath, reminiscing about the memories they had created together, then stepped closer to the mirror to check his appearance, smiling at his reflection before finally exiting his room. He found Cedrick and Alex seated and waiting for him, their smiles brightening when they noticed him carrying the aluminum case that held his pistol and other equipment. He observed Cedrick's reaction but returned their smiles and nodded in acknowledgment.

"Ready?" After he posed the question and listened to their reply, he began to stroll towards the windows and veranda, finally reaching the main door. Once he was content that he had secured their home, he headed to the kitchen, following their usual path to the back area, which led to the farm and the nearby training lot. He sensed that the two were trailing behind him. The sunny afternoon and the soft breeze made it a perfect day for Alex to relish their walk, while Cedrick kept her entertained by pointing out various trees and wild plants. She was delighted to learn that he knew some of their scientific names, as wild birds chirped from the branches, some darting to chase others or moving to different trees.

"That tall one is a Bull Kauri, scientifically known as Agathis Microstachya. Next to it is the common tropical tree found here in Queensland, the Palms Arecaceae. Oh, and look at those Lilly Pillies!" He gestured in another direction, and Alex followed his finger with her gaze. "They come in various types but are all part of the Syzygium group."

"Wow, Cedrick! I had no idea that you might become a botanist in the future!"

After hearing the heiress's reaction, Osmond was suddenly filled with irritation. He couldn't understand why she was treating him so differently compared to how she had on the day they first met, and this strange behavior persisted even after several days of getting to know each other. Moments later, he spotted the gate, retrieved the key from his pocket, and quietly unlocked the padlock while the two of them continued their conversation about plants and trees behind him. He recalled her outfit from that day; it seemed like she hadn't put much effort into it—a loose white shirt paired with black jogging pants and the baseball cap he had given her previously. In contrast, Cedrick was dressed in a long-sleeved black shirt, white walking shorts, and black sneakers. Osmond chose not to change his clothes, eager to return to their residence as quickly as possible, wearing a grey singlet, black shorts, and the same sneakers he wore yesterday.

"Alright, finally we are here!" Cedrick said as he started to prepare his firearm from holster after taking it off from his body and put in on the wooden table as he looked to Osmond getting the equipments from aluminium case.

"Good thing, even I did not bring my protective ones you have an extra here mate!" Cedrick said after he took two pairs of each from earmuffs to protective eyewear, then gave to Alex and saw her starting to wear the protective equipments. As the two preparing the empty cans on the rock Cedrick saw Osmond glancing at him but he chose to ignore it, and then Alex came over with a smile.

"Osmond, I think I'll let Cedrick teach me this time since you were my teacher last time, right?" Alex casually proposed, turning her gaze to the other agent, then Osmond nodding in agreement before he walked back to the table.

"So, mate, is that alright?" Cedrick asked Osmond.

"Yeah, mate, that's absolutely fine." He responded with a thumbs up to his colleague.

"So, since my mate has already shown you the proper steps, we can definitely move forward to aim the first can," Cedrick stated in a professional tone, "okay so let me hold your hands now." Cedrick said after he moved toward at her back and saw she automatically did the weaver stance which made him nodded. "Great, Alex! That's the perfect stance, then now let me hold your hands while we are trying to hit the first target."

"Sure!" Alex replied while she was now assessing the can with the gun's rear sight to her eye level.

"Ready?" Cedrick asked, after seeing her head nodded in agreement, then he pulled the hammer.

"BANG!" The sound from gun was echoing to the surrounding, while Osmond's feelings were screaming from deep within as the same time, he remained calm as they saw the can was now on the ground several metres away where it was situated.

"Wow, Ms. Alex, you did it great, huh?" Cedrick happily shook the shoulder of Ms. Alex, and he saw her reaction about what he did, it was clearly telling him about discomfort.

"Of course, you're good at teaching and also Osmond's instructions were very consistent last time, so I got it right away." And she shot the last can on the rock after pulling the hammer and looked at Cedrick and she smiled at him after. It was appropriate that she was able to succeed for the second attempt without help from the other agent.

"Wow, you did the right timing when you pull the trigger even without my instruction! High five Ms. Alex!" Cedrick happily told her.

Osmond was now turning as an outsider between them or shall he say, a chaperone. Then he gradually walked to get near to them while the two were on their way to collect the two cans.

"Wow, that was almost the same what we did last time, but the last shot? I was really surprised!" Osmond expressed himself while looking at her, he directly mentioned the last shot as a hint to Cedrick, but the next thing happened in unexpected form of surprise from his colleague.

"Well, for sure the way you teach her for the first time helps a lot! And also, by assisting her today for the second time, was surely a great way for her to managed to shoot the can without any assist from us." Cedrick replied as he checking the cans.

Osmond was just looking at him, trying to analyse if he would respond or not of what he heard but he opted to smile at them.

"Yeah." He replied then glanced at the woman next to him. "So, Ms. Alex ready?" He asked as he cocked the pistol he was holding.

"Absolutely! I think just one or two more, and then we can finally make our way to the stream. How about we take a dip there? The timing couldn't be more perfect for it," Alex proposed, adjusting his protective eyewear.

"Oh, I love that idea!" Cedrick chimed in after finishing his inspection of the two cans.

"But is that really necessary?" He asked Cedrick, prompting Alex to jump in.

"I came prepared! I'm wearing swimming shorts under my trackies!"

"Well, that's fantastic!" Cedrick replied after making adjustments to the two cans he had left.

Osmond simply nodded, choosing to avoid any awkward conversations. He wasn't worried about any lurking dangers; rather, it was the sight before him that made him uneasy.

"So, Osmond, I'm ready!" She said, her gaze fixed on him.

"Alright." He replied and moved closer to her.

"I miss this, Alex." He softly murmured as he finally grasped her hands, aiming at the can.

Alex beamed at Osmond's words, then she casually glanced at their friend Cedrick, who was a few metres away, before responding.

"Then, I have to say this now: it's not fair." She answered.

"What do you mean not fair?" He confoundedly asked.

"Oh, forget it." She said, "let's concentrate on this so we can finally make our way to the stream." Then Alex shook her head after adjusting her grip, looking at him and then at the two remaining cans, as her plan was coming together.

"Alright, but I mean it." Osmond replied, and to his astonishment, a loud bang erupted as Alex didn't wait for him to say another word while he held her hands, then her hands moved to his pistol.

"Take it easy, Alex." He said, sensing something was off with her.

"Relax, just like I am. I apologize, but I was simply thrilled to take a shot at one of the last two cans."

"Alright. I was merely worried," Osmond replied.

Then she gazed at him closely, noticing a change in the way he looked at her. She felt the intensity of his stare and responded with a smile and a nod.

"Okay, then. I'll allow you to do it just like we did at the beginning," she said, eager to move on to the next location.

Cedrick sensed a connection between the two but chose to overlook their conversation, his excitement building at the thought of visiting the nearby stream, a place he hadn't been to in ages. Suddenly, a loud bang echoed, bringing a smile to his face as they finally set off for the spot.

Once he felt content after stowing his gear back in the case, Cedrick made his way toward them after clearing the cans from the ground as Osmond was just looking at him and assessing his next move later.

"So, are we ready to go?" Alex inquired of them.

"Yeah, since I forgot my phone," Osmond responded, a sudden idea sparking in his mind. "Can we keep it to under half an hour?"

"No problem at all," Alex replied, glancing at them. Cedrick nodded in agreement after securing his holster, while Osmond carried his firearm case.

Osmond intended to walk next to Alex, but it was Cedrick who ended up beside her as they made their way. They began chatting, but the term *"chaperone"* kept resurfacing in Osmond's thoughts. He shot a few sharp glances at Cedrick after he locked the gate, relieved that the stream was nearby; otherwise, Cedrick might seize the chance to make it seem like he and Alex had been spending more time together than they actually had. Still, he allowed Alex to lead the way since she was familiar with the route and until he heard the sound of the stream then Alex was now pointing it out to Cedrick, excitement lighting up his colleague's face. Then Alex turned to him and asked.

"Osmond, can I go there? As I am just gonna take my trouser off."

Osmond followed the direction of her finger, which pointed to the thick wild grasses beneath the tree. He nodded and moved to ensure it was safe for her. Suddenly, he sensed someone behind him and recognised it was her. After examining the tree and its surroundings, he found no signs of creatures, whether insects or venomous reptiles, and turned to her.

"It is safe," he stated, stepping towards a nearby spot where he could quickly reach her if anything went awry.

"Alright, thanks," Alex responded with a smile. After removing her track pants, she beamed at him again while observing him and the area, his back turned to her, before swiftly folding her garment and walking away.

"I'm done, let's go," she called to him as she walked, noticing Cedrick already shirtless and waiting for them. A smile spread across her face, recalling how the other agent had been unable to take his eyes off her since their first meeting. The next moment, she watched as Cedrick dashed towards the stream, filled with excitement.

"Ms. Alex and Osmond, come over here and join me! Wow, this place of yours, Osmond, is truly unique! I could easily spend a long vacation here."

Then, Osmond smiled upon hearing her words. He noticed that Alex was finally joining Cedrick after placing her trousers beside him. He decided to wait for the right moment and opted to watch them while sitting on a rock.

"Osmond, come join us!" Cedrick called out, waving at him. What he saw next completely took him by surprise. Alex was having a great time with Cedrick, splashing water at him with her hands, and Cedrick responded in kind. Their laughter echoed throughout the area.

"Sure, maybe in a few minutes!" Osmond replied as he observed how intently Cedrick was looking at her while they continued to enjoy their time together. It seemed like the right moment to express what he felt, especially after noticing more signs that confirmed his suspicions. Cedrick needed to understand his boundaries when he was around her. His fists clenched tightly, and he could no longer contain himself. He strode quickly towards the two, pushing his colleague and launching a surprising series of rapid punches at him—first to his face, then a kick to his stomach, followed by another to his right leg. However, his colleague skillfully dodged each of his attacks.

"Hey, take it easy! What's the matter, mate?!" Cedrick asked while bewildered, shaking his head as his hands instinctively prepared for a fight. Yet, despite his readiness, he remained composed, carefully observing Osmond's posture.

"What's the matter? You're acting very unprofessional mate! This is my territory, and you should have recognised that the moment you arrived! Behave like a guest and stop vying for her attention, because she belongs to me!" Osmond shouted.

Alex watched in astonishment as Osmond glared at his colleague, shocked by his words. As she witnessed Osmond showcase his fighting skills, she was taken aback by their speed and intensity, far from the ordinary strikes she had seen before. Turning to the other agent, she remained speechless, realising too late that her intentions had led to this unexpected confrontation.

Cedrick thought the fight was over until he witnessed the next strike; it was a rapid and devastating blow delivered with Osmond's right elbow, aimed directly at his head. Instead of retaliating after dodging, Cedrick found himself facing another punch aimed at his face. Finally, he managed to reposition himself to counterattack after executing a quick sidestep with his left foot. He unleashed a straight punch with his right fist, followed by an uppercut from his left hand. However, Osmond deftly evaded those strikes until it was too late for him to avoid the incoming hook punch, which landed squarely on his face. The impact forced him to step back, and he felt the sting of pain, shaking his head slowly in disbelief. Seizing the moment, Osmond ensured Cedrick couldn't execute his next move. A tornado kick was all it took to turn the fight in his favour. He observed Cedrick's reaction to yet another unexpected attack, knowing that Cedrick was about to endure another painful blow as his kick connected with his chest. Without hesitation, he then seized Cedrick by the neck and plunged him into the water.

Osmond witnessed Cedrick's struggle as he relentlessly pushed his head underwater, until he saw Cedrick was desperately reaching for his hand, gasping for air. Determined not to let that happen, Osmond swiftly twisted Cedrick's wrist with his left hand, observing as Cedrick's breath began to fade beneath the surface. Just then, he heard Alex approaching, and she forcefully shoved him.

"Osmond, Cedrick! Stop that ridiculous fight!"

"Then tell this guy to stop being so friendly with you! Or maybe you actually enjoy it, huh?!" Osmond retorted in frustration, glancing at her before quickly releasing Cedrick and striding away from the stream towards his pistol.

"Wow, Osmond, is that all? Is that really the reason? You're so immature to think that way." She shot back, slapping Osmond as she followed him. Yet, a pang of guilt washed over her for the way things had turned out, with the two of them fighting over her.

Osmond was gazing at her, the pain still lingering—not from the slap, but from witnessing how effortlessly his colleague spend his time with Alex. He scoffed before speaking.

"I'm not foolish enough to ignore that he's subtly vying for your attention and trying to flirt with you! Isn't it obvious? Unless, of course, you enjoy what he's doing." As he shook his head while looking at her, another slap landed on his face from Alex.

"Slap me as much as you want, but it won't alter my feelings!" Osmond shouted.

Cedrick was trying to process everything he heard, until a realisation struck him, leaving him astonished.

"Mate, please, can you stop being so nice to Alex? We have a mutual understanding, even if we're not officially a couple yet! Is that understood!?" Osmond directed at Cedrick, jabbing his finger at his face, then saw Cedrick's glance towards Alex, a look that seemed to seek confirmation.

Alex took a deep breath and nodded.

"Now, do you understand?" Osmond inquired of Cedrick.

"Yeah, I understand, and I truly apologise." Cedrick replied as he began to walk over to retrieve his shirt.

Alex was in shocked at how quickly everything had unfolded; the truth about her and Osmond was now out in the open for Cedrick to see. This revelation would undoubtedly escalate matters, especially when her father eventually learned about her relationship with Osmond. Cedrick's gaze was fixed on her, and he began to speak.

"Ms. Alex, I sincerely regret my actions. If only I had known that—"

"Cedrick, it's completely fine. I don't see anything wrong with your kindness or your ease around me, especially since someone else doesn't seem to tolerate that trait unless they're burdened with guilt." She looked at him knowingly, aware that her words could strike a chord, particularly regarding his secret about the recent call from his sister. Even without directly mentioning it, he would confess once she found the right moment. For now, though, Osmond would have to keep guessing. When the time came to confront him with the truth, she would certainly ask him to clarify her significance in his life. It was painful to acknowledge that Isabelle undeniably held an irreplaceable spot in his heart. After taking her jogging pants, she walked away in silence, leaving the two men trailing behind her.

"Mate, I truly apologise for my actions. I had no idea that you and her shared a mutual understanding." Cedrick conveyed his remorse to his colleague with genuine sincerity, gently patting him on the back. Osmond gazed at him, recognising his sincerity, and felt there was no reason to reject his apology.

"It's alright. Let's just move forward, and you're already aware of what's happening between us," he responded, laughter escaping their lips as they playfully ruffled each other's hair.

"Now I get it. So, I promise, mate, you can rely on me if you need anything, even if you truly win her heart, though it does break mine a little," Cedrick said with a smile, his hand resting on the left side of his chest.

Osmond couldn't resist hugging Cedrick after hearing his words. "Mate, I apologise if my jealousy turned into aggression; we shouldn't have let it escalate, but I just couldn't control myself."

"I completely understand. I would probably react the same way if I were in your shoes," Cedrick replied, and they resumed walking, following Ms. Alex.

When they about to enter the door from the kitchen they heard a conversation followed by their laughters, and Osmond smiled after knowing that his parents had finally arrived. The rest of the day was another normal day for them after Alex stayed inside of the room while his parents decided to take a rest and notified them that they might not join the dinner later as they wanted to take long rest after the camping. The night became quiet for them as Alex ate her dinner inside of the room while the two men Cedrick and Osmond had their dinner at the kitchen. It was almost midnight, and Alex couldn't sleep. She sat in the chair, staring at the silence of the dark front yard while the calm wind bracing her. She made sure the two men in their respective rooms were asleep and then walked towards the veranda. She wanted to spend minutes assessing things, taking the chance to get out of the guest room. It bothered her about the recent incident today, which had given her a reason to disregard the mutual understanding she had with Osmond.

She let out a deep breath. "This can't be happening," she thought, just as she was about to conclude her next realisation, the lights from the lounge room quickly flickered on, revealing where she was.

"Sorry for disturbing you," Osmond said, standing there. "I've been standing here while watching you. Is everything alright?"

Alex was in disbelief that she had never felt any presence or noise. She quickly managed to respond.

"Yes, I just couldn't sleep and realised I needed to spend some minutes here. It might help me fall asleep when I go back to my room," she replied.

"Okay, but please, Ms. Alex, next time, just a soft knock on the door then call my name to let me know whenever you want to leave your room during this kind of hour. I must ensure that I can always keep an eye on your safety. Please, don't do this again," Osmond said, his voice casual yet firm. Behind his firm words, he tried to keep his emotions in check, not wanting her to repeat the same thing a couple of days ago.

"My apologies," she replied, realising that Osmond was fully aware of what she had tried to do. It was evident in the way he had uttered his words, she knew there was no way to disagree. It was part of his responsibility, and she attempted to compose herself as she walked back toward the room. When she was just a few steps away from him, she gently nodded and wished him good night, to which he responded.

"Good night as well, Ms. Alex. By saying this, I hope you fully understand where I am coming from with those words."

Their eyes met, and she searched within herself for a way to articulate her response, ultimately deciding to keep it casual.

"It's alright, and there's no need for an explanation; I completely understand you," she said, smiling at him before continuing her walk. At this point, she found herself feeling quite confused. Once she entered her room, another thought crossed her mind: if she were not a client, would Osmond still show her the same level of care and attention that he gives to Isabelle? She sighed, troubled by this realisation.

Thirteen

The Celebration

In the morning, around nine o'clock, Cedrick was assisting Osmond in tidying up the kitchen while the Gomez couple was in the lounge area with Alex. Suddenly, his phone rang situated on the bench top and after drying his hands with a towel, he answered the call.

"Morning, General!" He greeted cheerfully, casting a glance at Alex. Seeing her every morning made him feel that each mission would be thrilling, despite the inherent dangers. However, he reminded himself that Alex was soon to become his best friend's girlfriend.

"Good morning, Agent McKain! I was trying to reach Osmond, but it seems he's occupied, so I decided to call you instead," the General-Director replied, glancing at Osmond, who was finishing up their chores.

"Well, yes, sort of. Is there something urgent, sir?"

"Yes, indeed. But it's also good news. Where is Ms. Alex?"

"Sir, she's watching television with Osmond's parents in the living area," he responded.

"Alright. Could you please pass the phone to her? Mr. Enrique has something to discuss." Cedrick saw Osmond looking at him, signaling that it was the Director-General on the line.

"Sure thing, sir." He then made his way to the lounge area.

"Excuse me, Ms. Alex, your father would like to speak with you," he said politely, smiling at her and also at Osmond's parents as he handed the phone to Ms. Alex. He was taken aback by her reaction to the words from the lady in front of him.

"Oh dad, is that for real? You mean, I can finally return to Melbourne tomorrow?" Alex exclaimed, brushing her hair with her hand, the surprise was evident as she glanced from the couple to Cedrick.

"What a fantastic breakfast, followed by even better news!" Cedrick said while smiling and seeing the shock on her face transforming into pure joy after receiving the news from the other end.

"Cedrick, I can't thank you enough for preparing two different breakfasts this morning! What a delightful morning for all of us, especially seeing Alex's reaction to the news!" Celine said with enthusiasm, her eyes sparkling as she looked at her husband and then at Alex.

"The egg and trout croissants, along with the sweet cinnamon omelette filled with berries, are absolutely amazing! Thank you so much, mate! I'll miss you even though we've only spent nearly three days together since you're heading back to Melbourne! But I might celebrate my birthday there, so I'll see you!" Martin said, hugging Cedrick to express his gratitude, having heard so many wonderful things about him on their graduation day. He was the one who rescued his son from bullies, and it turned out that the General-Director had given them a fitting code name: *"The Combat Duo."*

"I miss them so much, especially Osmond's nephew Andrew. He's such a wonderful young man, Cedrick! Once you meet him, you'll definitely like him! So, Celine, can they come over later this evening?"

"Absolutely, they can. I'll give Cathy a call later." Celine happily replied.

"Wonderful to hear, Ms. Alex! As you mentioned the young lad the other day, I'll finally get to meet Osmond's sister later."

Osmond was now making his way to the living area, intrigued by the commotion he heard from the kitchen and sensing that they were in a joyful conversation while Cedrick stood beside Alex, and his parents were seated nearby.

"Osmond, fantastic news! Alex is heading back to Melbourne tomorrow. Her father is on the line," Martin informed him.

He smiled at the surprising news, feeling happy for Alex as he saw her walking towards the veranda, chatting with her father on the phone.

"Finally, after nearly a month, the enigma has been resolved. I'm relieved that your client can return to her everyday life," Celine said affectionately to her son.

"However, I still need to consult the Director-General regarding the information, specifically the name and the intent," Osmond responded to his mother, then Cedrick attempted to catch his attention, and he turned to look at him.

"Mate, let that go for now and let's celebrate today. We should be happy for Ms. Alex, right?" Cedrick suggested, wrapping his arm around Osmond's shoulder.

"Absolutely, I agree." But then a thought struck him; Alex would be going back to her world tomorrow. This would create a distance between them. He was determined to find a way to discuss and resolve things with her, and he noticed Alex hanging up the phone, her face radiating satisfaction.

"Osmond, my dad will call you later," Alex said as she handed the phone back to Cedrick.

"Alright. It's great that the General and his team managed to resolve the issue," he remarked while gazing at her.

"Yes, it actually happened last night when they raided the hideout. All the evidence against him was there," Alex replied.

Osmond nodded after hearing her response, and he thought of Isabelle. He hoped that one day, or even sooner, he would uncover the details too; that could lead him to her, especially since his sister had seen someone who looked just like her, which was a valid reason for him to keep searching.

"Excuse me, I'm just going to the room." She hurried towards inside to turn on her phone so she could finally reach out to her best friend Elissandra. However, Elissandra wasn't answering her calls; instead, she sent a message to inform her about an update. After an hour, she saw Elissandra's reply and was eager to see her again, once they were both not busy. She also mentioned the ring was given by her mother the last time they met, then she composed a text message and once satisfied, she pressed the send button.

It was nearly four in the afternoon when Celine and Alex cheerfully began preparing the food, as Cathy would finish up after five and they would arrive around six in the evening. Cedrick and Osmond were assisting them since Martin had gone to gather some extra vegetables from the farm, as they were short on ingredients. Osmond had offered to help his father, but Martin declined, assuring him he wouldn't be long.

After almost two hours, they finally completed the preparations. Looking at the table, they had a traditional roast lamb, a classic one-pot beef stew with rice, and an easy beef chow mein. Cedrick was just about to finish making a dessert, the Tim Tam cake. Suddenly, they heard voices coming from the main door as Martin greeted the newcomers. After their formalities, Cathy and her son Andrew headed straight to the kitchen, and greeted them. Meanwhile, Andrei and Martin was still in a conversation at the front door.

"Hi everyone! Oh, we have a new visitor here!" Cathy exclaimed as she noticed the unfamiliar face. She approached her mother to give her a kiss on the cheek, then glanced at Alex and did the same. Finally, her eyes landed on the cornucopia of food laid out on the table.

"Oh my! What a delight to see these dinner selections tonight!" Cathy exclaimed as she set her bag on the table. "What's the special occasion?"

"Cathy, this is my idea since I'm finally heading back to Melbourne tomorrow. I thought it would be nice to celebrate and show my appreciation to the whole family," Alex replied to her.

"That's so thoughtful!" Cathy responded, giving Alex another hug, both of them smiling. "So, has the conflict in Melbourne finally been resolved?" Alex nodded after the hug.

"Honey, your Aunt Alex made your favourite dish! The sausage casserole, just like I told her!" Celine mentioned to her grandson while holding the white medium-sized bowl and showing it Andrew.

"Wow, thank you Aunt Alex!" The young boy exclaimed as he dashed over to Alex and embraced her.

"You're always welcome, Andrew!" Alex said, lifting Osmond's nephew, just as Cedrick approached and introduced himself to the young boy.

Osmond couldn't help but feel happy seeing her so comfortable with his family again. He then looked at Cedrick, who was also smiling and chatting with his nephew, showing him the dessert, while his father and Andrei walking towards them.

"Anyway, Andrei, we have a visitor and he is agent Cedrick McKain, my son's closest friend. And Cedrick, he's Andrei the husband of my daughter Cathy."

Then Cedrick stepped forward to extend a handshake, which Andrei gladly returned. Meanwhile, Osmond made his way to the fridge to get a couple of bottles of beer for them, and he also poured apple juice into a glass for his nephew. His mother grabbed four bottles of sparkling water for the rest of them. After nearly thirty minutes of conversation, they decided it was time to begin their dinner since Cathy and her husband had work the next day, but young Andrew would stay the night as Alex had asked to spend time with him on this Friday evening.

"Young man, I recall how you ended up with my shirt on top of the cabinet!" Martin chuckled as he loaded his plate with his favourite dish, while little Andrew simply smiled at his grandfather.

"Haha! Really? Oh, what a silly child!" Cathy laughed, gently caressing her son's head, while Alex couldn't help but laugh at the heartwarming bond she witnessed between them. Although she was excited to return to the state of Victoria the next day, she knew she would miss them dearly.

Celine felt a wave of joy wash over her as her son's mission came to an end, and she hoped that Osmond would assign him a new task once they returned to Melbourne. Meanwhile, Martin noticed his wife lost in thought after they had shared a hearty laugh reminiscing about their youthful adventures. She had managed to push aside her worries for the moment. After dinner, they were now enjoying dessert, with Cedrick and Osmond busy collecting the side plates and dessert forks from the drawer. Cathy excused herself to take Andrew to the living area as the adults began their discussion, bringing along two plates of dessert. Celine grabbed a bottle of dessert from fridge while Osmond took a several glasses from cupboard.

"Alex, since you're heading back to Melbourne tomorrow, I think it wouldn't hurt to ask you for a favour," Martin said just as they were about to dive into their dessert, unable to suppress a chuckle as he glanced at her and then at the two agents.

"Hey, cut that out, Martin! Haha! I know you!" Celine playfully warned her husband, though she couldn't hide her amusement at his antics, giving his right shoulder a gentle spank with her left hand.

"Actually, I don't mind at all Martin since that would be a very memorable for all of us." Alex replied then Cedrick interjected.

"Well anyone could ask anything to anyone they think that they must answer the question as much as best that they can."

"That's a good idea Martin, and also I have been enjoying my stay here in a sense of unity about purpose!" Cedrick replied gleefully about the pun he mentioned.

Then Osmond stared at his colleague, and he simply shook his head. *"This lad, never learned."* Then he recall how they ended up in a duel while he can't no longer bear what he witnessed on that particular day. Cedrick reflexes saved himself from getting a swollen bruise to any part of his face as he targeted that area for his first blow from his fist. Meanwhile, Alex was now comfortable with Cedrick after the revelation that she never thought that might happened and she saw how Osmond simply glanced to Cedrick; so he knows how to feel jealous! Then she smiled, until she heard the unexpected question from his brother-in-law; Andrei.

"Mate, your sister just recently saw someone who really exactly looks like your childhood best friend, given the chance that was really her, what would be your first question?"

Before Osmond starts to speak his answer, he slowly looked towards the woman who were sitting next to his mother; while the rest was completely looking at him waiting to respond. Then he let the small smile came from his lips seeing that her expression was completely normal, so he guess it was just okay to spill out what he feels behind that simple and yet a very profound question.

"Where have you been all of these years? And what happened?" Osmond answered followed by heavy emotion to his mind while trying to contemplate himself to maintain the neutrality just not to ruin their night. Until Martin started to speak as it was his turn, then he looked at her after he smiled.

"This question of mine will be far more different from the previous question." Martin stated and gazed to the two men; Andrei and Osmond since the question created a tension and discomfort to the heiress.

"So, Alex this is my question. How can you help your father to be able to manage the stability of the business to make the country's economy going more progressive?"

"Martin, I never anticipated such a question from you! Haha! You and my dad are nearly identical about that kind of question. Alright, here it goes: I will discuss the significance of judgement through utilitarianism, as I reflect on his business leadership in the past, and it's no surprise that the family business has become the most valuable corporation in the nation." She concluded her response with certainty, as it greatly assisted her in managing herself, given the seriousness of Osmond's father question to her. This was a contrast to Andrei's question directed at Osmond.

"Wow, that was quite convincing, Alex!" He smiled at her, then briefly glanced at his son; despite the social status disparity between them, he was confident that his son would tackle any challenges. He was also aware of his wife's silent disapproval regarding the situation, but he understood Celine and also well enough to know he could manage her.

"And also I am truly pleased that you found joy and had an experience that is rarely felt in the city."

"Indeed, Martin, and given the opportunity, I can see myself returning here! I truly admire how charming your daughter is, and Andrew as well! He is playful yet always a delight to be around!" She replied while smiling then glance to the young boy with his mother in the living area after casting a warm look at her protector's father.

"Oh, that was quite flattering, Alex! I appreciate your admiration for the cozy and relaxed lifestyle we have in our town. It is such an honour to hear that from you," Martin replied, and he gently tapped his wife's shoulder to ease the tension while listening to Alex's heartfelt response.

"Celine," Alex began, adjusting her position from where she sat before reaching out her hand, surprising Celine with her unexpected gesture. However, the woman simply nodded. "Thank you for everything; I had a wonderful stay here."

"Oh, please don't mention it, Alex! I also believe in treating every guest to the best of my ability," Celine responded, gently holding and squeezing Alex's hand with warmth.

"That's why if there's any opportunity to return here, I will as soon as I can." After expressing her thought, a gentle smile was forming from her lips as they embraced.

"That would be wonderful, Alex! You are always welcome here, as you have shared such great memories with us!" Soon, the kitchen was filled with laughter, and they raised their glasses for a toast.

"Cheers!" Everyone exclaimed.

"We will miss you, Alex!" Martin said as he approached and hugged her tightly.

"I will miss everything about this place, Martin," she replied, unable to resist hugging him once more.

Osmond smiled as he quietly observed them, feeling content and grateful for the warm and indescribable experiences Alex had brought.

"Don't worry, Martin and Celine; Ms. Alex can always make a call, right? We have phones, and it's easy and quick to stay in touch anytime," Cedrick said, trying to lighten the mood amidst the heaviness.

"Haha! Okay, sorry," Alex said, attempting to compose herself while looking at him.

"Alright, so don't worry, Martin, okay?" Cedrick replied.

"Great news!" Cathy exclaimed excitedly as she made her way to the kitchen, holding her phone, while Andrew followed closely behind, carrying a plate of dessert.

"What is it?" Andrei inquired.

"I've decided not to go to work tomorrow since it's Saturday, and your friend Kenneth just informed me that your shift has been cancelled," Cathy responded, grabbing an extra glass from the table and pouring some dessert wine.

"So, cheers to that, Alex!"

"That's wonderful to hear, Cathy! Cheers!" Alex replied, clinking her wine glass with Cathy's, while the others raised their glasses for another round of toast.

"Aunt Alex, is it true that you're leaving tomorrow?"

Alex saw the sadness to the young boy and smiled after setting her glass of wine on the countertop to embrace him.

"Actually, yes, my father told me this morning. But don't worry, your Pops mentioned he might celebrate his birthday in Melbourne, where I live. So, we can meet there and we can have another fantastic time!" She said cheerfully, ensuring that this night and the next day wouldn't give him any reason to feel blue.

"Did you hear that mom? We could see her again!"

"Yes, of course honey! And to spend more time with her, we will sleep here tonight."

"That's great Cathy, so Andrew and I could spend so much time tonight before I leave tomorrow."

"I don't mind sleeping in the living room since we have a mattress pad," Andrei remarked, as Cedrick casually suggested the room he was occupying.

"Actually, I can sleep here, allowing the three of you to use the bedroom."

"It's alright, Cedrick. You're the guest," Andrei declined his offer.

"Yes, and I prefer to sleep in this area because it's near the veranda; I want to relive that experience," Cathy added.

Then Alex made her way to the living area while still holding Andrew, glancing around until she spotted the veranda, and smiled as she walked back toward the kitchen.

"Wow, Cathy's idea was fantastic! I really want to experience that tonight!" She exclaimed, taking a sip of her wine.

"Ms. Alex, even though you are now finally safe from the mysterious threat, I'm sorry, but I still can't allow you to sleep there," Osmond casually rejected her suggestion.

"Why not?"

"It's the protocol we must adhere to while you are still here," Osmond replied politely.

"Yeah, he's right, Ms. Alex," Cedrick concurred, approaching her to take Andrew, who willingly allowed him to carry him.

"I'll see you when you arrive in Melbourne! If I'm not busy, we can spend a lot of time together," Cedrick said while refilling his drink.

Osmond smiled quietly as he observed them, until he recalled his discussion with the Director-General prior to their dinner preparations. He planned to follow through with his intentions once he had the chance to do so, while the rest of the evening was filled with overwhelming joy with their laughs before the celebration came to an end. In her room, as Alex closed her eyes, she recognised that her time in Queensland had been truly remarkable for the rest of her life. It was a period filled with happiness, revealing to her what she had been yearning for, as well as the real events that opened her eyes to the reality of her feelings for her bodyguard, rich with memories.

Fourteen

Back to Melbourne

As Osmond opened his eyes, he was greeted by the sound of crickets, while the curtain swayed gently in the early morning breeze. Soon, he heard a commotion that he recognised as coming from the kitchen. After yawning, he was enticed by the delicious aroma of breakfast. He casually got out of bed and headed to the bathroom for his morning routine. Once finished, he returned to his room, changed his clothes, and grabbed his phone, remembering that the General-Director had texted him the night before about a call this morning. When he finally left his room, his sight welcomes him by seeing his sister and her husband, Andrei, were removing the mattress pad from the living area.

"Good morning!" He greeted them. They both responded, and he nodded with a smile before making his way to the kitchen. There, he found his mother and Cedrick preparing breakfast, while his nephew drinking his milk and while watching cartoons on his iPad.

"Hi everyone, what a beautiful morning! But it seems a bit early to prepare the food." He mentioned after glancing at the analogue clock, that it was almost five thirty.

"Good morning! It's actually better to get things ready now, as I know everyone will be busy later," Celine replied.

"Yeah, she's right," Cedrick added. "Mate, would you like some coffee?

"Of course, please. A long black would be perfect, mate, thank you," Osmond responded, gently tousling his nephew's hair while still focused on his iPad. He then retrieved his phone from the pocket of his tracksuit as it began to ring; it was their commander when he checked the caller ID.

"Pardon me, I need to take this call; it's the General-Director." He moved to a nearby corner after pressing the answer button.

"Good morning, agent Gomez."

"Good morning as well, General."

"The flight is scheduled to be on time this morning at eleven thirty, and I've already provided instructions to the airport staff. However, remain alert and vigilant until the three of you reach your destination later. Also, if you notice anything unusual in the area, stay calm, as there are snipers; I've assigned two of them to secure the area until the jet departs," the General-Director concluded his briefing.

"Thank you for the update, General," he replied earnestly, then nodded.

"Additionally, we will address the issues later when your group finally arrives, and the patriarch will be present as he is involved in this matter. Therefore, I must conclude this call for now. You will receive a notification later, an hour after eleven thirty."

"Understood, General. Everything is clear." He responded, and after hearing the beep, he casually placed the phone into the pocket of his track pants. He noticed Cedrick preparing two cups of coffee while his mother took a sip from her cup and set a plate of pancakes with syrup in front of Andrew.

Celine overheard her son's conversation with their commander, hoping it would pertain to his duty and that today would mark the end of his responsibility to protect the heiress. She smiled at him as he returned to the nearby table and picked up his drink.

"Mom, I hope dad decides to celebrate his upcoming birthday in Melbourne so we can all be together that day," he said while continuing to sip his coffee.

"Well, let's wait and see," his mother replied as she began to set the table, and he moved closer to Cedrick to help him.

"Mate, the flight is scheduled for eleven thirty. The General has already informed the airport staff. Additionally, there are two snipers in the vicinity to monitor us until the plane finally takes off." He said while gathering the plates and cups from the cupboard, and Cedrick watched him while holding the set of cutleries.

"That's wonderful news, mate. So, we shouldn't feel any threat."

"Well, we still need to remain vigilant on our way to the airport, as he instructed," Osmond responded.

"Alright, of course. You can rely on me." Then Cedrick saw the couple, Cathy and Andrei.

"Good morning, everyone!" Cathy began. "Is there anything we can assist with?"

"Good morning to you too! Well, we are just about done here," Celine replied.

"Wow, another feast for such an early hour!" Cathy exclaimed. "I will miss this moment and, of course, your client, my brother. She is such a delightful person to meet." Then she watched her brother smiling and nodding at her.

"Well, anyone could easily be fond of her, right mate?" Cedrick chimed in.

Instead of feeling any negative vibe, Osmond smiled at his best mate and gave him a thumbs up after placing the stack of plates on the table, then he replied.

"Yeah, even though we had many disagreements about the protocol at first, I am glad we are heading back to Melbourne now that the issue has been resolved.

Then they heard someone from the back door, and when they looked, it was Martin.

"So, how's the crops?" Celine asked as they were not able to tend it for three days.

"Martin, it's so unfortunate that I wasn't able to visit the farm, but for sure when I come back here, I would be able to do so." Cedrick expressed his interest to see the Gomez farm.

"Haha! For sure, next time." He replied to Cedrick then he looks to his wife. "Well, good thing we managed to prevent the spread of insects." Then he looked at the other agent, as he knew he had seen their farm during the night when he visited them.

"Hello everyone, good morning!" Alex greeted them.

"Morning too Alex!" Celine answered, "it's still early to wake up though."

"It's okay Celine as I just had a phone call with my parents." Then she gazed to Osmond until she saw him took his phone from pocket.

"Isabelle," Osmond whispered after seeing the text message from Lester. He gave his number to her and will contact him the soonest.

Then Alex asked Osmond, about the message and why she mentioned the name of his childhood best friend.

"Nothing, a person I knew just texted me that he would provide an update once he sees someone resembling her, as my sister believes she truly was her over the past few days while encountering someone from a specific location." He then offered to make her a coffee, which she accepted, and sat down next to his nephew. Her original intention to inform her parents about the mutual understanding between them was now filled with doubt about whether she should still tell them, as mentioning his childhood best friend had the potential to ruin her day. However, she attempted to calm herself as much as possible, knowing there would be an appropriate time to discuss her concerns with Osmond. For the moment, she decided to let it go.

"Ms. Alex, the flight is scheduled for eleven thirty," Osmond stated after placing the cup of coffee in front of her.

"Thank you, yes. I am aware of that, as my parents informed me," she replied. She then gazed at him for a few moments before shifting her focus to his nephew.

"Andrew, always be a good boy to your mom and dad, alright?" She adjusted his plate and noticed him nodding while looking at her, but soon they heard him stutter, and he appeared on the verge of tears.

"Oh, don't cry. We will see each other again," she reassured him, embracing him and feeling grateful that her irritation towards Osmond had shifted to comforting his nephew. Suddenly, an idea struck her, as she remembered she knew the owner of the retail toy shop.

"Cathy, I will let you know when you can come to the shop and allow Andrew to take whatever he desires." She then turned her attention back to the young boy. "However, you must behave yourself and complete your homework before you can play or watch your favorite cartoon, alright?"

"Oh, Ms. Alex, you really don't need to do that," Cathy declined her offer.

"Cathy, I insist. At least for this gesture to bring him joy, it makes me feel like I have a younger sibling," she said with a smile as she hugged the young boy.

"Thank you for pampering my grandson, Alex," Celine mentioned to her, before glancing at her husband and then to Osmond.

Osmond ignored the look his mother gave him and instead urged everyone to begin their breakfast since they needed to prepare later. The morning meal went smoothly, with everyone enjoying the food and discussing various topics to make it a memorable occasion for Alex, as it was her last day there. However, she assured them that she would keep her promise to visit them whenever she had the opportunity.

Once they finished packing their belongings, Martin offered to accompany them with Andrei to the airport, while Cedrick agreed to drive the Jeep, with Osmond sitting in the front to keep an eye on their surroundings while Osmond accepted his father's offer.

"So, Celine, Cathy..." Alex said softly to them as she exited the room, pulling her suitcase.

"We will miss you, beautiful!" Cathy exclaimed as she rose from the couch, and Andrew hurried to embrace her.

"I will miss you all," she replied, overwhelmed by the affection Cathy and her son were showing her, which brought tears to her eyes.

"Oh, please don't cry, Alex!" Celine said as she approached to join their heartfelt moment.

"I'm okay, just tears of joy, Celine," Alex responded, quickly moving to hug her bodyguard's mother as well.

Celine felt the deep emotion from Alex during their embrace and chose to gently caress her back.

"I'm so glad you're heading back to Melbourne. Thank you for the wonderful memories we've shared. Martin and I will miss you too." After their hug, Alex looked at her and smiled, wiping away her tears.

"I will miss both of you. Celine, if you ever need anything or any assistance, please don't hesitate to reach out to me." She then handed her a piece of paper, which Celine accepted with gratitude.

"Thank you, Alex, and please send my regards to your parents."

"I will." Then she fix herself and nodded to the two agents and made their way to the main door and waved to the three, from Celine, Cathy to her son Andrew.

The weather was the same as the normal day while Osmond gazing to every corner of the road and Cedrick driving attentively then he looked to the rear mirror and saw Alex was just busy on her phone, and he was happy for her since she was finally back to her normal life.

Alex felt the gaze that Osmond gave to her, but she casually ignores him, but later she will insist to know what's really behind the message he got earlier in the morning until after few minutes she saw the familiar place, the airport. Then she composed herself while the vehicle was now entering the gate until they reached the tarmac then she looked at the back and saw Andrei's car was behind them, when the SUV finally stopped she didn't wait for Osmond to open the door for her, she opened it and walked towards Martin and Andrei to bid her goodbye.

"Martin, and Andrei." She said while approaching them, "thanks a lot for escorting us."

"It's okay Alex, as I have also to ensure the safety of my guest." Martin replied after the handshakes between them which also Andrei hugged her to extend his appreciation the way she treated his son.

"He will definitely enjoy the visit to the store once you confirm to my wife about the date."

"Oh, yes. As I gave my number to your mother-in-law, so just tell her message me when she can. Again, thank you."

Osmond was just observing them after he took the luggage from the Jeep, and he glanced towards his best mate and saw he was glancing towards the plane.

"Whew, it is my first time to see this kind of jet. It is top of the line mate." Cedrick said.

Osmond looked at what he was glancing then he nodded, until the three was now heading towards them and he hugged his father then Andrei. After exchanging their words, Cedrick smiled to the two men followed by their laughs while in hug.

"Alright, so everything is set?" Alex asked the two agents. Then they both nodded at her, and saw the pilot; while the flight attendant waiting at the door, and he checked the time on his watch, it was nearly eleven thirty and saw Alex was now ascending to the jet steps then they waved their hands towards them before they followed Alex.

Inside of the jet, while the sound of the engine can be heard, Alex cast a meaningful stare towards Osmond, then she called his name.

"Osmond,"

"Yes, Ms. Alex?" Osmond asked then he looked to the woman who was now walking towards the kitchen, but Alex instructed her to go to the seat to the nearby door of the captain's cockpit.

Cedrick sensed something was off between the two and he opted to wear the headphone and grabbed a piece of magazine while he was sitting then saw the two cars was now finally leaving the airport.

Alex felt a wave of gratitude towards Cedrick for acknowledging the situation between her and Osmond. With a gentle stride, she approached the man who had ruined her day, with her gaze fixed on him.

"Osmond, just tell me the truth. Why did you say her name? I mean, Isabelle? Since the text message was about her, it wasn't really necessary to say her name, especially in my presence," she stated her concern, while maintaining a distance between them.

"Well, Alex, it's just a natural response when you see someone making an effort, and that was merely to provide an update by chance," Osmond responded, trying to keep his composure as best as he could.

"Really? Or perhaps that wasn't the complete story of the message?" Alex questioned, disbelief washing over her as she observed his reaction, shaking her head gently.

"Ms. Alex, please, what's the purpose of bringing this up?"

"The purpose? Isn't it clear? It's tormenting me because I love you," she whispered softly to him.

"Well, don't be. Please? Because I love you too, but I can't make any promises," Osmond replied gently, as Alex shook her head once more, filled with disappointment.

Cedrick sensed the tension between his friend and their client, deciding to help them in other way by approaching the flight attendant to create a distraction, ensuring she wouldn't witness any suspicious tension between the two. It was time for him to use his tactical charm on the woman, which proved effective after he introduced himself. As the jet began to push back and the pilot announced the flight details, he and the woman started to bond, asking her about the jet's features and other details, which she happily shared with a smile, flipping her hair. Moments later, the woman glanced in another direction as the aircraft finally soared into the sky.

"Excuse me, Cedrick, Ms. Alex is calling me." The woman began to walk towards their client until she was finally close to the heiress. Together, they made their way to the kitchen area, while Osmond sat quietly, gazing out the window in confusion. He kept gently tapping the laminated wooden table. To satisfy Cedrick's curiosity, he decided to sit in front of him, and smiled.

"Is everything okay, mate?" He asked.

"Well, not really, since I don't know how to explain things to her after we both confessed our love for each other, and she keeps insisting on the text message I received this morning."

Cedrick nodded, understanding the cause of his distress. An idea struck him, and he wondered what would happen if Alex's parents eventually discovered their relationship.

"For now, I don't want to think about that mate. I just want to resolve the main issue between us."

"So, tell me, mate, what was in the text message that made her so disappointed?" Osmond glanced in the direction where Alex was, then finally responded to his question.

"It was about Isabelle, mate. She's alive."

A wave of overwhelming joy washed over him, as his feelings for Alex now had a chance to find a place in her heart. But then Osmond mentioned something he wished he had never heard.

"However, I also have a deep affection for Alex, which is love mate, and Isabelle holds a unique place in my heart. I have no doubt about that. My journey as an agent began because of her to find her and now, the timing seems perfect, doesn't it? I was able to safeguard Alex during our time here, and with your assistance over the past few days, I can finally look forward to reuniting with Isabelle now that she has reached out to Lester." Osmond concluded his thoughts while Cedrick was taken aback the way he opened up about the situation.

"But please do not misconstrue this as me being unfaithful to Alex; my sole desire is to reconnect with Isabelle. That is all."

"Yes, I understand you. Regardless of your motivations, I hope she can understand your viewpoint. And what about her parents? Do you intend to inform them?"

"Certainly. However, it requires a gradual approach. At present, I find myself torn between two worlds: loving her and protecting her, during this mission while also I'll be seeking the answer to uncover the truth behind Isabelle's abduction fourteen years ago and ensuring that those people will experience the appropriate consequences for what they did to my best friend." He finally wrapped up his thoughts just as he heard footsteps approaching their seats.

"Gentlemen, I trust you will enjoy the light refreshments that Ms. Alex has thoughtfully selected," the woman announced as she laid a white tablecloth on the table, followed by a set of cutleries from the tray she was carrying.

"Thank you," Osmond said while gazing at her. She smiled back and returned to the kitchen. Out of the corner of his eye, he noticed Alex sitting casually with a glass of sparkling water, not looking in his direction. He chose to remain quiet until the crew approached them, beginning to serve their food. Upon inspecting the selection, he was satisfied seeing the veggies and dip, including sliced carrots, bell pepper strips with a small container of hummus, then celery, and an assortment of dried fruits, nuts, and seeds.

"Thank you," Cedrick smiled and while Osmond did the same gesture.

"What drinks would you like?"

"Anything non-alcoholic will do. Thank you," Osmond finally replied.

"Of course. I'll return shortly."

Once the staff settled in the kitchen, he turned to Enrique's daughter and asked her,

"Ms. Alex, aren't you going to eat? It's been a few hours since our last meal." He offered.

"Don't worry about me, Mr. Gomez. Do you really think I could help the flight attendant by telling her what to prepare if I wanted to eat?"

Cedrick listened quietly after taking a bite of carrot.

"I apologise. I merely wish to—" but Alex swiftly interrupted him to prevent him from completing his sentence.

"It's alright. We'll resolve the matter once you're truly ready to reveal the truth. For now, please serve as my bodyguard."

Osmond simply nodded in response; it was a painful reminder for him. Yet, he had to accept it for the time being.

As the two agents finally finished their snacks, the silence among the three provided him a chance to reflect on his issues with Alex, then her parents, and finally with Isabelle. It wasn't until he glanced at his watch that he realised, in just a few minutes, the altitude would begin to decrease. He noticed on the flight tracker that they were now close to the state of Victoria. He prepared himself while Cedrick remained asleep, casting a brief glance at Alex, who was preoccupied with her phone. He then shifted his gaze to the window, contemplating the upcoming events once they reached their destination, having already informed Cedrick about the message from their commander.

Unbeknownst to Osmond, Alex was deep in thought, her annoyance towards him simmering beneath the surface. However, she decided to hold back her feelings for now, knowing that one day her rage would be unleashed against him. She then noticed the two men getting ready as the jet finally landed and heading to the final destination. Osmond stood up, ready to fulfill his responsibilities, and moved towards the door to assess the area. Once he was satisfied that everything was secure, he send a signal to Cedrick by pressing the button on his earpiece.

"Agent McKain, nothing is peculiar, proceed after Alex," Osmond stated after scanning the surroundings for the second time as the jet finally stopped at the bay.

"Roger that, Agent Gomez."

"Ms. Alex?" He politely asked, while the flight attendant standing beside them. He saw her staring at him, raising an eyebrow just before he descended the steps, and he felt she was started to follow him then another footstep from Cedrick.

Fifteen

The Tragedy

He was reminiscing that day when he uncovered the truth inside the drawer—the first one from the top. An urge had been growing in him ever since his grandfather forbade anyone from accessing it. Then one day, everyone grew worried when his grandfather was hospitalised due to exhaustion. The doctor, however, reassured them that he only needed plenty of rest and that everything would be fine. Seizing that opportunity, he decided to satisfy his endless curiosity.

Before opening the drawer, he whispered, *"I am so sorry, grandfather, if I have to do this."* To his surprise, inside was only a single folder—not a stack of documents as his grandfather had claimed. Immediately, questions flooded his mind: Why had his grandfather lied? He quickly opened the folder to inspect its contents. Inside, he found the name Mr. Enrique de Ayala and a short paragraph typed on a piece of bond paper:

"Mr. Enrique de Ayala, the youngest of two sons of Mr. Carlos de Ayala and Mrs. Sofia de Ayala, assumed the spotlight after the tragic suicide of his older brother, Mr. Emilio de Ayala, who took his own life the day after the celebration of their mother's birthday due to failing to fulfill a promise to their parents. Subsequently, Enrique sought to impress his parents, but another incident occurred under his direction. He arranged for Mrs. Esmeralda Courteney, wife of Mr. Felix Courteney, to perform a song at that event. Afterwards, an accident happened at the local bookstore involving the couple

Mr. Felix and Mrs. Esmeralda, Mrs. Claudelle Vanderbilt the foster mother of Esmeralda and Ms. Eleanor Taylor, Lucas's teacher." The document was signed by Detective Gregory.

Lucas could hardly believe what he had uncovered. As far as he knew, after his own kidnapping, he had read the news about the tragic accident involving his family and teacher Eleanor the following day. He found another paper beneath the first—a report detailing his abduction by a group of thieves. He opted to close the folder, convinced he now understood everything.

But then he realised tears were streaming down his face, and feelings of hatred surged toward Mr. Enrique—the very man he had once admired, a grave misjudgement. A plan suddenly formed in his mind. Leaving his grandfather's library, he headed to a familiar place he used to visit—only this time, with a different purpose.

Lucas took a deep breath before knocking on the door. He had already identified the witness to the accident and knew where to find her. According to his source, the woman had been on the opposite side of the road and had informed everyone she knew nearby about the scenario. As he waited, he noticed the door was opening by the woman in her late forties.

"Hi, good afternoon, mam," Lucas started.

"Oh, hi there. How can I help you?" the woman asked, still not fully opening the door.

"I'm sorry if I'm disturbing you now, but your help would be very meaningful to me if you could provide it today," he politely replied.

"What kind of help?"

Lucas couldn't hide his emotion. His face turned into sadness.

"It's just a statement about how you witnessed the horrible accident six years ago," he said.

"Oh my god!" The lady exclaimed. Her two hands covered her mouth in shock. "It seemed like the accident is relevant to you. Come inside, but I'm leaving soon, maybe in less than twenty minutes?"

"Mam, that would be a big help to me. I'll be so grateful," Lucas answered. The lady offered him a chair when he entered the house.

"Thank you so much."

"Would you like something to drink?"

"Well, anything mam." He replied.

"Alright, I'll be back." Then he saw the woman walk towards the nearby kitchen. Then he glanced inside, it was a simple home, the vibe was vibrant. The different ornamental plants were situated in each corner. And then, he gazed at the nearby table and saw the different picture frames were all maintained very well, as it had already been a few decades old.

"I am Shiela, and you?" The woman asked while preparing the two cups of coffee on top of the bench.

"I am Lucas and nice meeting you Shiela," Lucas replied.

"How so polite you are," the woman replied to him with a smile.

"Thank you so much. As my parents raised me well." He said plainly.

"That's sweet! I could imagine how proud they are now that you became the man that they wanted you to be."

Then he nodded to her gently and smiled and he continued to look inside of the place to refrain himself getting emotional at that moment then again, glancing at the picture frames it was a family portrait, he quickly assessed that the lady next to the man in his mid-twenties was her. She was gorgeous as her long blonde hair was simply loose on each side of her long white shirt, then below them as they were sitting in the chair while the two young children were on their laps. A young boy with a wavy hair and while the girl was on the lap of her father.

"Oh, it is unfortunate today that you won't be able to meet my husband, since we will meet later after his work. Then those are our children, both of whom are living in Sydney with their families." The lady said while starting to stir the cups of coffee and then went back to the lounge room and put the two cups on the coffee table in front of them.

"Thanks," Lucas said and took his drink, and it was such a nice black coffee.

"Alright, I should start now as I have to leave soon," the lady said after she drank her hot drink.

Then Lucas nodded in agreement while preparing himself to hear what he needed to know, then saw the woman deeply sigh.

"I was walking on the other side of the road while carrying a bag from the supermarket when I saw how the glass shattered as the truck crashed through it. Some of the people inside were struck. A loud scream erupted before the truck finally entered the store. But it didn't end there—everyone inside was nearly run over by the massive vehicle. The couple, Esmeralda and Felix, were both thrown several metres and impaled by multiple steel poles. I just saw their names in the newspaper the following day, but I cannot forget how the interior of the store was almost completely covered in blood, and a few others groaned faintly before ultimately succumbing to their injuries and that's all I can remember," the woman said and looked at him while shaking her head, showing how it was awful to experience the tragic accident.

"Thanks for telling me how you witnessed the ill-fated incident that day," Lucas said, standing up from the chair. He then reached into his pocket and pulled out his wallet, grabbing a few fifty-dollar bills to give to the woman. However, she declined to accept them.

"That's not necessary," she said. Despite the horrible experience of witnessing the accident, she was genuinely open to sharing it with him today because she believed it was relevant to him. After touching his hand and gently closing it to show her sincerity, Lucas felt a sense of relief, despite the heaviness within him. Her grace and kindness reminded him that the world is still full of good people, no matter what. Then he nodded.

"I hope that after our meeting, you can still find a place within yourself to discover a better or more peaceful way of living," the woman said. To his surprise, she then hugged him, gently tapping his back. He remained motionless when their eyes met, until he realised, he was also hugging her.

"I can feel that you are in pain, Lucas. I am hoping for the best after this," the woman said as he started walking toward the door. Before he finally stepped outside, he smiled at her and waved. She waved back and smiled.

"God bless you, Lucas," she said, still smiling.

"Thank you, Shiela, and God bless you too." He then shifted his gaze toward the car, already considering his plans for the day.

Looking at their old home, he saw it lay in ruins. Gathering his resolve, he stepped inside. Furniture and kitchen items were scattered haphazardly, turning the space into a chaotic mess. A foul odour hung in the air, but he pushed it aside, concentrating solely on finding something of great importance. He shrugged off his jacket, rolled up his shirt sleeves, and began sifting through the debris with his hands, tears streaming down his face at last. "Please, I have to find you," he murmured, aware that what he sought could become invaluable someday. Minutes slipped by, then half an hour, yet the items remained elusive. With determination, he reminded himself this was the only way to preserve the memories of his mother and grandmother—the very women who had taught him how to craft riddles, using the examples they had penned inside. He recalled it was contained within a black leather bag. Suddenly, an idea came to him: perhaps it was hidden beneath the furniture. Changing his position, he began lifting tables and chairs one by one to peer underneath. The sun was dipping low, thick grey clouds clustering above; he needed to hurry before the rain arrived. After shifting the last piece of furniture, his eyes caught sight of something familiar—it was the bag! But he failed to find the other one, the photo album that holds of their priceless captured memories, but he still lunged forward to seize the last item, but the zipper was stubbornly stuck, corroded by rust. Gently shaking the bag, he heard a faint rustle inside. Hope and relief washed over him as a smile broke through his tear and the notebook was still there, he shook the bag once more, listening to the soft sound of pages moving, sure he had found what he was seeking. Yet he couldn't bring himself to leave just yet; waves of memories began to flow over him, holding him in place a little longer.

"Grandmother, please, I don't think I can make it," Lucas said after he tried to make at least one stanza of poetry then he scratched the back of his head in frustration. It was the weekend after lunch, and he even finished his assignment earlier, until when he was about to stand up from his chair, where she prevented him from leaving. His step-father and mother went to the supermarket to buy what they needed for the entire coming week, they were not poor or belong to any average kind of income but they were in a harmonious way of living as his grandmother was a retired teacher while his step father was struggling to get a full time job thought he had a lot of experience from hospitality, small retail stores, door to door cleaning to their suburb so same as his mother, but nevertheless they always make it whenever there was a job opportunity for them. Then plus the pension of her grandmother was really a big help. So, he couldn't ask for more that moment of his life, as their home was full of loved.

"Alright, I have a deal. "If you can make it, then I have a reward for you!" His nana said while smiling and caressing his back while looking at him dearly. Meanwhile, from frustration, his face went to a joyful expression from what he heard. He knew what it was, a honey joy florentines. Then he took a deep breath while glancing at the notebook, then nodded and looked at her.

"Good boy! Alright, I'll be back after a couple of minutes while preparing your reward, but also I would check the status of your writing, so I would definitely know if I can still continue to make your favourite snack." Then he silently watched his nana while she was on her way to the kitchen, then he looked at his writing and started to work his mind while holding the pen. Then until something came to his mind as he reflected on himself. He was still a teen; then he tried to analyse something. Then he smiled. She was right, he could do it. Then, out of nowhere, he found himself continuing with what he started earlier.

"I am no titan; therefore, I am not connected to humans from numbers and letters, but mankind is skeptical whenever my name is on the table."

"I can't find the reason behind those emotionless eyes and subtle smiles; then how can I see and feel their depths if you belong to an unknown celestial?"

His eyes widened after reading them twice, then he even tried to scratch the pair of his eyes to see the reality of what he had created on his notebook. Then he stood up from his chair after taking the notebook and rushed towards the kitchen.

"Nana! Look, I did it!" He joyfully exclaimed while jumping in mid-air after he gave his notebook to his grandmother which she accepted and looking at her while silently assessing what he had written.

"This is so beautiful Lucas! I am so happy with this! See? I told you!" Then until they hugged each other while laughing,

"Hey, what's going on here?" Felix asked while carrying two baskets that contain fruits and vegetables.

"Seems like you two are having a good moment here in the kitchen." Added by his mother after putting a small carry bag on the dining table.

"Look Esmeralda, finally he did it! Remember the last time he was struggling to make this?"

Esmeralda knitted her eyebrows after she accepts the notebook from Claudelle then upon glancing at it, she looked to her son then to the thing that she was holding.

"Mom, tell me that this is yours!" Esmeralda said.

"No, it is not mine. It was your son who wrote that!" Claudelle replied and gave the paper to her then Esmeralda was in awe after seeing the content of notebook, then a tears with smile and she looked towards her husband, and she passed the paper to him, then the moment was another joyful to them as the unexpected gesture of Felix surprised Lucas.

"Wow! Such an excellent work my son!" Felix exclaimed, and ruffled his hair.

Then the silence occurred, while looking at the sky, he tried to communicate with God and asked Him: "What have I done wrong to experience this kind of unthinkable suffering!?" Then he shouted as much as he could, as the downpour came with a strong thunder above the lightless, dark sky, until he realised, he was kneeling down on the ground while his tears kept falling down on his face with every countless raindrop. Then he paused for a few seconds while shaking his head until he started to scream again from the top of his lungs.

"Why?!!!!" Then a few moments later, a collection of thought about his plan, but for now everything will change as he would start the second step by tomorrow after he gathered the details that he needed.

He smiled when he sees the incoming middle-aged man wearing a casual dress, as he expecting him today, as he reached the ground floor area he smiled at him then the man also smiled back at him.

"Thanks for coming today, Doctor Blaine and I am extending my appreciation that even though you are not sure yesterday, but now look you've made it today." Then he offered his right hand for a handshake, which the latter accepted it with sincerity.

"So, what can I do for you Mr. Lucas?" The Doctor asked after the man motioned his arm toward the couch in front of them until they were finally seated.

In the scene with the doctor, Lucas warned, "Don't do anything that could lead him to death. I can literally impose punishment on you that's worse than death." He was referring to someone who can't say what he wanted to hear but he already knew that he was part of Enrique's desire and yet, he was not able to say to Enrique that he needed to know about his mistakes that day.

Sixteen

New Protocols

They reached the de Ayala estate without any issues, greeted by several staff members along the driveway. Alex spotted her parents and quickly exited the SUV, a Bentley Bentayga. The three of them met in the area and embraced, tears flowing. The General-Director stood behind them, while the two agents saluted their commander, who returned the gesture.

"Oh my, finally! You are here now, honey!" Evangeline exclaimed as they broke their embrace. "So, how was your stay there?"

"Well, it was actually wonderful. Just like a typical vacation, but the way I was treated was spectacular," Alex replied, referring to the Gomez family. "And I adore Osmond's nephew!" She suddenly realised something but composed herself on how to finish her statement. "I mean, Agent Gomez's nephew."

"That's sweet!" Evangeline thought, dismissing the idea after noticing how Alex exited the vehicle; it was unusual. While she was always thrilled to see them, this time felt different until her husband interrupted their conversation.

"Shall everyone get in?"

"He's right; the four men here need to discuss a specific protocol for today," the commander concurred.

"Before we get into that, should we have some welcome drinks or does anyone want to eat?" Enrique inquired.

"I think so, yes. Thank you, sir," Cedrick responded.

"Excuse me, I just need to go to my room," Alex said, excusing herself and asking one of the house staff to carry her suitcase.

Everyone then entered the house, followed by the staff. Cedrick looked around and noted that every corner of the residence was highly secured, equipped with CCTV and powered windows. Finally, they arrived at the main dining hall, where everything was beautifully arranged on the table. Evangeline asked her husband if he would like any liquor with his meal.

"No, thank you. How about you gentlemen?" Enrique inquired of the commander and the two agents, who both graciously declined the offer.

"We are all good. Thank you, Mr. Enrique." Osmond said.

"Mr. Gomez and Mr. McKain, my husband and I cannot express enough our gratitude for looking after our daughter," Evangeline started and saw how her husband to the members of the secret intelligence to take a seat as the staff began serving the meals onto their plates.

"So, Mr. Gomez, did my daughter give you any trouble while she was there?" Enrique asked.

Osmond smiled upon hearing the unexpected question from the family patriarch, then recalled something that made him feel guilty—the relationship between him and his daughter.

"Well, initially, yes, it was quite frantic. But as time passed and I remained steadfast in my duty to her, she eventually accepted the situation. The thought of her getting along well with my family was truly delightful, Mr. Enrique."

"That's wonderful to hear, Mr. Gomez. Actually, my daughter isn't really a spoiled brat; I mean, it's true that she's our heiress, but I know deep down she inherited the gentlest qualities from my beloved wife." The patriarch gazed at his wife and smiled at her.

"That's correct, Mr. Gomez. I know my daughter well, my husband and I have agreed that from now on, she will always be by our side since her schooling is complete. This week, our daughter will return to her responsibilities at the company."

"And that's why I'm here," the commander interjected, as the couple nodded in agreement, "to share the important details while ensuring her safety."

The two agents then politely nodded to their chief until they felt the presence of heiress finally approaching the main dining area.

"It's great that you're here now. We all have something important to discuss, and saying 'no' will not be an option, especially when you declined my suggestion before about Mr. Gomez to be your personal bodyguard Alex," the father stated firmly to his daughter.

"Alright, Dad. Let us move past that. Shall we?" Alex responded as she pulled out the chair, taking the napkin from her plate and placing it on her lap. Osmond then returned his phone to his slacks after notifying his parents that they had arrived safely.

"Anyway, my dear, what are your plans for your upcoming birthday at the end of this month?"

Alex glanced at her mother, who casually shrugged her shoulders.

"Well, I suppose it will be the same as usual," she replied, sipping her juice and smiling.

"I have an idea, but we can discuss it another day. Since it will be in three weeks time. For now, let us begin our meal," Enrique stated, raising his glass to propose a toast.

"Welcome home, Alex!" Evangeline exclaimed, followed by the sound of clinking glasses as they took a sip of their drinks, filling the area with a formal atmosphere while enjoying their light meal.

After Alex's welcome meal, the matriarch excused herself from the discussion and headed to the lounge room to wait for them. Meanwhile, in the study room, everyone was seated at the six-seater table, with a double door in front leading to the main library.

"So, Agent Gomez and Alex," Enrique began. "Earlier this morning, we spoke over the phone with the General-Director regarding Osmond's new duty, which will be five days a week. And you Agent

McKain," Cedrick nodded to the patriarch, awaiting the continuation, "will serve as a backup until you return to your primary duty at the Australian Intelligence Agency. However, it is entirely up to you whether you accept this offer or not."

"There is no way I can decline such a task, Mr. Enrique," Cedrick affirmed firmly.

"Thank you, agent McKain."

"Furthermore, my response aligns with that of my colleague, sir," Osmond stated with assurance as he directed his gaze towards the heiress, seeing her neutral expression, and then to her father, awaiting further instructions.

"In the event of an emergency or urgent situation, my daughter's code name will be *"Precious."* Meanwhile, Agent Gomez will utilise a permanent decoy to mislead any potential intruder, allowing us to gather essential information to secure our advantage."

Upon hearing the additional information, Osmond had anticipated this and now merely waiting for the patriarch to conclude their discussions.

"Then, Mr. Gomez, an enhancement to your appearance," he said, retrieving an item from the drawer and placing it on the table; within the transparent case was a dark brown moustache.

Osmond smiled when he saw the object, glancing between his employer and the head of Central Intelligence.

"This was my suggestion, Agent Gomez."

"Understood, sir," he responded, as Alex began to inquire about the individual behind the threat. Her father then shifted his gaze towards the commander in chief.

"Actually, Ms. Alex, allow me to clarify the entire operation from last night. The magazines featuring your photographs taken in Europe with your best friend, along with another collection of your images, both printed and digital, from the controversy in Madrid involving Elissandra, were gathered."

Osmond nodded in acknowledgment of what they've heard.

"In fact, we encountered difficulties in locating him, as he was situated overseas. We eventually discovered him in a remote area of Malaysia, alongside his team, while they were securing their hideout."

After hearing the final detail, even though the perpetrator was apprehended and his associates, something felt off in his mind. However, since their commander was behind the operation, but Osmond casually brushed aside the thought, then Enrique finally speak while looking to his daughter.

"While your mother and I will file a case against the team to ensure they can never give us any kind of trouble again, in every possible way, Alex. I promise you that," Enrique added then his daughter stood up to hug her dad and then she approached the chief commander while remaining to his chair.

"Thank you so much for assisting my dad, General," Alex said, extending her hand to the man as a gesture of gratitude.

"It is my responsibility to assist and protect. Besides, the three of us have been close since high school, so I am always willing to offer my help when needed."

Then Alex recalled the other man he was referring to, the most significant politician in the country, the Prime Minister.

"Also, Mrs. Celine Gomez sends her regards to you and to mom. I almost forgot to mention it earlier," she said, eager to leave the room as she still felt irritation earlier morning from Queensland.

"Oh, thank you for that. It's great to know that they have been liking you. And Osmond, lastly, you need to stay here; you will be staying at the guest house. It has everything you need. Just make sure to bring more of your personal items as soon as possible. Can you manage that by tomorrow?

"Absolutely, sir," he responded, but in the back of his mind, he was wishing that Isabelle would reach out to him before he got too busy until tomorrow.

"Agent Gomez, I can return here if you really need some of them to use, since I collected your items the last time I was here, right?"

"That would be a great help, Agent McKain, but it's alright because I brought some of my things," he replied, relieved that he had decided to pack a few items in his small suitcase.

"Alright, I will do that on my next duty day." Cedrick replied.

"Thank you."

Alex was about to say something when Enrique finally wrapped up the briefing.

"Okay, so this meeting is concluded, and thank you to your team, General," Enrique announced as he rose from his chair, followed by a handshake, and then everyone exited the room. Osmond was instructed by Enrique to follow one of the staff members to the guest house.

As he lay in bed, Osmond reminisced about a past event, smiling despite the significant misunderstanding he had with his nana, but ultimately, everything turned out well. It was nine in the morning, and his grandmother was in the kitchen washing dishes since he couldn't do it while waiting for the bus. He felt happy that the day was sunny, a stark contrast to the previous rainy day. He also remembered packing his clothes and other items he planned to take with him the night before.

"Hi Osmond, is there anything I can help you with?" Her question caught him off guard, reminding him of a time over a decade ago when no one supported his dream to find a certain person in his life. He answered while arranging a pile of shirts on the bed.

"Thanks, Nana, but I'm good here. I just need to finish packing these things into my bag, and then I'll be done," he replied.

"I understand your parents may not approve of your plans, but I hope you can see their perspective. Over the years, I've realised that without support or encouragement from our family, what is the point of being part of it?" He inhaled deeply after hearing her words, and with a nod, he felt reassured that everything would turn out fine. As the youngest sibling, he was the only one brave enough to pursue this life purpose, which was both risky and felt like his was his destiny. He recalled the individuals who had passionately supported him, and that was enough to convince him there was no turning back. And he was certain that one day, he would make them all proud of his journey. It wasn't just for himself; he felt there was something greater at stake, even if it was still vague. Eventually, everything would become clear to him.

"In any case, be good and break a leg, okay?" As his Nana came over for a hug, he held her close. Yet, a specific memory from his past emerged, reminding him that he would achieve what he needed to do one day, and for now, he was clinging to hope. While riding the bus, he thought, *"I will succeed in choosing this path, to find you, Isabelle, and to fulfill the rest of things once I finally succeed."*

After he got out of the taxi, he saw his fellow candidates making their way to the main entrance of a single-story building, which was surrounded by local pine trees and set in a well-kept Zoysia grass while in front of the building there were two flags displayed: the indigenous flag and the national flag of the country. One particular individual caught his eye just as he was about to enter; it was a blonde curly-haired man standing alone, while the others and their friends had already gone inside. Their eyes met, and they both smiled.

"Hi mate!" The man greeted him, waving his hand.

"Hello there, mate," he replied casually, noticing the man extending his hand for a formal introduction.

"I am Cedrick McKain, and you are?"

"Osmond Gomez," he responded, accepting the handshake as they walked in with an officer, when they reached the closed door in the middle of hallway they turned right until the uniformed man opened it for them with a smile.

"Good luck, gentlemen."

"Thanks," they replied in unison before stepping into the room, where the total number of candidates was fewer than thirty, including themselves. Once everyone was seated, the General-Director began introducing the members of their organization. They recognized two of them just as the projector turned on, displaying a photo.

"Ladies and gentlemen, congratulations on making it here today. Everyone has successfully passed the written exam, and it is crucial for all of you to grasp the importance of the Australian Intelligence Organisation's role. Furthermore, a comprehensive understanding of the history of the Australian Military Force is necessary," he said, glancing at the two individuals beside him. "And everyone recognises these two, as you have all seen their faces during the exam. For those who will endure the rigorous training, the final phase will be conducted in a military manner, but there is more to it. The head of military intelligence has provided us with our directives." The General-Director continued, "after World War I and II, leaders from various countries and under monarchies, along with several organisations worldwide, convened to establish peace. Their goal was to mediate conflicts between nations and their territories, ensuring civility and upholding rights when duty calls. This agreement led to the formation of the United Nations."

"Do you have any suggestions or ideas? Please share what's on your mind," the commander requested, noticing someone raises his hand and stand up with a salute.

"War is like a force of nature; it represents a conflict among humans, yet being resourceful is vital in every aspect as I believe that nothing can be higher with the truth if we are really keen to show what we really got." Then the General-Director smiled at him after his response, then turned his sight to the two officers, while nodding in agreement.

Osmond was astonished by the response he heard. From that point onward, the two formed a friendship, sharing similar qualities as candidates, especially with Cedrick, who had given such a considerate and fulfilling answer.

Then a man in uniform appeared after replacing the head of Military Intelligence and everyone was fixated on the large monitor as it displayed a pre-recorded message.

"Congratulations to all, and in a few months, once the military training concludes, the next phase will take place at our headquarters, Thames House, located in central London in Westminster. So, once again, good luck, and to those who will pass the initial initiation, I will see you there." The video concluded, and the following day, everyone was dispatched to the field to undergo the demanding training. The physical and tactical exercises were designed to enhance strength, endurance, and combat abilities, including bodyweight workouts like push-ups, squats, and burpees, weightlifting, along with skill-based activities such as ruck running and mountain climbing. Out of nearly thirty, only about twenty candidates remained. Subsequently, everyone who completed the first training was now en route to the United Kingdom.

Thames House, London. Within the high-secured room the phrase *"the harbinger of duty"* can be heard, then a high ranking official is in front while walking back and forth and looking to each of them while seated in their respective seats; then he continued, "is frequently crucial for this kind of training. While all participants undergo military training, the similarity ends there; but the key difference is the necessity for puzzle-solving, which calls for an *investigative skills training.*" This point was highlighted by the officer at the start of his speech before the training officially began. "The course will shift between classroom learning using non-verbal techniques and practical time with the investigative team to enrich the educational experience."

Osmond felt fortunate that Cedrick was part of his team, adept at managing the puzzles, and occasionally there were riddles to uncover the clues, as he excelled in that area. Then, he looked at the wall clock, and the final scenario he recalled from the past was the ceremonial venue. It was just before noon, and everyone had gathered to commemorate a once-in-a-lifetime victory after the national anthem of Australia, "Advance Australian Fair," concluded and everyone was surrounded by several significant people in their lives until Osmond closed his eyes and drifted off to sleep.

Seventeen

The Reunion

When he arrived in Sydney early in the afternoon a message appeared on his phone, it was unregistered number from his contacts. And glad that before he left, Mr. Enrique informed him that he can returned the following day instead of coming back later at night.

"I'll see you later in the evening. Just tell me the convenient place for you. And for sure, you already knew who I am." Then Osmond smiled while constructing his reply then he locked his phone after pressing the send button and resumes from eating his snack.

If the lights within the sophisticated restaurant were shining brightly, it was a reflection of the emotions he experienced at that moment; if Alex resembled a goddess in the photograph, she surpassed that instantly when he laid his eyes on her in reality. He had canceled his business appointments that day to finally meet her after the patriarch had kindly informed him a few days prior that he wished for him to meet his daughter. Watching her delicately part her lips to enjoy the food was captivating, and each bite of the red meat steak she took was even slower than his own, which only heightened his satisfaction; to top it off, the gentle melody of music wafting through the VIP room made the experience unforgettable until Mr. Enrique began to speak as he glanced in their direction.

"I am pleased that you two have finally met,"

"Well, if I could clear my schedule every day just to see your daughter, why not, Mr. Enrique?" He smiled after taking a gentle sip of his Penfolds red wine.

"Haha! Take it easy, Hugo. As you know, my daughter is quite busy, especially since she is under my watch whenever she's in the office."

"Oh, come on, Dad, don't say that in front of him; it makes me sound like a teenager." She remarked, furrowing her brows and delicately wiping her lips with the napkin before smiling.

"I didn't mean it like that. But naturally, you are my successor, so I have to fulfill my responsibilities."

"Actually, I changed my mind when he asked about you and knowing him then why not giving Hugo a chance to know you better. And I think this is the best first step, right?"

Alex answered her father by smiling while looking at him until Hugo shared an idea to her father while the man looking at her, and Alex was aware how Hugo was showing his deep interest in her, then shifted his eyes to her father and then to her.   "So, perhaps we could go out early in the evening once you finish at the office?" Hugo asked after taking a sip of his wine.

Alex didn't respond immediately, gazing at him as she flipped her medium-length hair, contemplating her plans with Osmond, even though she wasn't keen on that direction, but felt she had no choice. Cedrick had become her friend after he had a fistfight with Osmond in front of her, leading her to a realisation.

"Well, why not, Hugo? Since my dad knows you quite well." She replied.

"Of course, Alex, your dad is very familiar with me after some of our mutual business associates introduced us that night, and we have a lot of things in common, then followed by their smiled and continued to eat their meal.

After Osmond organised his clothes and other things, that day, he took a shower and chose to wear a black cotton long sleeve, a white tracksuit then a sneaker before he went out from his apartment, and ordered fish and chips then a bottle of soft drink from the nearby restaurant before he continue traversing to the meeting place, it was the park.

The fast approaching of their meeting time was aligning to every rhythm of his heart, as he glance to every one in the vicinity, then he decided to sit on the bench while next to it was a lamp post so he can see her then took several bites to finish his snack while facing the water and Osmond checked the time on his watch, five minutes more before the meeting time; nine o'clock and good thing Cedrick was able to guard Alex then after he got a text message from her it was only a normal message that saying *"Okay, I'll see you tomorrow."* Then he heard someone calling his name.

"Osmond.."

He quickly put on the bench the bottle of his drink and he looked around and saw the woman who called his name, and it was her! Isabelle. His sister was right, her face was almost still the same, and her shiny blonde hair just set plainly, while the wind was gently kissing every inch of it, then he stood up quickly and rushed towards to hugged her.

"Isabelle.." he softly whispered and he felt she started to tap his back, and he remember his answer to the question of his brother-in-law.

"Where have you been all of these years? And what happened?" Osmond asked her, then she smiled at him. Contrary to what he feels, he saw a radiant in her, and she took his hand and started to walk toward the bench.

"Osmond, can we skip from those questions please?"

Meanwhile, Osmond knitted his eyebrows and it was unexpected from her, opposite from being missing so many years and yet she doesn't want to discuss what happened.

"Isabelle.. please! I want an answer, and if you are scared of them then don't, as I am finally succeeded to achieve my dream. Remember, when we were young I want to become an agent?" Osmond pleaded while holding her hands until Isabelle gently raised her right hand to caress his face and tears was forming in her eyes.

"Osmond.." then followed by smile and looking at him deeply. "I am so proud and happy for you. And there's no need to punish the people who abducted me. And believe it or not, they never ever hurt or did anything bad. I assure you that. Please, let us leave at that. Is that okay?" Then she wiped his tears, and stood up. "I remember from your text, you just live nearby, can we go there?" She asked just to alleviate his emotion from what happened before.

"Yes, of course." He answered, then he smiled at her and they both started to walk, then his phone rang, and when he pulled it out from his pocket, it was her, Alex. Then he looked at his best friend.

"It's okay, you can take that call." She said and made her way to the nearest bench to sit down until Osmond prevented him from doing so after he texted Alex that he was about to sleep soon.

"It's okay, it's not an urgent." He said, then he felt an extreme guilt towards Alex, but he had no choice. Isabelle was also important to him and this time was crucial since he doesn't know when he can meet her again.

"Osmond, there's a lot of changes." She mentioned, as they continue to walk.

"What do you mean?"

"I mean, in our lives. Yours, and mine." She smiled at him.

"Yeah, that's true. And because of you, from that day since you have been kidnapped I made a promise to myself, that I'll pursue my dream to find you and yet, you are here even I had a lot of trouble to find any clue about any information when you were gone."

"And also, I was able to find you when I visited the hometown, I asked your neighbour. Then Lester mentioned that you are staying here in Sydney." She replied until they both looked at the road and Osmond smiled while pressing the button of stoplight.

"Wow, that was such a memorable place for us Isabelle." He said and they continued walking until they finally arrived in the front of the building where his apartment was situated to the second floor.

When they entered his place, he casually gave the photo album he got that contain photographs during his trainings up to their graduations and saw the immeasurable happiness in her eyes as she flip every page of it, then he proceed to the kitchen to make drinks for them and he opened the fridge to get something for them to eat while discussing the upcoming talks between them.

"Thanks, and actually Osmond they already forgive you." Isabelle started after he gave a cup of tea to her while took a sip when he seated.

"Oh thanks, for letting me know Isabelle." He said while looking at her.

"Well of course they must be. Since it was not your entirely fault." Then a sudden thought lingering her mind, but she dismissed it and smiled at him.

"Hopefully one day, we will meet again as I truly missed them a lot. And of course, my dad owed your father a lot when we were down." He said, as he recalled when his dad lost his job and turned out that her father hired his dad.

"And of course, that would be a great idea. For sure, in the near future once everything is settled."

"Where do you live?" He asked, then Osmond saw she was taken aback of his question, but he patiently waited for her answer.

"I don't live in a permanent place,"

"Why?"

"Osmond due to the nature of my work, I mean as a representative of company, so I have to relocate in each state once the company requires me to do so." Isabelle replied, "but do not worry, from now on you will always see me once there is chance. And of course, the nature of your duty is demanding same as mine."

"Yeah, it is. Actually, I am coming back to Melbourne by tomorrow for my work." He added.

"That's great to know. I am also coming there tomorrow with a friend, and I am staying there for about two weeks. And you can see me as well." She replied.

"Good to hear that Isabelle. So, I'll see you then." After an hour of conversation that full of satisfaction with each other and they talked random experiences when they were in their teens, until Isabelle gazed at her watch and looked at him as an indication that was her time to leave anytime soon.

"Osmond, I have to leave soon and I'll see you in Melbourne. But I'll text you which place the day before we would meet."

"Yes, sure. So, I'll see you then?"

"Absolutely," then she hugged him for the second time that night, and they both walked towards the ground floor to make sure, that she will be safe until her taxi arrives.

That night, after agreeing the following meeting, this will be his chance to gather anything as much as he could, he will never set his mind in peace without knowing the whole facts about the mysterious abduction of Isabelle, and he would start it later before the whole night concludes.

Then he opened his laptop, and tried to open some database to gather about Isabelle, then to his surprised, it was still the same as the last time he checked on it. Name, the address and other details. And a surge of question ran into his mind. "Where did you really go and how come you managed to reunite with me and to your family?" He asked himself, then a hypothetical conclusion came up to his mind but he quickly ignored it. Then he yawned, and turned off the lampshade next to him, and gently placed his wrist on forehead and started to closed his eyes.

He was glad that the airport at that time wasn't busy as the queue for check-in went smoothly, until Osmond finally boarded on the plane and he checked the time on his watch, as Alex texted him to proceed to the main office as she was heading to that place at that time and he started to eat his business class meal once the flight attendant finally put it on the foldable table.

Inside of the board meeting room, the oval shaped table was consisting of the full member of the company as Alex was in the middle of her presentation, this was her first day since yesterday they had to meet Hugo and she can't wait for Osmond to witness the next event later.

"As the file's subject is about the expansion of business to the continent of North and South America, it gives us a better approach to any international markets; so in the process we can offer more goods and services abroad since the market access will increase and therefore the trade barriers will reduced. And the probability of economic growth will be the result. Then as what I have mentioned before, by reducing the cost of products by applying the lost-cost effective marketing would be an advantage to any competitor inside and outside of Australia."

Then the couple Enrique and Evangeline was amazed and could not contain their satisfaction while gently squeezing each other's hand on how their daughter presented her analysis, even they just gave the folder when she arrived that morning. Then their daughter continued.

"Political-business relation was also included since in 1933 hence; some merchant manufacturers then workers had vested interests in individual colonial markets which they were reluctant to see jeopardised by the unifying of the Australian market under federation. In that year, as the business of my grandfather Mr. Carlos de Ayala was becoming popular within the country, he learned from the public service act when it was provided after amendment that one-tenth of each year's appointments should be open to university graduates under the age of twenty-five, so therefore he invested to help every sector for the mandatory training of economics and statistics or shall I say, suitable for Australia's foreign service when it is applicable." Then she smiled after placing the folder to the nearest table and she heard the big round of applause from people inside.

"That was excellent Alex!" Her father commented while she was on her way to her seat.

"Thanks dad," she replied when she finally seated.

"Anyway, Hugo just called me before this meeting started since you were not answering his call, and he was inviting you for an afternoon tea today, then I don't mind if you would say yes."

Then Alex glance to her father and nodded before she respond.

"Well, I was about to text him now," then she took her phone from the table and saw a notification text, that was from Osmond. He was just outside of the room while inspecting the premises. Then she chose not to reply as she composed a message for Hugo to confirm the time, then she smiled, "Now Osmond it's payback time." Followed by her malevolent smile and she returned the device on the table as the other member started to speak in front of them.

As Osmond walked along the hallway, chatting with the building's security, his cell phone suddenly rang. It was the Director-General. "Excuse me, I'll just take this call," Osmond said, stepping a few steps away to answer.

"Yes, General?"

"Agent Gomez, I've already spoken to Mr. Enrique about this morning. Tomorrow night, Agent McKain and the other agent has a delicate and difficult mission that requires your backup, it's really an urgent. I've already sent the information to your email. Bye."

"Alright, noted, sir," Osmond replied and the call was ended when he heard the beep sound and curiosity running in his mind, since Alex was his priority to watch but tomorrow night, they have a mission, and knowing it involves three agents it was a clear indication it was a highly stake mission that they need to fulfil!

As Osmond looked around, he thought of a way to make an excuse to get Alex away from that place. He didn't really like his hunch and briefly turned his gaze to where she was while talking with the arrogant man, which caught him off guard as he realised, he was staring at them.

Alex was facing the man with her back turned to Osmond, and she saw the sudden change in his face. Meanwhile, Osmond saw that he seemed to have said something to Alex, and the latter turned to him. Alex's forehead furrowed while looking at him, and she suddenly stood up and approached where he was standing.

"Osmond, what's wrong? And why are you looking at us?"

"Nothing. Is it bad to do such a thing?" He replied, while gazing around the VIP room.

"Yes, he's not comfortable with your stare."

Osmond looked at her deeply in her eyes for a moment, and then he answered. "In that case, that's not my problem. It's just him. I'm doing my job of keeping an eye on you, especially when we're outside." After answering Alex, he turned his gaze to another direction.

"I see. Is that all? Or are you jealous, Osmond?" Alex asked him with a smile, and he answered directly.

"Yes, I am experiencing such feelings while fulfilling my responsibility to keep you safe."

Then Alex saw the mixture of sadness and seriousness in his eyes. She didn't say anything more and turned away from Osmond, returning to their table with the man she had recently yesterday.

Osmond felt an extreme anger of how the events transpiring, then for tomorrow night the criminals will witness no mercy if he needs to execute his fatal strikes!

Eighteen

The Immersion

In the next state of Victoria, specifically Sydney, another figure sat quietly, taking a deep breath after glancing at a message on his phone, which led him to reflect on the past. The father of his personal assistant could no longer fulfill his duties due to health issues, prompting Mr. Amadeus to appoint him immediately that day when he volunteered to step in after his father relinquished the responsibility. He was selective about finding a replacement, concerned for the Emsworth clan, as a gesture of gratitude for the respect shown to his father and the equal opportunity provided as an employee. Well, it was mentioned to him when he tried to know the reason why, instead of pursuing other kind of duty, which he appreciated much from that day.

The trek took less than fifty minutes, and it was nearing midday, with sunlight filtering through the dense foliage of the surrounding trees. The wind was gentle, yet the sun had begun to heat up since summer commenced a few weeks ago, and he had been the one to suggest this location when asked, having visited the area several times before. Just a couple of days earlier, his boss's grandfather had firmly instructed him to keep a watchful eye on him at all times. He understood his responsibility and was determined to uphold it, as Mr. Amadeus had expressed that Lucas was incredibly dear to him, and he genuinely admired Amadeus's affection for his grandson. The moment shifted back to the present as he heard a sound. Upon looking at it, his boss's backpack was now resting on the thick wild grass, and watching as he removed his white shirt, walking shorts, and sneakers, his face alight with excitement, leaving only gray underwear on his body. He then dashed into the water to revel in its embrace, expressing his appreciation for nature as he finally submerged himself.

"Wow! Hahaha! I really appreciate to bring me here, Darek! It's been an ages since I last visited this kind of nature!" Lucas exclaimed.

Then Darek saw Lucas was diving into the depths of the water. A smile spread across his face, knowing he had brought joy to him that day.

"Come over here! Join me, Darek!" Lucas called out after he plunged into the water, and he politely shook his head, having not checked the safety of their surroundings, and he replied.

"Maybe later, Lucas." He said casually as he began to unpack his bag, sorting through items like the tent, food, clothes, and his firearm.

After enjoying their meal that they grilled over the bonfire, they sat on the grass. Lucas couldn't help but admire the loyalty and effort of his assistant. He recalled their first meeting vividly.

"Hello, Sir Lucas! I'm Darek, and your grandfather has assigned me to assist you with your daily tasks. Also, since my father taught me boxing and street fighting, I can serve as your bodyguard too. My father was a boxer, but he had to give up due to a lack of support from his family. Thankfully, your grandfather later provided him with an opportunity." Even though he wasn't thrilled about his grandfather's decision, Lucas felt grateful to accept it, as the man before him showed sincerity and loyalty to him.

"I can't believe it! It's your first day, and yet your introduction made me speechless! Thank you for that, Darek." From that moment, their relationship transcended the typical employer-employee dynamic. Lucas treated him like a brother, and Darek reciprocated the sentiment. After the tragedy, Lucas found himself without close friends, and his cousin Lawrence rarely visited due to school commitments. However, weekends were always the perfect time for them to bond and Lucas extended his hand to gently tap his assistant's shoulder, expressing how thankful he was for the day.

"Once again, thank you for suggesting this place, Darek. I've been feeling quite burnt out lately until my grandfather urged me to take a break. I was reluctant because I was also worried about his health, but I'm grateful to have someone like Arthur who can step in for me while I'm away," he said, smiling as how his late father's best friend agreed to cover him for a few days when he requested the favour.

"It's my duty, sir Lucas, and this location really highly recommended for someone like you to relax. I'm always pleased to offer my assistance whenever needed."

Just then, Darek gave his shoulder a tap as well, and they both shared a smile before continuing to enjoy their beers, the short vacation was more than the word *"worthy"* when they finally left the place and memories will always be memories to anyone after the similar experience, just like what they had.

A few months remained before the year came to a close, and Lucas reached out to someone capable of organising their training needs. He was swamped with tasks at that time and met his Sensei at a rented house located near the sea in Perth. He had already gathered all the essentials for their training, particularly the traditional Hakama. With his backpack slung over his shoulder, he gracefully removed it and bowed respectfully to his Sensei as the door swung open after his knock.

"Kon'nichiwa, Sensei Satoshi, it is a privilege to be your student; for that, domo arigato gozaimasu," Lucas began, gazing at his teacher, who was clad in an all-black Hakama.

"You are quite formal, Lucas. Let's keep things casual for now, and we can save the formalities for our actual training and lessons."

Lucas was taken aback by both his Sensei's words and demeanor, which amused him.

"I never anticipated this on our first day, Sensei," Lucas responded.

"Why? Did you expect it to unfold like a scene from a movie?"

Lucas smiled softly and nodded in agreement.

"Forget that notion. This is how I interact with my students. However, during the actual training, things will be entirely different."

Lucas noticed a sudden shift in his Sensei's expression and tone until he spoke again.

"I understand that your journey took over an hour, so please take a moment to rest. I look forward to seeing you later for dinner at seven and again tomorrow morning at eight for your first lecture."

"Yes, Sensei," he responded respectfully, bowing to him. The instructor returned the bow and casually made his way towards the lounge room, then he glance back at him.

"I commended you for transforming the entire house into a dojo."

He simply nodded in acknowledgment. The sensei resumed his walk, and he witnessed how he settled onto the floor in a traditional seiza position, and smiled after seeing the walls adorned with Japanese calligraphy, known as Shodo. On the other side, there were Katana Kake with a real swords in it, while the right was set of Bokken and Tanto. Lucas smiled how his trusted associate had meticulously arranged the space, ensuring everything aligned with his vision after extensive research how does the dojo should be exactly look like. It was nearly nine o'clock in the evening, and they had dined two hours ago, as he lay on his bed, a futon, the traditional Japanese sleeping bed while he could hear the sound of waves from the sea, accompanied by the chirping of crickets near his window. The stars were visible from his position, prompting him to recall their first dinner together. The atmosphere had been pleasant, as his grandfather had introduced him to Japanese culture, making him well instructed in table etiquette from the proper use of chopsticks and the correct way to handle each bowl or plate on the table. He was currently dressed in his uniform, having changed earlier from casual attire to a traditional Hakama.

"I am not surprised by your familiarity with Japanese table etiquette. Before I accepted your request, I conducted my own research about you. It is also an honour to be here as your Sensei, and I have no doubt about your commitment to this journey." This was the last thought he had as his eyes began to gently close, lulling him into sleep.

As he opened his eyes, he heard the ringing of his analog alarm clock. He promptly turned it off, stood up, knowing that it was seven in the morning after gazing at it, after folding the blanket, he adjusted the pillow to the middle position and went to the bathroom and changed his attire before heading to the kitchen to prepare their breakfast. Along the way, he spotted his Sensei, both of them dressed in their uniforms, leading him to assume that his teacher was also on his way to the same location.

"Good morning, Sensei," he greeted him politely, followed by a bow.

"Good morning to you as well, Lucas. It is quite fitting, as I require that my student accompany me for breakfast every day. This is an essential part of your training. If you would like to assist me in preparing our breakfast, I would be pleased with that," the Sensei replied, his voice warm and full of energy.

"Sensei, definitely, as I am quite capable when it comes to kitchen tasks." He responded, and together they proceeded to the area.

"Before I finally sleep last night, I inspected this area, and I must say, I am genuinely impressed by how well-equipped the kitchen is with various resources for preparing Japanese cuisine, whether for breakfast, lunch, or dinner. Therefore, this morning we will be making Asagohan, which is a traditional Japanese breakfast. I kindly ask you to prepare the rice, the ingredients for miso soup, and the pickled vegetables, while I will take care of the remaining ingredients."

"Hai, Sensei!" He replied respectfully and moved towards the cabinet to gather the necessary ingredients.

"Lucas, allow me to explain why I selected this particular menu for breakfast. But first, let me ask you this: what did I show to you when you saw me?"Lucas smiled, after he assessed what he was referring with, and nodded gently, placing the item he was holding on the countertop before responding.

"Sensei, I sensed and observed your chi; it was vibrant, illustrating how to embrace the early moments of the day." He answered with assurance and confidence.

"Great! The reason why I asked you is to tell you this: that this kind of breakfast is fundamental as a traditional meal for every morning, it is like a thought that could cultivate the person by its nutrition, and the rest of its consistent flavour and texture."

"Hai, Sensei! I will certainly keep that in mind, as starting today, I will be more exposed to the various aspects of the Japanese way of life." He replied, then watching his teacher gesturing towards the item placed on the table. He gracefully picked it up and returned to his previous task. When he glanced over, he saw that him was also engaged in his part of the preparations. Suddenly, a thought crossed his mind, but he made an effort to suppress his emotions, having promised himself that day when he left the city to concentrate on this matter to completely avoid any distractions when necessary. During the lecture, however, he found himself without pen and paper, but his Sensei motioned his hand at him to remain calm as he was about to stood up to get a paper and pen, and his Sensei started to speak.

"The purpose of this lecture is all about facts and memorisation. So, the presence of mind and the familiarity of each set will be your nature when you need to execute it, the samurai mindset."

He nodded after he remember the note that he read last night after he changed his clothes.

"To cultivate a mindset required dedication and continuous effort, and the martial, cultural, and spiritual practices of the samurai, if practiced with sincerity, could lead to such an elevated state of mind."

"In order to master the eight rules of the samurai warrior you must possess the core of it, and that's the mindset." The Sensei added during their first day of lecture, "then also the effort and dedication by a student could lead him into a spiritual practice." During lecture sessions it was his usual response, reciting and to enumerate his answers. While the rest of training was excruciating painful, the sweat, the exhaustion and the gap of their experience from being student and sensei, but he endured every inch of his sacrifice.

As the sun cast its light upon the earth, the sound of their blades was piercing, and it could irritate anyone's ears. Yet, the two fighters appeared unfazed from the moment they began, with a palpable tension filling the air as their swords remained locked against one another.

"Lucas, I can't believe you've come this far and wielding such power with katana!"

At that moment, Lucas struggled to contain his excitement at his Sensei's words, but before he could respond, he was caught off guard. Fortunately, his reflexes kicked in, and he executed multiple sidesteps, successfully blocking the sudden flurry of strikes from his Sensei's weapon.

"Lucas, remember this: in any fight, never allow a single distraction to throw you off! You must withstand them to achieve victory at all costs!"

Lucas remained silent as he defended himself by dodging against any possible injury, fully aware that even the slightest cut from that blade could provoke his enemy to attack relentlessly until he was vanquished. Thus, he waited patiently for his moment, having never spotted an opportunity to counterattack, until they both reached the sea's edge. Before that, he swiftly rolled in the sand to grab his weapon and after splash of saltwater became yet another reason for him to concentrate, soaking their Hakama, which sparked an idea in his mind. All he needed to do was recognise that opportunity, and a single strike would give him a chance, seconds ticked by as the sound of water drew his attention, rising with their heavy footsteps. He observed it closely, stepping back while his weapon remained his greatest ally for defense.

Then, until his instinct struck his mind like lightning upon witnessing the reason to claim his turn, he swiftly dropped his weapon, and his two hands moved as quickly as the wind within a second to execute his next move. Instead of blocking the incoming attack, he shifted his position by simply allowing the law of motion to guide him from his toes. He then grasped the arm of his Sensei, without any brute force, as he understood that the momentum would flow from the direction of his simple technique. Finally, he watched as the blade fell into the water, accompanied by its sound and a quick splash on their faces. Sensei's expression was blank, and he gazed at him without confusion until he posed a question.

"Why didn't use your weapon and chose to disarm me with your atemi?"

"Because I understand that I can find my own means of self-defense and also to stop my attacker from causing harm to any of us," he answered softly, seeing his Sensei looking at him with an approving nod.

"You are indeed a samurai warrior; you recognise when to use your weapon and when not to."

"What are the eight rules of the samurai also known as Bushido?"

"The eight virtues of that are justice, courage, benevolence, politeness, honesty, honour, loyalty, and self-control. Rectitude (or justice) is the strongest virtue of it, as it shows one's power to decide upon a course of conduct and act without wavering." Then Lucas kept in his mind the word "justice" after the training and then he knows that the war will be not easy as Enrique is currently the most influential entrepreneur, so then he collected everything he needs to succeed.

After completing his performance on the final day, his Sensei finally delivered his verdict while they were both seated in a seiza position.

"Domo arigato gozaimasu, Sensei!"

"Dōitashimashite, Lucas!" This was followed by a moment of silence as the gentle breeze from outside began to envelop the area and their bodies.

"Can you feel and hear it?"

"Yes, Sensei."

"Then you have truly grasped the essence of its existence."

He then nodded.

"Sayonara," they said to each other before bowing. When he finally completed the training, he confessed to his grandfather, Amadeus, about his experiences, and his eyes sparkled with pride at what he heard from his grandson.

"This is a remarkable moment that I want to share with you, Lucas. I've been contemplating this for a while, but I never anticipated it would arrive so quickly! I take great pride in who you have become." Amadeus then gently tapped his grandson's shoulder and gestured towards a specific cabinet in their library. They both approached it to unveil what lay inside. Lucas was astonished when his eyes finally laid on one of the most exquisite weapons he had ever seen.

"Wow, grandfather, this blade is truly magnificent! I can't believe I'm actually seeing such a masterpiece!" He exclaimed, still captivated by its beauty. In a swift motion, he watched as his grandfather drew the blade from its wooden case, pointing its tip towards the bookshelves before them, then he turned to Lucas.

"This sword has been in our family since your great-grandfather obtained it from our ancestors. It is fitting that you are done of your training about Bushido. From this moment on, this sword is yours, Lucas. I have no doubt you will wield it with the same courage and precision as our forebears had for over a century. The Nagasone Kotetsu, this blade dates back to the seventeenth century."

There was a time that Amadeus instructed his secretary to give the folder to his grandson after meeting then the lady obliged and left his office, several moments passed a thorough assessment of every detail was done by Lucas then he slowly shook his head and began to speak with clarity.

"Cultural heritage holds significant importance to the people, and I will not allow this project to be built, regardless of its future probability. Therefore, I must firmly oppose it," he said to the secretary of his grandfather and asked her to return the contract.

Amadeus was amused by Lucas's decision, he looked at the papers and then at the secretary, the final test was over. "As deserving as my successor," he smiled. And gently resting his right hand on his chin and caressing it slowly as he continued his contemplation, nodding in agreement.

Nineteen

The Raid

Upon discovering the mission details, Osmond realised he needed to act swiftly. He had to reach out to Agent McKain and several officers from the Australian Federal Police to strategise their approach. A verified report revealed that the terrorists were hiding in a remote location in Melbourne, planning an attack on Sydney within a week. The alarming quantity of explosives they intended to use would lead to numerous explosions and a significant loss of life. Osmond's fists tightened in anger towards the terrorists. Given the situation, Cedrick and his team found themselves unable to fulfil the task due to the nature of the terrorists involved. He understood that this was no ordinary mission and recognised the potential for fatal consequences, either for himself or the enemy. The worst-case scenario involved multiple bombs detonating while they were still engaged in their operation. He hesitated to inform Alex about his mission that evening, knowing she would be worried. Yet, he also pondered the difference between the missions he had previously undertaken and his current responsibility as her bodyguard. The distinction was negligible; he remained vigilant and dangerous whenever he was protecting her. Upon arriving at the designated location, Osmond saw a contingent of police officers. Despite being in civilian attire, he was accorded a respectful salute as a sign of recognition for his status as a top-secret agent of the nation. In response, he reciprocated the salute and proceeded to enter the premises. Inside, he saw Cedrick and another colleague, the Agent, engaged in conversation.

"Agent Gomez now that your presence is confirmed, we can finally commence planning our subsequent actions." Cedrick said and nodded to the police officer to summon the numerous officers stationed outside the house and for tonight, they need to focus to succeed; the city of Sydney will be in danger if they do not accomplish this mission.

After seeing the nearly six-foot-tall steel fence, Osmond leaped onto it with a quick run, taking a moment to adjust his eyes to the darkness, few seconds passed and he scanned the area and spotted three armed men patrolling the rear of the warehouse. Osmond devised a strategy to quietly disarm them, but just then, one of the men began to walk away after signaling to the others. Keeping his eyes on the man, Osmond watched as he moved towards the shadowy corner close to his hiding place. He had already prepared a counteraction. As the armed man lit a cigarette, Osmond carefully climbed down the fence without attracting attention. He stealthily approached the man and swiftly twisted his neck.

"Arrgh!" The man's response was abruptly silenced by the sound of his cervical fracture as he succumbed to death. Osmond pulled the body of his first victim to the nearest thick shrubs and cautiously moved closer to the other two. He was now positioned behind the broken machine, he silently observed them while they continued their conversation, until the taller man began to speak.

"Hey, can you check on him? He mentioned he was just stepping out for a quick smoke, but he's taking too long," the man said to his partner, who was armed with a .45 caliber gun.

"Okay."

Osmond was just waiting as the man approached the location where he killed his companion and when he saw the man passing close to him, while the darkness was in his favour. Osmond swiftly evaluated the situation to ensure everything was in control, then, in an instant, hurled his dagger at the man's neck, causing him to fall silently to the ground. Osmond quickly dragged the man into the shadowy corner and then glanced at the last remaining guard, who was preoccupied with his phone, and he aimed his dagger at the guard's neck. Osmond then pulled the third body next to one of his lifeless companions near the machine. Without wasting a moment, he set off to find the other guards.

A few metres away, Cedrick witnessed what Osmond had done with those three and took a deep breath; Osmond's skills were undeniably lethal. He could do the same thing, but his weakness lay in accurately targeting the main point. He then turned to his companion, and they exchanged nods, having already eliminated two men when they spotted them smoking under the tree and they quietly approached the warehouse to evaluate the situation while observing to plan their next move.

Meanwhile, Osmond spotted a room from the outside while he stealthily navigated through the dimly lit area along the fence. Upon hearing some voices, he slowly approached the room without making a sound with his footsteps. With a swift motion, he quickly neared the area and glanced through the open window, observing four individuals playing cards while laughing. He quickly formulated a plan when the fusebox caught his sight, and he turned it off.

"Hey! What the hell! Elmer! The lights just went out! Go check, and to see what's going on!" Shouted the man in the black jacket and jeans to his companion, handing him a flashlight.

The man scratched the back of his head and stepped outside. In an instant, as Elmer arrived to inspect the fusebox with the flashlight, Osmond struck him by his fist, targeting a vulnerable spot. He carefully pulled the body to the side of the room and then peered at the others inside through the window. It was dark until one of them lit a cigarette, and Osmond anticipated his next move. They weren't armed, but any misstep could provoke for them make a commotion. He couldn't afford to waste any moment; in a split second, he entered the dark room after the man exhaled his smoke. With calculated precision, he eliminated three of them in mere seconds using his ultimate technique, the rabbit punch, leaving them unable to retaliate. He had now taken out seven in total and swiftly made his way toward the warehouse. In the distance, he saw someone lying down and recognised that Cedrick had taken him out while wearing an earpiece headset. He then contacted the rest of his team.

"Men, stay vigilant and await my signal. Then everyone can enter," he instructed the eight policemen stationed outside, waiting for his command. "Understood, agent Gomez," a response from the leader of the seven officers waiting by the gate. He then contacted Agent McKain.

"Agent McKain, what's your location?"

"Agent Gomez, I'm at four o'clock," Cedrick answered. He checked his position, noting he was at around nine o'clock, indicating they were about to eliminate the entire guards around the warehouse.

"Alright. Inform me when you reach the six o'clock position. Remain alert and wait for my signal."

"Copy that, agent Gomez," Cedrick replied.

Osmond felt a chilling sensation at the back of his head, before he takes for another step. Instantly on high alert, he realised he had been cornered by the enemy.

"Put your hands up if you want to keep your head intact," the assailant warned him.

Without hesitation, Osmond raised both hands, waiting for the right moment to disable his captor. As he noticed the enemy's left hand shifted, Osmond sprang forward, seizing the man's gun and quickly ejecting the magazine with bullets. He understood that this action would signal his teammates that they had breached the warehouse, and he forcefully kick his hand to prevent him from getting his pocket radio.

Then, the man swiftly unleashed a flurry of punches aimed at his stomach and face, but he skillfully deflected the blows until the man was caught off guard by his counterattacks. He stomped down hard on the man's stomach before delivering two rapid punches, hitting both sides of his face. Following that, he executed a forceful knee kick to the abdomen, causing a significant damage to his several internal organs. Soon after, the man was seen vomiting blood in the dim light, and he concluded the fight by striking the back of his neck with his hand, as he needed to bring the duel to an end. As he gazed at the man sprawled on the ground, he made his way to the front of the warehouse. There, he saw another two additional guards stationed by the window. Time was of the essence; he couldn't afford to delay any longer. Without a moment's pause, he drew a dagger from his holster and hurled it at one of the men. The blade pierced the neck deeply, ending his life in an instant. Without a second thought, he aimed at the other guard and dispatched him as well.

Then, he heard a signal from Cedrick: the two were positioned around the five o'clock mark, ready for his command. He swiftly advanced toward the seven o'clock position and spotted three guards directly in front of him. He had to devise a plan to take them out quietly. After a brief moment of contemplation, another clever idea formed to his mind.

"Agent McKain, I will attract the attention of one or two of them, while you and the other agent, handle the rest. Just to ensure neither from us or from could make any noise. The leaders are inside, and they must capture tonight." And he swiftly picked up a stone from the ground and threw it towards the front of the gate. The man met his end quickly when subdued with a dagger when he walked towards it, he then looked at the other two, who were now lying on the ground, signaling him to notify the police to enter the rear and front of the warehouse. As the three of them entered, they were greeted with multiple shots of gunfire, forcing each to run towards the wall where they cannot be shot by bullets. But it doesn't matter anymore as the guards outside had already been eliminated by them. They retaliated fiercely, coming out unscathed from behind a wall, and he pulled out his .45

caliber and fired back, hitting an opponent in the chest just as he attempted to fireback at him.

He also heard gunfire coming from the front of the warehouse towards the rear. This indicated that the police officers were engaged in a shootout with the remaining guards. After a brief exchange of gunfire, the group of criminals began to dwindle, then he saw how the man leaping out of the window with an attaché case; the detonator was inside. It was certain, and he quickly followed him, running outside and shooting him in the left thigh.

"BANG!!"

"Ahhhh!! You bastard!" The man yelled at him.

"BANG!" Before the man could retaliate, Osmond had already taken cover behind a large tree. The man was tough, leaving Osmond with no choice but to take his life if he did not surrender. Spotting an opportunity, Osmond aimed for the hand that held the gun.

"BANG!!"

"Ahhh!! My hand!" The man cried out in agony from his injury and dropped the firearm. Osmond moved closer, aiming his gun at the man's face.

"If you attempt to fight back again, I won't hesitate to blow your head off!" Osmond shouted at the man lying on the ground, kicking the gun away from him. He watched as the man closed his eyes in surrender.

He sensed that his companions were exiting the warehouse as he heard their voices. At that point, they had accomplished their mission, and after seeing that a few were handcuffed when he started to walk when the last man with the attaché case surrounded by several police officers, while some officers had also arrived to handle the remaining task. Subsequently, he and the other two agents began walking separately until Osmond felt something and quickly dodged, telling himself, *"you never learned,"* while smiling as he grasped the last piece of his dagger, which was now aimed at his target and he smiled when he saw how he simply catch the pointed weapon by his short and quick dodge.

"Whoa! That was a close call, mate! Haha!" Cedrick chuckled as he gripped the blade. He swiftly retrieved a rock from his pocket with his other hand and tossed it into the air. Then, with a kick from his right foot, he sent it flying towards Osmond, who effortlessly dodged it while shaking his head. But that wasn't the end; he casually tossed the sharp object, and he executed his tornado kick for the last item in his hand when it reached his eye level, he then saw how Osmond rolled on the ground, giving him a laughter as he did.

"Well, that was a commendable effort, Agent McKain, and I appreciate your assistance tonight," Osmond added as he glanced at another agent standing beside several large trees, who gave him a casual nod. He then recalled the man, a reserved type of agent; yet undeniably lethal, as he had noted from their very first day of training.

"It was truly an honour to enact this risky task with both of you. I'll leave for now, and till next time." The man then began to walk into the darkness, and Osmond sensed that Cedrick was attempting to approach him for another silly game, but he managed to warn him.

"Oh, come on, mate! It's getting late, and I need to send a message to Alex soon."

"Haha! Alright, alright," Cedrick responded, now also heading in a different direction, while Osmond chose to navigate through the central part of the dark area, having parked his motorbike a few hundred metres away. Osmond returned to the guest house at two in the morning. When he checked the time on his phone, he saw three missed calls from Alex and one text message.

"Sorry if I missed your calls. I was busy with my colleagues. I just got to my place, and I will sleep soon. I'll see you later. I love you." Then after he replied, he took a shower so he could finally rest and able to wake up early later.

As Osmond closed his eyes, he recalled the moment he was taken aback by the sight of a man in a finely tailored suit approaching Alex as they got out from the room. He had anticipated that this man was merely a casual acquaintance or a business associate, but his expectations turned to disappointment when he heard the man call her name, 'Alex.' This indicated that there was something deeper at play. Osmond glared at him particularly noting how he touched her elbow while following them to the basement after they exited the elevator. Alex remained silent, even in the presence of her parents, who had suggested that he must keep an eye on them for their afternoon tea. He had hoped that the de Ayala couple would be with them; it was painful for him to see Alex with another man after Cedrick. Taking a deep breath, he opened the vehicle's door for them.

"Thanks." It came from her, and he nodded at Alex without casting a single glance at the man who smiled as he closed the door. Each step felt heavy for him; if only he could only dash towards them to seize the man's neck to assert his claim for Alex. However, he chose to maintain a formal in their presence. Taking a deep breath, he pressed the power button to start the engine. He glanced in the rearview mirror, hearing the sound of her laughter mingling with their conversation in the back. As the car ahead slowed down, he slammed the horn button with all his might.

"Hey, mate, please don't do that again. It's really irritating," the man said to him.

"I have to, and we need to get to our destination quickly since Alex has to go home soon," he replied, keeping pace with the car in front.

"It's okay, Osmond. My parents talked it over with me, so we can take our time," Alex interjected, and they returned to their discussion.

"But I need to ensure your safety, even though you're finally free from the previous mysterious threat," he shot back as he turned the vehicle left onto the main road.

"I can protect Alex," the man asserted.

"Wow, is that really like what I could do?" He thought to himself, opting to stay quiet and ignore the man behind him. His thoughts were now focused on addressing to Alex regarding the matter at the earli-

est opportunity, as he was uncomfortable with the notion of Alex being involved with that specific man. He sensed a darkness in the man's character that could reveal itself at any moment.

Twenty

The Crusade of Suffering

It was nearly ten o'clock in the evening when the group of men made their way to a specific hideout near the city of Melbourne. The cold, pitch-black winter night was intense, yet it seemed insignificant to them as they laughed and walked together. One man, wearing a bonnet, draped his arm around the shoulder of his companion. It was Sean, the one he trusted the most in their group, clad in a black leather jacket, who leaned into whisper.

"Hey, just keep in mind that according to my source from last week, it has a significant price compared to what we have," the man nodded until he recalled how Sean took the item from the bag before they left, and they kept walking until they arrived at their destination.

"Where is the other one?" The leader asked Lucas when he handed over the black bag that night, but he had come too late to notice what was missing, then he replied.

"I don't know. But I know for certain I had it while we were coming back here and-" the leader gestured with his hand for him to stop explaining. Then he nodded to Sean.

"I am telling the truth!" Lucas exclaimed after Sean punched him in the stomach, and before he could say anything more, another punch hit his stomach again. He bent over in pain, realising their leader had signaled to Sean, his assistant, to hit him once more.

"Ahhhh! Please! Stop! I'm sorry! I'll find the missing one—just don't hurt me!" Lucas pleaded, his voice strained with pain.

"No need!" The leader shouted, and he motioned his hand towards Sean then step forward, leaning into whisper instructions to him.

"There's a major operation next week—our biggest this year. Once it's completed, get rid of Lucas. You already know what to do; we discussed this two weeks ago. And I remember I said this before, the "idiot" word. But now, I apologise for it. Since he is useful for the upcoming task." He said before stepping back.

"Sure, and it is okay boss." Sean replied, smiling at him.

"Lucas, as usual, you may go now. I expect you to be back next week for the big task. Once it's done, I'll have a reward for you," the boss said firmly.

The young, impoverished man nodded politely before turning to leave their hideout.

"How pathetic and gullible," the boss muttered since it was known to him about what Sean did. They used to steal only jewelries, but this time was different. A book, but not an ordinary book, it was a holy grail since it was written in the early 17th century.

He strolled through the alley amidst a throng of people, and his appearance had changed; it had been three months since his last visit to the barber for a haircut. The slacks he wore were from the time he was abducted by the gang, while the jumper he had on was a gift from someone on the street. He paid no attention to the stares, as he had grown accustomed to it from the moment, he found himself in that dreadful situation. Soon, he began to feel hungry and exhausted. He was aware of where his feet would lead him. He took his time, not hurrying, knowing the situation could worsen. He realised it had been nearly six months of this, as he recalled being told he was always welcome to come by if he needed food. When he inquired why, the response was, "I have already been heartbroken seeing you in this condition, and I can't hold back from saying this to you. Living as a beggar on the street is not a solution, as I can see that you will end up feeling self-pity every day, and it will completely ruin you, Lucas."

After their paths crossed that fateful night, the weight he carried began to lighten. The simple fact that he has two or three selections of meals to enjoy each evening is more than enough to give him something to eagerly anticipate. The staff member inside, dressed in red from her long-sleeved top to her slacks, noticed him outside as he took a moment to rest in front of the window, wrapping his arms around himself. She smiled at him, and he shyly returned the gesture with a nod.

"Lucas, hi! Why are you still out there? Come inside; it's really cold!"

He looked at her, smiled, and nodded in agreement. Once they entered, the restaurant was relatively quiet, with four tables unoccupied while three others were filled with customers.

"Oh, finally you're here, Lucas! Perfect timing, as I just finished packing your meal into the container, and it's still warm," said Max, the restaurant owner, who had just come out from the kitchen. "I even added an extra just in case."

Lucas beamed as his fatigue dissipated at the sight of him once more, appreciating his kindness and the way he treated him.

"Thank you so much for this, Max, but I hope that one day I can return the favour."

"Oh, it's nothing, Lucas; the important thing is that I can assist in whatever way I can," Max replied while wiping his hands on his apron. "We are about to close soon, once the customers at three tables finish their meals," he added.

"Alright, let me help with the chores then, Mr. Max."

"Sure, it's your choice even though you really don't have to, as I have staff to handle the cleanup for tonight. But first, you should eat something," Max gestured towards a nearby empty table.

"Thanks, Max," Lucas responded, taking the plastic bag. Once seated, he opened a container and smiled at the sight of the Chinese noodle soup; it was perfect for the chilly winter evening.

"Savour your meal, Lucas, while I return to the kitchen to assist my team," Max said before turning away and heading towards the kitchen. In the meantime, Lucas was unable to hold back his enjoyment as he relished the delicious food before him; he was famished, and with each bite of chicken, he felt a wave of relief wash over him, while the soup only intensified his desire for more.

"What have you been up to, Lucas?" the waitress inquired after he finished drinking from his glass. He noticed her standing in front of him, balancing a tray filled with empty bowls, plates, glasses, used cutlery, and plastic chopsticks.

"Oh, just hanging out with friends," he responded, but the woman looked at him with a hint of skepticism.

"Are they truly your friends? I mean, no offence, but finding a genuine friend is quite challenging. In this perilous world, it's rare to encounter the real ones."

"Don't worry, I can take care of myself."

"Alright, Lucas. Just a quick reminder, since both Max and I are aware of the real story behind your family's tragic death. I truly hope you're in safe hands."

"Absolutely, I am. One of them is my cousin," he asserted confidently while he lied to them, knowing the leader had threatened him that if he sought help from any local organisation, they would kill him. He was determined to keep these people out of his true predicament. The restaurant owner had provided him with an abundance of food, and when he spotted a homeless couple asking for help, he didn't hesitate to share his meal so they could eat that night. He spent a few moments chatting with them before continuing on to a safe place where he could spend the night. As he gazed up at the night sky, he was grateful that the rain had ceased while he sheltered under a tree, wrapped in a blanket to fend off the cold. His mind drifted to the past, reminiscing about the wonderful memories of his family when they were all together. There was a time when he contemplated ending his suffering by giving up on life, but one fateful night, the universe worked a miracle for him. That was when he met Max while strolling along the sidewalk; the food menu in the window had caught his eye, and then the face became an unforgettable figure from his life before he met his grandfather.

At last, the much-anticipated night arrived, and he found himself and the rest of members in front of their leader, ready to cite his instructions.

"Lucas, as you previously mentioned your fondness for riddles, Sean, you will be taking on this task together. The owner acquired it at the last auction for nearly seven grand."

Lucas was taken aback by the item's price. Typically, the total value of the jewellery they had stolen was no more than five hundred dollars, but this time, things would be different.

"It is hidden in a location that requires solving a riddle to discover its secure placement. The other team from our group attempted to locate it, but I am confident that with your assistance, you and Sean can finally secure the biggest prize of the year."

The journey took nearly three hours, and after they split into two groups: him and Sean, while the driver along with the other two headed towards the nearest suburb for their mission. Once the vehicle finally stopped in front of the two-story house, Sean and Lucas hurriedly dashed inside. His companion was typically the one equipped with the tools to unlock doors or windows, but this time he attempted to open the door first, holding the flashlight. Eventually, Sean succeeded in opening the main entrance, and upon discovering what they sought, they found a note to the nearby living area, nestled among a pile of various magazines, books, and other reading materials on the table. Lucas then directed the light onto the note and carefully examined the contents of what he was holding.

An extreme temperature is unstoppable whether it's daytime or nighttime and I exist no matter what the season.

I look up to the sky, but I found nothing only the vast emptiness behind that cluster of stars of the universe.

And I ask myself, if I walk the whole night just to see the wrath of stormy seas, shall I be able to feel fear of its wrath? When there is nothing to fear?

I have seen too many faces but the graces of experience from aches was multiple acres that filled of invisible grains, then I shall not be worried since it is nothing without four corners.

After reading the note, Lucas smiled; it served as a reminder for the owner in case they forgot where it was stored, but it also acted as a deterrent for anyone wanting to claim this unique item for themselves or add it to their collection. He surveyed the entire room before casually making his way to the specific area. At the bottom, he discovered what he had been searching for, but then he heard footsteps. When he turned to look, he saw Sean, who was holding several watches and pieces of jewelry. Lucas nodded at him, while Sean grinned, pleased to have successfully located the item that was the focus of their operation that night.

"Look at this, Lucas! There's a bonus! Haha!" Sean exclaimed as he approached him. He casually turned his back to stow the item in his bag and handed the book to Sean for a quick glance. After a nod, he zipped up the bag, securing the book inside.

"Alright, this is going smoothly!" Sean added while ruffling Lucas's hair before following him toward the door. They needed to reach the location where the rest of the team was conducting another operation in a different suburb. However, things took an unexpected turn when Sean called out his name and suddenly punched him in the face, twice. The pain was intense, and he was taken aback as he felt the familiar sting of a syringe injecting an unknown substance into him. The last thing he remembered was falling into a specific area of a snowy mountain.

Twenty One

Unique Punishment

It was the ancestral house of Emsworth family that built during in late 1890's his grandfather informed him when they visited it a year ago, then Lucas was planning to renovate the place once he finished his dubious activity, he knew Amadeus, his grandfather would totally be disappointed once he discovered this, but as long as he had done his first purpose then it doesn't matter anymore if he could forgive him or not. Since the feeling of fear doesn't bother his mind anymore, not even exist to every plan of action that he wants to experience.

Following his initial encounter with the first man in the library, Lucas was devising a new interrogation strategy for another individual, but this time it would diverge from the previous two men. He recalled how his assistant had apprehended the second man while en route to the event, and how the man in the white suit had readily accepted his proposal. Convincing him to accept the offer was not a challenge, as Lucas was well-acquainted with him, allowing him to effectively outline the necessary steps for the next upcoming grand event.

The man found himself in the library, pondering why he was there as he awoke and surveyed his surroundings, realising he was alone. He then made his way to the window to look outside, seeing the sun was about to dip below the horizon. As he gazed around, he saw the beautiful garden filled with ornamental plants and the neatly arranged eastern white pines that adorned the front yard, then a memory struck him; he had just been on his way to the event after the unknown man approached him and then he did something that turned himself unconscious and now he was here. He struggled to piece together the events, feeling a wave of anxiety wash over him, reminiscent of his time at the event. *"Oh my god, what do they want from me?"* He questioned himself as he approached the door to open it.

"Where am I?" He muttered, glancing around at the unfamiliar surroundings that didn't resemble his home at all! He continued to explore the area, noting the Victorian architecture both inside and out. His eyes landed on a pair of doors nestled between two towering shelves filled with books, but he ignored them and cautiously moved toward the door. When he turned the doorknob, it wouldn't budge; it was locked. A new wave of questions flooded his mind as he tried to devise a way to escape. Just then, he felt a strange sensation at the back of his head, but he brushed it aside, focused solely on leaving this place. Until he heard footsteps approaching from outside, prompting another question: *"Who could that be?"* His heart raced as he felt a familiar flutter in his chest, and he instinctively stepped back from the door, his heart pounding faster than usual as the eerie sound of a creaking door echoed in the silence. Then, to his astonishment, he spotted two figures, a raven-haired man and the familiar face next to him was the one he saw before he lost his consciousness.

"Who are you? Why am I here?" He asked while looking at them in confusion.

"How can I answer someone, if it gives me a lot of questions?" The black-haired man responded to him.

"Why am I here?" He asked again.

"Alright, there you are. That's the right approach!" Then he saw how he smiled, which gave him a feeling that he had never felt before. Then his heart was now pounding more loudly while he was approaching him. Then the man stopped as he took the chair and seated, then he motioned his hand to another chair and looked at him.

"Please have a seat," the man offered casually.

He was hesitant to obey his command, while still looking at him.

"I said, have seat." For that time, the tone of his voice changed, it was now colder and full of authority.

"What do you want?"

"Alright, let us make it simple. You know something, shall I say I'll give you a hint since it happened about six years ago." The man replied to him, then his face changed into sadness.

"Hold on, almost six years ago? How can I remember that?"

Then Lucas took a deep breath when the man replied. He's right, maybe there were lots of event that time before and he carefully analyse his next response.

"It is connected to Mr. Enrique de Ayala," he answered and starting to tap the square antique wooden table then looked at him while saw how the man was now in confusion when he gave the hint.

"About my former employer? And it was almost six years ago?" The man asked him, then Lucas just silently nodded.

"Oh god, no! You must be the-"

"So, you finally absorbed everything?"

"But why did you take me here? Instead of my former boss?" Then the man in front of him didn't answer, instead he saw him how started to laugh slowly.

"Good question! But don't worry about him, as I have another plan. But for now, I want to start with something, or to someone that I can show about what I am really capable of, as the result of my immeasurable rage! If before I made a wish, then it is your turn to make a wish that you never did to Enrique, and that led me to this kind of suffering and hatred!" He said exasperatedly, then he stood up from his chair and walked around gently then he glanced at the window then before he continues to speak, he shook his head then he smiled bitterly while looking at him.

"They said, once we hear and see something we must say it since we are capable to spill it out." Lucas started and trying to conceal his emotion towards the man in front of him.

"What do you want?"

"Wow! That's' it! I like that question! Bravo!" Then he started to clap, while nodding at him.

"You already knew the truth, so what's the point of taking me here?"

"Oh yes, I know the point and you, you will experience what I have been through, and it is worst of ever you could imagine once it is finally done." Then followed by an insane laugh, while his eyes saw the confusion of the man, but his fears were also apparent, but he just dismissed what he saw. Then followed by one clap before he continued.

"I am done here; men take him inside of the room!" Then several footsteps were now approaching, and the helpless man turned his glance at the door shaking his head upon seeing the two-armed men entering the library, while the pitch-black haired man left the area without glancing or saying to anyone.

"Please! Sir, let me go! Mr. Enrique is the one you should blame, not me! Please!" The man begged while the two men was forcefully taking him to the room in front of them while the man in his right side was retrieving the key from his pocket for the key and after pushing him inside, he locked the door followed by banging the door and pleading to let him out of the room.

The following morning, after he had done his morning routine and now, he was finally changed his attire to casual long sleeve white shirt, a dark blue wool pants and a pair of sandals. He smiled when he sees the incoming middle-aged man wearing a casual dress, as he expecting him today, as he reached the ground floor area, he smiled at him then the man also smiled back.

"Thanks for coming today, Doctor Blaine and I am extending my appreciation that even though you are not sure yesterday but now look you've made it today." Then he offered his right hand for a handshake, which the latter accepted it with sincerity.

"So, what can I do for you Mr. Lucas?" The Doctor asked after he motioned his arm toward the couch in front of them until they were finally seated.

"That's too fast and blunt Mr. Blaine, but I don't mind that all. Well, I shall say this way; it would be the most expedient way to make it short, since I am quite sure that you have never done this before." Last night, he quickly concluded the best approach for the following day after he finally discover the other person behind Enrique's desire.

To the doctor before he departed, he only mentioned the word "complementarity of principle." Then the doctor nodded at him before he finally closed the door.

The next afternoon, it was almost five when they entered the room, rather the specific room about the procedure that will take place soon, the man automatically expressed his reaction after seeing the room when they put him inside. Then he nodded at his men to leave the room as he wants to savour whatever he can see from him.

"Shout, yes! Shout as much as you can! Hahaha! I want louder than that! Louder!!" Lucas yelled while expressing his amusement how the man was running inside of the room, and he was now starting to give him the moment about being frightened, as it was evident what he saw from his eyes. Then he gave him a round of applause.

"Continue! Nonstop! I want more! Hahaha! The last time I saw you, you were enjoying the event. And now, continue it! Enjoy! Hahaha!"

He was looking to the bottle that contains of general anaesthesia, he was now looking to the doctor and both of them were clad in a lab gown.

"You know something and yet, you never tell him about the suffering of people left behind. Scared of it? Then you can write them if you are and let that letter reminds him about his sins! And yet, you never did! You let Enrique enjoy all the finest things on earth that he acquired in an unfair way!"

As the day passes by, it was satisfying for him how he finally got what he wanted, then he recalled the first day while he silently watching him, and then he walked in front of the man while seated.

"It such a beautiful outside today, but you can't see it right? This is the first phase, and there are others to come." Then it shifted to the second process of his desire, while taking his glance to the outside by window, he smiled then he looked at him while taking his steps to get near him after having a thought of his next move.

"You can't feel the sensation of what I'm experiencing right now. And remember this: there are other phases to come." He coldly said, while facing him, followed by the echoing scream inside of the room. But he just disregarded how loud he was, it doesn't matter to him anymore. As long as the sight in front of him was fulfilling enough for him to witness.

The next day as someone hearing the footsteps from outside of the room, he whispered "please kill, me I don't want my family to see me in this condition." Until the door finally opened, and if only he could talk, he would gladly to wish on him that it would be better to end his life rather than this kind of out of this world to experience.

After plucking those eyes out, and kept them in a small transparent jar with preservatives to preserve them, and after healing the next was the sense of his touch by paralysing him and the final after a month were the two hands and kept hidden in the huge glass box with chemicals to preserve as well and also, to remind him something about the big event. Instantaneously, he had a sudden thought to himself while the pacing of his glance was in rhythm.

"Now, I don't know myself either and that is gruesome since I don't totally understand why I did what I did," then he walked casually towards the things and took an ample amount of time for himself to examine carefully each of them followed by sudden paused that causes himself to seek further action of plan.

After he completed the phases, Lucas nodded to someone as he already gave the instruction to him. Then he reviewed the notebook, and carefully assessed the necessary, then he smiled. An opportune is now on the table, as his plan will always be on his favour.

"The empire will burn soon, and the number of lifeless bodies must be countless," then he fiendishly smiled. He exhaled a thick cloud of cigarette smoke, likening it to the anger he had kept for so long. It had to be different, to shock the whole planet with his mercilessness. The aftermath would become an international headline, eventually entering a gruesome kind of history about him, he was only widely known for his leadership as an entrepreneur, but seeing the evilest of them all is about to unleashed, when a conclusion came into his mind.

"I can't find the reason behind those emotionless eyes and subtle smiles; then how can I see and feel their depths if you belong to an unknown celestial?"

"I wanted to witness the shedding of blood while kneeling before me," then he maniacally laughed and stood up from his executive swivel chair, gazing at the beautiful sparkling lights of the city skyline as the sun began to fade from the horizon until it completely dissipated.

Twenty Two

Heiress's Birthday

"What was that about?" Osmond asked Alex after her parents left the veranda just as Cedrick was arriving when he replied to him by text message. He was still somewhat irritated by the events of the previous day. Though the early morning could have been delightful if he hadn't overheard the name of Alex's supposed suitor after a phone call.

"Oh, are you referring about yesterday?" Alex responded, meeting his gaze with no hint of remorse.

"Yes," he replied firmly, determined to convey how significant the matter was to him, regardless of what she might say.

"Well, my dad introduced him to me while you were in Sydney. What's the issue with that?" She shot back.

Osmond was taken aback when one of the staff approaching them with a tray of breakfast. His frustration mounted further when Alex asked the uniformed woman to stay with them. She then flashed to Osmond a victorious smile as the woman began to arrange various plates and a selection of drinks on the table.

Within his thoughts, he understood how to brighten the way she treated him. A kiss, sweet and full of passion; just like the one he had shared before on the hilltop. A smile crept across his face as he reminisced about that enchanting moment they had together.

Rather than savouring her meal, Alex found herself in shock at the sight of Osmond smiling after she had successfully stirred feelings of jealousy in him. She then began to mash a piece of fruit while casting glances at it.

"Ms. Alex, are you alright?" The staff inquired, standing beside Osmond. She was on the verge of replying but chose to stay composed, needing to uncover what was going on in Osmond's mind.

"Yes, I'm fine. I just recalled something that really irritates me."

He was already aware of her intentions since Cedrick had informed him through a text message; she wanted to relish the morning workout in the botanical garden near Flinders Street Station. He secretly wished that Hugo wouldn't join them, as his presence only served to highlight how deeply it affected him, especially after witnessing how he held Alex's elbow. With a sigh, he thought that if he could erase such memories, he would do so in an instant, just by snapping his fingers. Ultimately, he reached a conclusion—a request he would make to her: to leave Hugo behind, knowing full well that he could bring about a sinister twist to any plan aimed at him or anyone else. He meticulously scanned the corners of the second level, and all he needed to do was wait for the moment she finally emerged from that specific room. He had no clue what kind of room it was, as it was located just a few meters from her bedroom.

"What do you think you're doing?" Alex asked Osmond as he cornered her, he then kissed her with fervor and depth, revealing his true feelings. And as for the CCTV? He was certain that whatever transpired, it would remain undiscovered. Despite Alex's attempts to push him away, he remained determined to have his way, until he was taken aback when she playfully bit his lower lip.

"Ouch! Why did you do that?" He exclaimed, rubbing the spot where she had bitten him, while Alex seized the opportunity to create some distance between them.

"What were you thinking, Osmond? Did I give you permission to kiss me?" And glancing around to ensure no one was nearby.

"It's just a natural reaction when I miss someone like you, isn't it? But what are his true intentions towards you?" He shifted the topic, hoping to steer Alex away from any accusations against him.

"Oh, Hugo? Isn't it obvious?" She smirked as she gazed at him.

"So, you have feelings for him? What about me?"

"I believe I should be the one to ask that first, don't you agree?" Alex shot back.

"What are you saying?"

"Forget it, Osmond, and step aside." She responded assertively, giving him a push. Just then, they heard footsteps approaching, prompting both to straighten themselves up.

Cedrick had just parked his sleek dark blue Audi. After stepping out of the car, he took his time to looked around and soon spotted Alex making her way to the entrance to greet him.

"Hi Cedrick, good morning!" Alex called out to him.

"Good morning, Ms. Alex!" Cedrick replied cheerfully.

"Anyway, I appreciate you coming. I plan to work out for about an hour, and afterward, maybe we can grab a bite? Unless you have other plans today." She wrapped up her thought. "Would you prefer to eat before we head out?"

"Oh no, Alex, I've already eaten, but I appreciate it." Deep down, he was undeniably enchanted by her character. Sure, she might display a tough exterior or provoke some negative reactions, but that's just who she is. Everyone has their good and bad moments, yet she genuinely knows herself. As an heiress and the future CEO, she must reveal her authentic self as the successor to the vast conglomerate whenever necessary.

"Cedrick, I just need to get a few things ready, and in less than an hour, we should be on our way. So, make yourself comfortable, alright? I won't be long, and Osmond will arrive as soon as he can. He's currently occupied with the butler and the head of our security team, discussing important matters he needs to understand, especially since handling emergencies is his top priority."

"Of course, take your time, Alex. I'll be in the living room waiting for you." Once seated, he picked up some reading materials from the table and began to flip through the pages. Just as he reached the middle of the content, he heard the familiar voice of his best friend, prompting him to stand up and exchange their customary greetings.

"Good morning, Agent McKain!"

"Good morning to you too, Agent Gomez! I must say, while we are on duty, I can't help but mention this. I hope you understand, especially considering what you said on our way back here about Isabelle. I hope you can see the distinction between her and Alex in your life."

Suddenly, Osmond was puzzled by Cedrick's words, but then he smiled while giving him a reassuring pat on the shoulder.

"You know, I really value your perspective as a friend on this matter, but I think you might be in for a surprise regarding what I witnessed yesterday. Just wait and see, mate. Today, I won't let this day go by without uncovering what I truly need to find out."

"Hold on, is there something I missed?

"Yeah and just wait for it. And I'll see your next reaction." Osmond replied and heads toward the place where he was staying to prepare his things.

Alex was satisfied as she gazed at her reflection in the full-length mirror. Since the moment yesterday afternoon when she first witnessed Osmond's reaction to being with Hugo, she felt a sense of satisfaction. Unfortunately, the timing was off this morning; he couldn't accompany her because he was unwell. Lucky Osmond, he would miss out on another dreary day, but at least she had finally figured out how to make him feel that way. She then strapped on her digital watch to track her exercise later on.

"Now that the biggest threat has passed, do you think it's alright for just the two of us to guard her today?"

Osmond glanced at Alex, who was making her way to the ground level as he observed her. He then replied to Cedrick.

"I believe so, and I see today as just another ordinary day for us. But we must stay vigilant at all times."

"Alright, noted."

That day marked the second occasion she saw Osmond with the fake moustache, which surprisingly suited him well. Yet, she constantly reminded herself that her plan was far from complete. But what if the situation between Osmond and Cedrick were to unfold similarly with Hugo and Osmond? That would certainly change things, especially since she had witnessed the prowess of her main guard. Hugo would undoubtedly be taken aback when that moment arrived.

"The vehicle is ready, Ms. Alex." Mentioned by Osmond.

"Great. And Cedrick will be sitting with me while you take the front seat next to the driver."

He glanced at her, and she simply smiled back. Meanwhile, Cedrick was doing his best to pretend he hadn't seen or heard anything, trying to adapt to the dynamic between the two. He mused to himself, *"navigating a relationship with this type of partner is incredibly challenging."*

They arrived ahead of schedule due to the light traffic, and after the two guards confirmed that the area was secure for them for an hour, they proceeded through the entrance.

As Alex made her way to the location she had indicated, they passed the Guilfoyle's Volcano at the Royal Botanic Gardens, and he followed her closely until he experienced a familiar sensation reminiscent of the time, he took Alex to the beach. It felt as someone was observing them, a feeling that he felt before, prompting him to become more vigilant. Meanwhile, another figure also sensed the same presence, aware that someone was watching the three of them. After a quick assessment of the other observer and a glance at the various individuals and groups around, someone concluded that none of them were the watcher and an idea began setting out to uncover the truth.

After jogging Alex was staring in the breathtaking view at the Shrine of Remembrance, she realised how much she had to be thankful for. A smile spread across her face as she looked at Osmond and Cedrick, wishing that her best friend Elissandra could join her someday when the opportunity comes. Then, as she gazed at the stunning scenery, a brilliant idea sparked in her mind; the Melbourne Metropolis has so much to offer at night. The skyline, historic monuments, the iconic Flinders Street Station, and across from it lies Federation Square, along with the giant Ferris wheel in Docklands and other city landmarks.

"Dad, we're heading out later, just before sunset," Alex said, as they finished their afternoon snack while the staff cleared the table.

"Oh, really? And where are you off to?"

"I'm just meeting up with Hugo," she replied.

"Wow, that's great! I'm really glad you two are going out again."

A wave of regret washed over her as she realised, she had lied to her father in that moment, but she felt she had no other option. She and Osmond needed to resolve their issues quickly, spending time together and allowing the right moment to reveal itself for discussing the misunderstandings between them.

The dazzling city skyline was breathtaking when the helicopter finally reaches more than three hundred metres from the ground as Osmond grasped Alex's hand, while Cedrick looking at them recalling the camera Alex had handed at him before the aircraft took off. He urged them to capture a photo by motioning his hand as they were all wearing an aviation headset and the breathtaking cityscape as their backdrop, stretching from Crown Casino to Marvel Stadium until they saw the iconic Melbourne Star, the colossal Ferris Wheel nestled in Docklands, as the aircraft glided towards Flagstaff Gardens. It veered right past the Melbourne Cricket Ground, then onward to the Royal Botanic Gardens, until they caught sight of Albert Park Lake until they reached the Brighton area and the chopper made its way back to the helipad in front of the Casino. That night, Alex drifted off to sleep, comforted by the thought that they were finally returning to the closeness they once shared.

The following morning, she made her way to the Royal Children's Hospital after seeing a news segment about the charity event. She opted to arrive later, after the media had departed, to prevent any spotlight on herself and to ensure the children's situations remained the main focus. For a few hours, she engaged in conversations with the kids and the hospital staff, and she was overjoyed when a young girl asked her to read a story to the group. Meanwhile, Osmond couldn't help but smile as he observed Alex; he found himself at a loss for words to convey how fortunate he was to be a part of her life. She had it all, and even though their relationship had its flaws, he held no regrets about his decision to love her.

The next day, Alex made her way to the kitchen in the early morning and was taken aback to find boxes of gifts and several bouquets of flowers in the middle of their living room. As she examined the cards, she recognised the names of people she knew, but one particular card stood out—it had no sender's name. Just then, a staff member approached her with a cheerful greeting.

"Good morning Ms. Alex! Happy birthday!"

She turned to the staff member, still clutching the bouquet.

"Thank you! And good morning!" The staff offered to help by arranging the flowers on the nearest table, closing her eyes to inhale the delightful fragrance of the blooms. A smile spread across her face as she carefully placed them in a vase provided by the staff. The rest of her day was filled with activity as she prepared her belongings in her room, assisted by her best friend Elissandra over a video call. Meanwhile, at the guest house, Osmond took a selfie and sent it to his father, wearing an all black suit paired with maroon necktie. After a brief wait, he received a thumbs-up icon along with a message: "*Good luck tonight, son!*" This made him smile. After sending a reply, he slipped on his shoes and took one last look in the bathroom mirror before stepping out of the guest house. Just then, he received an incoming call from the Director-General regarding the main suspect in a recent death found in his cell, which was ruled as no foul play. Osmond hurried to the scene, eager to uncover any clues that could help him.

"I never got the opportunity to speak with him one on one!" He exclaimed in frustration while driving and sensing that there was something more beneath the surface. It felt so odd; after arresting him and his group, he was found dead today. Upon his arrival, he swiftly evaluated the room, inspecting both the window and the ceiling. Everything appeared to be in order; no one had murdered the primary suspect. In fact, the knife was present, and a forensic officer confirmed that he had taken his own life that late afternoon. Disappointment washed over him as he shook his head; what if there was more to the story? Now that the room had been thoroughly cleaned, he requested to review the CCTV footage from the past 24 hours to see if anything suspicious had occurred, but to no avail. The investigators reached their conclusion justly and Osmond left the area.

Upon entering the venue, Alex was greeted by a meticulously arranged setting that exuded a serene atmosphere with the warm white of ceiling lights were also made her smile. With fewer than sixty guests in attendance, each of the seven round tables accommodated a maximum of eight people. The elegant white linen draped across the tables, complemented by breathtaking centerpieces featuring a delicate blend of blush and white flowers, alongside white candles nestled in glass holders. This was precisely what she desired for the evening: an intimate gathering that held great significance for her. However, Osmond had yet to arrive. She attempted to reach him by phone, but it appeared he was preoccupied. In the meantime, she decided to mingle with her guests, making her way to their tables as the wait staff began serving the entrée. Just then, Hugo approached her, greeting her with a gentle kiss on the cheek.

That night, as Osmond beheld her in a stunning white Greek-style gown, he was utterly captivated. Her hair was elegantly styled in a bun, with a delicate curly strand framing the right side of her face, perfectly accentuating her two-threader earrings. The soft pink hue of her lips added to her allure. Osmond smiled, glancing around his assigned table, and spotted Hugo at the adjacent table with the de Ayala family. Just then, he noticed the father and daughter rise as the emcee announced the event's first program.

The patriarch took to the dance floor with his daughter, captivating the attention of all the guests. Enrique caught sight of Osmond, who was stealing glances at his daughter, and a clever idea sparked in his mind as he shifted his gaze toward his heiress.

"I am so fortunate to have you as my daughter," Enrique expressed warmly, "happy birthday."

"Thank you, Dad," she said with a bright smile. "And I thought this before that we were not celebrating because of the threat. But look at us now, we're celebrating."

"I know since my team was determined to resolve that big problem, so we could enjoy this moment, just as I asked them to do."

"That's so sweet of you, dad!" She then embraced him, just as the smooth jazz music began to fade and a new song started playing in the room.

"Stay here, as I need to ask someone to dance with you." Enrique whispered to his daughter, which she just nodded at him.

Enrique walked over to the table where Osmond was sitting and he gently tapped him on the shoulder and whispered.

"Osmond, tonight you're not just my daughter's bodyguard. Since Agent McKain is here for the evening and we're celebrating, you may now approach my daughter to the dance floor and dance with her," Enrique instructed. Osmond hesitated for a moment, then lightly tapped his shoulder for the second time before saying, "come on, go for it. It's just for tonight; by tomorrow, you'll be back on duty."

"Alright sir. Thank you for that." He then rose from his chair and made his way towards the heiress.

Meanwhile, Evangeline relished the sight of the two as they twirled to the sounds of classical jazz music, until her attention was drawn to someone—Mr. Lucas Emsworth, who was deep in conversation with a group at a nearby table. She then redirected her focus to her daughter and Osmond, just as her husband finished speaking with Hugo, who was now heading outside to take a phone call.

"Are you feeling a bit queasy?" Osmond inquired, noticing her nod.

"Alex, just breathe as you usually do; it brings a different kind of calm, but it's simple, right?"

"Alright," she replied to him.

"This is finally allowing you to be free from anxiety or tension."

"Yeah, you're right," Alex responded.

"So, my father texted me this afternoon; they're coming this weekend for his birthday celebration. I suppose after this event in a few days, you might join us since he mentioned your name."

"Of course, I'll be there. Just let him know, though."

As they danced in slow motion, each step they took cast a soft, flickering light across their faces, her eyes locked onto his while his gaze remained on her, and then they both shared a smile.

"Before I forget, your enchanting charm is always captivating, but tonight it feels boundless. I can't help but wonder what lies beneath that beauty."

Alex shook her head and beamed at him.

"Oh, come on, Osmond. Would you dare say that in front of my father?" She laughed lightly.

"Absolutely. I'm just waiting for the perfect moment."

"I hope that when you finally get the chance to speak with him, he will see and feel about your genuine intentions in his heart."

"Don't worry, I will show him just how much you mean to me."

While the guests in the hall were busy enjoying themselves with conversations and drinks, one person was intently watching the two—it was Lucas. The man with curly hair with the rest of guards inside was certainly someone of importance, as he had already instructed his trusted assistant to gather information about him. Once he received the details then it's time to change the plan if something was off then he smiled, deducing that the newcomer dancing with the heiress was indeed part of her social circle. Just then, the father of the birthday celebrant waved at him, gesturing for him to join them. As he made his way to the table, he noticed that Alex was also heading in the same direction.

"Lucas, I appreciate you being here with us. My daughter, allow me to introduce Mr. Lucas Emsworth, the heir to the largest construction firm." At that moment, Alex recognised someone she had seen on television multiple times, and she was taken aback to find him among the guests this evening.

"It's truly an honour to meet you, Ms. Margarette Alexandria de Ayala," Lucas expressed warmly. Shortly thereafter, the couple from the other table came over to Alex, embracing her just as they had done with everyone else. After exchanging pleasantries, they excused themselves, needing to depart early for their morning obligations the following day, as they were prominent mining magnates from Darwin.

"So, Lucas, maybe we can go over the proposal I've been wanting to discuss for a while now?"

"Haha! Enrique," Lucas chuckled lightly before answered "to be honest, I still have a stack of documents waiting for my signature regarding the pending contract, and accepting your offer at this moment would be entirely unfair to those involved," he explained to Enrique, catching the attention of the wait staff. "Could I please have a glass of red wine?" The waiter nodded politely, responding in his customary manner. "Thank you." Meanwhile, Lucas thought to himself, glancing over at the de Ayala family, *"There you are, Enrique. You seem to have it all in business, yet you still want me on your side. I'd prefer to assist those who truly need my expertise to enhance their competitiveness in the industry."* Just then, someone addressed him—it was the heiress of the de Ayala family.

"Mr. Emsworth, thank you for joining us this evening," Alex began.

"It's my pleasure to be part of this event Ms. Alex," Lucas replied.

"What a wonderful celebration we have tonight, Mrs. Evangeline, wouldn't you agree? And your daughter is absolutely stunning, just like you," Lucas remarked to the matriarch, though he saw that familiar sight whenever he spoke to her husband.

"Oh, thank you, Mr. Emsworth," she responded with a casual smile, taking a sip of her drink.

"You're welcome," he said, a thought brewing in his mind. *Indeed, Mrs. Evangeline de Ayala, you never seem at ease when I am around, for I will soon unleash my fury upon you all.* After chatting with several guests for a while, the couple shifted to another table to mingle with others, and he flashed a smile at Alex.

"I hope you're enjoying the evening, Mr. Lucas."

"Yes, I am. Thank you."

"And also it is nice to know that my father is quite serious to establish a partnership with you in the near future. I sincerely hope you will respond to his request, as I believe that when it occurs, you and my dad will achieve something truly great and noteworthy."

"Ms. Alex, I appreciate your kind words. However, before I take my leave, as I need to wake up early tomorrow, I want to share this with you. The presence of your father's ghost is the very reason my own exists."

He then sipped less than a quarter of his wine from the glass and offered her a gentle smile.

"Good night, Ms. Alex, and once again, happy birthday."

Alex felt completely bewildered and confused by his words, which seemed more like a subtle suggestion, until the entrepreneur took his leave, extending his hand to her, which she happily accepted. She glanced over at Osmond, who was engaged in conversation with a group of gentlemen at the other table.

Hugo was following them, driven by his curiosity after Enrique mentioned that his daughter would be meeting her best friend that night after the event, yet Alex had not sent him a text. To quench his curiosity, he decided to follow Elissandra, and it turned out to be the right choice. He witnessed the model parking her car in the building's basement and caught a glimpse of her inside the Bentayga, with the light from the lamp post glinting off the back passenger seat. It stung him to realise he was merely a second choice. Consequently, he turned down the invitation to dance with Alex when her father said that he would be the next to dance with the celebrant and opted to take the call. After they parked the SUV beside a row of trees, the four of them strolled casually through the park, until he saw the couple began to each other's hands, with Elissandra trailing behind after speaking to another bodyguard he recognised. His eyes narrowed, as he sensed something that might prove useful to him in the future.

When they arrived, Osmond texted her to reveal that the second bouquet of flowers she received that morning was from him, as it had no sender's information. Now, she finally knew it and that night, she fell asleep with a smile after they exchanged sweet words of affection by text message then Cathy greeted her too and thanking her how Andrew had enjoyed yesterday when they finally visited the toystore. At the other side of state, Osmond smiled after reading the text message he received before sleeping that night, the day had been demanding for them, but it was fulfilling as Alex's birthday concluded well. Then it was perfect timing as for sure Isabelle will also confirm about their incoming meet up, it was weekend and surely by Monday she might send her confirmation, it has been a week since their reunion happened.

Twenty Three

Maximillian Williams

It was Friday in the morning at nine o'clock in the bustling city of Sydney, and Lucas found himself staring out of the window, lost in thought as the world moved on without him. He wore a black suit paired with a crisp white shirt and tailored black slacks then a black leather shoes an ensemble that exuded dignity and decency—a stark contrast to the disheveled man he had been just five years ago. The reflection in the glass revealed someone he barely recognised, a version of himself he never imagined possible. The transformation wasn't just in his appearance; it was in his demeanour, his choices, and the quiet confidence that had replaced the chaos of his past. For Lucas, this moment of stillness was a quiet triumph, a reminder that change, no matter how unimaginable, was always within reach. The streets hummed with the rhythm of a city in motion, a symphony of hurried footsteps and rolling wheels. People of all kinds filled the sidewalks—some briskly weaving through the crowd, their eyes darting to wristwatches, while others strolled with a carefree gestures, unbothered by the ticking clock. Students in uniforms and professionals in tailored suits clustered at corners, anxiously waiting for taxis or buses to whisk them away to their daily obligations. The tram screeched softly as it came to a halt nearby, spilling out a stream of determined passengers, while fresh faces climbed aboard, eager for the journey ahead. In the background, the faint hum of the metro pulsed through the air. Letting out a deep, heavy sigh, his attention drifted to something by the roadside next to the stop light pulling him from his thoughts.

As the sleek black car glided smoothly along the busy street, Lucas leaned forward slightly, his gaze fixed on something outside the window.

"Caspian, please find a spot to park the car," he instructed, his voice calm yet tinged with urgency, unable to tear his eyes away from the scene unfolding beyond the glass. Caspian, the ever-composed driver, responded with a brisk nod, his hands steady on the wheel.

"Absolutely, sir," he replied, his tone reassuring as he scanned the chaotic street for a suitable place to stop. The air inside the vehicle hummed with quiet anticipation, the unspoken significance of the moment hanging heavily between them, A few minutes later, he felt the car come to a stop, one block away from the spot where he had seen a particular person. Before stepping out of the car, he chose to put on his visor. Then, without waiting for his driver to open the door, he opened it himself. The two of them began walking toward the place. When they finally arrived at the establishment, they both stopped. While the man inside busied himself placing a sign on the large window, Lucas stood silently watching. The man's movements hadn't changed, though his face had aged slightly. Nonetheless, Lucas smiled—he had finally found him: Mr. Max.

Meanwhile, Caspian observed his boss and the man in front of them who just finishing his task. He had no idea who the man was or what connection he had to the heir, but it was clear that he held some significance to Lucas. Lucas stepped inside with an air of calm confidence, his movements deliberate, as though every step carried a purpose. The man inside, clearly unprepared for the arrival of two unfamiliar figures, shifted his glance between Lucas and his companion, his curiosity barely masked by a polite demeanour. His eyes flickered with questions, but his tone remained measured as he broke the silence.

"Sorry, gentlemen, but I think you missed the signage I just put up."

Lucas, unfazed, offered a small, knowing smile.

"I saw it," he replied, "but there's something I left behind before—something unfinished. Let this unexpected reunion be the reason for me to start coming here more often." With that, Lucas removed his sunglasses.

"Max, I finally found you," he said with genuine emotion, moving closer to embrace the man.

"Wait a second, mate. Who are you? And how do you even know my name?" Max asked, bewildered, the growing unease evident as he awkwardly attempted to pull away from the unexpected hug.

"You don't recognise me anymore, Max?"

"Sorry, but no. I don't think I know you," Max replied plainly.

Meanwhile, as a realisation slowly began to take shape in Lucas's mind.

"Alright, I understand," he said with a gentle nod, his gaze fixed on Max. He had to admit, Max was right—his appearance had changed significantly over the past five years. Slowly, he removed his visor, hoping the man would recognise him, but it didn't work.

"Max, what about my voice?" He asked. "My face might look completely different, but my voice should tell you who I really am." He watched as the man's expression until it gradually shifted to one of surprise.

"Oh god, Lucas! It's you!" Max exclaimed.

"Finally, you remember me!" Lucas replied with a laugh, and before he could react, Max was hugging him, laughing as well.

"Damn! I'm sorry I didn't recognise you, Lucas! I just never thought I'd see you again and now you look different!"

Meanwhile, Caspian observed the unfolding scene with quiet intrigue, his sharp gaze capturing every subtle detail. It was a rare moment to witness, one that left him both curious and oddly amused. As far as he knew, Lucas was not the type of person to initiate interactions with strangers, let alone approach them with such ease. Reserved and often appearing distant, Lucas rarely offered a smile unless it was directed at someone he genuinely knew and trusted. Yet here he was, defying expectations, his demeanour unusually warm and engaging. Caspian couldn't help but feel as though he'd stumbled upon a hidden layer of Lucas's personality, one he hadn't seen before—an enigma unfolding in plain sight.

"Anyway, would you guys like something to eat? I think we still have some food left. Luckily, one of my staff is still here to help me to prepare." Max offered as they finally pulled away from their hug.

"Sure, that sounds great!" Lucas replied. Then he remembered his companion. He had forgotten to introduce him to Max. Smiling at Caspian; he quickly corrected his oversight.

"Sorry about that, Caspian. It's just been such an overwhelming reunion for Max and I. Anyway, Caspian, this is Max. Max, this is Caspian," he said, watching as Max stepped forward to offer Caspian a handshake and the latter genuinely reciprocated Max's gesture.

"Please, take a seat," Max said, gesturing with his right hand toward one of the seven tables in the restaurant. "I'll be back after I check what we've got left in the back."

"Thanks, Max," Lucas replied as he sat down, his gaze soon landing on Caspian seated across from him.

"This is a great spot for a restaurant," Caspian commented.

"Yeah, totally," Lucas agreed, glancing around the room. The space was sparsely decorated, with a few adornments scattered about. Some chairs were neatly stacked in a corner, and a pile of menus rested on the nearby table. Lucas shook his head slightly. This place shouldn't have to close, he thought, silently firming his resolve. After a brief stretch of silence, Lucas stood facing the window when he felt the presence of someone approaching from behind. Turning around, he spotted a woman in her mid-twenties holding a black tray with two steaming cups of coffee.

"Thank you," Lucas said as the woman set their drinks down on the table.

"You're welcome," the staff replied then it went back to the kitchen area as Lucas watching her.

And Lucas saw Max was now heading to their table.

"Lucas, Caspian, I'm sorry, but all we can offer is Twice-Baked Cheese Soufflé. It's all we have left, and we're officially closing tomorrow."

"That's absolutely fine, Max. Thank you," Lucas replied with a warm smile.

"By the way, Caspian, do you have any dietary restrictions?"

"None at all," Caspian assured Max.

"Perfect! I'll get it started now and bring it out to you shortly once it's ready."

"Okay, and take your time Max," Lucas answered, and watching him while walking back to the kitchen.

Until finally the waitress was now approaching to their table, carrying a tray filled with their food, and she carefully placed the cutlery right in front of them.

"Thank you," he said to her, and she smiled before he turned his gaze to the table.

"From Chinese cuisine to a Western menu," he thought to himself as the wait staff set three plates on the table.

"Enjoy your meal, sir," she said, and he nodded at her with a smile, realising that Max had likely shifted to this type of food to offer customers a chance to try something different. However, it wasn't what he had anticipated, especially since it was their last day to pack up their belongings. Just then Max was now returning to their table, carrying a pitcher and water glasses in his other hand.

"Alright, everything is finally set," Max said as he took a seat next to him, while Caspian gently took adjusted his plate.

"Very timely, as we were just about to eat after my appointment today," he remarked as he began to enjoy his meal.

"It's great to hear, and we're fortunate to still have this," Max replied as he poured water into their glasses, placing them beside his plate and in front of Caspian, who was seated across from them.

An idea suddenly came to him again. But for the moment, they would relish and take their time enjoying this reunion between him and Max.

"Where have you been all these years, Lucas? We were quite concerned about you. There was a period when you disappeared, and it took us several days and nights to find you while we were still in Melbourne, I mean with Nancy."

Then he recalled her, the one who always served him food whenever he visited them.

"Where is she now?" He posed a question instead of responding to his inquiry.

"Well, she's quite satisfied and happy with her family and chose to remain in Melbourne, but in the countryside since her husband is a farmer. So, what about you? Where did you go?"

"Max, I must say that something unexpected occurred, and I sincerely apologise for not being able to inform you about my sudden absence, until when I finally had the opportunity to visit your restaurant in Melbourne, I discovered it was closed. After a week of checking back, I felt as though I had missed my chance to accomplish what I truly needed to do. I noticed some tradesmen working on renovations, and when I inquired, they informed me it was under new management." There was a silence after he finished his drink, then Max's voice brought a reason for them to continue their conversation.

"But look at what happened today, Lucas. While on your way to the restaurant for lunch with Caspian, and the fact that you saw me without even realising it?" Max said, smiling at him.

"It truly feels surreal," he responded, and they enjoyed their meals filled with joy and light until they were done. Suddenly, he recalled something, and his right hand instinctively went to his suit pocket, retrieving something he felt Max truly deserved. After jotting down the amount, he signed the check and handed it to him with a warm smile.

"Max, you shouldn't have to shut down this business. You don't deserve to go through bankruptcy," he gently said, then he continued, "when I had nothing, you extended a hand of generosity without expecting anything in return, and that act of kindness has stayed with me ever since," Lucas said, his voice steady with gratitude as he addressed the restaurant's owner then he continued, "in my darkest days, your unwavering support gave me hope, and now that I have the means to give back, I want to help you re-establish this restaurant and bring it back to its former glory. Let me be the one to repay the favour, not out of obligation, but because your kindness deserves to be honoured," he added.

"Lucas, this is too much. I cannot accept this," Max stated, shaking his head as he reached for Lucas's hand. However, Lucas smiled and grasped his hand firmly.

"No, I cannot accept that you are rejecting my assistance," he continued, smiling to alleviate his emotions, aware that he was on the verge of tears. Subsequently, he shifted the conversation. "Anyway, how come you ended up here in Sydney?" He asked.

"Well, I took that opportunity when my wife asked me to move here since she couldn't relocate to Melbourne due to certain matters, even though she could have contributed greatly to the expansion of my business back in there," the man began, his tone reflective yet resolute. "But you know, sometimes life has a way of surprising you; I was on the verge of closing this restaurant due to bankruptcy. It felt like everything was slipping away—this business, my dreams, and even the future I wanted for my children, who are ready for college. Then, as if by divine intervention, you came into the picture. You didn't just save this restaurant; you saved my family's future. It's moments like these that make you believe that no matter how tough things get, there's always a way forward. I am very thankful Lucas."

He finished his answer with a sense of quiet satisfaction, his gratitude evident in every word.

Lucas couldn't help but feel a sense of serendipity as he smiled at the man sitting across from him, their conversation flowing with an ease that felt both natural and momentous. The air carried a quiet hum of familiarity as Lucas tapped Max's shoulder, his gratitude spilling into his words.

"I feel very grateful that our path finally crossed," Max's easy smile deepened as he introduced himself formally.

"Anyway, my full name is Maximilian Williams," prompting Lucas to extend his hand.

"I am Lucas Emsworth," their handshake was warm but brief, and Lucas noticed Max's expression shift slightly, his brows knitting in thought.

"Hold on," Max said, curiosity lacing his tone.

"Are you associated with AE Company? I mean, the owner of that company is Mr. Amadeus Emsworth, right?" The question hung between them, sparking an unspoken connection that neither had anticipated. He hesitated, grappling with the weight of the question before him. Deep down, he wanted to cling to the familiarity of who he had always been, resisting the disruption that honesty might bring. Yet, he felt indebted to the man before him, someone who had been a significant figure in his life, and he feared that giving the truthful answer might create distance between them.

"Well, not really," his tone measured and cautious, "Surnames are scattered all over, in so many places. It's just a coincidence that Mr. Amadeus and I happen to share the same surname."

"Okay," he said, then nodded. Leaving the conversation at that.

Lucas seized the chance and dedicated his time to discussing business expansion with Max. He even attempted to share his ideas, which Max happily agreed after Lucas elaborated on some unfamiliar strategies for the future success of the establishment.

One time Lucas had witnessed the woman was crying in the hall-way, and he approached her and asked about the situation. They then proceeded to the office to address the matter.

"I believe everyone has the right to say, 'I am human.' However, the real question is, are you truly living by that principle?" Lucas posed to the supervisor as they finally entered the office after calling his name. "It's humiliating to criticise someone for being late when there is a valid reason behind it. Her mother was unwell, and she had to care for her, which meant she couldn't wear the appropriate uniform since it was still in the laundry, and she had no option but to wear some-thing different. Yet, it was still decent attire. Let me emphasise this: before we take action, we must listen to the other side of the story, like in this case with the woman. I want to prevent this from happening again. As a supervisor, please allow her to return to her duties. If you continue to insist your unfair judgment, I will have no choice but to let you go. Remember, the final decision is always with the owner of this building." He said then turned his glance to the helpless woman, "once you are done with your task, then you can leave early." Then the grandson of the company left as the matter has finally been resolved.

Twenty Four

Avoid it or Confront it

Alex was wondering why Osmond extended his day off and would be back to his duty tomorrow through text message. She simply replied with "Okay, I'll see you then. I love you." She was about to asked the reason but just realised Osmond might still want to bond with his parents so she'll just hang out with Cedrick later after lunch which her friend did not reject the favour after she sent an invitation via text message, and simply put her phone on the bedside table then continued watching her favourite television show, and still have more few hours to prepare herself.

Osmond was inside a restaurant, sitting in the corner at the end of Reine & La Rue, anticipating a meeting with someone that early evening. They had arranged to meet at six o'clock, and he arrived thirty minutes early. Despite having seen each other just the day before at his place—a heartfelt reunion that nearly brought him to tears—he clung to the promise she had made to meet again that evening. He glanced at his watch; it was ten minutes to six then he let his left hand rested in his jeans pocket, brimming with excitement, while his right hand lightly tapped his phone on the table. He kept his eyes on the entrance, watching as everyone turned their attention to a stunning blonde woman who entered the elegant restaurant. She wore a knee-length red dress with black high heels, and the golden strap of her classic black Chanel bag sparkled under the chandelier's light then a waitstaff member in corporate attire approached Isabelle politely, clearly about to ask the usual question and saw how she elegantly reciprocates the waiter's gesture, until their gaze met.

Osmond smiled when he saw Isabelle was now approaching together with busser and quickly stood up to hug her. Then he pulled out a chair for his childhood bestfriend

"Thanks," Isabelle said casually, flipping her wavy blonde hair. "What time did you arrive?"

Osmond smiled at her question. Should he tell the truth or choose to lie?

"To be honest, I arrived at five-thirty," he confessed, unable to take his eyes off his childhood best friend. Isabelle was even more beautiful than the night before, her straight hair now styled in soft waves.

"You look wonderful tonight," he complimented with a smile, his gaze still on her.

"Oh, thanks! You also look handsome and stylish," Isabelle expressed her gratitude, then smiled as she silently appreciating Osmond's overall look tonight. He was wearing a long-sleeve white polo shirt rolled up at the elbows, black fitted denim jeans paired with black leather topsiders, and his hair styled in a classic manner using wax.

Her radiant smile made Osmond's heart flutter. It was always a joy seeing her since their teenage days then especially now, catching up after all the time they had spent apart.

"So, how have you been since yesterday?" He asked, a playful tone in his voice, "since we last spoke, of course," he added.

Isabelle laughed softly after settling into her chair with elegance. "It's been a whirlwind, as always. Work is relentless, but it feels good to unwind and catch up with you. I've missed our chats," Isabelle replied, but deep down in her mind was a certain wish of courage; then she dismissed the emerging emotion.

Osmond nodded, feeling a warmth of familiarity and comfort between them.

"I know the feeling. Life's been quite the ride, but moments like these remind me what really matters," their conversation flowed easily, like they hadn't spent years apart, beautifully wrapped in the glow of the evening. Osmond cherished these moments, basking in the serendipity of life bringing them back together in a corner of a beautiful restaurant at the end of Reine & La Rue.

Meanwhile, along St. Kilda Road, Alex and Cedrick were on their way to the CBD while pop music played, and the SUV's window was halfway opened. As usual, Alex was wearing a yellow turban and sunglasses. Two and a half months to go before summer starts, and the sun was still up due to daylight saving.

"Alex, where would you want to eat?" Cedrick happily asked his friend after they bonded and went on a long drive earlier. Since it was twenty-five degrees, he saw how wind gently blew Alex's hair on her temporal point area.

"Well, I'm not sure yet, but I'll have a look on my phone," Alex replied.

"Okay, when you see something, you like, just tell me and we'll be there," he said as he was driving and after a minute, Alex gently locked the screen of her phone, as it was only an eyeshot away from him.

"I remember this. I've never tried Reine & La Rue on Collins Street. Let's go there, since someone I know invited me before, and I can dine without needing a reservation," Alex said to him.

"Sure," Cedrick responded with a nod since anyone who's aware of the stunning former stock exchange would definitely know where Reine & La Rue is. Then after few minutes, Cedrick turned left two blocks away from Flinders Street train station then he went to the nearest parking space and they walked for a less than five minutes to get in the upscale French restaurant.

When Alex and Cedrick greeted by the security staff at the main entry, Alex felt an inexplicable feeling when a wait staff approached and escort them to their table. Unbeknownst to her, Cedrick had already spotted Osmond in a corner. Despite Osmond's back being turned, Cedrick recognised him, Osmond was engaged in conversation with a beautiful woman. Who is she? Cedrick wondered in his mind, but he needed to act before things got complicated. He sensed something was off and had a bad feeling for that early night.

"Alex, can we go somewhere else? To be honest, I'm not a huge fan of French cuisine," Cedrick suggested, hoping to coax Alex away from the area.

"Cedrick, we're here now. I promise you'll like my favourite French dish. Excuse me for a moment; I need to use the restroom," then Alex stood up and smiled at the waiter stationed by their table.

"Wait, hold on," but it was too late. Cedrick couldn't prevent Alex from heading to the restroom, so he followed her, feeling even more anxious.

As Alex walked, she noticed a man with his back turned, speaking with gorgeous blonde woman, and she paused for a while and carefully gazing at them which was not normal for her to do such thing but there was an urge within her.

"Wait, is that Osmond?" She asks herself wondered and squinting at the woman then her face seemed vaguely familiar, though she couldn't recall where she had seen her before. Just then she turned and saw Cedrick walking towards her.

"Come on, Alex, let's eat somewhere else," Cedrick trying to conceal his reaction from Alex since she had possibly recognised the man behind her.

"Hold on, Cedrick, as I am trying to recall about something," as she spoke, the memory she had been grasping at clicked into place. The woman from the photograph, it was Isabelle!

She felt an extreme of surge about anger. How long had her boyfriend lying to her? Without hesitation, she moved toward where they were sitting, but Cedrick grabbed her wrist and started to speak.

"Alex please, don't," he pleaded as he looked into her eyes.

"Do not worry, Cedrick. I know what I'm doing, and I won't cause any trouble," Alex shrugged off Cedrick's hand, but it remained firmly.

"Cedrick, please let go of me," her voice was firm as she forcefully removed Cedrick's grip on her arm. Then she quickly slipped into the bathroom; after composing herself, she exited the restroom.

Osmond's attention was drawn to a woman approaching— it was Margarette Alexandria! He could see the sharp gaze in her eyes, which only made him anxious as she moved closer to where he and Isabelle were sitting.

As she neared their table, the fear on Osmond's face became clear. An idea sparked in Alex's mind, she was a decent woman and has a reputation to maintain after all; so, she would not make a scene.

When she reached the table, Alex smiled mischievously before she spoke up.

"Oh, hi Osmond! Good evening and what a small world." She said with apparent decency in her tone.

As Cedrick watching the unfolding scene, unsure of how to react.

Osmond found himself at a loss for words in that moment. Amidst the countless restaurants in the city of Melbourne, why was Alex here? and who was she with? Mustering his courage, he finally spoke up.

"I'm good, Alex and how about you?" He concealed his shock and anxiety from Isabelle, who sat opposite him before he answered, "I- am okay, who are you with?" Osmond replied calmly, hoping to diminish his bewilderment.

"I am with Cedrick, we were just spending time together for a few hours," Alex answered exuding with confidence as she responded to Osmond. Whatever their business for that night was entirely fine but lying to her was a different story and she was determined to keep her own matters private, casting a meaningful glance at Osmond.

As Alex spoke, Osmond saw Cedrick in a few steps away, which apparent the visibility of uncertainty of how to react. He waved and smiled at him, which Cedrick quickly reciprocated. Turning back to Alex, Osmond smiled that only heightened the tension—one that seemed forced and masked a deeper frustration.

Cedrick stepped closer, hoping to ease the emitting tension between Osmond and Alex it was the only solution he could devise, or perhaps he could suggest moving to another place to eat.

"Alex let's head back to our table; the waiter is waiting, and this is getting awkward," Cedrick whispered without getting near her.

Alex glanced at Cedrick.

"Alright, Osmond we are now heading back to our table. Enjoy your dinner," when Alex and Cedrick were about to leave, then the woman in red interrupted them from leaving.

"Wait, why don't you just join us? Since you're friends with Osmond, right?" Isabelle finally spoke.

Alex halted and turned to acknowledge her, offering a smile.

"Sure, thanks," as she returned to the table, deliberately sitting next to Isabelle to keep an eye on Osmond's expression, she looked at Cedrick, who seemed hesitant to sit with them.

"Cedrick, come take a seat," she smiled at him then shifted his gaze to Isabelle.

"By the way, I'm Alex and you are?" She extended her hand towards her, a smile plastered on her face, as concealing her feeling and emotion. Osmond's childhood bestfriend exuding a blond goddess of beauty and a sense of sophistication, evident in her graceful demeanour.

"I'm Isabelle, his childhood bestfriend," Isabelle gracefully replied, then looked at the man in front of her, then at Alex. Ms. Margarette Alexandria, to be exact. The famous sole heiress.

"Oh, my bodyguard's childhood bestfriend, nice meeting you Isabelle," after she and Isabelle shook hands, her gaze shifted to Osmond and Cedrick were next to each other and both silent. Though she wanted to ask about anything to Osmond or Isabelle, she just stayed calm and not do such thing, Alex chose to make the scene between them formal for that night.

Meanwhile, Cedrick's mind was now finally forming a conclusion and he was just trying to remain calm as much as he could as he knew Alex very well, the idea about intense confrontation between them will be so

"My mate's childhood best friend, such a big trouble!" He said to himself and took his cell phone from the pocket of his slacks to pretend that the situation was not on him, and he made himself busy with device.

"Have you guys taken your order?" And Alex took the menu cards and gave them one by one to her three companions at the table, and she gazed at Osmond eyes for a few seconds then turned her eyes to the menu.

"Not yet," Isabelle answered, then Alex just nodded, and she looked again at premium quality menu card that she was holding. Osmond watched as Isabelle and Alex chatted, while right next to him was Cedrick focused intently on his phone, Osmond wished he could vanish, as everything would have already unfolded. He would significantly face challenges the next day and beyond, uncertain about how to explain his meeting with Isabelle to Alex.

While eating, Alex was able to suppress the anger simmering within her toward Osmond as she silently watching Isabelle, with her impeccable table manners, was the picture of politeness, offering no grounds for criticism. Meanwhile, Osmond listlessly pushed food around his plate, while Cedrick silently consuming his food. Osmond's racing thoughts came to a halt when Isabelle finally spoke, prompting him to lift his glass for a sip of red wine.

"Osmond, are you okay?" Isabelle asked him gently. Her words pulled him back to the present, and he composed himself before he responded.

"Oh, I just had a thought about something," and he began to slice the red meat using the main knife with main fork despite the tangled emotions he was wrestling with, Isabelle's silence did not surprise Osmond; their dynamic had shifted from the warmth of their private meetings to a more guarded interaction with the other's presence. For Isabelle, the arrival of Alex and Cedrick was a welcome distraction, keeping Osmond from probing into a past she had no desire to revisit. This evening served as another reunion, ensuring everything was in place before she took action on her decision after fourteen years.

Cedrick, sensing the mounting tension, took a deep breath as Alex returned to the table, her expression a mixture of resolve and weariness. The air was thick with unspoken words, and Cedrick knew they needed to defuse the situation before it escalated further.

"It was such a pleasant dinner, everyone," Alex began, her voice steady yet firm, "and I think it's time we call it a night," she said with a smile.

Cedrick nodded, grateful for Alex's formality. It was a relief to see her taking control, and Cedrick hoped it would prevent any further confrontation. Osmond shifted uncomfortably in his seat, perhaps aware of the silent judgment in Cedrick's eyes. As they all stood up, Cedrick felt a mixture of relief and anticipation, eager to leave the tension behind and hoping would offer Alex some much-needed peace.

"Sorry, but Cedrick and I have to leave now. There's an urgent matter," Alex said. "It was nice meeting you, Isabelle." She hugged Isabelle and kissed her on the right cheek, then looked at Osmond. Alex still trying to maintain her composure, though deep inside, she wanted to slap his face. However, this was not the right time to confront Osmond about his hidden agenda that night. She approached him for a hug and pecked him on the cheek as a farewell with unexpected words of whisper from her to him.

"Enjoy the rest of your night with Isabelle as this juncture experience happened twice, not only once."

As Osmond reciprocates Alex's farewell, he could sense the tension crackling in the air between him and her gesture earlier already showing with unspoken words, had hinted at this confrontation. Despite his intention to clear the air, Osmond knew this moment was fraught with misunderstanding. Alex cryptic whisper about enjoy the rest of his night with Isabelle only deepened the mystery. Now, with almost a metre gap between them Osmond met Alex's fiery gaze with a calm demeanour, determined to defuse the situation.

"Alex whatever you think, you are wrong," Osmond said, as his voice begging to her and hoping his way would lessen her judgment. Meanwhile, Cedrick, standing nearby, watched the scene unfold with a mix of concern and curiosity. In that moment, the bustling sounds of the city seemed to fade, leaving only the echoes of unresolved feelings and the potential for understanding.

"It's okay. Bye for now, and you must go back inside as Isabelle is waiting." Then she turned to Cedrick and nodded at him, "let's go Cedrick."

Cedrick watched as Osmond went back to the restaurant, sensing the silent appeal in his friend's eyes. The night had taken an unforeseen twist, leaving emotions tangled and unresolved. He glanced over at Alex, whose tear-filled eyes reflected the night's turmoil. Although Cedrick usually maintained a respectful distance from his friends' personal matters, he couldn't turn away from Alex's current distress. He chose to offer his support and listen, as Alex meant a great deal to him. He knew the intense pain she feels and a reason for him to be with Alex, hoping the next day might bring a positive for them. As he started the car, Cedrick drove gently to get Alex home safely, to gather her belongings as she already mentioned that they were heading to Airlie beach, then he saw her making a call on her phone, and he heard the name of her best friend, Elissandra.

Twenty Five

Win You Back

After watching the Aboriginal cultural dance at Airlie beach Queensland, Alex remained silent. There was nothing any response she gave to Cedrick when they arrived that evening. Alex promptly locked herself in a room while the food he provided to her throughout the next day was barely touched, and then it was only a small a portion that she consumed when he collected the plate. Concerned about Alex's condition, Cedrick invited her out this afternoon to attend a show and to interact with some enjoyable activities. He hoped that by dinner time, she might feel inclined to eat, and fortunately, he was able to alleviate her pain. He stayed committed to doing his best to cheer her up, and Alex opted them to get there by a commercial plane, so Osmond wouldn't be able to find them just in case.

"Alex, would you be interested about scuba diving and snorkelling tomorrow? We could also explore this island," Cedrick suggested as they sat on the veranda overlooking the picturesque sea.

"I regret to inform you, Cedrick, that I am currently experiencing pain and may not be able to participate in those activities," Alex replied. She then looked up to the sky to prevent her tears from falling.

Cedrick saw what was happening and stood up to ease her feelings. He put his hand on her shoulder and patted her.

"You have not eaten well, cried all the time, and drunk alcohol since we arrived. Please don't punish yourself. I do not want to see you like this," he said.

Alex smiled slightly at him before turning the gaze back to the sea, then he replied.

"I understand that you are feeling hurt, and it is not right for you to treat yourself in such a manner. The surroundings are indeed beautiful, and I can assure you that we are in a truly idyllic setting. Compare your current circumstances to this paradise." He hoped that he could persuade her to regain her former enthusiasm. If only he were in Osmond's position, he would never have caused her pain and distress. He acknowledged that emotions are always unpredictable. He considered how he might help his friend feel better. He chose to take an object from his room after noticing the instrument the previous night.

"I will return soon," he said. Alex nodded in acknowledgment.

As time passed, she felt Cedrick return to her side while she continued to gaze into the distance. She turned to face him.

"To alleviate your discomfort, I intend to play this instrument, and perhaps you will find it enjoyable," he offered. Cedrick recalled the classic song and prepared to strike the string of the guitar he was holding.

After completing his musical performance, he carefully placed the instrument on the table and offered her a warm smile.

"How are you feeling now, Alex? I am here for you whenever you need me. Through both joy and sorrow, you can rely on my unwavering support," he softly said, keeping eye contact with her. He then gently took her hand to caress it.

"Thank you, Cedrick. I am equally here for you as your closest friend."

"Please, Alex, cease self-harm and find solace in the fact that you still appear visibly distressed. I urge you to cheer up," he said, offering her a comforting embrace. "I wish I could be Osmond." He said to himself and took a deep breath.

Back in Melbourne, Osmond could not find Alex and Cedrick. He had checked the Port Moresby airport's website for their flights, but there were none. He was even more uneasy since Cedrick was with her. Different thoughts raced through his mind. What if Cedrick was already trying to get her attention? Especially at this event, there was a possibility that Alex might fall for Cedrick. He quickly dismissed that thought.

"I can't let this happen!" Osmond suddenly parked the car on the side of the road. He had to find out where they were so he could explain to Alex the real reason for his meeting with Isabelle; it was about what happened behind the abduction of her fourteen years ago. But still, she declined to say any then Isabelle grabbed his hand and stared at him while the casual facial expression was evident in her eyes, seemed like nothing happened. "Osmond, this is the second time about the same question. Please let us not discuss it. Since even myself, I am no longer holding on from that past." Then it was the last conversation he had with Isabelle, and since last night he found himself ending up staying at the hotel and he does not want his parents to see him in that awful condition, so he just called them to say he was busy with his duty. Then he started to drive and decided to go back to hotel, but he would still try his best to find them, and to finally to confront Cedrick about his intentions.

Following dinner, Cedrick was now finally drinking red wine as Alex insisted him to drink. The agent, trying to avoid alcohol, discreetly poured a part of the liquid into the adjacent white vase whenever Alex's attention was diverted. Mr. Enrique had specifically instructed him to ensure the safety of his daughter. Alex persisted in her consumption and expressed her resentment towards Osmond and Isabelle, eventually succumbing to tears and rushing to the nearest restroom to induce vomiting. Cedrick, observing the door's opening, promptly entered the restroom. He subsequently assisted Alex in cleansing her face and carried her when she became unconscious.

"I hope you'll be finally okay by tomorrow," Cedrick whispered after wrapping a blanket around her. He felt the same fluttering sensation he had on the first day he saw her. His eyes were drawn to her mesmerising lips until he realised his head was slowly getting nearer her face. Then, Alex started murmuring, and it was Osmond's name. Cedrick quickly regained his composure, his respect for her overriding any other feelings. Then he took a deep breath and started to walk towards the two large windows while hearing the loud sound of crashing waves. Then he locked the windows, and before he finally went out of the room he turned off the light and switched on the lampshade then, his gaze landed on her before he closed the door and ensured that all doors and windows were securely locked within the suite. Then, he proceeded to his room to take a shower before finally succumbing to sleep for the night.

The following morning, she woke up with a headache upon opening her eyes. Upon observing the wall clock, she realised that it was nine o'clock in the morning. This was surprising, as she was still wearing the same shorts and shirt and recalled drinking with Cedrick the night before. She had subsequently vomited in the toilet and had a fragmented recollection of the events.

"Oh no, that was incredibly embarrassing!" She thought to herself after remembering that Cedrick had helped her cleaning up her face. She then slowly stood up and proceeded to do her morning rituals in the bathroom. However, she was interrupted by several knocks on the door after half an hour, but she was pleased to be already finished.

"I'm coming!" She responded, casually walking to open the door while brushing her hair. She knew that it was Cedrick and was attempting to compose herself after recalling the events of the previous night and when she opened the door, a boy next door vibe appeared in front of her as Cedrick was wearing a plain white shirt and light brown walking shorts, while carrying a tray with different choices of food for breakfast, one glass of orange juice, and a cup of coffee.

"Good morning, Alex! Breakfast in bed!" Cedrick said loudly.

"Good morning too, Cedrick! And thanks for the breakfast, come in!" She replied happily while walking towards the huge mirror to finish her routine.

"You're welcome!"

And shifted her gaze towards Cedrick, and the tray was now on the bedside table. Then Cedrick asked her to go back to bed to eat, and she casually obeyed.

"Cedrick, it's embarrassing. It's not your obligation to prepare my food, and I'm so sorry from last night."

"It's totally fine, then I have to since I understand. So, eat."

"Alright, but you have to eat with me, Cedrick." She said as she got back to bed.

"This coffee is mine. I'm not hungry yet. You should eat because since we got here yesterday, you haven't been eating properly. Or maybe you want me to feed you?"

"I am fine, and I will have my breakfast, I assure you!"

Cedrick insisted on trying to feed her, but she continued to refuse until she was finished. Finally, she noticed the medicine for a headache on the tray.

"For your hangover headache," Cedrick said, looking at her intently. She smiled and nodded.

With that, she felt guilty. The man was willing to do anything he could to make her happy and safe, and the person who loved her deeply that she could not reciprocate his feelings. Suddenly, she bowed down after taking the medicine.

Cedrick grasped Alex's hand as she suddenly bowed. He understood her reason.

"Don't worry, Alex. I'll do what I can for you. I won't expect you to love me back. Seeing you is enough for me." He smiled, took a deep breath, and squeezed her hand gently. After a moment, he said goodbye and took the tray, leaving the room. Alex realised she'd chosen Cedrick over Osmond given by chance. But she loves Osmond dearly and quickly dismissed that thought, and chose to rest for a while, and when she felt better, she immediately got up so they can explore the beauty of the place until the end of the day.

At that juncture, Osmond experienced a state of restlessness. He had undertaken numerous searches in an attempt to locate Alex, but his efforts had yielded no positive outcomes. But how? He checked the websites of various airports in Asia, but there was nothing. Until he realised to check the countries in Europe, then after less than half an hour he still couldn't get any details. In his frustration, he picked up the bottle of rum from the table and then threw it against the wall of the hotel room where he was staying.

"Shit! Where are you, Alex? I wish you had waited for me to explain!" Then he rushed towards the wall to punch until his fist bled, and he sat on the floor. He let the tears he had been holding back flow down his face, hoping that she was okay at that moment.

"Love, I miss you so much. I hope you come back soon so I can explain everything to you when you get here, and I promise I will not keep any secrets from you anymore." Then Osmond wiped his tears and trying to think of any possible way to win her back.

"Are you now completely okay and did you enjoy it?" Cedrick asked Alex happily after their last activity of the day. They were already in their private suite, resting in the living room.

"Yes, very much. Thank you, Cedrick," she replied, hugging him.

"It's nothing, Alex. I just did what I had to do, and I'm happy to see you back to your usual self," he said.

Alex instantly remembered the last time he saw Osmond with Isabelle. Now, she was ready to see him and whatever explanation he would give, she would ignore it after concluding a plan.

Past two in the afternoon, the private jet landed at Essendon Field. When it finally stopped, Cedrick answered the incoming call from Agent Gomez. He clearly instructed him about the usual protocol, ignoring the annoyance he felt towards his colleague.

"Copy, Agent Gomez," he replied. Then the call ended, and he saw Alex's reaction in his peripheral vision; she was rolling her eyes.

"So, he's here. The nerve," Alex murmured.

Cedrick tried to react casually by asking her.

"Shall we?" Then he saw her nod at him before he went ahead to the jet's door when it was finally opened after he put on his sunglasses. Then, while Alex was behind him upon descending from the jet steps, he was observing the surroundings and when he finally made sure that everything was entirely clear, his glance landed on Osmond. He could see his reaction since he was not wearing a visor, while surely, Osmond could not see how his gaze was sharp on him when he realised the event between Osmond and Isabelle.

Osmond, why are you here? Where is my driver?" Alex asked Osmond in a formal tone.

"Your driver is sick, and your dad asked me to pick you up. But I am glad that you just spent your two days within the country, and I am sorry from that night since–." Osmond wasn't able to finish his words as Alex quickly motioned her hand in front of him.

"Osmond, take the bag from her and put them now in the boot please," Alex replied then saw how the flight attendant handed her belongings to Osmond while looking at her which she casually ignored and to her surprise it was merely a few seconds passed when Osmond opened the door for her, and Osmond was about to speak again and she looked at him.

"Please Osmond, not now and there is no need as you don't have to say any,"

"But Alex please it was a–." Osmond saw how she was now looking at him, the way she glancing at him was cold and the good thing was he managed himself not to touch her where the airport's crew was just nearby from them.

"Osmond I am tired," she said firmly.

"Did you hear what she said? Now, please show your professionalism by respecting her decision to follow her order as our client. I am sorry, but this is not the appropriate time to discuss things that you want to settle," Cedrick warned Osmond as he was now really fed up with him after he witnessed the incident last time inside of the restaurant.

With a clenched fist, Osmond chose not to say anything of what he heard but he made sure about his stare was sharp as a razor blade to show as a forewarning for Cedrick to back off.

But Cedrick stays firmed and this time, he won't let the same thing happen again as he and Osmond exchanged intense glances.

"Osmond, shall we go now? I want to go home," Alex said to him and shifted her gaze towards her. Then he proceeded to the driver's seat and drove home. While driving, Osmond would sneak glances at Alex in the rear mirror, while her face was serious while looking out the window.

Alex felt Osmond stare, so she put on her sunglasses and told him to focus on driving. When they arrived at their mansion, Alex saw a particular car parked in the driveway. Then her disappointment faded because she knew that it was Elissandra. Cedrick opened the car door for her then when she alighted from the car their butler opened the two large main doors and rushed towards her best friend upon seeing her when the door opened.

"Hi honey! Finally, you're back!" Elissandra said loudly.

"Thanks for coming over! And I miss you too honey!" She replied, then she saw Elissandra motioned her eyes behind her.

"Hold on. Alex, I remember he was cheating on you". Elissandra murmured after they hugged then still smiling just to be civil in front of the staff, and to the two agents. Alex looked behind her and saw Osmond pulling her suitcase while Cedrick stood by the car with his suitcase. She nodded in response. Elissandra smiled as she watched them.

"So, do you still remember what I said before?" Elissandra asked.

Alex recalled their conversation over the phone last time but maintained her composure to avoid further questioning from Osmond once he heard the name of "Isabelle," or else her plan would entirely ruined.

"Yes, of course," Alex replied, and Elissandra waving to Osmond and Cedrick. The two men waved back.

"Now, you know what fate really is, don't you?"

"Yes," she quickly replied.

"Wow, and now that was not entirely coincidental. But do you really feel threatened of her presence? I mean let's be real here, with that kind of look anyone could possibly thought that she can be a famous actress to any romantic or a drama film and perhaps a model."

"Really, honey?" She responded sarcastically and saw Elissandra just shook her head while still amused by her reaction.

"Okay, you really love Osmond!" Elissandra whispered.

"I shall have an objection with that." She replied while nodding then all long she looked at Osmond when he gave the luggage to their staff.

Then, she must get something as like what Elissandra suggested last time when they had a video call and that was to get the contact number of Isabelle!

Twenty Six

Margarette Alexandria and Isabelle

That early night, Alex resolved to obtain Isabelle's number, no matter the cost. She aimed to put an end to the uncertainty once and for all, believing it was the best way to prevent any future disputes. A wave of irritation washed over her at the sight of the woman when she finally met her, but then she recalls how alluring Isabelle was, prompting her to shut her eyes. *"Oh, god!"* She thought to herself. It was a classic rivalry between two women vying for the same man. After regaining her composure under the shower, she pondered the potential outcome of her plan; if it succeeded, the confrontation would be straightforward. How dare that woman, after all these years? *"Osmond is mine, and mine alone,"* she reiterated in her mind, reminding herself that Osmond was still not her husband, and she had to secure her position before it was too late. The woman had been a source of a different kind of uneasiness ever since she heard the words, "childhood best friend," Alex closed her eyes again while showering, trying to suppress her incessant thoughts about her.

It was nearly eight o'clock in the evening when Osmond sent a text to Isabelle. He stood nearby as the two were busy in the kitchen area. He placed his phone on the side table nestled between two large flowerpots filled with peace lilies, scratched his neck, and adjusted the collar of his long-sleeved polo just as he saw Elissandra approaching him.

"Osmond, could you do me a favour, please? Is that alright?"

"Of course, what do you need?"

"It's regarding my car. I heard a strange noise when I got here this afternoon, and thankfully, I remembered it before I leave soon. Could you take a look at it?"

Before he could respond, Alex nodding at him, signaling to help her friend.

"Okay."

"Thank you." With that, Osmond began to walk, and before she followed him, Elissandra shot a meaningful smile at Alex while pointing her finger at the device on the table.

As soon as they leave the living room, Alex hurried to grab the phone, which was perfectly timed because it began to ring. The caller ID showed an unregistered number. She swiftly retrieved her phone from her pocket, copied the number, and set it back on the table. A hunch told her that this mysterious caller might be Isabelle, as she had seen that all incoming calls were usually linked to contacts whenever she glanced at the screen. The phone continued to ring as she made her way to the kitchen and sat in a bar stool. She double-checked to ensure she had the correct ten digits, nodded in satisfaction, and pressed the lock button. Almost three minutes later, the two were now returning inside, and she feigned nonchalance as if nothing had happened.

As she refilled the two glasses of champagne, her peripheral sight saw Osmond picking up his phone from the table, tapping the screen as he inspected it. Meanwhile, she discreetly signaled to Elissandra with her finger when she finally settled beside her. They both lifted their glasses for a toast. That night, she switched her number to private mode before dialing. When the call connected, she was right; it was her on the other end. The voice was familiar, almost like a ghost haunting her thoughts confirming it was indeed her. Before drifting off to sleep that night, she decided to send a message with a crucial warning: *"do not tell Osmond, no matter what."*

The following day, she devised the most effective strategy to create a distraction that would allow her to leave unnoticed. However, prior to that, she had already contacted Cedrick for help, and they planned to meet as soon as she managed to escape their home. When they finally convened at a specific location—the nearest petrol station from the suburb of Toorak—she turned off her phone.

Cedrick stood outside, having offered them a moment of privacy for their conversation, and he was taken aback when he recognised Isabelle waiting from inside.

Upon seeing the person, she was to meet that evening, dressed in the same color dress, Alex realised that Isabelle was deliberately pushing her buttons. It was even apparent how much more alluring Isabelle had made herself that night.

Then she let out a sigh and resumed her walk in her straight cut fitted denim paired with black stiletto, and under of her crop top black suit was a white shirt. The choice of meeting place was actually suggested by Isabelle, who had recommended a spot in the SouthBank area, but Osmond's friend was adamant. If only she hadn't made plans to get involved with this woman, Alex would have never felt the need to meet with her. Once this meeting concluded, Osmond would truly need to answer what she really wants. She can handle the dynamics between them, if only Osmond weren't so secretive. She truly understands her role as a girlfriend, while Isabelle is his childhood best friend. Her thoughts were abruptly interrupted when Isabelle rose from her chair and embraced her. In that moment, Alex sensed a peculiar feeling behind that action; Isabelle's affection for her was genuine.

"I apologise if I picked this location for our meeting, as I truly value our time together and prefer to avoid drawing public attention," Isabelle said, smiling as she flipped her wavy blonde hair and took a seat. The wait staff gently pulled a chair out for Alex.

"Thank you," Alex said to the waiter, returning the smile.

"You're welcome, Ms. Alex," the well-uniformed man replied and smiled at her.

"Please let me know when you've made your decision on what to order," the waiter said, casually walking to a spot near their table, while Alex's gaze fell on Osmond's childhood best friend.

"You know, the first time we met, and now this second time, it reminds me of the word tychism." Alex smiling at Isabelle, who appeared genuinely pleased by her comment. However, it irritated her to see Isabelle smiling back while still keeping her eyes on her.

"I completely agree with you Ms. Alex, and I'm really pleased about it. Don't you feel the same? Communication is such a valuable asset, isn't it? Therefore, I believe this meeting holds significance for you, Ms. Margarette Alexandria. As the future CEO of your father's company, I imagine you have a packed schedule. So, I must say, it's quite a compliment that you took the time to meet with me," Isabelle began as she flipped to the first page of the menu on the table, their eyes locking when she glanced at her.

Alex paused for a moment after hearing Isabelle's introduction, contemplating how their discussion would unfold.

"You're absolutely right, Isabelle. As Osmond's girlfriend, this meeting is indeed important to me. And feel free to just call me Alex," she responded with a smile, her gaze shifting from Isabelle to the menu she was holding.

"Oh, I was right then. The night when we first met," Isabelle replied.

"Wow, I am not surprised that you instantly concluded that fact. I am glad for that, Isabelle."

"Thanks. Well, you know what Osmond and I had shared— great memories back then; so that's why you cannot blame me for us being always inseparable, which led to a remarkable kind of friendship."

"Don't lie to me, Isabelle. What is your intention towards him? And let me remind you that Osmond is not to be shared with anybody else." She said firmly while looking at her, then she continued browsing the menu.

"Oh, that thing?" Isabelle remarked, a small smile creeping onto her lips before she added, "Don't worry, Alex. I'm content with my life as it is, and neither of us can be blamed for crossing paths at any time or place. And naturally, Osmond belongs to you. I promise you that." Isabelle responded, then she refrained from turning the menu page and signaled to the nearby waiter that she was ready to order.

As Alex decided to forgo the entree, she flipped to the main menu selection, glanced at the waiter, and smiled. She placed her order for the chicken leeks gnocchi with potatoes and carbonara sauce. Once she finished her main course and dessert, she planned to leave the restaurant; there was no need to extend the conversation since she had already discovered what she wanted.

The plane touched down in Melbourne around ten o'clock in the evening, and the Gomez couple hopped into a taxi that would take them to the address their son had provided earlier that day. It was an apartment hotel, a choice Celine favoured so she could prepare their meals instead of relying on room service. Even Osmond had suggested accommodations that would meet their needs. As Martin glanced to his wife, who's staring outside of the car's window, it was a familiar look of concern on his wife's face.

"I had seen that expression a few days ago. Is something troubling you?" Then the vehicle's headlights from the opposite side of the road revealed his concern while Celine took a deep breath before responding.

"Martin, do we really have to celebrate your birthday here? I mean, I have nothing against it being here, but I just have this uneasy feeling about it."

Then Martin nodded, reaching for her hand to reassure her that there was no need for such feelings.

"Celine, look at me." His wife turned her eyes toward him, and they locked gazes.

"It's been quite some time since we enjoyed a long vacation, and spending about a week here would be beneficial for us," he comforted her.

"Alright, I apologise. Perhaps I was just overthinking things."

"Yes, definitely. So, to keep your mind occupied, starting tomorrow, we'll wake up early and take a walk for about an hour, then do some grocery shopping?"

"Oh, that sounds wonderful," Celine replied.

"After we sort out the things later, we can finally relax, but are you feeling hungry?" His wife gently shook her head.

"Okay, me neither, as I was completely stuffed from the meal we had on the flight," Martin said.

"Knowing our son, it was definitely him. Without a doubt," Celine responded.

"Absolutely." His wife then rested her head on his shoulder as the taxi exited the freeway, signaling that they were nearing their apartment, situated at the edge of the city.

The following morning, Alex was having an early FaceTime call with her best friend, who had been unable to reach her the previous night.

"If you believe she wasn't showing any confirmation to about your suspicion, then why not just calm down and trust Osmond?"

"In a way, I do feel quite guilty," Alex replied while brushing her hair and making her way to sit on her bed.

"Of course, let's be honest. Do you really think she would have the courage to tell you about their history directly?"

Alex was taken aback by her friend's comment and let out a sigh.

"Stop being so paranoid, okay? But anyway, how is Cedrick?"

Alex raised her eyebrows upon hearing the question from the other end and smiled.

"And why the sudden change of subject?"

"Well, I just think he's really nice and accommodating guy."

Then she smiled again. Alex knew Elissandra very well.

"He was with me last night to help me," she replied.

"I hope to be able to visit there whenever I have free time, but this coming week my schedule is quite packed. The term 'camp arrest' is indeed quite demanding."

"Oh, the future beauty queen!" She exclaimed after Elissandra mentioned her training.

"You know, the pressure is really high! Can you believe there are almost twenty candidates competing for the title of Ms. Victoria? Two of them are particularly strong. If I recall correctly, one is from Hamilton and the other from Shepparton."

"Then, show them that you possess what it takes to be a beauty queen."

"Thank you. I will do my best, leveraging my past experiences as an advantage. Anyway, my time is up, Alex, and I need to prepare myself and take care of other matters. So, I have to leave for now. Goodbye. I'll see you after this camp-arrest, take care.

"Alright, see you soon and good luck! Bye."

At the opposite end of the state, Osmond was already dressed in his uniform. While Alex was on a phone call with her best friend, Osmond had just ended his call after admitting to his commander about visiting the main suspect's cell. To alleviate his concerns, the General-Director proposed that another agent will take over the investigation, which brought Osmond relief upon hearing the suggestion from the other end.

Inside the Phantom site, the agent on a mission arrived earlier than anticipated, and the uniformed man stood and saluted as the newcomer greeted him in their customary manner.

"Thank you for coming, as agents Gomez and McKain were unable to handle this at the moment due to their obligations, but something weighing on Osmond's mind, which I also sense. So, we will have an interim period of about a week when you have the time for it." He then handed the envelope to the agent before him.

"Consider it done, sir. Starting today, I will commence this mission since the involved is the primary suspect regarding the threat to Ms. Alex," the agent responded after reviewing the contents of the envelope.

"Thank you." This was followed by their customary salutations, and the agent exited the building.

She was rolling her neck and gently massaged the left side, knowing she had a big day ahead. She then glanced at Osmond, who stood outside the smoky glass door, but chose to tidy up the stack of papers on the table instead and she recalled how he reacted when they discussed his childhood best friend and the choice, he had to make between her and Isabelle.

"Alex, please, don't do this. It's so unfair!"

"Unfair? Seriously, Osmond? Was it fair that you secretly met with her without my permission? Now, choose her or me; it's that simple." She didn't hear any response instead seeing him shaking his head and made her realise he was uncertain about their relationship, while Isabelle already gave her certainty between the two.

"Alex, I love you, I truly do. Isabelle is important to me too, as she was my childhood best friend. She supported me when I dreamed of becoming an agent one day. That dream is also why I became your bodyguard. So, I'm sorry, but I can't choose just one."

Then she started to murmur and shook her head to show how painful it was to hear from the man that she'd really loved, next to her father. But actually, she was just testing his loyalty to her, after finding out the real score between him and Isabelle. Then another tease came up in her mind.

"I don't think I need you for tomorrow, so you should take day off since Cedrick is also my bodyguard. And by his presence, even you are not around I am sure I'll be fine.

"Why are you saying that?"

"Because I hate the fact that even I have you, but it is totally different and had to deal with Isabelle about the truth! Even though she gave me an assurance."

"Wait hold on, assurance? What do you mean?"

"We just met last night, and to ask her personally about things between the two of you."

"Then?"

"And why would I tell you the answer?"

"Because I want to know." Osmond replied, "Alex, I can't believe you can say such thing. How can you reply to someone like that?"

"Do you really love me? If so, love shouldn't be painful, right? Yet, you keep hurting me!" Alex exclaimed, pointing to her heart then she heard a soft knock, when she opened it, he saw Osmond who was hesitant to speak while looking at her.

"Osmond, it's over and don't worry, our meeting last night wasn't what you might think. It was quite civil. Let's head home; my parents want to have dinner with me after from their appointment later."

The following morning, Osmond called his parents to check in on them and was pleased to hear they were enjoying their first day in Melbourne. They were at the park, taking a break, and later planned to head to the supermarket.

"Your siblings are arriving today; we'll pick them up in two hours," Martin mentioned.

"That's awesome, Dad! I haven't seen my brother Larry in a while."

"Yes, and I'm also thrilled about this birthday year since we are finally complete. Plus, my future daughter-in-law, Alex."

"Oh dad, are you aware of the situation between Alex and me?" Osmond was surprised by how his father referred to Alex.

"Of course, I'm aware. Your mother knows too." However, Martin decided to hold back further comments, understanding that his son would be hurt upon hearing Celine's disapproval of their relationship.

"Wow, that sounds like an amazing celebration, dad. I'm really looking forward to it."

"Yes, just a moment, your mother wants to talk to you."

Osmond waited a few seconds until he heard his mother's voice on the other end.

"Hi Osmond, when is your next day off?"

His mother's question piqued Osmond's curiosity.

"This coming weekend, why do you ask?"

"Just asking."

"Alright mom, I'll come by tomorrow after my shift to see you and my brother Larry as well."

"That's great to hear, because we need to discuss something."

"Okay, sure," he replied with a smile, certain it was about him and Alex.

"I'll see you by tomorrow then. We need to go for now. Take care. Bye."

"Bye mom." The call ended, and as he glanced at his watch, he realised he still had an hour before they were set to leave. Just then, he received a text from Alex, informing him that they would be departing after ten thirty instead of nine thirty. He quickly replied, confirming he had received her message and added a term of endearment for her. "I'll see you around, I love you." He then made his way to the kitchen to prepare another cup of coffee, but a sudden, inexplicable feeling washed over him. Nevertheless, he continued to make his drink.

As he waited for Alex in the living area, the driver walking towards the garage, so he followed him since it was only ten o'clock and he asked Barron.

"Which one will we use?"

"Ms. Alex told me she wants to use the Rolls Royce."

Then Osmond nodded while still gazing at the Range Rover Sentinel, and a thought crossed his mind after an unfamiliar hunch began to nag at him. After brushing the thought aside, he made his way to the lounge area, until the driver spoke up, having gone unnoticed by Osmond due to the sudden distraction in his mind.

"I think we should opt for the other one, the Sentinel," he suggested just as Alex was coming down the stairs wearing an all over black attire.

"That's fine, it doesn't really matter," Alex replied after glancing at her watch, noting it was now ten past ten.

"We'll be leaving in twenty minutes," she added.

Osmond felt a sense of relief wash over him after she agreed with his suggestion instead of choosing the luxury sedan.

Twenty Seven

The Fall of Empire Part One

It was already past eleven when Alex was preoccupied with her phone, seated next to the driver was Cedrick, and Osmond was right beside her. Cedrick kept glancing at the rearview mirror to keep an eye on his best mate, sensing something unusual about him that morning; it made him uneasy as he had never witnessed this behaviour before, especially in comparison to past events.

In the major establishments within the CBD area, people were thrown into confusion by the sudden shift in what they saw on the screens. The message was different.

"I am no titan, so therefore I am not connected to humans through numbers or letters, but mankind tends to be skeptical whenever my name is on the table."

Shortly after, Enrique received a peculiar text message, reminiscent of one he had received before taking Alex to Queensland. After reading it, he reached out to the head of security and subsequently called Osmond, who answered the phone.

"Agent Gomez, where is Alex?"

"Sir, she's with me, and we are our way there."

"Return to the residence! I received a text message from the number of main suspect, the same strange e-mail before, and I have a feeling something might happen."

"Understood, sir." He then instructed Barron to pull the car over.

"What's happening?" Cedrick inquired.

"Ms. Alex, your father received a text message earlier, same as the strange e-mail before and it's best for us to head back. Agent McKain, stay alert."

Alex looked at him in confusion, while Cedrick stared into the distance as they entered the central business district. The car came to a halt at a red traffic light, and as he glanced at the digital advertisement on a two-story building, it has a strange phrase:

"From certain to uncertainty but there are times that uncertainty will be certain, and equinox shall appear to reign for eternity."

Then came another one, and he turned to the driver and the other agent behind them.

"Did you see that, mate?" Cedrick asked, gesturing towards the large screen. As the phrase shifted, Osmond experienced the same sensation he had felt earlier that morning. He then glanced at Alex who also appeared puzzled by what they had witnessed.

"I am no titan so obviously I am not connected to humans from numbers to letters, but mankind is skeptical whenever my name is on the table."

In just a few seconds, everyone on a specific street heard a deafening explosion in the distance. The people on the road were screaming and fleeing in all directions, completely overwhelmed by panic. The catastrophic blast was so powerful that it shattered the windows of nearby buildings. Meanwhile, a flock of birds can be seen by flying away from the area, seeking safety from the affected areas. Osmond and Cedrick quickly became alert, fully aware of where the massive explosion had occurred. It was one of the de Ayala buildings in the central business district! Without hesitation, Osmond pressed the microphone button.

"This is Agent Gomez; "Precious" is compromised! We are in an emergency situation! We need a backup now!" Osmond shouted loudly and he pulled out his gun and Cedrick retrieved his firearm while still looking outside and they both became more alert. Until the entire vehicle was shaken when a Mercedes Brabus Rocket P900 struck the Range Rover Sentinel, and bullets rained down on their vehicle.

As the police officers stationed at the nearest corner were fired upon by a group of men inside a vehicle, they called for backup after witnessing an explosion from three blocks away. Meanwhile, the rest of their colleagues throughout the city were already trapped by the armed group, rendering them unable to assist in the impending rescue as the attack commenced.

"Barron, fall back!" Osmond shouted as bullets pummelled their car. It now became clear why he had a lingering suspicion when they left de Ayala's residence and now the situation of danger justified his intuition while the black Mercedes Brabus still blocking their path, while bullets continued to pour down around them.

"Ms. Alex, get down!" Osmond shouted as yet another assailant emerged from the rear, prompting Alex to comply without hesitation. He then had to open the car door to shoot their aggressors. From the front seat, Cedrick locked in a gun battle, relentlessly shooting at the black SUV.

Alex was in disbelief, feeling like she was trapped in an action movie rather than real life. Yet here it was, an intense reality marked by the explosion and their desperate escape from relentless adversaries.

"Sir and ma'am, we need to evacuate this building as soon as possible!" One of the bodyguards urged as the couple huddled inside the panic room. Meanwhile, the other bodyguards outside were exchanging gunfire with the attackers. The scene was chaotic, with the lifeless bodies of employees, security guards, and assailants strewn about, along with various items shattered by bullets.

"My daughter, Enrique! What happened to her?" Evangeline cried, clinging to her husband.

"I can't unlock my phone!" Enrique shouted, and when Evangeline grabbed her phone to use it instead , she faced the same issue as her husband.

Osmond unleashed a barrage of gunfire as Barron tried to maneuver the car behind them. He then focused on the driver, ultimately striking him in the chest, which made him stagger back until his vehicle crashed into a lamppost. Following that, Osmond fired at the car's hood, resulting in a deafening explosion. The Brabus Mercedes became his new target as part of his mission to aid Cedrick.

Only one pursuer remained, and rather than heading towards the Melbourne Central Business District, they found themselves trapped in a lane across the street without a moment's pause, they accelerated away when Barron saw an opportunity to the nearest alley resolute in his commitment to safeguard their boss from the adversary.

"Cedrick, my parents!" Alex cried out, her voice filled with tears. She was certain that they were also in danger at that moment. As Osmond's gun emptied, he swiftly replaced it with a fully loaded magazine and resumed firing at their adversary. However, at a nearby corner, a car unexpectedly emerged, blocking the Brabus Benz. This unexpected turn of events brought Osmond a moment of relief, only to be short-lived as a man in all black alighted from the vehicle and proceeded to shoot the driver multiple times.

"Follow the black Range Rover Sentinel 777 towards Bolte Bridge. Eliminate the two bodyguards but spare Ms. Alex. The boss wants her alive," Darek commanded to the interlocutor wearing the headset while watching the moving car they were chasing.

"Cedrick! My parents!" Shouted by Alex again, then at that time, she saw he was now looking at her then glanced at Osmond.

"Agent Gomez! I'll get down to rescue them!" Then the driver promptly pulled the car over to the side of the road.

"Osmond, look after our boss. I'm going to rescue her parents. I trust you to keep her safe. I'll call you once they're secure," he swiftly exited the vehicle and spotting a motorcycle approaching, Cedrick tried to signal it to stop, but the rider showed no intention of halting. In response, Cedrick raised his hand with his weapon pointing at the motorcyclist.

"I'm an officer of the law!" Cedrick shouted, prompting the rider to stop abruptly. He jumped on, and they sped toward Collins Street. Cedrick's heart pounded as he clung to the back of the motorcycle, the wind rushing past him in a frantic blur. His mind was a whirlwind of urgency and determination, fuelled by the desperate cries of Alex echoing in his ears.

Only one pursuer was left, and they knew they had to get out of there fast. Instead of heading towards the Melbourne Central Business District, they found themselves in a lane on the other side of the street. Without hesitation, they sped off, determined to protect their boss from the enemy.

Alex got the chance to check her phone and by surprised, there was a lot of missed calls from her parents and Elissandra on the screen until when she tried to enter her passcode but to her dismay, the screen was freeze, then Osmond's phone rang, it was their commander.

"Agent Gomez, are you guys okay?" Osmond could feel his extreme concern on the other line.

"Sir, I'm alright and I am doing my best to protect Ms. Alex against those people."

"Great, and based on updated report, her parents are inside of the panic room of building, they are trap, but the Special Operations Units were now on their way."

"Sir, agent McKain is on his way now to the main office to get them!"

"Good, I'll contact him, bye."

While the armoured vehicle was now heading to a specific direction, but then a man inside of helicopter rapidly shooting it by machine gun and the countless gunshots echo along the road, a grim reality for those nearby. Onlookers from the inside of the building while under the table feel sympathy for the victims while running, then buses swerve frantically to avoid being caught in the crossfire. Sadly, some individuals are struck, and others died on the road due to their critical gunshot wounds. Following the turmoil in the city, another phrases appears on the screens.

"Vengeance is always inevitable, like death. Don't let your guard down, and so am I."

"When someone is hungry, an attack can be as fierce as a shark on a wounded target."

Amidst the relentless pursuit by both the enemy and law enforcement, Alex and Osmond navigated the city with a combination of desperation and determination. Each alleyway and corner seemed to breathe with menace; the pressure of impending captures a constant weight on their shoulders, as the newcomers showed from left and right of the alleys then another series of gunfires against them, until Barron's voice can be heard after the visibility of his blood was now dripping under his uniform.

"Oh my god, Barron!" Alex shouted.

"I am alright Ms. Alex, I can still manage to drive, I am not just a driver, but to protect you is also part of my duty."

"No, please let us take you to the hospital!"

"Alex, get down!" Osmond shouted as she was about to check the driver.

"Ahh!" Barron shouted, he was shot again, for the second time.

Despite the motorcycle riders' unwavering resolve to complete their mission, their fellow colleagues continued to provide cover fire from special forces. Meanwhile, the road was nearly impassable due to the chaos of gunfire, and news of the large-scale attack in Melbourne rapidly circulated globally, with international media already reporting on the shocking event.

Elissandra was watching a local news at that time and she quickly covered her mouth as she was watching, then shook her head.

"Oh my god, this is horrible, so inhumane." And she sat down on the couch and turned up the TV volume became even more worried about her best friend.

"Here now live in Melbourne's Central Business District there is no clue who's behind of these massive attack in metropolitan area. But there is a certain target of this group. The Enrique's family and their business empire." Suddenly, the clip featured a series of video explosions associated with the de Ayalas and the screen shifts to the face of the reporter. And the Australian Coast Guard has just released an updated news update. A large cargo ship in the Timor Sea has been involved in an explosion, they confirmed that the ship was bound for Japan, containing products from the business of Mr. Enrique. Back to you, Valerie."

"Thank you for the live report Julie. And we will be shortly and please everyone keep safe. God bless Melbourne, and our nation."

At the vicinity where the Gomez couple were staying together with Osmond's siblings and their families, Celine was started to look at her husband after watching the live report.

"This is what I am really scared of, Martin. I knew it! I knew it!" Then she slam the main door.

"What do you mean you knew it?"

"I had this feeling, remember? While we were on our way here?"

"Do not let that fright drives over you Celine! I really trust our son that he is capable enough to handle this, and the special forces are helping them." Then he hugged his wife to make her feel that everything will be fine.

"Barron , you must go to the hospital. Your arm is bleeding heavily. Please, save yourself?" Alex glanced to the driver with so much worry in her.

"She is right Barron!" Osmond said after firing back at their pursuers and he managed to hit two of them, and while their numbers had been growing, they were now dwindling, courtesy of law enforcement officers arriving in their vehicles. With only a few bullets remaining in his gun, Osmond focused intently and fired again. Almost the last shots from his weapon struck the remaining attackers. Osmond's mind raced as he turned to the driver, who was speeding down the road.

"Save yourselves. You might run out of blood. I can take care of her," Osmond said and rested his hand on his shoulder.

"Are you sure, Osmond?" Then he looked at the heiress.

"Ms. Alex?"

"Barron yes. Do as we say, please?" She couldn't bear to just watch their driver will soon running out of blood and die, then the SUV turn into another alley.

"Alright, Osmond don't take me to the hospital. What matters is, you would take our boss away. I can get to the hospital by myself." He got out of the car while one of his hand resting on his left wounded shoulder. Osmond hurried to the driver's seat and took off. As he drove, he gave a bulletproof vest to Alex that he had seen earlier in the back seat.

"Put this on."

Alex nodded, understanding its significance and hoping that Cedrick would reach out to Osmond promptly after rescuing her parents.

Yet, unbeknownst to them, Darek watched from a hidden vantage point, his lips curling into a confident smile as he retrieved a high-caliber weapon from its secure case.

"Let's see if they can handle this," he murmured to himself, the metallic clink of ammunition sliding into place echoing his resolve.

And now, Osmond quickly spotted a man who appeared to be the leader from SUV and armed with a heavy weapon—a bazooka. Instantly, he accelerated the vehicle, reaching speeds of over eighty kph. He had a strategy to avoid being struck by the bazooka. Unwilling to risk whether the Sentinel could withstand the hit, he decided to execute the plan he had devised.

The car hurtled down the asphalt, its speedometer needle quivering at almost a hundred kph, as Osmond's sharp eyes caught the menacing glint of a mini rocket arcing through the air, instincts honed by countless high-stakes chases kicked in, prompting Osmond to slam the brakes with a force that sent the vehicle skidding. The rocket-streaked past, missing them by mere inches, and collided with a towering truck ahead, triggering a cataclysmic explosion that painted the sky with flames. Inside the car, Alex, tightly strapped by her seatbelt, felt her body lurch and shudder from the abrupt halt, her senses reeling amidst the cacophony of the truck's fiery demise. The world seemed to pause in a disorienting tableau of smoke, heat, and adrenaline, as they absorbed the narrow escape from disaster.

"Osmond! Where are we heading now?!"

Darek was in dismay as he saw how he missed the target; this was the first time he meets this kind of adversary; the driving skills are capable enough to challenge them. Until he heard the incoming call from their boss.

"What's the status there?"

"My apology but my team is having a hard time to finish the task." He answered after pressing the button.

"Then, keep going!"

"Sure, sir!"

The bazooka's missile narrowly missed the SUV for the second time, striking the giant crane, which then fell onto several parked cars, including a truck carrying a gas cylinder at the rear, leading to a catastrophic explosion. Darek saw the tragic loss of several members of his team as they perished in the massive blasts, with some being hurled onto the footpath while their motorbikes spun wildly in the centre of the main road due to the sheer force of the impact.

Despite the major communications was not able to function, the authorities managed to relay messages to their comrades using their advanced earpieces. Lucas, however, felt content with the situation as the entire de Ayala family had lost contact, according to his source. He sat in the centre of the room, flanked by floor-to-ceiling glass walls. In front of him was a grey oak executive boardroom table with chrome accents, displaying a complete 3D map of the city. Wearing also a headpiece, he marked every update from his team with a red marker and highlighted a specific building then he commanded the two specialist to cover their team on the ground position.

Meanwhile, his assistant was actively pursuing Alex and her bodyguard. Snipers were now positioned in the area to assist the ground team in capturing the de Ayala couple, but they faced challenges penetrating the interior due to additional government special forces. An alternative, more sinister plan crossed his mind if his assistant failed to secure the main target within half an hour.

As Cedrick made his way to rescue Alex's parents, the Director-General reached out to him, instructing him to meet another agent near their extraction point, just two blocks away and he witnessed a brutal exchange of gunfire between elite government forces and a group of private armies clad in sophisticated black gear, while their allies donned in a dark blue uniforms. Alex's parents were in grave danger, and he observed some of his comrades being taken out by snipers positioned on rooftops of two nearby buildings as he scanned the area. He double-checked the situation and realised he needed to act quickly to eliminate the threat. An idea sparked in his mind as he glanced at his companion.

"Distract them; I need extra time to set up an ambush," Cedrick instructed before moving towards his first target. He surveyed the surroundings, determined to reach the top of the building without being detected by the two snipers, then they both nodded to each other before he left. He was lucky to reach the first building and grateful for the vehicles and street bins that provided him cover. He quickly composed himself and opted for the stairs since the elevator was out of order. After ten minutes of hurrying to the location, he cautiously opened the single door and spotted him, every step he took was deliberate to avoid making any noise. Then he noticed him poised to pull the trigger; and a playful tactic came up to his mind before he finally reveal that he was not alone in that spot.

"Hey man, are you enjoying killing my comrades from this vantage point? Then, taste this!" He smashed his head with the gun after he swiftly seized the rifle from his hands and shot him in the head. He then quickly grabbed the earpiece to contact the other sniper, who was positioned less than two hundred metres away.

"Any updates?" Cedrick asked.

"I'm having trouble finding a perfect viewpoint on the intruder."

"Oh, that sucks mate," he responded. "Can you see where I am now?" He commanded, then he pulled the trigger when he saw the other sniper adjusted his scope towards his position. It was a perfect shot to the center of his head, and he casually left the rooftop, radioing the other agent that he had successfully eliminated both snipers.

As the elevator doors slid open, the two men aimed their gun at them, but they swiftly retaliated with powerful punches. And a straight kick from Cedrick's right foot struck the man's belly, while the other agent expertly twisted his opponent's elbow, effectively subduing him as he witnessed the extreme pain on his face. With a decisive move, he knocked him out. They both exchanged a nod and pressed the button for their desired level.

"What's the situation?" Lucas asked as he pressed the button, glancing out the window to witness the chaos unfolding in the city.

"Sir, it's confirmed! They lost track of Mr. and Mrs. de Ayala when they reached the panic room."

"Are you all incapable of retrieving them? What happened to the two snipers?"

"Sir, I regret to inform you that they have been eliminated."

Lucas chose not to ask any more questions; instead, he ended the call, running his fingers through his hair in frustration as an idea began to form in his mind. Just then, one of his men in the room spoke up, maintaining his position at the nearby table adorned with a lampshade and a flower vase, with an intercom situated in the center.

"So, sir, why didn't the helicopter eliminate the couple inside their building with a bazooka? While the other is pursuing the daughter and her bodyguard?"

Lucas remained silent. Instead, he glared at him then a smile crept across his face. Everyone was taken aback when blood splattered onto their suits and finally onto the floor, as his katana swiftly pierced the abdomen of the one who proposed the idea.

"I really dislike being told what's best for my plans and what actions I should take! Clean up this mess! I have more important matters to attend to." He smiled again, his eyes fixed on the main door of his well-equipped room.

"Agent McKain, I sincerely appreciate your prompt rescue efforts, and to you also." the Patriarch stated, glancing at his wife, who was being consoled by his female assistant. At the same time, he summoned the leader of his private army to find his daughter by using a tablet.

"Subject AB are now both secured." Cedrick reported to their commander, then he nodded at the father of Alex. "This is merely a matter of course, Mr. de Ayala. Our sworn obligation is to rescue individuals from the clutches of malevolence." Then he saw the other agent gave an earpiece to the patriarch.

"Excuse me, agent McKain I have to talk with your commander."

"Yes, General?"

"Mr. Enrique, I extend my sincere apologies for the unfortunate events that transpired. The Prime Minister and I are actively engaged in devising a comprehensive plan to restore order and we are diligently investigating the perpetrators of this heinous act. In the interim, I have dispatched more elite military forces to provide protection for you and your wife."

"Thank you very much, General. However, I am deeply concerned about my daughter."

"And to that, I also sent a reinforcement for them as agent Gomez is doing his best to protect your daughter, and I will give you a constant update, Mr. Enrique. So, for now I have to speak with our leader and I'll call you later."

"Got that General. Thanks a lot." When the call ended, he glanced at his wife's assistant.

"Prepare a video camera and relay my message to the media," Enrique expressed in frustration, his mind seething with rage as he concealed his emotions. The woman took the tablet from him and nodded in agreement, before he began to speak.

"This is an act of war. You initiated this conflict, and now I will bring it to an end. No matter who you are, my men will track you down. I will not tolerate the slaughter of innocent lives! And do not ever lay a hand on my daughter! If you have the courage, confront me, and we will resolve this. Just tell me the time and place, and I will not retreat." When the recording ended, he approached his wife to offer her comfort and the video circulated rapidly, and Lucas caught it on television. He switched it off and spoke in a gentle tone.

"You're doomed Enrique. I will ensure that nothing remains of you." He gestured to one of his men and approached him.

"He's becoming increasingly frustrated, and I find it amusing," Lucas began.

"And I will repay him with interest," he added with a grin. "Bring me the video recorder." He then switched off the main light in the room, allowing the lampshade on the table to cast a glow over half the space while he waited for the suited man to return with the device.

"It's ready, sir," prompting Lucas to begin speaking from his chair.

"Enrique, Enrique, I truly apologise if I've made you feel this way, but I am quite sure that you and everyone on your side will completely grasp my perspective at this moment," he stated, his eyes went more serious, filled with deep emotion.

"Do you still remember your brother? Are you fully aware behind his death? Because of that, I have endured a life of misery that words cannot adequately describe. Greed!" Lucas stated resolutely, then began to stride towards his sword, which was resting in the Katana Kake, all the while avoiding the camera's gaze.

"Evangeline, let my message to your phone tell you about your husband, and for you, Enrique, will you tell your wife the truth? And let this sink into your mind, Enrique, take everything what I have now and bring back what I have lost before. Now, do you remember them?" Tears streamed down his face as his eyes revealed a profound mix of pain and loss. For those who knew him well, it was the first time they had seen him so vulnerable, and he glanced at his priceless possession, the katana while the man continuing to record the video then he gracefully took the weapon, and by his swift foot stance and timing, the end of the blade was now pointing to the lens of the camera while his head shaking slowly in pain. Then the clip was ended, cutting the worldwide broadcast and leaving Evangeline to confront her husband—sure to ignite a chaotic mess between them then by his phone he sent the message to Evangeline with attached documents that contained of his claim against Enrique.

Twenty Eight

The Fall of Empire Part Two

The entire room was filled with shock and disbelief as they caught a glimpse of the man's half face behind the camera. Evangeline, filled with confusion, turned to her husband, while Cedrick struggled to maintain his composure after witnessing the unsettling scene on television. At that moment, his primary focus was fulfilling his sworn duty. Suddenly, they heard a familiar voice—it was Enrique's wife, Evangeline.

"I don't know what to say, Enrique, but one thing is certain. I thought I really knew you from the very first day of our marriage. But now, I see that was a horrible mistake!" As she spoke, everyone had seen the matriarch's eyes welling up with tears as she moved closer to her husband.

"It was just an accident!" Enrique responded, trying to soothe his wife. He reached out to embrace her, but she pulled away.

"Really, Enrique? Lucas would never end up in this kind of madness without a valid reason!" Her voice echoing until the matriarch's phone beeped that caught everyone's attention. When Evangeline glanced at the screen, realisation dawned on her. She gradually shook her head, and the sheer shock on her face sparked curiosity among the onlookers about what she had seen. Handing her device to her husband, she slapped Enrique back and forth, all the while continuing to shake her head in disbelief.

"You are a monster! I can't believe this! Why Enrique? Why?!!" The woman burst into tears once more, pounding her husband's chest in anguish, oblivious to the onlookers around them. Meanwhile, Enrique stood frozen, rendered speechless by the shocking message he had just read.

"Evangeline, please! Enough already! I repeat, it was an accident! If I had known, I would never have done anything to lead to such a disastrous outcome, which is an absolute chaos!" Enrique implored his wife until they were interrupted by their confidante, who was holding her phone, and soon everyone could hear a voice blaring from the loudspeaker.

"He is correct; it was indeed an accident. Even though I don't have any fondness for you, I must admit that you are telling the truth. Your greed has led to my anger! Enrique, I have experienced the profound pain caused by your avarice, and as a result, the void within me will remain forever, and I will show that Enrique, take my life now as you have taken the lives of all that I cherish! Otherwise, I will be the one to strip everything from you! You need to make a decision today, as I am presenting you with a choice! I have endured suffering for many years, and there was a moment in my life when I wished my grandfather had never found me, so I could have finally perished that night. And now, I am setting your empire ablaze!" Lucas shouted before ending the call, and at that moment, he finally discovered how to identify the unknown bodyguard, and to track the new location of Enrique and his wife. He desires a grand reunion for the entire family, with a shocking surprise, he then dialed a specific number from his phone.

"Good afternoon, Mr. Prime Minister!" Lucas greeted him in a malevolent smile and waved his hand.

"What do you want?" The man asked when saw Lucas on a video call.

"Wow, I like that! You are quite the prominent political figure. So, you know what I desire," Lucas replied.

"I don't believe I can provide that."

"Then that's fine. I also have your wife's number, and also to the rest of your cabinet member to share your dirty little secret." He smirked as he recalled the day he saw the country's leader with his mistress.

"Please, don't put me in this position!"

"Then give me what I want!" Lucas exclaimed, running his fingers through his hair in frustration for the second time. "Remember, your reputation or my wrath?!" He ended the call, confident that the Prime Minister would soon succumb to his demands.

It was now past mid day as the police officers and the rest of the team securing the perimeter of the area, the influx of rescuers is increasing due to the overwhelming number of casualties visible on half of the television screen. Firefighters are also engaged in a critical mission to prevent the fire from spreading to nearby unaffected buildings and to rescue civilians trapped inside and followed by a panoramic view showing the extensive damage to the city, accompanied by billowing black smoke rising from the ground and buildings.

"I am here once again to provide an update on the latest events occurring in the CBD. Currently, I am with a victim who has been searching for his family since they were separated when the terrorist group initiated the first explosion. Sir, what message do you have for your family in case they are watching this from somewhere out there?" The microphone shifted to the front of the man, whose shirt and jeans were soiled with ashes, and his hair was in disarray.

"Ruth, I hope you and our daughter are both safe. I have charged my phone, so please call me to let me know that you are finally safe. This is the only way I can find peace once I receive a call from you." The man then struggled to maintain his composure, shaking his head and beginning to cry. Before the news anchor could speak again, the man shouted.

"This is the outcome of his perilous plan! Mr. Lucas, if you are watching this, you are worse than any other evil person! The number of victims throughout the city is utterly unacceptable! We will never forgive you, and we deserve to feel this, which is to hate and condemn you!" The man then attempted to take a deep breath as one of the media personnel approached to console him, offering a bottle of water, until the screen of huge advertisement from nearby displaying a new message.

"The untimely demise of innocent people that matters to me needs justice, while the responsible for it was free for so many years and wielded a vast amount of power within the corporate world. I shall inflict an immeasurable amount of suffering upon him!"

"The aftermath of my wrath are pointless and meaningless way of life for them. Thus, it is not futile for me, but glory!"

Then, following the message, an indescribable malevolence of laughter engulfed the screens throughout the city until they disappear.

"How may I assist you, Mr. Lucas Emsworth?" Addison inquired, referencing the unexpected call he had received less than thirty minutes prior from the CEO of AE Company. The number had been unfamiliar on his phone, but he had answered nonchalantly, thinking it might be one of his colleagues. To his astonishment, the caller identified himself and provided an address where he could formally disclose the complete details of his scheme.

"That's what I require from you, and I'll reciprocate in kind," Lucas responded while scrutinising the man in front of him. Dressed in a plain black long-sleeve shirt, complemented by grey fitted track pants and running shoes, the man offered a smile. It appeared to be an ordinary grin, yet upon closer examination, Lucas detected a sinister hint in his demeanor.

"This mission is quite serious and carries a significant cost. To be honest, I never realised you were the one orchestrating these events," Addison remarked, gazing intently at the man he was conversing with.

"A steep cost? Not an issue, especially since your organisation's name is quite fitting; 'World's Top Assassins.' Therefore, as long as one of your elite members can take out Ms. Alex's two bodyguards, along with the rest of their allies, I'll be able to obtain what I desire by tomorrow," Lucas responded. He then asked for a portfolio from Addison's organisation. Three individuals piqued his interest. He was already acquainted with a sniper, but this particular sniper, known as 'The Expert,' had a range of skills. Lucas kept perusing the file on Addison's mobile device.

The sniper's codename "The Expert" execute the mission in broad daylight, anywhere while the other "Hooded Pitohui" is possessing a devastating execution for the mission since this one can fulfill the task anywhere, anytime and the number of victims could reach hundreds or thousand of people including high ranking officials. The two of world's top assassins is a figure shrouded in mystery, operating with unmatched precision and skill that sets them apart from any ordinary killer. These assassins embody different shades of lethality—one a master of public execution, the other a harbinger of mass devastation—each leaving an indelible mark of fear and infamy in their wake." Then he nodded; the two of them are enough. Then he saw a code name "The Umbra" but then no specific details, but the name itself really captivated his eyes then he looked at the man in front of him, the way he looks at him was fully enough that he was seeking an answer.

"However, Mr. Lucas, as I have mentioned, both the Hooded Pitohui and The Umbra are no longer active as their resignation was finalised a month ago," Addison stated.

"Are there any restrictions?" His expression revealing a touch of disappointment.

"To be honest, Hooded Pitohui and I never talked about it; however, The Umbra is permanently inactive for a very valid reason," Addison responded, looking at the man in front of him, it was evident that he was determined to do whatever it takes to secure something for this event.

"Then give it your all. I can hardly envision satisfying my wish without witnessing the Hooded Pitohui's participation in this event after having missed The Umbra," Lucas replied.

"Let me convince the Hooded Pitohui." He then made a call from the phone Lucas had given him.

She was watching the live news when her phone rang. Taking a deep breath, she answered the call. The way he pronounced her name made it clear that a mission was underway, and she was right.

"Okay. Give me a moment to think and I'll call you back as soon as possible." Then the line was ended, then she meticulously considered her next steps; the first thought that came to her mind was none other than "The Muñeca," the most formidable of them all. She then waited for the second call before she could finally carry out the mission, but when she informed her first colleague, the response was so enthusiastic that they were eager to join the mission.

Martin was curious about the identity of the unknown caller, yet he chose to answer the call to quench his curiosity.

"Hello?" He started.

"Martin Gomez, pay close attention, as the world's leading assassins are on their way to eliminate the 'Combat Duo.' I can't say who they are, how many there are, or what their skills entail, but upon hearing this terrifying news, I risked my life to inform you." Then the call abruptly ended. Martin quickly formulated a plan to secure his wife and the other Osmond siblings in a safe location he was familiar with before proceeding to his next move, which was to aid his son. Overwhelmed with fear for the combat duo, he realised it had been more than a decade since he used his skills and experience as a marine. However, that did not imply he was incapable of neutralising any threats now. He seized his USMC Marine Corps Knife, ready to embark on the most dangerous mission of his life. For him, the notion of risk no longer evoked fear; rather, it ignited his bravery and his most lethal strike to assist his son and Cedrick!

"Hello everyone! I sincerely apologise for what has transpired today, but I must clarify that it is not entirely my fault. So, the public demands an explanation? Let the matriarch take charge on my behalf. As I prepare to sign off, there is one more thing! The final act, a curtain-raiser!" Then, once more on the advertisement screens, a video of a man appeared, causing everyone to cover their mouths in disbelief at what they were witnessing. Some were horrified to see the armless man, with both of his eyes missing, having been amputated.

Lucas then stated, "he's also paralysed and deaf. Enrique, I recall those moments from the past; were they truly evil? No! Not at all! It is time for all of you to see what a real demon looks like! Do you still remember him, Enrique? Oh, and last but not least, money is the most detrimental human invention; it turns people evil and leads them to suffer in hell. Right, Enrique? Hahaha!" The clip then came to an end.

"He is completely out of his mind!" Evangeline shouted, unable to hold back her tears as her thoughts drifted to her daughter. She approached her husband to slap him once more, but Enrique managed to grasp her hand before she could strike again.

"Enough of this, Evangeline! For heaven's sake! Do you really think I don't care about her? Huh?! I do! I am the head of this family, so never assume otherwise. I am trying to figure out how to resolve this chaos!"

"Oh absolutely! You must! After reading everything in the texts, I can't fathom how you can deal with that situation! Lucas is furious! Can't you see the turmoil in the city? Do you believe you can stop him without help from the authorities? No, Enrique! Instead of our daughter, I wish it were you been chasing not her!"

"Our daughter, Evangeline! She is my flesh and blood too! Don't forget that!"

"Then, put a stop to this! I can't fathom what I might do to you if..." Evangeline's voice faltered, and she chose to sit down once more, her body shaking as tears streamed down her face. After a brief pause, she turned her gaze back to her husband. "Just do the hedge of your bets Enrique and I hate saying the word what I am really afraid of. Please, do everything you can to save our daughter!"

Enrique came to his wife and hugged her to express how regretful he was for what he had done before that lead to this chaos.

Osmond recalled the training he had undergone previously; it was incredibly challenging. Fortunately, his father had taught him how to create his own traps, which turned into a vivid sequence of memories as he searched for a safe spot. When he glanced in a particular direction, something shiny caught his eye—it was a silver cross, though one part was missing. He then set out to find the other half. The concept of a causal chain popped into his head next. He discovered a hook and some string, but it was incomplete. It was just one piece until he located the missing part, and then he noticed a thread nearby, along with a hook. Suddenly, he was back in the present, smiling as he realised, he could bring them to the last battlefield. The bush! A thought of precedence struck him; instead of continuing down the road they were on, he quickly veered onto another lane, causing Alex to look at him in shock as her head nearly collided with the dashboard.

"My god Osmond! Where are we heading?!"

"Their reconnaissance was done very well. And I am now changing the battlefield."

The two towers are visible amidst a massive, radiant fire: the Eureka and Australia 108, followed by the remaining skyscrapers, with the Melbourne Star Observation Wheel being the last.

"If anyone fails to hand over the heiress, the helicopter will not hesitate to instill fear across the entire city!" The last clip concluded; he recalled Enrique's words before: *"Alex means everything to me,"* and he contacted the helicopter's pilot.

Osmond was now making his way to the suburban area when suddenly, a barrage of high-calibre machine gun fire erupted from a helicopter in front of them. He had assumed the military would come to their aid, but he was mistaken. Bullets were tearing through the windshield of the car. Behind them, the Mercedes Benz Brabus that had been pursuing them earlier was still in close range, while Alex lying face down in the front seat. He needed to eliminate one of the two threats to execute his plan. He rolled down the car window and returned fire at the helicopter. If he could take out the primary target, the pilot, it would make his escape much easier. Osmond fired a barrage of shots at the helicopter, one after another, until one of his bullets struck the pilot, causing the helicopter to alter its course. He then fired another shot, and as he observed the helicopter spiralling towards the road, it exploded with a deafening force.

Osmond disregarded the scattered fire and smoke that would pass by at that moment from the exploded helicopter as he had to carry out his plan.

"Regardless of the circumstances, we need to reach the target and eliminate her bodyguard!" Darek yelled to his teammates.

"Osmond, what's our next move?!"

"Alex, we're in a life-or-death scenario, so you have to trust me more this time, alright? I know what I'm doing," Osmond responded as he paused and noticed the expansive bush area to the left of the road. He quickly devised his plan, recalling his recent training, and a smile spread across his face.

"Routes, areas, reconnaissance-in force and special, the technique of his own decrement against the troops of Lucas!" Osmond said at the back of his mind and he found a spot on the road and halted the SUV after activating the smokescreen.

"We need to hurry!" Alex nodded to Osmond, until the two quickly got out of the car and headed into the woods.

"Sir, my apology but they are gone." Darek stated as he was inspecting and recording a video of the vehicle while the smokescreen was now starting to fade, then he glanced to the other side, and he concluded where they were.

"I am not fond of this type of capability. They managed to survive the assault in the city despite the clear visibility to complete our mission; he completely decimated our first group of troops! Now, I am certain it will be twice as difficult as before."

Lucas nodded after considering Darek's perspective, but it became increasingly thrilling after he received the confirmation about Hooded Pitohui from Addison.

"Continue the search until my top mercenaries will now finally be joining this game—one that offers me a whole new level of excitement," and a wicked grin spreading across his face while the thought of having his favourite, the world's finest beef; the Matsusaka wagyu after the confirmation from Addison a few minutes ago by text message and finally the grandest moment of his plan from very beginning of phase against Enrique, then he forwarded a video showing the SUV along the highway.

"Enrique, consider this as a means to keep you and Evangeline from panicking as I am still evaluating my next steps. Despite the chaos I have unleashed in the city, I am still considerate enough to limit my cruelty."

Twenty Nine

The Sacrifice Part One

As the sun began to set, he heard a distant commotion. The unknown man felt puzzled by the sudden upheaval and knowing he would need rest soon after a long day. A thought crossed his mind: *"I hope no one comes near my place tonight; I truly desire a peaceful evening."* Though darkness starting to envelope the vast area and without any source of light but he remained unbothered. The surroundings were entirely familiar—he even recalled how he had discarded objects that no longer served him, choosing the path where he was now. The memories of his past slowly faded with each passing minute.

A few moments later, intrigued by the commotion and scratching the back of his head, he nonchalantly rose from the hammock and strolled over to discover the source of the persistent noise from afar. And there it was, finally revealed, and he couldn't help but admire the man who had carefully set traps instead of questioning why they found themselves in the bushes fighting for their lives. It was evident that the woman held great significance for him, and there was no doubt in his mind, considering the man's intentional actions from several metres away. A smile crept onto his lips—such dedication was genuinely heartwarming. Caring for someone dear was a considerable responsibility; it required bravery to bear such a commitment. He continued to assess the protector's abilities, observing the accuracy in every step and movement. Soon, he witnessed several intruders meet a brutal and bloody fate—a grim but fitting outcome on such a perilous battleground, where danger lurked at every turn. Then, a familiar sound reached his ears, one he had grown accustomed to over time. Closing his eyes, he let the noise wash over him, —until he realised that a single misstep at this moment could spell his doom. Taking a steady breath, he began calculating his next move. A smile returned to his face. He knew his skills well, and the situation amused him. Reaching into his pocket, he swiftly retrieved an item, mastering its use within a heartbeat. He redirected his focus to the couple, noticing the woman start to scratch her arms. To his surprise, her guardian gently and lovingly inspected her arms, trying to ease her discomfort with care and dedication. Then, he removed his suit and offered it to her to protect her shoulders.

As darkness enveloped the untamed wilderness, he meticulously scattered the snares he had prepared throughout the area. He also discovered a suitable spot for him and Alex to take a break, and he crafted a method to sense any approaching individuals. By using nylon, he connected it between small trees to act as an early warning for him that they were near to them. At the same time, the remaining traps he set were specifically designed to effectively incapacitate any potential threats.

"Osmond, I am so thirsty."

"Don't worry, we'll be leaving soon."

Then Osmond glanced at his cell phone, realizing it was out of battery. He let out a sigh.

"Okay. I just hope the rescuers find us soon," she said as she moved to Osmond's side, resting her head on his shoulder and wrapping her arms around him.

"Don't fret. They won't just come near us. That's my promise to you," Osmond reassured his girlfriend, giving a gentle kiss on her forehead.

Meanwhile, in a certain part of the wilderness, a chilling scream suddenly caught the group's attention.

"Aaaaah!!" One by one, those struck by the unexpected sharp twigs in shadowy areas of the forest reacted. Darek witnessed the horrifying scene, one of his troops was pierced in the neck, while two others were simultaneously stabbed in the abdomen, blood pouring out profusely; a clear signal for them to remain vigilant at all times. A wave of intense fear washed over him, the thought of being the next victim looming large if he let his guard slip, until another scream echoed from the rear of his group.

Then another sound of a moan, echoing the finality of death, while another was also pierced in the chest by a shard of wood. He urged the remaining members to keep moving, uncertain of the whereabouts of the others and why they had vanished. This absence served as a grim indication to him that they were likely dead, especially after his attempts to reach out to any of them had failed. He then witnessed how others fell victim to gunfire from newcomers clad in military uniforms. Fortunately, they had three backups who assisted in eliminating any intruders from the authorities.

According to Hooded Pitohui, all she needed to do was follow their lead once she received the signal, which was a significant advantage for her as it allowed her to steer clear of any potential conflict with their organisation. As far as she was aware, "The Expert" could eliminate her at any moment, given that his skills were for a long-range. However, she could skillfully incapacitate any number of her adversary's joints. This was her true nature, her specialisation lay in close combat. As she meticulously surveyed the area and seeing their Superior joining the operation, a sudden realisation struck her: tonight could very well be her last if things went awry. Hooded Pitohui was indeed correct, and that's why no one could dispute the recognition of its codename as one of the most lethal assassins in the world—strategic and insightful in every mission she undertook. But for now, she had to wait for the go signal to finally start her mission. "Retrieve and leave; take the subject to a safe place." That was the deal between them.

The unknown follower finally caught sight of the two faces for the second time. The man was unfamiliar to him, but he recognised the woman, which brought a smile to his face. However, the man cautioned his companion to stay still as he surveyed the surroundings. Gradually, the moon illuminated the area, and the man became fully alert, continuing to scan the environment.

Osmond felt something that someone was following them and capable enough to handle his traps. Then he quickly drew his dagger from the holster after deciding where he could finally send the sharp object as a warning. Although it was not their enemies-he was sure of that. But the reason for following them was not entirely clear. However, as long as he gave some sign of warning, it was enough.

Soon, the follower witnessed several intruders meet a brutal and bloody fate-a grim but fitting outcome on such a perilous battleground, where danger lurked at every turn. Then, a familiar sound reached his ears, one he had grown accustomed to over time.

On the opposite side of the bush area, Hooded Pitohui and her partner, The Expert, scanned their surroundings with caution. They decided to choose a different direction from Darek's group to simplify their task.

"Hooded Pitohui, please be more cautious; I have concerns about the enemy's capabilities. It's too risky. Many of Darek's armies have lost their lives, which clearly an indication why Mr. Emsworth urgently asked our assistance."

Freya merely nodded in agreement with her companion's warning. They were already there at the location, and if they declined this mission earlier, it would have brought great shame upon their group, as they had never shied away from any perilous assignment. Over half an hour later, the two assassins detected a noise nearby. They exchanged glances and swiftly approached the location of the sound, and they saw the four men had fallen into a deep trap laden with booby traps, until they saw Darek was coming with his remaining troops.

"I can't believe this! And what kind of human he is!" Darek exclaimed. There were only five of his companions left, including their new backup.

"Let's separate again," The Expert suggested, as he was wondering where his father, Addison. As a sudden feeling of caution arose, as at any moment, either of them could be killed by a trap. However, their precise reflexes could avoid such a death.

"If only we had The Umbra, this mission would be so much easier. It's frustrating that we ended up here, and this is the first time we've had a target like this."

Meanwhile, Hooded Pitohui just nodded, assessing the vast area of bush before them.

"We shall take this as an enormous challenge. Remember, the organisation's reputation is incomparable to any other underground group."

"Okay, okay. That makes sense," the Expert responded. At the same time, Hooded Pitohui and The Expert dashed in opposite directions, dodging several incoming traps. Both took a deep breath, feeling the weight of the moment as they scanned their surroundings, only to hear another scream nearby. It had been less than five minutes since the last scream echoed; now, another one pierced the air. Every footstep was meticulously evaluated, and upon inspection, another group of men fell victim to the trap, another booby trap.

"This is for the best, let's separate since we might be the next and I cannot allow that to happen; I must see this plan through. I have anticipated this event, so, The Expert, I apologise, and I trust you can hold your own in this battle." Before moving in a specific direction, they carefully examined each twig, considering its size and weight, knowing it would provide a significant advantage in avoiding any potential deadly traps by using it to trigger the nylon. A smile followed, reflecting the amusement at how they found themselves in this situation.

After Martin alighted from the taxi, he opened the backpack and took the item he needs; a military shirt and camouflage fatigue and to be able to blend himself to the environment by putting a coal on his face.

While on his way, he saw several dead bodies from the traps, and assumed that it was his son, Osmond; as he exactly knew his capabilities to that kind of battle area. He was the one who taught him after he confided to him about the last part of their training and after he taught him how to make deadly traps.

Martin ascended the tree to set up an ambush using his technique. Perched on a large branch, he noticed someone approaching his position. In a swift motion, his sartorial became his support as he hung upside down, head facing the ground. However, he failed to seize the man's neck to twist it, as the target detected his movement. He then leaped from the tree, now armed with his military knife.

"Who are you, and what is your intention in ambushing me?" Ansel asked, biding his time to formulate a strategy to swiftly reclaim his rifle from the ground, which he had inadvertently dropped while evading a critical strike. He had to scrutinise his movements meticulously, as this man appeared to be one step ahead. Based on his looks, he seemed to be in his fifties, and Ansel concluded that he could be easily dispatched; it was truly an unfortunate evening for him. The man exhibited exceptional skills in close combat, an opposite of his own capabilities.

"Only one will survive," Martin stated.

Ansel nodded in agreement. He then prepared himself as best as he could. Meanwhile, the two figures in the distance began to engage in combat.

As the moonlight above grew increasingly bright, the thick clouds gradually parted, allowing anyone to witness the tragic deaths caused by the traps, and the dismembered remains of their bodies scattered in various directions after their agonising screams. Amidst this chaos, a struggle for survival unfolded, and Addison realised that his son was outmatched by the newcomer. His son's arms were bleeding and he was on the verge of exhaustion. Reluctantly, Addison pushed his son away, despite his hesitation to leave.

"Please, son, go! This opponent has far more experience than you do, and I can take care of him!" He shouted as he drew his weapon.

"Dad, please! I can handle this myself!" Ansel replied then he glanced at his injury.

"Now is not the time to argue! This is a mission, and as your Superior, you must follow my order! Leave immediately!" Addison shouted shoving Ansel away. After being pushed again, Ansel finally nodded and walked off. He then turned to face his opponent, quickly adopting his signature fighting stance, his eyes locked on the man capable of causing his son harm.

Martin saw how the man readied himself for their duel, who was also with a military knife. Then, he gave a sinister smile to him as this for sure would be an equal battle between them, so it was exciting for him as they were on the same tier. Then he raised his right arm holding the knife and motioned it towards the middle of his body as his way of warning for his new opponent that there was no time for him to concede at all cost, then his left was ready as well for any open attack while his left foot was already set in motion any time.

Addison knew that his son was capable of defeating this man with his most lethal skill, but this time Ansel met his match, the man who could defeat "The Expert" in close combat.

Addison was the one who started the first attack, but Martin aimed to conclude the duel as he sought to locate Osmond and Cedrick, making their task that night more effective. After dodging, he delivered a powerful kick, causing the weapon to be discarded, and executed a Corkscrew lock successfully. However, Addison retaliated by slashing his opponent's arm with his knife after reached for it nearby. Martin quickly rose to his feet despite the painful injury, and in a swift motion, he positioned his right foot behind his enemy's lower body and pushed him with significant force, inadvertently giving Addison an advantage: he was thrown close to a weapon, which was his son's spare firearm, the .45 caliber gun. With no other option, he had to end the duel. He retrieved the gun and shot the chest while advancing towards him, witnessing the final execution with the USMC Marine Corps Knife, followed by a loud bang.

Meanwhile, Osmond witnessed the entire incident as he heard the particular sound from nearby and rushed towards his dad as quickly as possible.

"Father!!" Osmond realised the gravity of the situation for his father when the moonlight's reflection was particularly bright at that moment.

"D-dad.." he uttered while grasping his hand, noticing his breath was gradually fading away.

"I'm glad that you're safe.." Martin replied, looking at him.

"Dad please.."

"And tell your mother that I truly regret if I cannot return to her. As a father, I had to make the right choice for you." Then his father firmly placed his hand on his shoulder, as his breath was getting more critical.

"Promise me, you will take care of yourself no matter what, and let our family know that I love them dearly." Osmond nodded gently as they exchanged glances, until the painful truth became evident; his father's eyes were slowly closing, and he smiled at him, then the grip on his hand faded away.

"No!!!! Father!!" Osmond shouted, hugging him tightly as his body shook violently bursting with tears.

"So, you are the main protector of the heiress. It's a privilege to meet you here tonight," Addison began.

Osmond remained silent after he softly let go of his father's hand, he then glared at the man filled with hatred, the one responsible for his father's death, and he was determined to demonstrate how he would end him tonight in a brutal way. Gradually, he rose to his feet and prepared himself for their duel.

Initially, Addison wielded the remnants of his weapon, the two sharp iron rods, aiming them at Osmond, but Osmond found it simple to evade those attacks.

Then Addison came to a realisation; this is the most challenging mission I have ever faced. If I were to be defeated by this exceptional agent, it would mean I was truly meant to lead the world's most dangerous underground organisation, as I have proven capable of handling such tasks. I had Hooded Pitohui, The Umbra, and The Expert; I couldn't ask for more. These facts alone are sufficient to earn that title, yet sometimes everything has its conclusion, so I am content with where this journey may take us." Then, he unleashed a right hook followed by a front kick aimed at his opponent, but the agent simply shifted to the side.

Osmond felt assured that he would take the assassin's life that night, having observed his stance and the combination of attacks directed at him was not entirely his best, it was for sure. He recognised that behind that was his father, who had previously made things difficult for him, but now the advantage was in his favour. With this realisation, he began to speak with conviction.

"A simple warning. Surrender, and tell me who sent you here and I will let you live," said by Osmond to the high skilled mercenary then Osmond did not hesitate, as it was his turn. Pivoting on his calcaneus, he delivered a devastating kick to his opponent's chest, the impact reverberating through the assassin's body as the sickening sound of cracking ribs filled the air.

The mercenary staggered backward, his breath ragged, but Osmond didn't lower his guard. "Who sent you?" Osmond demanded once more, his voice was sharp, a stark contrast to the fire burning in his eyes, but the man just shook his head while looking at him.

"I am here to do our mission!" He was prepared to pull the trigger, but the agent threw a weapon to him. It was too late to dodge when he felt the sharp object pierce the deltoid muscle of his shoulder, causing him further damage and weakening his stance. He quickly pulled the trigger for the second time, but his focus on aiming the target revealed to his opponent just how easily he could be defeated.

"For my father!!" After Osmond saw an open attack, he quickly punched the elbow of the man so he wouldn't be able to use his gun as he was already suffering from pain, until he seize his opportunity by swinging low then he quickly slashed the enemy's knees and by a swift calculation, he unleashed a strike by his left knee to the abdomen and by a swift calculation, he was able to slash the opponent's jugular vein, and within thirty seconds, he will suffocate to his own blood and he was the last person seen until his final breath and swiftly returned to his father in search of any useful item to communicate with his comrades. After obtaining the device, he promptly made a call to his commander.

Alex left her hiding spot as the enormous frog leaped nearby, but the sight of the two figures ahead was even more frightening, causing her to hold back a scream while she ran.

"Hooded Pitohui, at last! Haha!" Darek exclaimed, bursting into laughter as he seized their primary target. Along the way, they were taken aback to find Ansel with the remaining two troops, despite being injured.

"Alright, mission completed before midnight." He then updated Lucas, commanding that they must now bring Alex to him.

The Muñeca casually roamed the area when she noticed a group of men meeting their demise in a trap. It was amusing to her how entertaining the situation became, but she knew she had to stick to the plan until she felt a sensation at the back of her head.

"Who are you?"

Instead of responding, she swiftly executed a back kick to his manhood with her right foot, the impact was so severe that his agony was unmistakable. Now was her chance to turn around and deliver the final blow by punching his throat. She needed to avoid drawing attention, as she must not engage in any prolonged battle, just in case Hooded Pitohui signaled her to proceed with her mission.

Thirty

The Sacrifice Part Two

As they entered the hideout somewhere in Warrandyte area, but from the outside it was like an abandon three storey big house, surrounded by wild trees and tall grasses. Darek stepped outside to give instructions to the rest of the team, leaving Alex behind, blindfolded and her lips sealed with masking tape, struggling against her restraints.

She glanced at her once more before moving to the corner, ensuring that any conversation would remain private, and she reflected on their last moments together.

Why did you bring us here?"

"Well, it's complicated, but trust me, it's safe this way," Freya explained to her parents while her siblings remained in their rooms. She had already taken care of everything she needed to do; the final task was to ensure they stayed inside, no matter what. As she awaited confirmation from "The Huntress" regarding her decision, "The Muñeca" stood by, ready to assist her, and everything was unfolding according to her plan.

Meanwhile, someone nearby was observing the situation, and it appeared that Freya truly required her assistance. She recalled a moment from her arrival, wondering, "is this related to the widespread chaos in the city?" Just then, she spotted Freya at the door, embracing several individuals before departing the premises. She was prepared, having turned off one phone that allowed their Superior to reach her, while the extra phone in her pocket was designated solely for her comrade, Hooded Pitohui.

"Huntress, what is your estimated time of arrival?"

"As anticipated, I arrived either on time or early. I am currently in position and prepared to draw my bow if I see anything unusual within the vicinity."

"Thank you very much. Are all lights on?"

"Yes, and keep this in mind: If the Superior completes the mission for Mr. Lucas and discovers this, I will track you down, Hooded Pitohui."

Freya smiled at what she heard from the other end; every member has no boundaries! It's do or die, whether the mission is within or outside their organisation.

"I appreciate that, The Huntress. So, see you. Goodbye."

"Understood. I will ensure that I am deserving of this assignment."

Then she let out a deep sigh. If The Huntress secures the advantage on the battlefield, she could be eliminated at any moment without even realising it. However, she is determined to rely on her reflexes and heightened senses to neutralise the threat. After taking a deep breath, she exited the room upon hearing Lucas's command through her earpiece.

Once they stepped outside the room, Darek began instructing the rest of the team, assigning one man to keep watch over their hostage. In that moment, while Ansel thought of his father and attempted to call him for the third time, but the line just kept ringing. He held onto the hope that his father had survived the traps.

In under ten minutes, the man was fixated on Alex's face, then turned his attention to the already torn dress; he had been waiting for this moment. To fulfill his twisted fantasy, as soon as the three exited the room, he hurried to lock the door.

Alex was in shock when the man began to stroke her face, his gaze filled with a repulsive kind of desire, prompting her to fight back.

The man failed to comprehend the repercussions of his actions when Lucas used the spare key to unlock the door and caught him in the act with the hostage. Without uttering a word, he swiftly approached and with his left hand, yanked the man away from his position. In an instant, a powerful hook kick struck the man's neck while his right hand gripped the katana. Everyone who followed was left in disbelief as they witnessed the man's head soar through the air, followed by the sickening thud when it finally hit the ground.

"If I catch anyone doing the same thing, I won't hesitate to repeat what I did!" Then his gaze fixed on the headless corpse, as blood pooled on the floor and the scent of blood began to permeate the air. Then he continued, "yes, we find ourselves in a position about labelling us as a terrorist, but our primary goal is not to violate a defenseless woman! Everyone in my crew can easily hire a prostitute, so go ahead and do that! But under no circumstances should you ever rape a woman while you are under my command! Is that understood?!" Then his men nodding in agreement and then removed his suit, offering it to Ms. Alex to cover her body. Initially, the heiress hesitated to accept his gesture, her eyes fixed on him as he began to speak.

"Do not expect me to be the one to cover your body. Please, accept this, Ms. Alex." The woman nodded as she took the suit and began putting it on herself. He smiled at her and turned his attention back to his staff.

"Do not provoke me further today, gentlemen! I have already provided two samples." He warned them, then instructed one of his staff, "clean up the mess and bring her food, as I want everyone to treat her like a guest while I continue to evaluate the next plan. I insist on the best treatment for her. She is meticulous with her appetite, so the kitchen has everything she might want to eat." He concluded while observing them, then shifted his gaze to the door then he instructed The Expert and Hooded Pitohui to monitor their hostage and nodded to Darek before they both exiting the room.

Lucas found himself reflecting on that moment, recalling the night he entered the church to seek forgiveness from God. His plans were set in motion, and nothing could quell his impending wrath!

"I deeply regret the destruction and countless lives that may be lost because of my actions. Whatever punishment you deem fit for me, I will accept full responsibility for the consequences. However, I hope you can understand my situation, both then and now. This is my solemn vow: I will never allow any human to force me into submission. Only you, our almighty God, have the authority to punish me. I pray that you protect anyone who dares to obstruct my path." After making the sign of the cross, he rose slowly and exited the church in silence. A smile crept across his face as he recalled the deal he struck with a certain man during their last meeting the previous week. With the aid of advanced technology and skilled individuals, his plans had come to fruition. He had spared the man's life, for a purpose! Then Darek discovered the device, then he smiled while he had already anticipated this as he had devised a plan for the two scenarios. As agent Gomez goes to rescue Alex, the commander of agents will targeting the wrong person; this scenario would be gratifying for him, as he would face the agent in a one-on-one confrontation tonight.

On his way back, Osmond saw Cedrick and they headed to the spot where he had left Alex, but a wave of shock and fear washed over him as he approached the location. Alex was missing in the heart of darkness.

"Mr. Lucas is the one responsible for this chaos," Cedrick said to which Osmond nodded in agreement.

"Honour is walking the talk about morality, then I am on a rescue mission. To protect what matters to me." Then he took his device to check the location of Alex.

Meanwhile, Freya was planning her next step, and she discreetly sent a message to someone. Less than twenty minutes later, a knock echoed at the door.

Hooded Pitohui knew that Ansel had injuries on both arms, and she smiled then leaning in to whisper to the Muñeca.

"Do not make any movement, unless I give you a signal." Then she saw how the other comrade responded by giving her a slow nod then after, a casual look to the man in front of them and greeted him.

"Oh, hello there, 'The Expert!'

"The Muñeca, what brings you here?" Ansel asked, while taken aback.

"Oh, are you not excited that I am finally joining the party?" She grinned, poised to strike at any moment, eager to break numerous joints that night after witnessing the bloody events since before midday.

"So, did you two plan this?" Ansel asked gazing at the two men who had lost consciousness before the door finally shut. They had double-crossed their organisation! Although he was merely an adopted son of the founder of their group; the man who had raised him as if he were his own son! He understood that facing these two members would be challenging then he reminded himself not to let his guard down.

"Please don't as I'm still honouring you two as a comrade, but if both of you will insist that desire, then I have no choice but to eliminate any one of you!" Then he aimed his rifle at Freya's head.

The Expert's first shot missed, and the man was resolute in his intent to take her down. He launched several strikes at her face and stomach with both low and high kicks, but she easily dodged them. Ultimately, she showed him a surprising spinning kick to his injured shoulder, and without hesitation, Muñeca seized the moment to approach Alex to untie her.

"Muñeca, I am counting on you. Please guard Alex with your life." She then took Ansel's rifle, aimed it at him, and instructed him to sit down and bind himself with the rope.

"Oh, sure Hooded Pitohui, I can assure you that." She wrapped her arms around Alex's shoulders to help her walk, and they made their way toward the door. Once they finally exited the room, Muñeca spotted Lucas!

Lucas spotted Alex with an unfamiliar face, and he rushed towards them, sword in hand, fully aware that someone was aiding Alex's escape. However, the distance of over thirty metres made it impossible for him to reach them.

"If I were you, I wouldn't leave this place, or you'll regret the consequences!" Said by Lucas and he called his team by his earpiece, but the stranger paid him no mind. It was too late to intervene as Hooded Pitohui went out from the door, blocking his path. He regarded her with a satisfied nod, realising she was the mastermind behind this escape! Then, Addison must explain this, once he finally arrives after sending him a message.

Hooded Pitohui responded with a gentle nod, fully aware of the potential outcome of her actions. She shifted her right foot back, preparing for her next move. In an instant, she propelled herself into the air, her left foot following to execute a stunning butterfly kick! She swiftly drew a weapon from her waist, unfurling it just before her left foot touched the ground, and launched it towards her opponent.

Meanwhile, Lucas heard the sound of an approaching object and instinctively raised his weapon to deflect it. The projectile veered off in another direction, glinting under the ceiling lights. His eyes widened as it came perilously close, just half an inch from his face, igniting a surge of rage towards the one who had betrayed him.

"Hooded Pitohui, you have sealed your fate tonight, yet I cannot help but admire your unique abilities," Lucas said while pointing his weapon at her, he then shifted into a battle stance that revealed his true nature, but a thought suddenly crossed his mind.

"Cursed that Addison! He never mentioned this kind of skill possessed by his most distinguished group member!" He thought to himself, realising he needed to time his approach perfectly. However, he had to first neutralise the threat she posed with her weapon—the dart rope.

"Feeling like a sweat bullet?" Hooded Pitohui asked after the neck spin, as the man swung the weapon.

"Absolutely! I have to keep an eye on both my front and back with that type of weapon, and to be honest, it's a compliment to you, or should I say; Isabelle Lewis?"

"How did you know that?" The woman inquired, taken aback, her posture shifting as the pointed end of the dart rope dropped to the ground, yet she maintained a piercing gaze on him.

"Because I am Lucas Emsworth!"

"Indeed, and there is certainly no doubt that I am Hooded Pitohui!"

Then Lucas swung his blade to the left, then another set with one hand to the right while turning around followed by a grab with two hands then swing to left and step in then turning around and swing to the right he continued to swing with right hand and raises the sword, and swing to right while lowering left hand and knee, he was surprised after that precise combo, the notorious member uses her weapon against his weapon effectively, then it was the turn for Hooded Pitohui to strike, then when Lucas finally saw an effective counter move, he quickly took that moment; as he finally secured the rope with his sword, he began to twist the weapon and pulled as much as he can but the woman showed a remarkable resistance. He smiled when their eyes met. Eventually, he took the opportunity to grab her, only to be unexpectedly struck by a lethal and devastating blow; it was the scorpion kick! The impact nearly jolted his neck as the attack came perilously close, but fortunately, he managed to dodge it just in time. The force behind it was astonishing; it was a genuinely destructive technique. The intensity of the battle escalated as Lucas fought to counter every unexpected thrust of her sharp weapon. The turning point arrived when he attempted to evade the swiftly approaching object, only to be shocked to find her deadly weapon entangled with his sword for the second time. Before he could respond, it was too late; her next move was executed with such speed that she yanked her weapon away, sending him to fall on the ground. He attempted to retrieve his sword but was hindered by a sudden pain in his right arm. He watched as she twisted downward, prompting him to leap into the air to evade her strike. However, he felt another surge of pain as his left leg was now injured.

Meanwhile, Lucas's adversary took great pleasure in the effectiveness of her abilities, honed through extensive training in that field, which remained undisclosed to her organisation, as they were all cognisant of her ultimate skill. She understood that she required unmatched proficiency with dart rope. Instead of feeling disheartened, Lucas grinned at his injuries; it was evident why Addison had ranked her at the top of his list. That evening, he observed how this world's leading assassin was able to inflict injuries on him, not just once but twice, despite his background as a swordsmith. It was genuinely a privilege to confront such a powerful opponent!

By swinging low then readied his sword at hip thrust up while stepping in, then raising the katana to swing down, then drawing in reverse grip striking high then he turned the weapon around to swing left horizontally, then continued to swing while turning and stepping in same direction then he aimed the left part of chest.

However, the Hooded Pitohui was rightfully struck when the unexpected strike from Lucas after he rolled to recover his weapon then she evaded the rapid and adrenaline-inducing slashes from the sword which created a piercing sound in the air.

"I remember, you eliminated two hundred people at once including several high-ranking officials, what a great prowess to possess, Hooded Pitohui! But those are useful but useless in time when it needed most." Lucas said after piercing the left part of body using his katana. "I don't need any traitor, so I am happy to eliminate you." He whispered, then forcefully pierced his sword deeper until he saw the tip of the blade stained with blood from Hooded Pitohui's back, and he noticed drops of red liquid beginning to fall to the ground.

"Lucas!!" He saw the most malevolent grin he had ever seen.

"Where is Alex!?" He then turned his gaze to the woman wearing a silver mask, delicately caressing the wounded spot, just before he heard a voice coming from the mysterious figure.

"O-Osmond..." The voice he recognised as he looked at her, while kneeling on the ground, revealing the severity of the wound. The voice was familiar, and his eyes widened in shock, freezing him in place as he struggled to articulate his words until he finally managed to utter the name...

"No!!! Isabelle!!" Tears began to well up in his eyes as he rushed towards her and removed her mask.

"Osmond, I am truly happy that you're here." Isabelle began, smiling at him.

"Isabelle... please hold on, okay? Stay put." As he was about to press the button of his earpiece to radioed Cedrick to call an ambulance, then the woman motioned her hand towards his lips as signalling him refrain from it.

"Shh... stop, and it's alright. I'm happy since I achieved something meaningful in life. But I apologise if I have to go. There is a letter, as I already knew the possibility of this which is a reality in life that we cannot avoid. And that is my sacrifice." Then she gently whispered.

"Alex is now finally safe do not worry about her. Since you'll be with her once this is finally over."

After listening to her words, he continued to grasp her hands tightly, gazing into her eyes, and seeing that she was now having difficulty breathing.

"I am truly satisfied that I succeeded to my plan and I love you, Osmond, my dearest friend..." Isabelle smiled gently as she began to fondle his face, then offered him one last smile before finally closing her eyes.

"No!! Isabelle!!" Osmond shouted as loudly as he could upon seeing her eyes finally closed, then he embraced her tenderly.

Thirty One

The Ultimate Battle for Supremacy

"**I**f you intend to do the same to me, come and show me just how furious you can be!" Said by Lucas while his sword was pointing at the agent. As he strolled casually toward the main door, he was filled with excitement at the prospect of witnessing the man's deadly skills, having already taken down the most notorious assassin. The nation's leading agent would serve as yet another trophy in his collection for the evening, should he not be fortunate enough to overcome him.

"Osmond, I can't wait to face you as my next challenger! Please don't make me wait too long, as I'm truly looking forward to this! Hahaha!"

Upon hearing the mockery directed at him, he simply shook his head in silence, his gaze fixed on the woman before him, feeling the profound loss of someone who once held immense significance in his life.

"Isabelle..." he whispered her name softly. Tears streamed down his face as he gently caressed her forehead one last time then kissing it tenderly. After wiping his tears, he took a deep breath and carefully laid her head on the floor. His eyes began to narrow. Now that he knew Alex was safe, thanks to Isabelle's reassurance, he was ready to reveal what Lucas truly desired. It was he who had put Alex's life at risk, and the most painful part was losing the two most important people in his life—his father and childhood best friend. They were gone! The disaster he had caused led to countless casualties! Now, the moment of reckoning between them was now about to happen and no matter the cost, the mastermind had to face justice! He slowly rose to his feet, steeling himself as he stepped outside.

Meanwhile, at a different location, the General-Director gathered his team to search for Lucas, until he received an incoming call.

"Sir, we have found him!" One of the officers reported to the General-Director.

"Excellent work, let's move!" He then signaled to the two officers assigned to a specific mission. Maintain security around the perimeter, from the top to the ground," he commanded. "And you, once we arrive, make sure the basement is secured."

"Understood, sir."

"Yes, sir." The team then moved towards the designated location. However, they were soon met with disappointment; after infiltrating the area, they received a report indicating that Lucas was at a different site, only to find out that the person they had captured was an impostor, then agent Cedrick McKain finally called the commander about their location, mentioning that the heiress of Mr. Enrique was there.

Osmond was standing in front of Lucas, while both glancing at each other, measuring their capabilities and willingness to win.

"You want to know something pal, I'm wondering how long you can keep up with me." Lucas said, pulling his samurai sword from its sleek black wooden case. In an instant, it gleamed under the moonlight as he assumed the fighting stance known as 'Ko Gasumi.' A gentle breeze swept through the area. Meanwhile, Osmond inhaled deeply as they locked eyes, their gazes sharp enough to ignite a life-or-death duel between them, like an obsidian blade; until a playful grin appeared on his face.

"Well, I can keep this up for all night. Just to show you that I'm not a fighter for nothing," he replied and his right hand moving down to the underneath of his slacks retrieving his Bowie knife, followed by a defensive posture. Lucas, however, remained silent, still in his stance, and simply nodded in response.

"Pal, how far can you go for love?" Lucas inquired of Osmond, "remember, I have already taken the life of your childhood best friend, Isabelle! Should I call her Hooded Pitohui instead? Additionally, I've just found out that Alex is your girlfriend. What if tonight is the final time, you see her? I have a plan ready."

"I will fight for her, and everyone associated with her until my last breath, Lucas! Just make sure you can defeat me tonight; if you don't succeed, I promise you will never be able to repeat what you have done!" Osmond responded, the word "pal" stirring up memories from the past, reminding him of how he managed to attend private school all the way through college.

"Oh, what a gallant knight in shining armor! How romantic! But consider this, that type of love has led you to this fate tonight; you are weak, Osmond!" Lucas responded, shaking his head, then the agent smiled at him.

"Indeed, Lucas, I concur. Furthermore, your desire for revenge against Mr. Enrique is also tied to your affection for those who truly matter to you! So, I pose this question to you: are you weak or not!"

"Do not speak to me in that manner! You have no understanding of what has transpired!" He then swiftly launched two strikes at the agent, only to witness how effortlessly he dodged both of his attempts. A realisation finally dawned on him: this man undoubtedly has the stamina for such a unique mission; in fact, two missions. His initial assault on the city unleashed a tremendous chaos, yet the agent succeeded to protect Alex. Consequently, Osmond brought his forces to the bush to eliminate them one by one. This is evidenced by the fact that the country's Central Intelligence has ranked him among their elite agents. But now, the battleground between them is a territory of his own!

"Why are you calling me pal?"

"Huh! Are you really concerned about that term? Does it even matter to you? It was just a random choice!" Then a Jodan No Kamae stance before unleashing a third slash, aimed straight at his opponent's head. Unfortunately, he missed. Following that, he delivered a powerful kick to the stomach, observing the agent's reaction, but his second slash also failed as Osmond quickly ducked, creating an opportunity for the agent to gain the upper hand. He then directed his knife towards the chest but missed again. However, Osmond quickly adjusted his position and struck the lower part of his opponent's leg with tremendous force from his right foot. Seizing another opportunity, he landed a blow on Lucas's right jaw with his elbow, followed by another strike to the opposite side, causing his opponent to stagger from the sheer power of his attacks. Next, he executed a spinning heel kick, perfectly timed to deliver significant damage to the temple area of Lucas's head. To his astonishment, Lucas's sharp eyes were prepared for his next move, and the pain in his stomach made him aware of the distance between them.

Lucas seized the moment to swing the sword from below, then diagonally to his left, followed by an upward swing to the right as he stepped forward. He then executed a turning kick to the abdomen for the second time, followed by reverse grip sword maneuvers, and followed by a katana leg sweep.

Osmond struggled to keep himself agile enough to dodge the unexpected attacks, ensuring that he maintained a sufficient distance to anticipate any surprises, but his incoming movements towards the shoulder and neck with his military knife was ineffective as Lucas unleashed a counter moves against it.

"It's my turn!" Lucas shouted as he stepped forward, striking to the right. He then took a step back to regrip his katana before swinging it across to the right. Ready with his sword, he swept low to the left, pulling the sword back, and then stepped in to thrust at the agent's chest. However, the agent managed to defend against the strike. Lucas then swung low to the left and raised his sword for another attempt.

He swung low from the right, stepping forward before delivering one more high strike, aiming for his target as he recognized the perfect moment.

Osmond felt overwhelmed by the flurry of techniques but was relieved that his reflexes remained sharp after his Bowie knife had been thrown to the ground.

"Never fight back when you don't know how to defend yourself, Osmond! You're wounded! Both emotionally and physically! Just accept it, tonight is your end, haha!" He lunged at the agent again with his sword, fueled by a fierce determination to eliminate the man who had posed so many challenges to his grand plan.

The kick he assessed would be clear enough for him to deliver the next strike once he sees his advances against Lucas, the "rabbit punch." He then rolled on the ground to grab his weapon, and in the blink of an eye, Osmond felt another injury, this time to his right leg. After steadying himself, he quickly slashed his aggressor's right arm twice, back and forth, and then slowly stood up despite the pain.

Lucas was also injured, but in contrast to Osmond, his advances were in his favour. He was certainly getting drain soon at this point, having had to fight his troops before midday.

Osmond needed to keep his reflexes sharp after being wounded in the leg, and he saw the incoming slashes until someone has arrived unleashing a bodyguard combo towards Lucas. When he looked at it, it was Cedrick McKain! He witnessed their opponent nearly being caught by the second strike, a sweeping kick

"Mate, why is this quadragenarian still giving you a headache?" Then Cedrick smirked towards Lucas.

"At last! The Combat Duo is finally complete! One down, and two more to go. I enjoy this, as it allows me to easily eliminate both of you since I no longer have time for foolishness! I seek my revenge on Enrique, but these parasites keep getting in my way! Aha! This will make the game much more thrilling to consume in the end! Hahaha!" Lucas laughed, then directed his sword at Osmond and then at Cedrick.

"I must say, I'm quite impressed that you were capable enough to handle my best mate but without that, him and I against you are definitely even in hand-to-hand combat."

Then Osmond couldn't believe what he heard from Cedrick. Is he out of his mind? There's no place for arrogance here. Cedrick then nodded at him, and they both took their respective combat-ready stances with Lucas positioned in the middle.

"A decisive attack is crucial now; if we fail, one of us is likely to meet our end." He said to Cedrick after evaluating the situation, while keeping an eye on their opponent, then Cedrick's gaze finally settled on the weapon.

"That katana isn't just any sword, is it? I'm certain that's Nagasone Kotetsu."

Osmond was shaking his head slowly upon hearing Cedrick's comment, and he initially deduced that Cedrick had a strategy, which was to divert Lucas's attention! A glimmer of hope ignited in his mind as they now needed to conclude the duel; they had to locate Alex!

"Agent McKain, it is a pleasure to receive such words from you, but my weapon is not your concern!" He then surprised the agent by executing a low swing from above twice, stepping in and raising his sword for a mid-level swing, followed by another strike to the right. The agent's series of backflips provided him with an advantage, Osmond then redirected his gaze at the other agent, furiously shifting his stance to the opposite side before launching another strike to the right. He stepped back to regrip the katana, then struck across to the right once more, readying his sword to swiftly sweep low to the left. He pulled the sword back, stepped in, and aimed to thrust at the agent's chest, but the agent showed his reflexes by blocking with a Bowie knife. Osmond then executed a low left swing and raised his katana for one final attempt. Meanwhile, the other agent took his opportunity to strike but Lucas unleashed a jump spin back kick against Cedrick, landing perfectly as he heard Cedrick's reaction. He then refocused on Osmond, preparing his sword on the left before swinging low to the right with the same precision, stepping forward for yet another mid-level strike.

Osmond's objective at that moment was to position himself close to Cedrick.

"Cedrick, please find Alex," he whispered.

"I was just about to suggest the same, as I could not find her after inspecting the rooms. However, Osmond, I did see Isabelle. What is she doing here? And..."

"I will explain once this situation is over. For now, please locate Alex." Then he pushed him to leave the place.

Lucas was aware of their strategy, and he instructed Darek through the earpiece.

"Secure the area. Locate Alex and eliminate the other agent while I am still dealing with agent Gomez." He then glanced at the agent he was referring with, after Cedrick had left.

A swing low while sliding his back foot then swinging the blade upward followed by diagonally across and he stood up and readied the sword swinging horizontally and continuing while spinning on his front leg and switching his stance behind from starting point while the agent was evading his blade, then until Osmond find an opportunity to disarm Lucas, by kick to his wrist and by swift calculation, he managed his blade to make sure that he can slash the target area in front of him, which was the lower part of shoulder but Lucas was able to strike back by a sharp and forceful punch to his stomach, then he was taken aback while seeing Lucas retrieving his samurai then an aerial cartwheel to avoid the sharp weapon, while in mid air he attempted to execute his last resort, but Lucas was aware about the technique and he forcefully punch his opponent's hand when he managed to dodge, then followed by another slash to the agent's shoulder, when Osmond's set his foot on the ground he felt the extreme pain, while touching the wrist he started to twist his fist. Then he took off his long sleeve when he stood up, he ripped the sleeve into two to prevent the continuous bleeding of his wounds.

"Another slash." Lucas said, then he wipes the blood on his blade by his two fingers while looking at him.

"Surrender, before I make countless slashes to your body!" Then he pointed his sword at the agent and started to laugh.

"Why would I?" He asked. He was now in a crucial moment; any wrong step it could be his demise.

"I will never forget the cause of this everything! Are you aware what Enrique had done to me and to my family? That caused me so much pain until I die! Now kill me, while you still have strength! Or worst, I can do so much that anyone can ever imagine once I succeed to eliminate you! Remember this, God doesn't exist without destiny!"

"Then, let us finish this!" Then he rolled on the ground, and he threw his knife towards Lucas, aiming to his chest; then the target just simply took a sidestep to evade the incoming object.

Until Darek came while they can hear the gunshots from nearby, and for sure it was the other agent, Cedrick.

"Sir, I am sorry, but they found the double about more than ten minutes ago, the General and his team will be arriving anytime soon, and we don't have a choice, but only the plan B."

"We are not done yet." Lucas said while seeing the agent looking at them. "Let's go." He said to his assistant.

"I hope my sacrifice won't be in vain. God, I leave everything up to you." Osmond said to himself in exhaustion, then he fell on the ground and closed his eyes, while the rest of his wounds were continuing to bleed.

The Muñeca eliminated the two men within the security control room, ensuring that all paths were clear as they approached the main entrance to exit the area. Suddenly, a thought crossed her mind, reflecting her nature as an assassin: The Muñeca, and her art of being a seductress.

She instructed Alex to conceal herself in the dark corner and whispered, "do not make any noise or movement, regardless of the situation. There are two of them, and if they manage to kill me, do not flee. Remain here and only leave if you feel secure about your next step." Then the heiress nodding in response, and she proceeded towards them after opening the door with the access card from Freya.

"Who are you?" The man inquired, his gun aimed at her.

"Hooded Pitohui has sent me here as a reinforcement, as the mission remains incomplete. Therefore, I am here to assist and also to amuse the men with firearms." She responded gently, with her playful demeanor towards the two men. With a sweet smile, she then gazed directly into his eyes and subsequently began to raise her arms to stroke the gun, casting another glance at it before looking back into his eyes.

"Oh, what is this? Is this how you ask such a lovely woman standing before you?" She then pouted her lips, which were adorned with red lipstick.

"Oh man. This is thrilling, we are just chilling here inside of this room then look what we've got!" The man said to his companion, lowering his weapon and stepping closer to the woman before them.

"What's your name, hottie?"

"I am Muñeca," she stated, positioning both of her arms on his shoulder, then gradually lowering them to his chest to play with it.

"Oh my, what an unusual name! What does it mean? And please, do not stop as I truly enjoy it! Subsequently, she anticipated his next action. He intended to kiss her lips as he raised his arms to caress her face, but she playfully restrained them while maintaining her gaze into his eyes.

"Oh, hihi! Take it easy!" She chuckled, "and I apologise for not telling the meaning of my name. It is a Spanish term, and it means "doll." She replied while persisting with her strategy.

"Wow, it truly complements you!" The man was preparing to kiss her for the second time when she seized the opportunity after taking the gun from his other hand and shot him directly in the center of his forehead. Subsequently, she discarded the gun onto the ground, and she quickly anticipated the next action of the other man; to shoot her with his weapon. However, she merely smiled at him, followed by a sidestep with her upper body while one of her feet was poised to take him down as soon as she takes the right moment to strike. At that point, she swiftly grasped his hand holding the gun, then promptly executed the kotegaeshi technique, and the man was now finally disarmed and next was an elbow strike from her right hand.

"Damn!! Ahhh!" The man shouted in agony as he attempted to strike her. She merely smiled, for the perfect moment she had anticipated was right before her eyes—a vicious kick to his left toe by her right foot, clad in a combat shoe with a titanium outsole. This time, the victim began to scream loudly, but she was accustomed to it. Next, she aimed for his other toe, followed by several fingers, twisting them simultaneously, and executed another kotegaishe, this time more ferociously, choking his throat with her foot as her final strike. The man struggled to breathe then he finally became unconscious, and she proceeded to her intention before exiting the place.

"Who are you?" Alex asked the woman again.

"I am fulfilling my mission, I kindly request your cooperation, as any possible assailants may pursue us; we are not yet secure in this location." She then extended her right hand to indicate that she posed no threat but rather sought to be escorted to a safer area. After nearly twenty minutes of walking, she estimated that they were now over three hundred metres away from the hideout at which point Alex brought up the need to relieve herself, prompting her to roll her eyes.

"Alright," she said, scanning the surroundings for a secure location, and her gaze fell upon a large tree nearby.

"Go, there. And be quick." She instructed her, observing the woman hastily move towards the tree. Throughout this time, she could hear footsteps approaching from the nearby trees, far from Alex's position, and a smile crept onto her face, another target! While the heiress was preoccupied, she too would keep herself occupied—by eliminating a potential threat!

Cedrick had just arrived in the area and set himself behind a tree. *"Where is Alex?"* Then, he recalled the two men he had seen inside of the security control room, disbelief washed over him as he see them on the ground. One had been shot in the head, while the other has no visible wounds from any weapon, yet the joints of his five fingers were dislocated, along with his elbow and two toes. This was the first time Cedrick had witnessed such a victim, and an overwhelming sense of fear for Alex engulfed him, as it was clear that someone could be targeting her! Just then, he spotted a woman from a short distance and readied himself behind the tree. Upon closer inspection, he realised that she was not Alex, and she appeared to be no ordinary woman; she wore a black fitted long-sleeve blouse, denim shorts that matched her top, and Glasgow boots.

As the woman approached him, Cedrick readied himself. *"This woman is dangerously deadly!"* He thought to himself, observing her as she stretched her ten fingers, cracking them in the process. A smile crossed Cedrick's face; he recognised her as another worthy opponent, much like Lucas! Just as he was preparing to make his first move, a swift kick aimed at his neck came flying towards him. Reflexes kicked in, and he narrowly evaded the strike, missing the target by mere inches. He had not anticipated such a powerful kick! It was evident that this woman was an expert in close combat, as the force of her attack comparable to Osmond's kick. It was clear that the unknown fighter intended to conclude the duel with aggression.

As Muñeca prepared to launch another fierce attack on the newcomer, Alex shouted from behind them.

"Don't! I know him!" With that, she rushed forward to embrace Cedrick.

Thirty Two

Farewell

Inside the clinic, Alex shook her head as Hugo was caught by her mother and their security trying to kiss her while she was asleep.

"Alex, please! You love me too, right?" Hugo pleaded, struggling to resist against the two guards who were pulling him out of her room.

"You are completely out of your mind, Hugo! I will never forgive you for taking advantage of my situation! And you misunderstood how I treat you as a friend!"

"No, I didn't! We have a mutual understanding, don't we?" Hugo insisted, still resisting against the guards.

"Please, leave!" Alex exclaimed, "please, take him away from me." She said to the guards, while her mother comforted her after the distressing experience.

An hour later, Enrique was taken aback when he received a call from Hugo, who wanted to visit him. Enrique agreed, after receiving a call from his wife about the disrespect he had done to his daughter. Even though he had a meeting with authorities and the General-Director about their cooperation with the International Criminal Court to locate Lucas and his assistant.

"Mr. Enrique, you have to see this," Hugo said as he pulled his phone from his pocket, brushing his hair in frustration.

"Hugo, please, not now. As you can see, my family is in serious trouble!"

"Listen! The man you trust so much is actually an asshole! I thought we had an agreement."

"Then don't speak to me like that! We don't have an agreement!" He then pointed his index finger at Hugo. Seeing Hugo smile sparked his curiosity.

"What are you doing here?" Until the man placed the device on the table, and Enrique picked up the phone to understand what he was talking about. Enrique then was in disbelief the two in the photo: his daughter and agent Gomez were holding hands, with Elissandra also visible in the background. He abruptly set the phone down on the table, overwhelmed by yet another unexpected revelation. He had already been carrying too much since yesterday, and this truly shocked him, especially coming from someone he trusted deeply, second only to the General-Director.

"I can't believe this..." he whispered. "So, why didn't you show this to me before?"

"It no longer matters. All I desire is to love and care for your daughter. After that one mistake? They never gave me the chance to share my perspective! So, I'm finished here. Osmond and I are finally even. In fact, you and I are too." He then laughed, not even glancing at the man he had invested so much in just to be with the woman he once deeply desired after the loss of his fiancée last year.

"Are you sure about this?" Cedrick asked Alex the following day, as she voiced her desire to visit Osmond.

"Absolutely, why not? And naturally, Cedrick, I have every right to see Osmond since I'm his girlfriend," Alex replied. Cedrick merely nodded, understanding that Celine was infuriated after he had informed her about the situation concerning her husband and son.

Celine was watching her son asleep, and alongside Larry and Cathy, witnessing him in such a state was heart-wrenching for her, seeing his injuries and the fatigue that was still evident. Just then, they heard a knock on the door. She was taken aback when she opened it, and a smile crossed her face before she slapped Alex across her face from left to right.

"You have no right to be here! Get out now! Leave!" Celine shouted showing her anger and having pushed Alex while Cedrick stood behind her.

"But I need to see Osmond, Celine. Please, let me see him," Alex requested as she reached for her hand.

"No, you are the reason why my husband is dead and my son was nearly lost! Do you really think I would allow you to come near us?" Celine then turned to Cedrick. "Cedrick, please. Take Alex away from us now!" Meanwhile, Larry and Cathy were trying to calm their mother down from her hysteria.

"Alex, I believe we should go now. This isn't the right moment to visit Osmond," Cedrick suggested, though Alex hesitated to comply.

"I promise I will do my best to get you in next time, I swear. But for now, please try to understand Celine as a grieving wife who has lost her husband and as a mother to Osmond." Alex nodded to Cedrick wiping her tears.

"I apologise, Osmond, but I promise to return next time, and I will ensure that I can take care of you." She reassured herself, "alright, Cedrick. Let's go." Then she turned back to Celine.

"I truly apologise for everything."

Days went by until Martin's remain was cremated before Osmond finally discharged from the hospital, and that day was the most painful experience for the Gomez family while Alex and Cedrick had no opportunity to visit him, as Celine was adamant that she would never allow Alex to see his son.

He stood there quietly, watching Isabelle's parents and siblings, their grief was heavy as she was finally laid to rest. It was a deeply devastating moment for him. He had gathered information about his childhood funeral and managed to be present for this day. From yesterday until now, he spent his time watching over her until her final farewell. Then he vowed to himself, that once he settled everything; he would hunt Lucas.

At the de Ayala residence, a tense argument unfolded between the father and daughter as he prohibited her from contacting Osmond, even going so far as to change her phone number without her permission.

"From this moment on, you are grounded, no exceptions! You have betrayed me as well!" Enrique exclaimed to his daughter.

"You can't keep doing this to me! Whether you approve it or not, dad, you will never change the fact that I love Osmond!" Alex then hurried upstairs, while Enrique set up a meeting with someone he needed to talk to.

He was lost in thought when Osmond received a text from Mr. Enrique the day before their return to Queensland. The curiosity swirling in his mind didn't bother him at all after he knocked on the door, and then he heard a voice inviting him inside.

"Mr. Enrique, thank you for meeting with me today; I have something significant to discuss." He started after Enrique declined his offer of a handshake. However, he got no verbal reply, just a nod paired with a cold gaze, which left him feeling confused.

"When did you start your relationship with my daughter?" This was a question he hadn't seen coming, as his primary goal was to reveal that truth today, but instead, he found himself caught off guard.

"Mr. Enrique..." he said as he finally got in his seat.

"Simply saying my name isn't what I was hoping to hear! How long have you been treating me like this, Osmond?"

"Sir, I sincerely wanted to have this conversation with you, but your busy schedule hasn't permitted even a single one-on-one discussion about what you really need to understand."

"But it's too late!" Enrique replied, his anger was evident. "Why, Osmond? After everything, you still chose to betray me!" He then pulled out his gun from the drawer, pointing it straight at the agent's forehead.

"Did you realise that I could end your life right here in my office?" Enrique said, his intense gaze locked onto him.

"If that's what gives you pleasure in your anger, then so be it," Osmond responded, having already lost his father and Isabelle, and knowing that Alex would soon be taken from him; he felt he had no reason to keep living.

"Unbelievable, Osmond. After everything you've done to me, you still have the audacity to say such things? Leave! From this moment on, I won't permit you to be near her or any member of my family! Get out!" Enrique shouted, pointing towards the door, but Osmond hesitated to leave.

"I repeat, leave or I will end you right now. And if you still have any respect for me, do not dare to disturb us again, understood?"

Hearing those words caused him pain. He started to walk, finally reaching the door, and as his hand rested on the doorknob, he looked back at the patriarch.

"Sir, I truly apologise. If loving your daughter was a mistake and as betrayal to you then I will never regret it, not until my last breath." Enrique stayed silent, looking at him, and then Osmond nodded as tears began to fall while he closed the door. After that, he saw the matriarch and approached him.

"I'll see you tomorrow morning. I'll send you a message about the location later today, and it's important." She then left quickly without looking back.

With each tick of the clock, Osmond sat gazing out the window, watching as the sunrise was about to break, bringing hope to everyone as a symbol of something to anticipate. He was waiting for someone that early morning, and he picked up his drink, glancing at the window once more before standing up. Hearing the sound of a vehicle, he turned to see the person he was meant to meet that day—it was her. The matriarch of the de Ayala family. She was accompanied by three bodyguards, who she instructed to wait outside. After they nodded, there was a knock on the door, and he walked over to open it.

"Good morning, agent Gomez. It's nice to see you."

"Good morning to you as well, ma'am. Please, have a seat." He gestured towards the chair and was about to grab a cup of coffee from the nearby coffee machine, but Evangeline quickly reminded him that it wasn't necessary since their time was limited.

"Osmond, I need to talk to you about something."

After turning his head, he casually placed the coffee cup back on the table, nodded, and began walking towards his seat.

"Ma'am, if this is about your daughter and me, I really—"

The woman in front of him interrupted him with a wave of her hand.

"Osmond, I understand what you're trying to say, and there's no need to explain. I'm actually pleased that things turned out this way when my husband chose you to protect her, but for him, it was a significant error. However, for me, it was not. So, I'm seizing this opportunity for her and for you to spend at least one night together. I've already arranged everything, so if you're worrying about my husband, just set that aside for now."

"What do you mean, ma'am?"

"Alex is utterly shattered," the woman replied, beginning to dab at her tears with a handkerchief she retrieved from her bag.

"Ma'am, what happened to her? Is she okay?"

"Yes, she's alright. I mean, Alex is completely broken because you're not there for her." As the matriarch struggled to contain her emotions for her daughter, she inhaled deeply and managed a smile.

"You know, as a mother, and with her being my only daughter, it's absolutely tearing me apart inside to see her like this, feeling helpless to ease her pain. Now, I'm taking this risk. I don't care if Enrique goes into another rage; this time, I must stand up for my daughter," she declared, taking another deep breath.

"I have arranged everything. All I require is your confirmation, so I can finally bring joy to my daughter when I got into her room later, delivering news that I know will ultimately lead her to despise me."

"Thank you, ma'am. I understand your perspective, and I truly appreciate this opportunity to be with your daughter. I am very grateful."

"Alright, everything is in place then. However, I must remind you, Mr. Gomez, that this will be the final time you see my daughter," Evangeline stated before departing. He then approached the door, watching as the car finally drove away until it was completely out of view. In a moment of frustration, he yelled and struck the wall to release his emotions, while the matriarch's last words continued to resonate in his mind. *"This will be the last time you see my daughter."* This implied that they already had plans after he spent his final moments with Alex.

As the moonlight shimmered on the water and waves crashed onto the shore, the night became unforgettable for Osmond and Alex. This magical moment continued until the main light in the room was turned off, leaving only the lamp in the corner to illuminate their surroundings. Osmond gazed deeply into her eyes, wishing he could freeze this moment in time, making it last forever. He was captivated by every inch of her, their eyes locked in a tender embrace.

"Osmond..." she whispered, her fingers gently caressing his face.

"Alex, I truly love you."

"I feel the same way, Osmond..." she replied, noticing how his face drew closer to hers, ready to seal their kiss. They both savoured the love they shared, a bond so strong that nothing could tear them apart. Yet, deep down, Osmond felt a pang of sorrow, knowing this was their final moment together, a truth he kept hidden from Alex.

Meanwhile, outside, Cedrick smiled and shook his head, knowing that this was truly a well-deserved moment for Osmond and Alex. They had earned it after the unimaginable battles they faced since becoming agents. He then volunteered to the matriarch to keep an eye on them, as the authorities were still searching for Lucas to bring him to international court once he got arrested. For now, no one could disturb the two, as he had completely secured the area under his watch.

"How many children would you like?" Alex asked him, smiling as they shared the essence of their love.

"Maybe four or five?" He responded, catching Alex off guard, prompting her to playfully smack his shoulder.

"Are you serious?" She asked, leaning her head against his chest.

"You asked me, so I gave you my honest answer. I truly mean it," he said, kissing her hand. And I hope for as many as we can have; I want our firstborn to be a boy, so I can name him after me: Osmond de Ayala Gomez Jr." He winked at her.

"I have no objections to that, my future husband, Mr. Osmond," Alex replied, snuggling closer to his chest with a smile.

Yet, in the depths of his mind, guilt washed over him, knowing this was their last night together. *"Alex, I'm so sorry. I realise I've lied to you countless times, but I never intended to hurt you; it was all due to the circumstances."*

"What if we go to our wedding ceremony tomorrow? I'm talking about a civil wedding," Alex proposed, "and then we can definitely have the church wedding afterward, since my parents and your mother won't be able to refuse that?" He then gazed at her with a smile.

"Let's not talk about it right now, Alex. For the moment, let's enjoy another round," Osmond replied with a smile, leaning in to kiss her passionately as Alex closed her eyes and embraced him.

The next morning, while Alex was still in slumber, Cedrick was sipping his coffee at the cabana when he saw Osmond preparing to leave. Feeling something was off, he hurried over to him.

"Where are you heading? Where is Alex?"

"She's still asleep," Osmond answered.

"So, where are you going? You didn't respond to my first question." Cedrick asked Osmond for the second time while shaking his head.

"It's better this way, and please promise me, mate, that you will look after her no matter what happens."

At that moment, Cedrick was finally piecing together a thought in his mind, reminding himself of how this situation might unfold.

Then Osmond gazed at him before he began to step into the cabana.

"I am the greatest fighter and marksman in the nation, yet I am unable to protect those I cherish—the ones who truly mean the world to me. Tell me, Cedrick, am I worthless?" Tears filled his eyes and streamed down his cheeks. He inhaled deeply, and in a sudden surge of frustration he released another pain that had taken root within him, he began to hit the wall with fist, his strikes becoming quicker and more intense until his knuckles bled.

"Yes, I am brave and strong," he went on, his voice quivering. "But no one realised that deep down, I'm dying inside at this stage of my life." Osmond said in tears, as if his emotions could somehow lighten the burden of his suffering and help him endure his pain.

Cedrick stood in stunned silence at the sight before him. He could sense the overwhelming agony and frustration radiating from Osmond, yet words failed him. He let out a deep sigh, his mind wandering to Miss Alex, and an unshakeable wave of worry.

"I truly apologise, mate. I wish I had the strength to ease your burden," Cedrick said, letting out a deep sigh as he contemplated the unimaginable ordeal Osmond had faced.

"But I kindly ask you to do me a favor: please take care of her, as that is the only way you can assist me," Osmond urged, gently tapping Cedrick on the shoulder, and he noticed Cedrick nodding in agreement with his plea.

It was already after eight in the morning when she woke up with a smile, realising that soon her morning routine would be looking at Osmond when she wakes up everyday. She glanced to her right, but Osmond was nowhere in sight. Her gaze moved to the closed bathroom door; maybe he was just inside. Standing up, she went to check, but he was not there. As she turned to return to bed, her eyes landed on a white envelope resting on the bedside table. She quickly approached it to see what was inside. As she settled onto her bed and opened the letter, confusion furrowed her brows at the way Osmond had addressed her; he had never spoken to her like that before. In that instant, her heart raced, and a whirlwind of emotions swirled in her mind as she attempted to grasp the feeling. Summoning her courage, she inhaled deeply before starting to read the letter in her hand.

Margarette Alexandria,

"Love is a wonderful feeling that a person could ever feel." I realise it might sound clichè to start with a simple hi or hello, followed by the hope that you are doing well as you read this letter of mine. I still vividly recall the day we first crossed paths; it was a serendipitous moment when our worlds collided. You seemed to harbour some irritation towards me, especially when I responded with sarcasm, and I ended up leaving the cafeteria abruptly due to an emergency call from the General-Director, unaware that I was about to be assigned a very specific duty by your father: to protect you from an unknown threat. Many theories about you swirled in my mind, but they began to dissipate the moment I truly saw and understood the real you. Eventually, we grew comfortable with each other, cherishing every single day spent in our hometown. What made this mission so admirable and fulfilling? It was witnessing how my family adored you—not as the heiress or Ms. Alex, but simply for who you are.

I believed it was merely a client and a bodyguard dynamic between us, yet the power of human nature is undeniably relentless, and that force was love. A love that will never grant us tranquility or any semblance of happiness, as those closest to us do not support it due to the conflict we both wished to avoid. If only we could own this world, a realm where we could make choices without needing their consent, especially regarding your father; for I have shattered his trust. My mother shares the same sentiments about our relationship, as my father sacrificed his life to save me, so I could rescue the one who truly matters to me, and that is you. Please, never doubt that I did not fought for this love; I have done everything in my capability to save our relationship, but how can we see a future together when both of them are opposing it? How can we live each day? Choosing that path would be selfishness. I cannot imagine we living that way. I have already lost my father and my childhood best friend, and I cannot bear to allow anyone else to make another sacrifice. I am not selfish. Additionally, I have spoken to Cedrick about looking after you, and I trust that he will fulfill that promise. My dearest Margarette Alexandria always remember this:

"As stars above in twinkling dance, their sparkling light recalls our chance.

No matter where our hearts may stray, our story lingers, bright as day. And this I vow, with all my might. To love you beyond day and night, not just when near, but through all time, forever yours, in endless rhyme."

Eternally,
Osmond

Then she exited the room, tears streaming down her face, and didn't even think to check on Osmond as she made her way to the ground level and dashed outside. Once there, she glanced around, but the beauty of the surroundings felt completely out of place given her emotional turmoil. In a rush, she sprinted towards the beach, hoping to catch a glimpse of Osmond, thinking he might still there, hesitating to leave. But once again, there was no sign of him. Only the stunning scenery remained; the seagulls soaring above, the cheerful chirping of birds nestled in the nearby trees, and the gentle sound of waves lapping at the shore. Yet, she couldn't appreciate them.

"Osmond!!" She cried out, her voice echoing in the air, until she felt a hand on her shoulder. When she turned to see who it was, her heart sank—it wasn't him.

"Alex, I'm so sorry," Cedrick began, attempting to offer her some comfort.

"Cedrick, where's Osmond?! He just disappeared... he left while I was asleep, and I know it's for good. He left a letter for me..." Alex said, tears streaming down her face. "And Cedrick, please tell me, do you know where he is?"

Cedrick shook his head, feeling the weight of Alex's tears as the sea breeze tousled her hair. It pained him to see her like this.

"Alex, I did everything I could to find out where he went. But I swear to God, he doesn't even want me to know. All I can do is look after you, as he asked me to, and that's a promise I intend to keep."

"No!! He can't do this to me!" Alex screamed. "I know you know where to find him! Please, Cedrick, where is he?!" She pleaded again.

"Alex, how I wish I knew, and that you wouldn't have to ask. Because I would take you to him; it tears me apart to see you in such pain," Cedrick replied, seeing her nod slowly. Then, Alex hurriedly ran inside the beach rest house with so much grief.

Meanwhile, in a small remote island Lucas was thinking about the conversation after receiving the information he required; and promptly instructed Darek to enact about his plan, concluding with a satisfaction. He was eagerly anticipating the forthcoming events. At the other side of location the man he had spoken with from the previous day was now at the airport, then there was a man next to him waiting for someone..

Thirty Three

Love Conquers All

"Alex, why did you fire her? She is the best in that department, and I cannot believe this! Additionally, I have heard that you have declined several offers; why is that?" Enrique inquired, pacing back and forth while shaking his head. In response, Alex approached the table beside them and picked up a stack of folders that contained information related to what her father was discussing.

She smiled as she realised it had been nearly a year since she last saw Osmond. After work, her routine had been to consume alcohol while isolating herself in her room, a pattern she maintained throughout the entire year.

"Dad, I am merely following in your footsteps, am I not? Or perhaps you would like me to list the justifications for my decision, as I am confident that what I did was in the best interest of our company, which is what truly matters to you, correct?" She asked him with sarcasm, then casually extended the folder to her father, still smiling at him but with an underlying insult.

"Never dare to make that kind of gesture or hurl your words at me like that again!" With that, Enrique slapped his daughter. But then, another voice broke through, rushing towards them.

"Enrique! Stop! If you ever lay a hand on my daughter again, you will live to regret it!" Evangeline warned her husband, attempting to comfort her daughter while embracing Alex.

"Then tell your daughter she needs to learn how to address me properly! She's becoming so disrespectful! I am still your father, Alex! Don't forget that!" The father said while pointing his finger at his daughter's face.

Alex scoffed, raising an eyebrow as she looked at her dad, while her mom was pulling her away from him.

"Those words, Dad? Another slap? Go ahead! And let's talk about the word 'properly' and 'respect'? Wow, coming from you! After you disregarded my choice to pursue what I truly want, despite my efforts to meet all your expectations! But when it comes to something that genuinely brings me joy, your pride has destroyed what could have been the best for me! I will never forgive you, Dad! I'd rather not inherit anything from you since you've taken away everything that mattered to me!" With that, she walked out of the room and grabbed her phone to make a call as she headed towards her bedroom.

"Alright, thank you Cedrick, please hurry up." She said, as soon as she stepped into her room, Alex swiftly locked the door, ensuring no one could interrupt her plan. Tears streamed down her cheeks as she entered the walk-in closet, beginning to pack her dress. After several minutes, she felt content with what she had packed into her suitcase. Without glancing back, she exited the room, still able to hear her parents arguing in her father's office.

Cedrick spotted Alex waiting for him along the driveway, and he initially thought that her situation with Mr. Enrique had deteriorated.

"Cedrick, thanks for coming. Please, lets go," she said, wiping away her tears.

"Alex, please don't do this!" Cedrick said to her as he watching her putting the suitcase in the back of his car.

"Cedrick, I have already made my choice, and I can no longer with them for now. It serves only as a reminder of my painful past, so it is preferable this way. Only time can mend my wounds," she stated.

Cedrick remained quiet, recalling his promise to Osmond to take care of her until he saw Alex's mother coming from the main entrance.

"Alex, please, do not conclude this day in such a manner. Stay, and we can resolve this; eventually, reconciliation between you and your father is likely to happen," Evangeline implored while reaching for her daughter's hand.

"Mom, please, it will not work. I have already made my decision, whether you approve or not. In fact, I despise you as well, since you have given me something that ultimately brings me immense pain. You are just like my father. Therefore, there is no reason for me to remain here."

"But Alex, I really need you to see my perspective."

"Mom, please. That's enough." She ran her fingers through her hair in frustration. "You know where I'm heading, so any of you can come visit me there. But living in this house with both of you? After everything that happened, I need to go and let dad know that I've already convinced my cousin from Spain, Ciara will be taking my place. So, there's no reason to be concerned." Evangeline nodded, tears streaming down her face. She then opened the passenger door and got into the car after embracing her mother, then Cedrick approached the matriarch for their goodbyes.

"Oh, my god, Cedrick, I can hardly believe that today is going to be the worst for my daughter and husband. I feel utterly hopeless, and I apologise, but I can't help but express how deeply worried I am about both of them," the matriarch said, shaking her head slowly.

"It's alright, ma'am. When it comes to family matters, it's something we can't avoid, and it's completely natural to express your true feelings," Cedrick replied.

"Thank you, Cedrick. I am putting my trust in you regarding my daughter and your updates."

"I promise, ma'am, I will keep you informed." He then extended his hand for a handshake before heading to the driver's seat.

Evangeline stood at the driveway, watching the car leave, her heart aching unbearably as tears streamed down her face.

Inside the car, Alex was also in tears, while her eyes closed. Leaving was painful for her too, but this time she chose peace, not just for herself, but for her parents as well. While Cedrick concentrated on driving safely, he made sure to be there for her, especially now when she felt so alone, knowing that no one else could truly understand her feelings except him.

A few months have passed since he accompanied Alex to that destination, the very place where Osmond and Alex shared their final night together. Cedrick stood there, observing Alex, as the situation grew increasingly complicated since Lucas was still missing. According to the Australian Central Intelligence, on the night of his disappearance, he was on a boat with his most trusted assistant, Darek, making it impossible to trace him for now. However, his grandfather Amadeus reassured them that he would cooperate once he had the opportunity to find his grandson. He then glanced at the other agent and nodded before leaving the area.

She carried it with her wherever she went after Osmond left her, until the sky turned unkind as she walked along the shoreline. She took Osmond's letter from her dress pocket and kissed it softly, a part of her daily routine. From morning until sunset, a sadness pierced her heart as she watched the sea birds flying in formation, smiling as she realised, they enjoyed freedom no matter where they traveled, surely accompanied by their loved ones. Envy washed over her, and she wiped away her tears before continuing her walk.

At the other place, everything felt devoid of meaning the moment they're gone from his life. His father, Isabelle, and Alex were out there somewhere, yet it seemed impossible to reach out to her, even through a normal call or video call on his phone. He then closed his eyes, realising how this whimsical fate had drastically altered his life since he became an agent; it was only when he sensed a hand on his shoulder that he recognised it was his older brother, Larry. He felt a wave of gratitude that Larry had arrived before his tears could begin to fall.

"Osmond, are you okay?" Larry asked gently. But Osmond just looking at him smiled fairly.

"Come on. Don't hold back. I know what's happening, and I completely understand the situation between you two." Osmond met his brother's gaze before replying.

"Thanks, but I really hope that one day our mother can stop blaming me entirely." He then settled onto the wooden outdoor bench while Larry gave his shoulder a reassuring tap before sitting beside him, with the beach just fifty metres away from where they sat.

"All I can do is listen to every perspective of you and I wish the incident were merely a recurring nightmare during our sleep. However, my brother, this is what we refer to as fate. If only we could turn back time; to restore everything from the fragments of pain, transforming those sorrows into joyful moments for each of us, as I deeply miss our father. It has been nearly a year since I last spent time with him before his passing."

Then Osmond saw his brother taking a deep breath and glanced at him before he went on.

"But I understand, as you previously mentioned, that when he passed away in your arms, he felt no regret, only satisfaction in seeing his son and being able to leave a message to the rest of the family. You were unharmed and strong enough to complete the unfinished duel with the leader of that notorious organisation, as our father did his utmost, which was showing of a father's love for his son." Then Larry smiled at him and nodded.

Initially, Osmond was at a loss for words when his brother finished sharing his thoughts, then allowing a small laugh to escape his lips, after remembering a joyful memory with their father.

"I have missed those smiles, my brother, and now I finally get to see it again. Don't worry, alright? One day, our sister and I will arrange a conversation with our mother, and we will do everything we can, and

I truly believe in destiny; the right moment will come and to end this kind of misery." Just then, his brother's wife approached them, bringing two bottles of beer and some snacks. Tomorrow, he would be leaving, as this visit was part of his weekend routine, having moved to Cairns, which was near his brother's home. Meanwhile, his mother was with his sister and her family. Months went by, and another day for Osmond to make himself busy. He was getting his farming tools ready after finishing his breakfast. Then, he recalled the letter from his childhood best friend, Isabelle, and this time he felt compelled to read it again.

Osmond,

I'm uncertain whether I'm still alive by the time you read this. However, I want you to know how truly happy I am to see you and have fulfilled your dream, one that I wholeheartedly supported during our younger days. But Osmond, I must ask for your forgiveness on behalf of my family, in case I don't make it through, as my last mission was for Lucas. By the way, I have witnessed how happy you are with Alex that day. It was the most beautiful moment I've ever witnessed between you two on that secluded beach; I did everything I could to ensure your happiness by saving the woman who brings you joy. Do you recall when I declined to participate in the play during our childhood? I was afraid everyone would see my true self, and I never told you about my passion for martial arts. The rest was history, especially after my kidnapping. I believe that one day, things will come to normal, and I trust that my parents will eventually forgive you one day. But for now, I want you to take care of Alex. If I could turn back time to alter my destiny and yet, I find happiness in knowing I did the right thing, and it's an honour to have done this for you. I was able to reunite with my family, filled with joy and love once more. Please, choose happiness and peace whenever you can. I love you, my dear friend.

Your forever best friend,

Isabelle Lewis

After reading the letter, he felt a smile spread across his face as he realised how fortunate he was to have Isabelle in his life, even with the negative opinion of being an assassin. Ultimately, his friend's choice was a difficult yet selfless act. He then stepped outside, walked closely to the seashore, and offered a prayer for her, closing his eyes as he gazed at the sky.

That late afternoon, Enrique felt a sense of satisfaction with his niece's performance from Spain, but he knew things would have been completely different if Alex had been involved. He sighed after smiling at her, and then she returned his smile, raising her glass in a toast to their drinks.

"Uncle, I apologise for saying this, but I know what happened, as Alex informed me. Please consider the consequences for your daughter, despite our family's wealth. I believe you should learn to forgive Osmond, and I truly admire how he really cares for my cousin and fighting those mercenaries just to keep her safe. I wish my husband were like an agent or knight in shining armour too! But that was for Alex. Haha!" Then her uncle beginning to laugh with her, Evangeline shook her head in happiness after hearing their conversation behind the door. She sensed it was a positive sign for better days ahead for them. She then approached one of their staff members and requested another round of drinks and food for them to enjoy, having anticipated brighter days after reading Cedrick's text last week.

When Larry brought their mother to the location, she was taken aback by the sight of his son's best mate, agent Cedrick McKain. She exchanged a meaningful look with her son, filled with questions, until Cathy took her hand and began to explain.

"Mom, I believe it's best to start anew. This way, we can move ahead. Surely, wherever he is now, he wouldn't want this situation for either of you. It was his choice, mom, and we can't change that fact.

What we need is acceptance; he acted out of love, even if it caused us pain."

"I apologise, Larry and Cathy. I struggle to accept things easily, but I've come to some realisations lately. There was a time I dreamt of Martin; I saw him happy, holding my hand, and in that moment, I felt his love when we embraced before the dream faded."

"Do you see that, mom? Dad came to you in your dreams because he disapproves of what he sees between you and Osmond," Larry added, nodding at his mother with a smile as he glanced at his sister.

"I have no doubt about that, Larry. So please, mom? It's time," Cathy urged, moving closer to their mother for a hug.

"I apologise for being difficult in forgiving Osmond, and I realise I caused them pain. I mean, Alex too, since I prevented her from seeing my son."

"Yes, we understand that mom." Larry chimed in, "and it's not too late, haha!"

"And also, I have already made arrangements," Cedrick stated, a look of satisfaction illuminating his face as he realised their mission had been successful that evening.

When he opened the door, he was greeted by Mr. Enrique, but his expression shifted to concern as the General-Director, Agent McKain, and several police officers standing behind him. His gaze then locked with Mrs. Evangeline's, who was staring directly at him.

"You are under arrest, Mr. Gomez," the Director-General said, as an officer approached him with handcuffs in hand, eyeing him intently.

"Wait, what is this about? I haven't done anything wrong," he replied, maintaining his composure and gesturing for the officer to step back.

"You did, because you refused to marry my daughter," Enrique replied and started to smile at him, then he looked at the other agent. "So, Agent McKain, I believe I am done here and If he refuses again, I am instructing you to take him into custody." The patriarch turned to the Director-General, who simply smiled back at him and at Cedrick.

"Alright, men, let's go! And agent Cedrick McKain, we're counting on you," the commander said.

Osmond was at a loss for words, yet the joy he felt at that moment was beyond of his imagination. Then he thought of his mother, and Cedrick flashed him a knowing smile, aware of his thoughts.

"I understand what's holding you back, mate. Don't fret; we've already sorted it out. I mean, with your brother and sister."

"Cedrick..." Osmond replied, recalling how he had treated him when he sought his help to protect Alex, which had culminated in a fierce fight between them. He shook his head and embraced him.

"Damn!" He muttered to himself, realising that the man he once despised was now the source of his happiness.

"So, let's go, mate! I'll take you to where she is."

It was late afternoon when Osmond spotted someone special, gazing at the view. He smiled and paused for a moment, wanting to watch her, even though he longed to call her name and rush to her side. But this time, there was no need for that. This was their perfect moment. Osmond continued to watch her, feeling an overwhelming sense of peace while Alex was engulfed in deep sorrow, watching the sun kissing the horizon of the ocean. Then he inhaled deeply and shook his head. This has to be enough; they have suffered for such a long time.

"We will never experience that again," Osmond said, his voice strained as he grappled with his emotions while still keeping his gaze on her. He ensured she could hear him despite the cacophony of crashing waves with the ocean's breeze.

Alex recognised a familiar voice, prompting her to stop and glance over her shoulder; and she closed her eyes, wondering if she was merely imagining things. But when she opened them again, there he was, standing there with a smile.

"Osmond..." she whispered softly.

"My love, I've missed you so much, Alex!" He exclaimed, gazing deeply into her eyes, ensuring she felt his sincerity.

Fate had playfully separated them, turning their lives into a nightmare, and neither could take the first step, yet he continued to smile at her. Then, they both ran towards each other, sharing a passionate kiss as they embraced.

"How did you find me?" Alex asked him after their kiss.

"It was him!" Osmond said, pointing to Cedrick, who stood beneath a cluster of palm trees.

"But Osmond, they're still not—"

"Don't worry about them. It's finally over, my love, and for now, we need to stay here to savour this moment," Osmond reassured her, winking, which made her giggle by surprised.

"Oh, look at that place! I remember our first night there," Osmond said, unable to stop smiling.

"Wow, after you turned me down that night? Well, come and chase me!" Alex laughed, taking off her beach sandals and started to run.

"Oh, absolutely! Why not? I could do this all day and night long!" He laughed heartily as he watched her and then began to chase her.

"Once I catch you, must be hugs and kisses before we move on to the next level! Haha!"

"Well, if you're lucky enough!" Alex replied, still laughing.

Then, before he started to run, a thought occurred to his mind; however, for the moment, he just took it aside.

From afar, Cedrick witnessed about their happiness. At last, they were reunited, the two were inseparable until the tragic events came into their lives, but now it was over. They stood the test of time. After an hour, he received a text message from Osmond, and he scratched the back of his head before replying.

"If you were not truly my best mate, I would not do this! Haha!" He then pressed the send button on his phone's screen, and that would be for tomorrow.

The following day, while it was after sunset, Osmond and Alex were sitting on the sand after discussing their wedding plans through a video conference with their families the whole day. Alex felt a sense of contentment when they agreed on her idea, which was both simple and meaningful, regarding the wedding at Whitsundays beach, until Osmond broke the silence.

"I believe it would be better if this area had additional lights," Osmond whispered to her ears.

"Yes, I agree. However, it is fine since the moon is exceptionally bright tonight."

"What if I told you that is possible? I mean, aside from that," Osmond commented, gesturing towards the moon.

"What do you mean?" Alex replied, leaning her head on Osmond's shoulder, but she did not hear any answer from him; instead, she saw him glancing at his watch before smiling at her and looking up at the sky again that starting to filled with stars.

"There it is, look!" Osmond responded while pointing his finger towards the sky.

Suddenly, the sound startled her as the light from the fireworks began to illuminate the beach. From peony, chrysanthemum, crossette, to comet and brocade, etc.

"Oh my god! Why did you do this?" She asked in confusion, but then she beamed a radiant smile at him.

"Just to let you know that those fireworks also symbolise our love. Since yesterday when we reunited, and every day I promise that we will never be apart, I am here to make your day special, like fireworks." Then Alex quickly embraced him, and he gently reciprocated the tenderness of her affection for him, then Cedrick interjected.

"So, I am completely finished here. You, owe me a great deal, mate! Haha!" While shaking his head, he then sat next to Osmond and tapped his shoulder. "Thank you for what happened, because if you hadn't requested a backup, I would never have had the chance to meet her best friend."

"Yes, I am aware of that as what you've mentioned before. Do not worry, as I know how I can assist you in return." He smiled, then glanced at Alex, who was also smiling at their friend. They heard an incoming call, and Alex smiled when her best friend Elissandra confessed to her about what's going on between her and Cedrick then prompting the other agent to stand up to take the call.

"Okay, hold on." Cedrick said while covering the mouthpiece of his device by his right hand and turned his gaze towards them.

"Sorry guys, I have to leave, I need to return to Melbourne. I will see both of you on the wedding day!" Cedrick waved goodbye to them, and the two waved back as they resumed watching the fireworks.

In just a few days, it will be their wedding day and the selected guests they truly knew are coming after receiving confirmation, aside from their families. Of course, Elissandra will be her bridesmaid, while Cedrick will serve as the best man.

It was early morning, just before the sun began to rise, as Osmond and Alex sat on the shore, both sharing a blanket, and they felt a deep sense of tranquility, welcoming by the gentle morning breeze, until they started to share a soft kiss.

"Finally, I found someone who will watch every sunrise with me, until the sunset of my life... " Alex whispered at him, after they kissed. Then Osmond smiled, then he replied to her.

"Before, every beat of my heart was full of emptiness but this time, every beat of our hearts will always be full of love and joy."